AMONG THE FALLEN

AMONG THE FALLEN

HENRY MITCHELL

ALSO BY HENRY MITCHELL

Novels:

The Summer Boy – Alfie Dog Fiction (UK)

Between Times – Alfie Dog Fiction (UK)

Laurel Falls - Alfie Dog Fiction (UK)

Slick Rock Creek – Solstice Publishing

The Winged Child – Creative James Media

Short Story Collections:

Dark on the Mountain – Alfie Dog Fiction (UK)

Early Dark – Alfie Dog Fiction (UK)

Anthologies:

"Winter Light" – This land is my Land, Alfie Dog Fiction (UK)

"Shard" – The Day Death Wore Boots, Alfie Dog Fiction (UK)

"Fairy Tale" – Thrice Upon a Time, Alfie Dog Fiction (UK)

"Dark Fork" – Fall Fiction Anthology, Dark Ink Press

"Púca" – Happily Ever Never, Creative James Media

"Abigail's Guest" – Dark and Stormy Night, Creative James Media

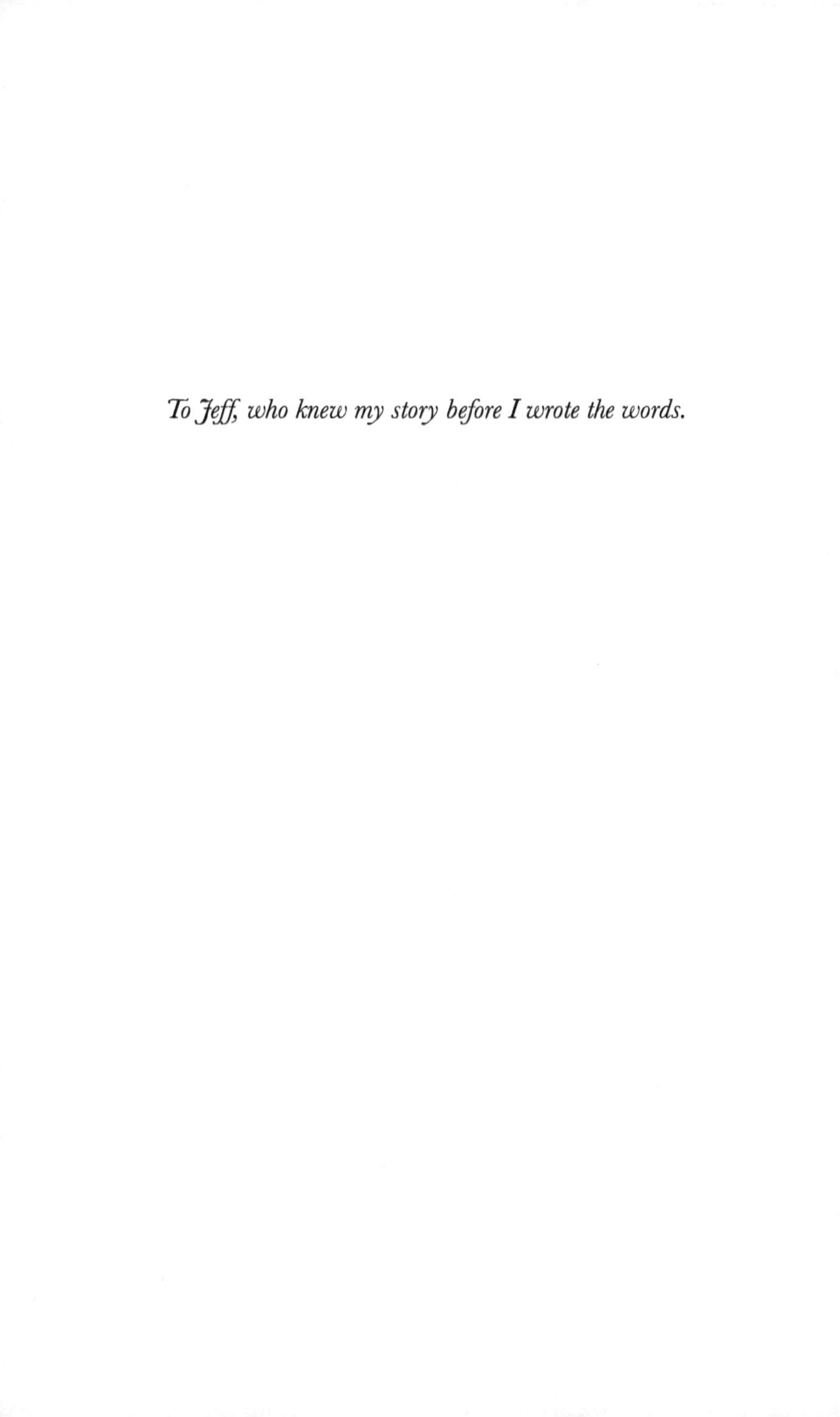

To Jeff, who knew my story before I wrote the words.

ONE

Wendl was reading the story aloud. It was an old story. He knew it by heart. After a while, lost in the flow of his remembrance, he no longer even glanced at the ReadPad. Mid-way through the tale, he felt something wet and warm and viscous in his palm. Wendl stared down at the ReadPad. A thick red liquid oozed out of it, dripping off his fingers. He raised his hand to his face and inhaled. Wendl had been in the War, a long time ago when he was still young. There was no mistaking. He had never forgotten the smell of blood.

"Are you alright, Grampa?" said the child sitting beside him. There were two of them, a boy and a girl. The boy had spoken.

"I'm sorry, children," Wendl smiled down at them. "I must have dozed off."

"You were talking funny," said the girl.

"It was the Old Tongue," Wendl said, "as we spoke it among the Fallen."

"But the Old Tongue is not allowed," said the boy. His voice tremored with fright.

"We should report you, Grampa," the girl admonished, looking suddenly very serious and grown-up.

"Are you going to report me, children?" asked Wendl, chuckling, as if they were sharing a joke.

"Oh, no, Grampa," the boy said shaking his head, vigorously. "They would cut out your tongue."

"Then how would you tell us stories?" asked the girl, wild-eyed and giggling.

Wendl laughed himself awake. "What a strange dream," he mused aloud. There were no grandchildren of course. Never had been. There were no ReadPads at the Abbey, either. The Trier had seerbowls. They felt no need of the screens and devices ubiquitous among the Fallen.

Wendl suspected this, like most of his dreams, was a Summons, albeit not a clear one. He would tell his dream to Goodmother Wandalena when he saw her at Lauds. Perhaps his Superior would know what to make of it.

Thunder rumbled in the distance. Through the window, he saw light flickering the sky. Wendl stretched out his mind to it until his awareness became another attribute of the storm, gathering it closer, savoring its energy. He shut his eyes against the strobing lightning bolt that for a single infinitesimal instant, rendered the world outside his window naked and darkless. Wendl counted, one . . . two . . . and not quite three when thunder shuddered his cell, rattling the jars and pots on the shelves across the room.

He felt the shift in the air, held up his arm as the next burst of heaven's fire limned the silver hairs standing straight and erect across the back of his hand. This was no ordinary storm, but a deep tempest tumulting both the Two Worlds. After this blow, the Separation would be open and passable for at least a day, maybe several. Before he sought enlightenment from Wandalena, he reckoned he should gather all that might be needful for travel. She would not pass any opportunity to restore a Fallen to the Stream.

Wendl sighed, threw back the blanket and found his feet. He worlded himself enough to know the chill of the stone floor, but not to be distracted by it. He padded across to his brazier, removed the snufferlid, and held his right hand low over the coals until they offered their pale blue flame to the night. He took down a jar from the shelf, removed a spoonful of aromatic twigs, filled his cup from the waterjar, and dropped in the twigs. Careful to keep his hand present to the cup while absent to the fire, Wendl held the cupful of water and floating twigs over the coals until the twigs sank and the water began to steam.

"We've found Gobnait," announced Goodmother Wandalena without preamble. Wendl hadn't needed to request an audience. At the conclusion of Lauds, she waved him summarily into her study. "Quit hovering about and sit down," she commanded while Wendl steeped in his astonishment.

"After so long, Superior. Are you certain?" he murmured as he obediently settled into a chair.

"You've spent so much time among the Fallen, Brother Wendl, that you're beginning to think like them," Wandalena snapped. "Seven hundred years is no time at all for us."

"Does she know, then?" Wendl asked.

"Hardly," said Wandalena. "After a few generations among the Fallen, none of them remember what they were. "She doesn't even recall her bees."

"How did you manage to find her?" Wendl queried.

Wandalena manifested a wry smile that didn't look quite at home in that habitually severe face. "The bees told Owl," she said. "They are upset because their Keeper has forgotten them."

"Is that why they are so prone to sting Brother Owl as he tends the hives?" Wendl asked.

"They sting Owl to remind him of his sins and his need for penance," Wandalena declared.

"They don't sting me," Wendl said. "Surely I have

committed transgressions to the Rule far more numerous and grievous than Owl's."

"Bees are not moral creatures," countered Wandalena, "They don't keep score." She seemed on the verge of laughing, something no soul at the Abbey had ever seen her do. "They mercy you, Wendl Von Trier, because they sense your kinship."

Kinship? I doubt that. Wendl didn't quite say it aloud. However, his thought did not escape his Superior's scrutiny.

"Like the bees, Brother, you can fly between the Two Worlds," said Wandalena, "which is what you are about to do again."

"You want me to bring Gobnait back into our Stream?" Wendl said it like a question, but he already saw his place in the story.

"We want you to guide her," said Wandalena, waving a bony finger in his face. "She must choose to return. Your mission is to enlighten her choice."

"And maybe leave a door open for her?" Wendl ventured.

"You may open a door, if you will, but don't shove her through it," admonished Wandalena. "The Fallen know her as Abigail."

"How will I find her?" Wendl asked sincerely.

"Ask the bees," said Wandalena and clapped her hands. Wendl thought she was starting to laugh but immediately found himself in the Abbey apiary immersed in the humming drumming thrumming song of the bees.

Two

On an August afternoon that rendered the whole world a sauna, Abigail Trammell labored in her front garden, pruning back her roses now reduced by the unrelenting heat to a failure of withered blossoms and limp yellow leaves, though not even the Japanese beetles had been able to dull the thorns. Those remained sharp as ever.

She possessed shears some place that eluded her memory, so wielded the sharp butcher knife she liberated from her kitchen, a sin she'd only forgive herself. Startled, she nearly slipped and sliced her fingers when she heard the unfamiliar voice behind her.

"Miss Trammell?" A man's voice only maybe, with a peculiar lilt, obviously not from around here.

"You're a quiet one," she said, turning to face the tall, gangly figure who'd snuck up on her. Abigail was proud that she had kept her acute hearing into her elder years while she had to shout at most of her friends, couldn't fathom why she didn't hear a car come up her drive or footsteps on the gravel. "Can I help you?" As much accusation as question. She assumed this was one more lost tourist, reduced to asking directions of a local because his GPS app was off-line.

The spinyspindly maybe-man—a closer look left her still not quite certain of the gender—said, "VonTrier. I reserved your room."

Abigail remembered the name because it was odd. "Yes," she agreed, "Wendl. You're set for the week." She subjected him to a frank inspection. *How did he get here? I didn't hear a car because there isn't any.* "Luggage?" She wouldn't rent a room for a week to a man without luggage and started to tell Wendl VonTrier precisely that.

"Here," he said, lofting his suitcase as if it were empty.

Abigail wondered how she'd missed it. It was almost as if it didn't exist before she named it.

She dropped her trimmings into the basket at her feet, waved her knife in the air. "I'll show you," she said, remembering to smile.

"You have a renter," Rhonda Shaw accused as she handed a book of Forever stamps across the post office counter.

"Yes," Abigail conceded, "Don't see many trippers this late in the season. He's different from the lot of them."

"He's strange. That's what he is," Rhonda said. "What's he here for?"

Abigail permitted herself a laugh, "I didn't ask and he didn't say. He's paid his room for a week, so whatever it is will take a few days. This time of year, I can use his money, let me tell you."

Another customer waited in the queue, seemingly engrossed in their conversation, so Rhonda expanded on the subject, "Gloria Proudfoot said he was in her store yesterday, browsing old books. Windy, I think she said his name was."

"Wendl," corrected Abigail, suddenly and for no obvious reason, feeling protective of her peculiar lodger, "Wendl VonTrier." She spelled it for Rhonda, who wrote it down,

"What kind of name is that?" the postmaster asked as Abigail tucked her Forevers into her purse.

Exiting the post office at the south end of Main Street, Abigail started walking toward Hemlock Cottage, her home and Airbnb at the other end of town, four blocks away. Halfway there, she stopped in front of Vintage Reads, Gloria Proudfoot's well-read bookstore. "Morning, Gloria," she said with practiced cheerfulness.

Gloria, culling her Battered and Bartered table just outside her door, peered up over her glasses and released one of her carefully rationed smiles.

Abigail took that as an invitation to chitchat. "I hear my current renter has been prowling your shelves," she ventured.

"I reckon you must mean Windy," Gloria said, not denying that her shelves had been scrutinized by an outlander.

"Wendl," said Abigail.

"Wendell," repeated Gloria, "Like the Berry." Before Abigail could spell it for her, she went on, "He only bought the one book. Looked long and long. Laid hands on every cover in the store, must've, but only bought the one. Said he'd come to Drover's Gap because he heard I had it."

"Peculiar," Abigail said because she thought it was.

"Yes," Gloria agreed. "No way he could have known about that book. I didn't know it was in the store. Don't remember having seen or heard of it. It wasn't even marked for price. Windy . . ."

"Wendl," Abigail corrected.

"Wendell. Laid three twenties on the counter and asked if that was enough to cover the book. I reckoned it was."

"Peculiar," Abigail said again, because the taste of the word was still on her tongue, and she couldn't think of anything else to say.

"And then . . ." Gloria paused, dangling the words in the air between them like a fly floating in front of a mountain trout.

Abigail took it. "Then what?"

"You won't believe this," Gloria warned.

"I might, even if it is you telling me," Abigail murmured.

"Then," as a huge grin swallowed Gloria's face, tugging and stretching her words. "He offered to buy my shop. Said to think on it and he'd be back if I want to name a price."

"Goodness," breathed Abigail, thinking this was all indeed peculiar.

After a quick stop at Dolf's Market to buy some half-and-half for Wendl's morning coffee, Abigail arrived back at Hemlock Cottage to find him sitting on her front steps as if he were right at home, intent on a battered old book she assumed was the one he'd bought from Gloria.

"Hello, Mister VonTrier," she called cheerfully as she came up her walk, sincerely glad she'd taken in a reader instead of a gambler or drinker or some kind of kinky predator. "That must be an interesting book that has you reading out here in the heat of the day."

Wendl looked up, smiled, closed his book, holding his place with a long spidery finger, "Yes, it is. In fact, it is the last existing printed copy of this title. I was fortunate to find it."

"Are you a collector, then, Mister VonTrier?"

"Wendl, please." He stood, unfolding like a growing plant. Holding his book in front of him as if presenting evidence in court, he answered, "Not of books, necessarily, but I do collect stories. This particular book happens to contain one of my favorites."

Abigail fumbled awkwardly in her purse, searching for her keys while trying to keep her grocery bag from slipping through her arm and making a splattering mess on her porch floor. Wendl dropped his book onto the big wooden rocker beside the door and reached out with both hands.

"Let me hold that for you," he said. The grocery bag appeared in his grasp before Abigail realized she had released it.

Slightly flustered, she opened the door and Wendl followed her down the hall and into her kitchen, still clutching her bag. He set it on the table, turned to go as Abigail, who never offered hospitality to her renters beyond an orderly room, clean linens and a decent breakfast, heard herself saying, "I'm going to fix myself some iced tea with fresh mint. Would you like a glass, Mister VonTrier . . . Wendl?"

"I never refuse hospitality," murmured Wendl, which wasn't precisely an answer to her question. Abigail counted it sufficing as acceptance. She hoped a glass of iced tea would generate opportunity to glean some intelligence regarding her mysterious guest. If there were any intriguing secrets connected to Wendl VonTrier, she wanted to be the first in town to know them.

She stirred the pitcher, was about to reach into the refrigerator, but saw the glasses already filled with ice, although she didn't remember doing it. *You're getting old, dear girl. The knees are first to go, then the mind.* She poured the tea into the glasses and, after brief interior deliberation, hauled out into the light the last surviving portion of her winter's fruitcake which had only improved with age, thanks to regular annointings from an ancient bottle of whisky that flavored and preserved the cakes of many winters though it had never filled a glass. She cut a thin slice for herself and a slightly thicker one for her guest, set them on their little plates beside the tea glasses.

Sitting to table, Abigail was immediately embarrassed because she had forgotten forks. Wendl promptly reached out, broke a piece of his cake with his fingers and delivered it into his mouth, held it there as he sat for a moment in rapturous silence, gazing through the window at Abigail's sunny yard. His expression assured her that he savored her cake with all the appreciation it was due.

She waited, mute and expectant, was not disappointed when, having received his bit of cake deeper into his being,

Wendl whispered, "This is exquisite, Miss Trammell. It makes me homesick for the Abbey."

Now we're getting somewhere. Aloud, she queried, "The Abbey? Where's that now?"

"Oh, now, it isn't in this world," said Wendl, his smile all in his eyes, "but in one of my former lives, I resided in an intentional religious community for a time. Among our other activities, we made fruit cakes and kept bees in order to earn our keep in the larger world. Honey and cake. Our life was sweet."

"You were a monk?" said Abigail, craving details.

"I was a visitor," Wendl said, pausing mid-sentence to sip his tea, "who stayed longer than anyone intended when I arrived. Do you keep bees, Miss Trammell?"

Abigail permitted herself a chuckle. "Mercy, no. They just come here for my flowers."

"You have a lovely and intriguing garden," Wendl acknowledged. "I wish I might be here long enough to get acquainted with all your plantings."

Abigail laughed. "Perhaps I should warn you, Brother Wendl, that more than a few who pass through Drovers Gap on their way to someplace else are drawn to stay awhile. Some of them, in fact, never get around to leaving." *Like me.*

Wendl looked his soundless laugh at her, then lilted, "Dear Miss Trammell, I'm not on my way to any place I know."

Later, after Wendl excused himself with profuse thanks and went off to his room carrying her instruction, "Breakfast at seven," Abigail went out to sweep her front porch as she did every morning and evening, always in hope she might exchange some friendly insult with a passing neighbor. She found Wendl's book lying apparently forgotten on the chair. The worn cover evidenced a hard life. From the look of it, she thought it might well be the last surviving copy of its kind. She picked it up, read the title, *The Forest Soul, by Millicent McTeer.*

The tattered old volume seemed on the brink of escaping its binding, but curious, she opened it carefully, looked at a page, then another, then several. All the pages were blank.

THREE

Wendl's unwordy book still lay on the chair by her front door as Abigail went out for her morning porch sweeping. Her chore done, she dropped the book on her hall table as she came in. It would stay dry there from the misty rain beginning to fall, and he'd see it on his way out.

She hoped to feed him questions with his breakfast, but Bernice Abner phoned as Abigail was setting the asparagus omelet and grapefruit juice on the table and she had to scurry to answer just as Wendl came down the stairs from his room. By the time she managed to extricate herself from Bernice's meandering and monologenous gossip, her guest had finished his breakfast and disappeared.

She heard her front door close as she hung up the phone and looked out the window in time to catch a glimpse of Wendl VonTrier dissolving into the foggymisty day. She began clearing the breakfast table, noticed the cup and plate looked as clean as if straight from the washer. She held up the juice glass to the light and peered through its sparkle. *How'd he do that?*

Wendl had eaten everything she put out for him and not a

trace left behind. *He might look like a bird but he has a man's appetite.* She carried the glass and silver back to the kitchen and, though everything from the table appeared clean as clean, loaded it into the dishwasher.

Wendl, she figured, would be gone until evening. Abigail burned to find out what he did with himself all day in their little town, besides trying to get a monopoly on used books. She went to the linen closet and pulled out fresh sheets, pillowcases and towels. She could clean her guest room while Wendl wandered.

As she started up the stair, she saw Wendl's mysterious little book still lying on the hall table. She dropped it onto her laundered load and arms full, began to climb up her morning. She thought she heard something rustling in the air during her ascent, maybe the gusted rain on her metal roof, maybe her own breathing. *You're getting old, you are.* Thinking that she who had once climbed mountains might now be winded by her own stairs brought no comfort.

It wasn't the rain she heard. Her breath steadied as she set her burden down on the little table, just like the one in the hall downstairs, to unlock Wendl's door. The rustling sound persisted, like leaves trembling on a breeze. Abigail feared something buggy or mousy had gotten into her linens, then realized the sound was coming from the book. She stepped back, hesitated, finally reached out arm's length, extended a finger to flip open the cover.

The rustling suddenly louder, she couldn't tell if she heard it from the book or in her own head. Almost fearfully, she gingerly turned a few pages. They were all still blank and unmarked as a baby's conscience. As she stared, the rustling rattle morphed into whispers, then syllables, words, sentences, a woman's voice, not her own, speaking in her head, saying something about war and weather. Half afraid of the book now, Abigail summoned courage to turn back to the first page. The book dutifully began to recite itself from the beginning.

She saw the words now as she heard the woman narrator say them, not in the book, but behind her eye.

THE FOREST SOUL
By
Millicent McTeer
Chapter One
What Trees Know

Abigail stood transfixed, book in hand, as the voice behind her eyes clarified and settled in her mind. She gazed at the blank pages while the book spoke on, relating a hidden, though omnipresent world of microbes and mycelium, eukaryotes and anaerobes, luring her toward euphorias of knowing beyond the boundaries of egocentric selves, where the distinctions between book and beholder are rendered permeable and transparent.

It seemed to Abigail that she was as much author as reader of *The Forest Soul*, that the book was becoming as she read it, if their intercourse could be described in any sense as reading. She wondered if every soul who opened this book had encountered their own unique story. Was the voice in her head Millicent McTeer's, or maybe the voice of Abigail Trammell's own undiscovered self?

The voice stopped mid-sentence. Abigail turned the page and the story continued telling its world, alien as an Eocene fern forest and familiar as her own flower garden. After the first dozen or so pages, lines and figures began to waver and consolidate before her gaze, not quite on the paper and not exactly behind her eyes, but by some mysterious process of the book, projected into her perception. The words, though not exactly English, sounded to her at least close enough to the American twenty-first century version that she could comprehend.

Abigail stood suspended between two moments, caught in

the spell, the book feeling like a live and breathing thing in her hand, pulsing in her thought for a time she couldn't measure. When she finally broke her trance and put the book down, the light said afternoon and her feet ached from standing. They moved reluctantly, as if she had become rooted like the trees in *The Forest Soul*. She felt winded, gulped in air like somebody who had forgotten to breathe. She barely had time to clean and tidy Wendl's room before he came in.

"Your book's on the table by your door. I brought it in from the weather," she blurted as soon as she saw him.

"How do you like it?" he murmured, in that forest voice of his, so soft and deep in his chest she wouldn't have heard it but in quiet and still.

Abigail blushed, something she never did. Being found out reading a book without the owner's invitation made her feel inexplicably guilty. "I didn't read it all," was all she could summon in her defense.

Wendl picked up the book and held it out to her. "Then, you should finish it. We'll have something to talk about over breakfast."

Wendl left Hemlock Cottage early next morning before Abigail woke. She found a note on her kitchen table that her renter would not need breakfast. She poured buttermilk over left-over cornbread crumbled in a bowl. When her coffee was ready, she filled a cup and sat down to breakfast with Wendl's book for company.

This time, when she opened it, she could see text, dim and wavery, seeming not quite anchored to the page but floating a hair above it. The print shifted slightly as she read, as if floating on a thin layer of water. After a while she discovered she didn't need to turn a page, the text would scroll along as she read. As an experiment she closed the book, waited a moment then opened it again to a random page. The sentences resumed right where she'd left off. The book knew she was reading it.

"Beats Kindle," she said to the book, who paused for a moment to verify her attention, before continuing.

While Abigail Trammell was finishing Millicent McTeer's treatise on arboreal sentience, Wendl VonTrier explored Drovers Gap and surrounding environs seeking connections of another sort. By mid-afternoon, he finally concluded that he might be hungry after all and stepped into a snug and shadowed establishment behind a sign declaring it to be Home Ground Suds and Java.

At three o'clock, most of the inhabitants of Drovers Gap found it too early for suds and too late for java. Only a couple of patrons sat at the bar, nursing their untimely brews. In a far corner, on an abbreviated triangular stage, a young Viking with a brilliant red beard perched on a stool, breathing heavily into his saxophone, practicing for his evening gig.

Wendl let himself go dim, hoping he wouldn't be noticed while he let the bluesy moaning of the instrument soak into his attention. As he listened, melancholy, outright sadness, dark and astringent as old wine, welled up inside him. More than the music turned his feeling. He caught the joy that found the musician as he played, but it grieved Wendl that this ordinary glory was so transient and fragile, that too soon, very soon, none of this would be here, that these wanting and seeking souls would be displaced to wherever souls are exiled when the last music dies in silence.

His concentration broken, the solitary server suddenly realized she had a customer and timidly came over to his table, looked him in the eye and promptly forgot her spiel. Silently, she laid a menu on the table, peered at him from under her purple hair while she considered whether to risk taking his order or simply to flee.

Wendl ordered a beanburger and a glass of retsina. She asked him to repeat his order, just to make sure she heard right.

He did and she said, "I'm not sure we have retsina," although she was certain that her boss stocked no such thing.

Wendl said, "You did last time," although it was his first time.

"Let me check, then." She pretended to check in the cooler and to great surprise spied three unopened bottles. Meekly and promptly she returned with a full glass and a few minutes later was back with the beanburger. She set the burger down as Wendl sipped his wine and looked up at her and she drowned in his gaze. Curiosity overwhelmed professional etiquette. "Is that stuff any good?" she blurted, gesturing at the glass.

"You won't know before you try it," murmured Wendl VonTrier.

FOUR

Abigail glanced out her kitchen window. *Where did the afternoon go?* The narrow band of trees between her yard and Bernice Abner on the next street already cast a shadow across her herb garden. A figure bent over one of the beds, inspecting her artemisia. A second look verified it was her enigmatic renter, Wendl VonTrier. Although it violated her self-imposed house rule, she thought she might invite him in to share her supper. She was eager to discuss Millicent McTeer's marvelous book that still filled her head with mysteries and miracles.

She found it hard to fathom that the world Millicent described in *The Forest Soul*, so deep and complex and miraculous, was the very same world Abigail had lived in all her life, although that world, too, contained charms and beauty enough to elicit gladness and love. She was grateful for her garden and her life, and for the most part, content with it as it was, but if *The Forest Soul* was something more than a fairytale, there was a lot that Abigail Trammell had overlooked on her journey to the present, and it occurred to her now that perhaps more than that she had forgotten on the way.

She set two plates on the table, looked out her window again. Wendl was nowhere in sight. She added water to the kettle to make more tea. Abigail already had a meatloaf in the oven. She wondered if it was enough for the two of them. She had observed that the spindly Wendl could disappear a prodigious amount of groceries. Abigail had lettuce. She would make a big salad. Wendl always ate his green stuff first.

When her timer chirped and she pulled the meatloaf out of the oven, she still hadn't heard Wendl come in. She stepped out her back door and called as loud as she dared, "Wendl . . . Mister VonTrier?" Abigail hoped Bernice hadn't heard. Her gossip-hungry neighbor kept her keen eyes and ears ever tuned in the direction of Hemlock Cottage and its parade of transient occupants from other worlds than hers.

Only frogs and crickets answered Abigail's call, so she stepped down into her dusky herbarium among the rosemary and marjoram, chives and chamomile and a dozen other species and varieties flavorful or medicinal. She looked back toward the house. The rental room window up in the gable was dark. Her paying guest must still be out here someplace.

She peered into the deep shadows among the trees, saw a flicker of light through the branches, perhaps from Bernice's house, then noticed a little path she had never seen before, winding from her garden's edge up through the trees. *It must be new*, Abigail thought. Had Bernice Adams been poaching her herbs? "You only need ask," she said to the trees.

On impulse, Abigail plunged ahead along the path, as if she might catch her neighbor slinking down to her garden, shears and basket in hand. She expected every step, to see the light again from Bernice's window and step out into the neighbor's yard, but when she stopped and looked back toward her own property, she couldn't see her garden at all. Ahead, the dimming path wound only deeper into the rising night.

"These woods are dark and deep at least, Mister Frost,"

Abigail said to the crowding shadows. She could barely see the path now in the gloaming wood. Whistles and growls and moans and howls from invisible and unfamiliar throats dissipated her calm. Twigs scraped her face as she blundered off the path. Momentarily she lost her bearings, couldn't recall which direction was homeward. Something only slightly darker than the air hurdled at her out of the deepening night. An owl? No, a crow, who settled to the ground right in front of her and croaked what may have been warning or command or plea or invitation.

This way, it translated in her mind, as the corvid lofted again and flew away toward an opening in the canopy, that grew brighter as she followed. It seemed to Abigail that she had been walking for hours, but when she emerged from the indeterminate wood, the waning afternoon was still as bright as when she crossed her garden in search of her boarder.

Standing among her familial flowers on ground that she named her own, she saw across the garden, the crow guide, perched on her porch railing. She stopped, panting, looked down aghast, commenced brushing away the spider webs and leaves her apron had accumulated during her sylvan perambulations, and when she looked up again, there was no crow, only Wendl VonTrier standing on her porch, his face, that might, in another world, have belonged to a crow, emulating a human smile,

"I've been wandering," Abigail wheezed breathlessly, as she approached, having thought of nothing beyond the obvious to communicate.

Wendl's changeable and unsettling face manifested an expression resembling human mirth. "Not all who wander are crossed," he murmured, and opened the screen for her to pass through to her kitchen. The first thing she saw was that her oven was still on and no meatloaf sat on the counter. She was certain she'd taken it from the oven before she went out.

"Dear Lord," a whispered exclamation. "My meatloaf!" a

louder urgency. She grabbed a towel from the back of a chair, dashed across the room and threw open her oven door, felt a wash of relief when no smoke billowed forth and she didn't smell burning, only meatloaf. Folding the towel around her tender fingers she hauled out the hot pan and set it atop the stove. The meatloaf was the proper shade of golden, and

. . .

"Just right," said Wendl over her shoulder.

Abigail turned off the oven, sighed a wordless prayer of gratitude.

"Will we eat this, then?" murmured Wendl VonTrier.

When she finally made it down to her kitchen next morning, Abigail's eccentric boarder was out and gone again without his breakfast. She supposed he might fuel his day at Home Ground or Wardlow's, the only establishments in town where a stranger could buy a breakfast, not counting the posh and pricey Apple Grove Inn, a mile down the mountain.

She was only mildly miffed that Wendl had chosen to forego her own culinary fare. The tired part of her was relieved that today she had only herself to feed. She had not slept at all well last night. VonTrier's unworldly book kept whispering in her head long after she laid it aside and turned out the light. When sleep finally arrived, it drowned her in a continuous sequence of demanding dreams about forests inhabited by dragons and elves. She woke feeling exhausted, as if she had actually spent the night wandering through woods wild and wondrous.

As soon as the sun cleared the ridge bright and unclouded, Abigail, coffee in hand, forayed out across her garden, but found no trace of the path that confounded her the evening before. Peering up the hill through the trees beyond, she could see her neighbor's back door.

"Did I dream it all?" she asked her garden. Okra and tomatoes and squash offered no opinion.

While Abigail pondered elusive paths, her absented renter waited outside Gloria Proudfoot's Vintage Reads bookstore when she opened the doors to customers. He insisted on helping her wheel out her Battered and Bartered sidewalk cart.

"I've been pondering your offer, Mister VonTrier," she said as she added an armful of worn and wounded volumes to the display. "Is it still open?"

"No rush," he murmured, sounding like some sort of large cat. I'll be ready when you are. Actually, I've come today in search of another book."

"Anything in particular?" asked Gloria, hoping the object of Wendl's search would be found somewhere on her shelves with no price marked.

Wendl recited a garble of syllables that she supposed was a title, but she couldn't sort the sounds into words. When he saw her blank stare, he clarified, "It's Japanese. The title translates roughly in English as Dragonfire Soup. Tadahito Kitamura is the author."

Disappointed, Gloria said, "I'm sorry, Mister VonTrier. Except for a couple of old German bibles, we don't have any foreign language titles in the store."

Wendl shrugged, raised his hands. "Perhaps if I might look around? Surely there is something inviting."

I might get a sale out of you yet, Wendl VonTrier. You find things. Aloud, Gloria said, "You just help yourself then. I'll have some coffee ready in a minute if you'd like something to warm your search."

"I'll look forward to it," Wendl purred as he disappeared behind a row of shelves as if headed for someplace he knew.

The coffeemaker beeped done just as a middle-aged couple, obvious daytrippers, made a tentative entrance. Gloria gave them her tourist spiel as they gazed aimlessly around her store, looking for something with pictures. Eventually her studied charm was rewarded when they left carrying two paperbacks, a guidebook of local hiking trails and a photographic history of the town of Drovers Gap, along with two cups of her free coffee. She went to find Wendl and offer him a cup. He wasn't in the first row of shelves, nor the second. There were only three, and when she didn't see him in the third row, she assumed he'd slipped out of the store while she was busy with the couple. She walked down the row to go back to her desk, sipping coffee as she went, then turning the corner, saw another row of shelves beyond.

But that's all there is, she kept insisting to her eyes as she stood between the shelves that simply could not be in her world. Nevertheless, they stretched away in front of her now into a dim and indefinite distance. Miles of books on either side and no end in sight.

"It is Found," proclaimed a familiar voice behind her. Gloria whirled about to see Wendl brandishing aloft a book with a vertical row of indecipherable characters trickling down the front. She followed him meekly to the sales desk as if she were the customer and he the proprietor. As she had suspected, when he handed her the book, she could find no price sticker.

"I don't know what to charge you for this, Mister VonTrier," she said. "Wendl," she modified, getting his name right and surprised by her own familiarity.

She didn't see him reach for it, but a crisp hundred-dollar bill fluttered between his fingers. "Perhaps this might be enough?"

"More than enough, I'm sure," Gloria said, wondering what other costly items she might have overlooked among her stock. "Would you like that wrapped?" she asked, not knowing why she said it, as he had not mentioned anything regarding a gift.

"You are a thoughtful human," he murmured, "And a

receptive mind as well."

She thought Wendl laughed then. He sounded like windblown leaves skittering across a pavement, but when she tried to focus her gaze on his smile, for a second in the changeable light, his face looked to her beaked and feathered like some huge, benevolent owl. Flustered and unnerved, Gloria concentrated on gathering paper and ribbon for the giftwrap. She flipped through a few pages of the book before she snugged the paper around it. Wendl had said something about looking for a recipe book, she was sure, but this one seemed to be full of strange maps.

"You planning to travel?" she asked as she cut the ribbon to make a bow.

"I'm quite contented to be found right here for now," Wendl said. "But a young friend of mine is about to commence a journey, and I think some guidance might be in order."

Gloria wondered who that friend might be and where they might be going. Before she could extend her interrogation, however, a babbling gaggle of young customers came in. She bagged the package and handed it across the counter, then gave all her attention to the customers, escaped college students by the look of them, hoping she could keep track of them all and that nothing would leave her store that hadn't been paid for.

As it turned out, they actually bought an armload of books between them and all their plastic met approval. Gloria was surprised and elated, and as soon as the tribe swirled out her door into the street, she went down her aisles of shelves again to find the longer than long one where she assumed Wendl might have located his book. Three rows of shelves all began and ended inside the walls of her store. The fourth and forever row was as gone as if it had never been.

Did I dream the whole thing? she thought, *Or did Wendl take it with him?*

FIVE

As soon as he emerged from Vintage Reads, Wendl VonTrier followed his shadow to Home Ground Suds and Java. The young Viking saxophonist of his previous visit wasn't in view, but Wendl went to the counter and ordered a double espresso from the purple haired server. While Purplehair engaged the machine, Viking came in and retreated immediately to his accustomed corner and began opening his instrument case. Wendl took the book parcel from his shopping bag, crossed the room and held it out to the musician,

"Happy birthday," he said

The young man looked up, his red beard flashing like an igniting flame with the sudden movement. "Who are you?" he asked in a voice that carried as much suspicion as inquiry.

Wendl just smiled his unquantifiable smile and gestured the book toward Redbeard's chest.

The Viking gazed at the wrapped gift. "How did you know it's my birthday?" he ventured.

"It was the same date last year," Wendl said.

Hesitantly, Redbeard took the book. His "Thanks" barely

more than a whisper as Wendl turned and went to the counter to collect his espresso.

Redbeard unwrapped his present and when the book didn't explode immediately, he opened it to find page after page of musical scores. The saxophonist had never been great at reading music but these immediately made perfect sense to him. As his eyes scanned the notes he could hear them in his head. He knew just how he might tug and stretch them to make music more and deeper than what he saw on paper. He looked up from the book astounded and full of thanks, but Wendl was nowhere in sight.

He asked the girl with purple hair, "Where'd the old man get to?"

She shrugged. "Gone, I guess."

Redbeard went back to his corner, opened the book on the table in front of him, and began assembling his instrument.

On the street outside, Wendl sipped his espresso as he heard the first tentative wails before the music caught and flowed out the door behind him, a river of sound like no soul in Drovers Gap had ever heard. Around him in the music, people and trees and cars and all the buildings in the town began to shimmer in the dancing light as if on the verge of becoming beneath some other sun.

Chloe Toibin hung her apron on the rack and shook out her purple hair. As she scanned the front of the house, she didn't see a vacant table. Home Ground Suds and Java was not usually packed out this late in the season. She almost wished her shift were not ending, and not just because of the potential tips. Her head was full of the music Ronan had practiced most of the morning, a delicious pain of being filled and wanting more.

Now he was back. He had come in early for his evening set

and had been playing for nearly an hour now without a break. The music possessing him apparently captured anybody who listened, as well. By ones and twos, the townfolk and daytrippers had drifted in, consumed their drinks and food, and as if they had no place else on earth to go, stayed on to imbibe Ronan's sound.

If there had been any words to Ronan's tunes, Chloe was sure she would have known them. She'd caught herself time and again humming and singing nonsense syllables as she bustled, companioning Ronan's saxophone with her own wee voice, softly, softly, as much in her head as in her mouth, careful not to annoy her customers.

Nobody she had ever listened to played such music as she heard from Ronan tonight. In Ronan's hands, his sax, on this evening, became a live thing, with breath and voice and a beating heart all its own. Watching him play, Chloe thought he was out of himself, that the instrument played the man. Where had all this gift and power come from? She reckoned it had to be more than Ronan found in that old book her strange customer had given him.

Tonight, Ronan's saxophone conjured a wailing, moaning, throbbing ecstasy that washed over the room like a sunlit waterfall. When she closed her eyes, she could see the sound, twining the air, binding all who heard in a bright warm rising of belonging, like a mother holding her babes, rendering each and every of them children of the same song.

Chloe handed off her orders to Greg, who had the evening shift, resisted an impulse to sit down and submit to the music with everyone else. Instead, since she had to go now and make supper for her grandfather Colm, she shrugged into her coat and stepped out into the rising night.

The sky, not yet dark, washed the town in a celadon glow. A scatter of precocious stars and a spilling crescent moon were echoed by the lit windows of houses atop the ridges flanking Main Street. Chloe had often wished and dreamed that she could sing the music she kept hearing in her head. Now, walking through the quiet town, she suddenly astounded herself by doing just that. A full-throated, soaring burst of aria answering the unworlded melodies of Ronan's saxophone, still splashing and tumbling in her mind as she walked home to her new life.

Abigail Trammell pulled her sheets from the line, dropped the pins into the little bag hanging beside and carefully folded them into her basket. She owned a new clothes dryer, but whenever a laundry day came clear and breezy, she preferred to hang out her bed linens. They came in then crisp and fresh from the mountain air and some of her guests, at least, those she would hope to see return, appreciated the difference. Wendl VonTrier was one of them, she was sure.

Not to overwork a metaphor, her peculiar boarder had been a breath of fresh air in her life. His unsettling and uplifting presence breathed into her days youthful feelings she supposed she had forgotten and outgrown decades past. Not that she had developed anything like a crush on Wendl, but his arrival stirred up the smouldering embers of a love for life. Her neighbors had long since ceased to be subjects of any particular curiosity or affection. They provided a relief to her aloneness primarily because she was used to them there. Even her garden had become more of a habit than an enthusiasm.

But on this day, as she cut back her bedraggled roses and pulled the last remaining blueberry leaves to dry for tea, she was thinking not so much of the bleak winter coming fast upon her but of the burgeoning green to follow after. She blamed her unaccustomed optimism on Wendl's Otherworldish book he'd loaned her, its changeable pages, wordy as a dictionary one day and unmarked as a fresh snowfall another. She hadn't just read *The Forest Soul*, she had communed with it. Through the book, its mysterious author, Millicent McTeer, became alive and present. The book wasn't just paper pages, numbered and bound, it was an incarnation, drawing together two women, worlds and times apart, into a shared soul.

That encounter wrought a mysterious enlargement in Abigail's life. In numerous and indefinable ways and aspects, she found a space in her days for the occasional unexpected joy, maybe even a small miracle. Once upon a time, long and far from this present, Abigail Trammell had anticipated the joyous and marvelous as her due, had lived and given herself extravagantly in assurance that she was so held. She had come to Drovers Gap alone, but in some season previous to that solitary arrival, she had traversed in beloved company.

She carried the burden of that not-quite-remembered joining to steel her long and present solitude. She dared not permit her mind to seek much after the joyous belonging left and lost in her past and other life. The tears she refused had pooled in her being over the years until they formed the calm and placid sea of sadness upon which her days floated now. Garden routines, quirky and inquisitive neighbors, random exchanges of small kindnesses, the distraction of those familiar strangers, her paid guests, all accumulated into the raft of flotsam that bore her across the depths of her quiet despair.

Wendl VonTrier's arrival displaced that past which she never spoke of to anyone she knew in Drover's Gap. Her abiding melancholy, which she went to great pains to render invisible to all she met, had receded for days at a time to the farthest edge of her awareness. Wendl had restored her to the world of unforeseen possibilities, where on any given day, anything might happen, the odds being better than even that whatever it might be would prove at least marginally worth waiting for.

So, on this particular day, a restored, if not actually reborn

Abigail Trammell hoisted her basket full of the clear clean light of late autumn and headed for her house, glad in her heart that Wendl VonTrier had just paid his rent for another month of room and breakfast. She would have some desired company through the shortening days into winter. Abigail learned long ago not to dwell on things too far into the future. A harder and later lesson had been not to stew and mourn over an irretrievable history. Abigail only knew for sure that she was alive now. She breathed and moved and felt in this moment, which held enough for endless exploration and exaltation.

Stepping into her kitchen, she gazed back over her garden, gauging the afternoon light, then checked it against the clock above her stove. In the laundry room, she folded the towels, ironed the sheets and pillow cases and folded them neat enough to sell. She gazeed out the window. She likely had time enough to do Wendl's room today before he came in. He left her house early this morning before she could make his breakfast. She thought she might invite him to share her supper tonight to make up for it. Abigail liked to keep all her accounts, business and social, balanced.

Carrying her basket of fresh laundry up the stairs, she indulged in her by now habitual speculation regarding what her boarder did all day in their little town to keep himself occupied. If the strange tales conveyed to her by Gloria Proudfoot and Rhonda Shaw were to be believed, Wendl spent a good part of his time upturning the carefully crafted routines of the local population. Outside the guestroom door, she set her basket on the floor, gazed down at the sheets and pillowcases, pressed and pristine, along with the fluffy towels and washcloths, still redolent with the essence of a mountain day. She wondered if any other woman in this town still ironed their sheets. Nobody but Abigail would mind the difference, but they fit neater in her closet if she ironed them first.

She pulled the keys from her apron pocket and opened the door. Wendl's room appeared just as she saw it last time. Virginally neat. The bed looked not to have been slept in. She changed the linens anyway and found the bathroom equally untouched. She replaced the unwrinkled towels there with the fresher ones from her basket. *Let none say I didn't do my part.* No sign of Wendl's luggage. Curious, she looked into the closet. No clothes on the hangers and no suitcase, either. She considered opening the dresser drawers and rebuked the temptation.

What does the man do in here? She spied a single red leaf on the carpet. Her ghostly boarder left some tracks after all. Abigail dropped her basket in the hall and went to the little closet at the end where she kept her vacuum. As she retrieved the appliance, a gusty breeze whispered down the hall and she heard Wendl's door slam shut. An involuntary chill rippled her shoulders.

She towed her vacuum back up the hall and opened the guestroom door again onto a moss bound path that trailed away among ferns and stones shadowed by close-crowding spruce and fir. Through the branches overhead she glimpsed scraps of blue sky and shards of brilliant white clouds. Abigail stepped through the door, felt forest underfoot, filled her lungs full of the scent of conifers after a spring rain.

A choir of invisible birds set the air ashimmer with their song. Glancing behind her, Abigail saw the door had vanished and almost wondered why it didn't bother her that the way she had come no longer existed in her moment. The path ahead was her only reality now. It beckoned and she followed between the sheltering trees.

Six

Abigail Trammell walked and walked, with no backward thought of the place or the people she'd left behind. The path snaked on and on through the trees on either side, and she followed it deeper and deeper among the watchful woods. Sometimes the trail lifted her up along bright ridges where birds clamored and sunlight dappled the ground and the leaves and her own body, and sometimes the way led her down and down among cool shadows where she could hear the insistent music of a boisterous stream and catch glimpses of white water between the shouldering boles of a forest as ancient, it seemed to her, as the earth that rooted it.

She walked until she forgot to count the miles and hours. The forest went with her, unbroken and unbounded. She rounded a turn and through an opening between the trees the setting sun struck her full in the face, startling her back to herself. She was far and away from any place she knew. Home might be just over the next ridge or on the far side of the moon. This world that looked so like the one she left in Drovers Gap answered to no name she had ever learned. Unrooted in any memory, this place was all the home she could claim. She knew no more of it than her two eyes could map.

Aware of herself again, Abigail realized she was hungry. More than hungry, thirsty. She'd seen ripe berries occasionally along the way. She wished she'd paid more attention, couldn't now recall what sort they were, if they were edible or not. Water, she supposed was more likely down slope. As she considered how far she could safely wander from the trail in search of a drink, she heard singing. From some hidden where up ahead, the tune lifted and wavered, gradually loudening as she stilled and watched for some glimpse of the singer. She judged it a solitary voice, probably male, likely past youth. The almost tune, a spare, strident rumble and hum, carried an edge, yet manifest oddly musical, cheerful, even comforting in this place apart.

Abigail stayed and waited. It didn't occur to her it might be more prudent to hide. And there he came through the undergrowth and into her view, first a round pate, bare and bronzed by seasons and sun, then two dark and piercing eyes set deep in a weathered face that merged into a long beard tumbling and swirling like a mountain waterfall until tucked into the singer's wide belt. Broad and angular, he strode toward Abigail, his legs emerging from the rough kilt, stout and knobby as tree trunks. Still singing at the top of his voice, an apparently empty burlap bag slung over his left shoulder, and swinging a long stick in his right hand, he gave no sign he saw her there, and she wondered if the man were blind, was about to step aside, when he stopped abruptly, practically nose to nose, and stared at her, motionless as moss.

Abigail held her breath, not daring to move or speak. After years and years, Singer stepped back, thumped the ground three time with his walking staff and with a smile that shouted down the gathering shadows, said, "Ganny ye're Gobnait."

"Abigail," whispered Abigail, finding no air left behind her voice.

Singer's smile erupted into a mighty laugh that seemed to well up from his toes, perhaps from the mountain beneath. When his mirth subsided enough for him to get a word in edgewise, he gasped and wheezed and recovered his speech. "That's what they call you among the Fallen, but at our Abbey, we know you by your true name. You're Gobnait here, and you've heard my prayer that you would help me with my bees."

"Bees?" queried a mystified Abigail, beginning to breathe again.

"That's why you're here," Singer said. "I'm Brother Owl, the keeper at Trier Abbey, yonderside of this wood."

"What do you keep there?" asked Abigail, trying to prolong the conversation with this crazy wanderer while she planned her escape.

He laughed again, as if she'd told a joke. He lifted the bag from his shoulder and waved it in the air between them. "The bees, of course, and I've lost 'em. That's why you're here, ain't it?"

"I don't have any bees," Abigail protested meekly.

"They told us you're a gardener."

"I admit to having a garden," she said.

Dark eyes flickered like coals on a hearth as Owl declared his obvious. "Then you have bees."

Before she could summon any additional denials, Owl whirled and started back the way he'd come. "We'll sing the bees home tomorrow," he cackled over his shoulder, waving his stick over his head for Abigail to follow. "I forget my Rule. Before else, we must take you to Goodmother Wandalena and get you fed and rested. Bound ye're purely spent after walking across the Two Worlds."

Wendl VonTrier walked up the drive at Hemlock Cottage carrying an armload of groceries. He'd intended to cook supper for his landlady tonight, while they were in the same world together.

He knew before he came into the yard, though, that the house was empty. He carried the groceries to the kitchen, set the bag on the table, and called out softly, though he knew she wouldn't hear, "Miss Trammell? Abigail?"

Faintly, the drone of the bees in the garden filtered in through the open windows. Wendl smiled to himself, crossed the hall, climbed the stair to his room, opened the door, gazed into the woods beyond.

"Welcome Home, Sister Gobnait," he said aloud in the Old Tongue, closed the door, went back downstairs to Abigail's room, opened her closet and dressed himself in her clothes, adjusting himself to fit. She looked into the mirror, and when satisfied the face she saw belonged to Abigail Trammell, said aloud to her reflection, just to practice her new voice, "My name is Abigail Trammell, and I feel so comfortable here, I've decided to stay awhile."

Then she picked up the phone and punched in the number for Vintage Reads. "Gloria? This is Abigail. I'm finally delivered of my peculiar boarder. To celebrate, why don't you come over tonight and let me cook us up something special for supper."

Gloria Proudfood showed up for supper with a blackberry cobbler, which she presented with her usual friendly aggression. "Here," she said as soon as the newly configured AbiWendl opened the door. Gloria thrust the pie forward as if it were a weapon. "You never serve sweets, so I brought some." although Abigail Trammell seldom served a guest without.

"How sweet, Gloria, and you baked this just for me?" AbiWendl cooed convincingly.

"I don't bake," remonstrated Gloria. "I picked this up at

Dolf's Market on the way here. I wanted to be sure I got dessert."

"Well, I'm sure you'll enjoy it," AbiWendl said. "It smells delicious."

"It should be," groused Gloria "Do you know how much that man is charging for these? You'd think he had to pick the berries himself."

"Well, it was mighty kind of you, Gloria, to go to such expense just to improve my little supper." AbiWendl already knew that sarcasm was lost on the bookseller and could be indulged in outrageously without fear of detection or retribution.

During the meal, the two women talked of many things, rather Gloria talked while the transmorphed púca mostly listened. After covering the entire catalog of Drovers Gap's rumors and scandals, Gloria expounded in protracted detail about her "Little Sister" in Florida, rendered chronically unwell by various self-diagnosed ailments. "Little Sister has been at me for months to move down there to Fort Fiesta and live with her, and I just might if I could get out from under the bookstore. These mountain winters are getting too much for my old bones. Your Windy pretended he might like to buy the place, but he skipped town without making an offer. I hope he paid you his rent."

"Wendl," corrected AbiWendl.

"That's what I said," sniped Gloria. "Wendell, like the berry."

The transpúca sighed just like Abigail would've, and asked, "Ready for some of your cobbler?"

"Oh, I don't eat blackberries," Gloria said. "I can't abide the seeds between my teeth."

AbiWendl dished out a serving of blackberry cobbler and set it at her place. She got out a sliver of her much diminished winter fruitcake for Gloria, The Wendl part of AbiWendl knew as well as Abigail would've that the fruitcake was what

Gloria had been shooting for all along. The bookseller sniffed at it and said, "I really shouldn't. I'm a teetotaler regards sugar," but she ate it with relishment and seemed disappointed when AbiWendl didn't offer her another piece.

And although it wasn't quite, "That's the last of it." AbiWendl said to Gloria's silence.

Not the whiskey, I hope, Gloria thought to herself.

The Abigailed púca caught the thought in the air. "There's plenty of that for next year's fruitcake," she said, and abruptly changed the subject. "Tell me, Gloria, are you serious about wanting to sell Vintage Reads?"

Gloria nodded, and as soon as her fruitcake left room in her mouth for words, said, "I suppose I am, but who would buy a used bookstore in this town?"

"I'll buy it."

Gloria stared open-mouthed for three seconds, took a long swallow of her tea. "You never struck me as much of a reader, Abigail Trammell," she said at last.

"Oh, you'd be surprised at the things I've been reading lately. Sure you don't want to try a bit of this delicious cobbler you brought?"

"You really want to buy my store?"

"Yup. What's your price?"

So she wouldn't have to answer immediately, Gloria said, "Maybe I'll have just a teenytiny taste of cobbler after all, just to sweeten our deal."

SEVEN

Later that night, the púca crawled into Abigail Trammell's bed and released her likeness to rest in his true shape, at any rate, the shape he could maintain with minimal effort. The forms the púca had assumed over his span of being were legion. Wendl had forgotten which came first. He found living in Abigail's skin comfortable enough, for all that, and suspected very soon it would become as natural to him as his own.

He ignored the subliminal glimmer near the ceiling in the dark above the window, wove his shield a little tighter just in case Wandalena persisted in her probing. She would be wanting to know why he hadn't returned to Trier, and he didn't have an answer. He only knew he wasn't ready quite yet. Perhaps, he thought, his Superior was right. Maybe he had spent so much time among the Fallen, he was becoming one with them. They were all broken, of course. And Wendl had not yet forgotten what brokenness felt like. It would be a while before the Goodmother sent her Vergers into Shadow to compel him back to Trier. Meanwhile, he intended to defy her stricture against meddling in the troubles of the Fallen.

Tonight, this púca would sleep, perchance to dream. With

dreams might come some enlightenment regarding his purpose here. Imagination loves the dark. Wendl breathed in the close and comforting night, and turned loose the world, blending with the mists over Abigail's garden, hovering, drifting ever so slightly on the faint breeze, shining under the waxing moon like a flock of fireflies or a swarm of miniscule stars.

In the World behind the world, at Trier Abbey, Goodmother Wandalena shook her head at the blank surface in her Seerbowl. Her púca was running silent again. *One day, Wendl VonTrier, you will wreck the Two Worlds.*

Wendl sank into his dream, down and down, past the moon, into the air, down beneath clouds where starlight didn't reach, down into a murk where the sun shone red at midday, down among the ruins of a still city where no one breathed, forgotten by all who had lived there. A metropolis of the deceased, habitable only for ghosts . . . and Púca.

Wendl hovered for a moment over the broken pavement, noted that nothing green grew up through the cracks, assessed his status. Yes, this was indeed a dream or perhaps a vision.

"Follow me and see for yourself," the Dream said.

Wendl gathered to a shape, recent and well recalled, and set solid feet just like Abigail Trammell's on fractured concrete. She listened, for Wendl VonTrier in this present form was consistently and convincingly she. Silence as only a dream is silent. No wind, no machines, no voices nor footfalls. Not even the sweet whisper of her own breath nor the comforting cadence of her heartbeat. It occurred to her then that she might be herself a ghost, or . . .

"Am I deaf?" AbiWendl shouted. She wasn't. Her voice still echoed among the gutted towers as she walked along the deserted street.

"Where am I going?" the dreamer asked the air, preferring to arrive at her destination, if not prepared, at least aware of her fate.

"Tell me who you are and I will tell you where you go," said the Dream.

"And who are you that I should listen?" queried the dreamer.

The Dream laughed. The city shook and shimmered with vast peals of cosmic mirth. The dreamer shrank under that onslaught of holy delight, almost losing her grip on her form.

"Don't you remember me, little one?" teased the Dream. "We were in the War together. For a while, I was afraid you'd been lost to me there."

"Of all our Galère who went to war," said the dreamer, "only I came home. At the end, I was alone."

"Answer me, púca," The Dream thundered. In the distance, one of the towers shattered and fell. "You wear a thousand faces to the world. Which one is you?"

"Not one of them are mine," confessed the púca in a whisper. "I have only the shape You dream me to be."

Wendl VonTrier woke to a cloud of fragrant mist filling the room, but by the time the púca settled and gathered and looked in her mirror, she saw Abigail Trammell again.

"Morning, Abigail, business must be good." Rhonda Shaw observed as AbiWendl presented the seven books she was mailing.

"Business is business and life is good," the púca who looked and sounded like Abigail Trammell said.

Rhonda took the books, looked over the address labels while she was thinking Abigail had been different since she took over Vintage Reads from Gloria Proudfoot. Abigail had never been much of a talker, but before she spent all her time with books, she had never talked in riddles, either. "Mercy," Rhonda said, "these are all going over the water."

"Prophecy is seldom read close to home," murmured the bookseller.

"What's that supposed to mean?" snapped the postmaster.

"I'm trying to be nice, Rhonda. It means most people in Drovers Gap have honed their minds on Fox News. They don't read books by anybody they wouldn't vote for. If I'm going to keep Vintage Reads open, I must cater to people who live in places where intellects are still cultivated."

"How do all these people find out about you?" Rhonda queried.

"Truth will out, Rhonda. The farthest star will shine bright on the darkest night."

Rhonda shook her head. "That's thirty-eight dollars and forty-six cents, Abigail. I declare, you've become a feisty old crone, not to mention hard to understand."

"Sounds like a compliment to me," said AbiWendl as she tapped her plastic on the cardreader. "You take care of yourself, Rhonda," as she turned to go.

"A couple of your out-of-towners were in here asking about you when I opened up this morning," Rhonda threw at her as she reached the door.

AbiWendl stopped, turned back. For a split second, she resembled a large bird. "What did you tell them?" she snapped.

Rhonda couldn't remember having seen Abigail Trammell appear unsettled before. "I didn't tell them anything. I said the Postal Service can't give out information on our patrons. I might have sent them down to your bookstore, but they were just . . . odd. I wasn't sure they needed to know."

"Did they say who they were?"

"No, but they asked me to leave their business card in your mailbox. I told them I could do that if they mailed it to you. They bought a stamped envelope and put the card in it. I wrote your name on it and put it in your box after they left."

"Thank you, Rhonda. You did good."

When the púcawoman checked her box she found three book orders, assorted flyers, and an envelope with *A. Trammell* scrawled across the front in Rhonda's barely legible hand. She opened the envelope and pulled out the card. *I'm surprised it took so long*. The card was printed in a High Speech script that read,

Corvid and Hawke Associates
Vergers Licensed and Ordained
7 River Street, Trier Ordinary

It was almost closing time at Vintage Reads when AbiWendl ushered the last of the day's customers out the door. The tourist couple carried an armload of books between them, having fallen victim of the Abigailed puca's talent for persuading potential readers that an author they'd never heard of happened to be the very one they had been looking for all their lives. She was about to lock the door behind them and slip into a more comfortable shape when she spied the two figures on the opposite side of the street crossing toward the store, oblivious to the traffic. She flipped the sign to *CLOSED* and leaving the door unlocked, walked back behind the counter. By the time Orville Hawke and Wilbur Corvid opened the door, the púca was solid Abigail.

"I'm afraid your friend Wendl isn't in at the moment," she said pleasantly. "He must have seen you coming."

"You'll do just fine, Púca," grated Wilbur Corvid.

"The Goodmother sent us to find out why you haven't been returning her calls." Orville Hawke said, leaning forward, resting his taloned hands on the counter, scratching the polished surface.

Wendl relaxed into a more púcaesque configuration. "Why hasn't Wandalena sent some of her own from the Abbey to fetch me, instead of scouring up the dregs of the secular town to come slinking across the worlds in my wake?" he asked in a how's-the-weather tone.

"Take you care now, Púca," cawed Corvid, allowing a hint of his native form to show faintly as he spoke. "We come not quite exactly in the service of the Abbey, but we do have your

Superior's commission, if you need to see it. Show us some due respect."

Hawke took from his jacket pocket a small glass vial, corked and sealed with wax and set it on the counter between them. "There's no need for ruffled feathers here," he said. "We haven't come to take you back. The Abbey has another job for you while you're among the Fallen, which you would already be about if you had deigned to answer the Goodmother's summons."

Wendl picked up the vial and held it to the light. The liquid inside was as clear as water.

"You going to open it for us?" Corvid ventured.

"I'll not break the Abbey's seal in such profane company," Wendl said. "Go tell your employer that Wendl VonTrier is about her business." He gestured at the door, which swung open as two large dark birds flew out over the heads of startled pedestrians.

Eight

The Abigailed púca dropped the transworlded vial into her purse, turned out the lights, except for the window display, locked the door to Vintage Reads and set out across town toward Hemlock Cottage. She hadn't rented out the guest room since taking over Gloria's bookstore, and wondered if, in view of the shift in inventory and customer base over the last twelve months, a rebranding might be in order. If the online business continued to grow, she might need to hire an assistant for the brick-and-mortar side of things. She could work the mail-orders from home, if need be, and have time to take in guests again.

The Wendl part of her was gratified to have Mother Wandalena off his case, at least until this current assignment was completed. With every intention to fulfill the obligation, there remained an equal resolve to be as leisurely as possible in the process. Wendl's nickname among the abbey congregants, Wendl the Fallen, he figured was apt enough. This púca found life in the fallen world much more fulfilling and intriguing than the cloistered routines at Trier. No play and all pray made a dull monk, whether púca, human, or other. It was hard to nurture compassion where there was no field for it to run in.

At this precise moment, the púca was consumed more with curiosity than compassion. What sort of game was afoot that would make the Superior go to the length of hiring townie thugs to convey her command? Wendl might be able to reach his seerbowl from here. If not, he would have to make do with whatever was at hand.

Getting home took longer than it should. Bernice Abner coming out of the post office nearly ran over AbiWendl in her eagerness to range about the town sharing the latest scandals. Gossip dripped constantly from her lips like the infectious slobber of a rabid canine.

"Abigail Trammell, you will absolutely not believe what I just heard from Rhonda." Bernice gloated.

"Probably not, Bernice," AbiWendl said. "Maybe you ought not tell me right now and wait for some moment when my incredulity is at low tide."

Ignoring the reposte, Bernice sank further into unfounded speculation. "Windy VonTrier has run off to Florida to be with your friend Gloria Proudfoot."

AbiWendl laughed like a púca. "I doubt you heard it from Rhonda Shaw, because I know for a fact, dear Bernice, that Gloria is living with another woman in Florida. If Wendl VonTrier has run off, it's just to escape your unbridled gossiping."

For three full seconds, Bernice stood with her mouth hanging open as if hoping some escaped word might find its way back home. Finding her breath again, she exclaimed, "Abigail, that is a horrid thing to say about somebody," but AbiWendl was already walking away, her mind all on getting home and opening a bottle.

She reached Hemlock Cottage without further interceptions by neighbors eager to talk, set the little bottle from the Vergers on the kitchen table, and gazed at it intently for several minutes. Whatever intelligence had been given to the bottle stayed inside. AbiWendl sighed, went to her room, undressed and immersed in a hot bath until Wendl emerged clean and clear. He would be better able to access his powers in his native form.

Back in the kitchen, he extended the tendrils of his awareness to his limits, attempting to reach his seerbowl in that other world. Barely, he could touch it in his cell at Trier, but try as he might, could not grasp it firmly enough to draw it back across the Separation. Eventually, he gave up, slipped back into Abigail mode and went out to her garden to gather a salad. On her way back in with her basketful of supper, and maybe breakfast, she picked up the old porringer Abigail had left out seasons ago to catch rainwater for the birds. She poured it empty of last night's rain, pleased to see that, although cracked from some past winter's freeze, it could still hold its water. Cleansed by the seasons, it would serve the purpose.

Faux Abigail washed the greens and made the salad but was Wendl again by the time he ate it, along with toasted slices of Abigail's buttermilk loaf. He saved the last swallow of the kukicha he drank with his meal. It wasn't the savory mountaintwig tea that heightened his perceptions at Trier Abbey, but it would suffice to bond him with the seerwater. Actually, any liquid he might have been drinking would have been efficacious, even Abigail's iced tea, so sweet it made his teeth hurt. Assuming Abigail's shape had not endowed the púca with her tastes.

Wendl cleared the table, leaving only the bottle, the porringer from the garden, and the cup containing the dregs of his kukicha. Deliberately, ceremonially even, he broke the seal on the bottle and poured the contents into the porringer. The clear liquid turned an impenetrable black as it settled. One might have been peering into a bowl of India ink, or into a hole in the world. He wet his lips with his kukicha, enough to get a taste of it on the tip of his tongue, then poured the rest into the porringer.

He watched the tea swirl and disappear into the black. When no trace of it was left, the bowl suddenly cleared and Wendl sat face to face across the worlds with Goodmother Wandalena, Superior of Trier Abbey.

"They told me you are a woman, now." Wandalena said, when she recognized Wendl.

"Most of the time, I'm Abigail Trammell," he said. "Would you like to see?"

"We have Gobnait back among us now," Wandalena almost smiled. "Your simulation could not add to that."

"Why did you send Corvid and Hawke after me instead of someone of our own?" Wendl queried.

"You would have been expecting that, and you would have evaded them. Besides, the Vergers are not inhibited by any Rule. They are efficient because they employ means and methods that, were they to speak of them to us, we would not find acceptable."

"Don't ask. Don't tell," murmured Wendl.

"What?"

"Nothing," he said. "Just an expression among the Fallen."

"I ponder at times, Wendl VonTrier," said Wandlena, wavering as her intensity disturbed the calm of Wendl's improvised seerbowl, "if you are still one of ours at all."

"If you really doubted me, Goodmother, we would not be talking now," Wendl said with frankness unbefitting his station.

"You have talents, Little Brother, that make you worth the risk. Take care you don't lose them."

Wendl bowed silently, hoping that would pass as an appropriate gesture of humility and contrition.

Abigail's cast-off porringer began to cloud. It wasn't a true seerbowl and wouldn't hold a thread intact much longer. Wandalena must have noticed it, too, and went straight to her point. "Badb Catha, has escaped the cloister and fled among the Fallen. The Vergers have located the old dragon but claim they are unable to contain her. She's in your vicinity. Watch her, but don't interfere."

The seerwater went gray, almost transparent. Wendl thought their thread had broken until Wandalena reappeared long enough to for Wendl to catch a fragment of her final sentence, ". . . sending Lugh as well. She will be dealt with." And the water was just water again and Wendl was not surprised to see the cracked porringer had mended without a trace.

The púca felt no rush to reconnect with Lugh Longarm, who had been an upper-echelon deity before the Separation War. To say they had been enemies in that other and past conflict would be an overstatement, but none who knew them there would have ever said they were friends.

NINE

First thing next morning at Vintage Reads, AbiWendl wheeled the Battered and Bartered table out front under the awning, went back inside, switched on her laptop to pull up the *Mountain Magic* website and order an employment ad for an assistant manager at Vintage Reads.

Just as she tapped *Confirm Order*, a covey of weekend nuisances swarmed the Battered and Bartered table outside, intent on finding some inexpensive mind candy to while them though an afternoon shower. She watched them through the window, especially the young man trying to grab-and-go a small paperback. AbiWendl concentrated, and the book slipped out of his hand and bounced off his feet. He scurried to retrieve it and jammed it into the pocket of his jeans. One of his friends said something to him and he laughed. The book fell out of his pocket and bounced under the table. As they all started walking away, the boyman glanced through the window and saw the bookseller watching him. He stopped, went back, bent down and picked up the book and sheepishly placed it back on the table. Before he could turn to catch up with his friends, AbiWendl stepped through the door, took the book and held it out to him.

"It's free if you read it," she said.

"I'm sorry," he stammered, looking at the book as if afraid it might reveal all his sins. AbiWendl smiled, took his hand, and placed the book in it. His friends were standing half-way up the block, looking back solemnly as if watching the aftermath of a traffic accident. "Thanks," he said, and fled, clutching his book to his chest. The púcawoman knew he would read the book. She had tasted his want for it in the air as she came out her door.

Neil Redding stashed his little book in the inside pocket of his jacket and ran after his friends. They had already turned and walked on down the street, were almost to Home Ground by the time he caught up.

"I thought that old lady was going to call a cop on you, Redding," Donny said, punching Neil in the shoulder hard enough to break his stride. It appeared a playful gesture, but present company agreed behind his back that Donny was a bully. His light banter veiled a deep-seated aggression toward the world in general.

Neil didn't answer, just reached inside his jacket, and held up the book. Donny was impressed. "I didn't know you had it in you, boy." They reached the restaurant and navigated through the crowd to a table. Neil's book was out of sight and forgotten in the wake of other pressing topics they never discussed with any of their parents.

Neil knew Donny assumed he'd stolen the book, and that he'd gained some cred with Donny on that account. The two girls with them, sisters, wouldn't care one way or another. Neil hadn't stolen anything since he was eight years old, and he didn't know why he'd swiped a used book that would only cost a dollar, except he wanted to be able to truthfully say to his father when he got home, that he'd spent no money except for a Mountain Dew and a hamburger. Lying to his father about something so trivial wouldn't have dented Neil's conscience, but he was afraid to be anything but truthful to Lewis Redding. His father always seemed to know, and Neil still carried hidden scars from his last foray into fiction.

If the elder Redding ever found Neil's book, and Neil would go to great pains to avoid that, he could truthfully tell his father now that the bookstore lady had given it to him. Lewis would check, of course, and the lady would tell him, yes, she did. Why had she done that, Neil wondered, and why had he taken the book? All he could say with any certainty was that when he looked at the title . . .

The Talking Trees
By
Alice Firehand

. . . he knew the book was written to him. The only thing now keeping him from being a shoplifter was the generosity of a woman who probably didn't even know his name. He hoped she didn't know his name. If word got back to Preacher Lewis, not only would Neil have to stand up and confess his thievery before his father's congregation, but for weeks afterward, he would wear under his shirt the marks of Lewis Redding's belt.

A week passed without any response to the ad for assistant manager at Vintage Reads. AbiWendl had about decided that good help was impossible to find. She was stirring up eggs in her kitchen for a Sunday morning omelet when she heard a knock at her back door and looked up to see a woman peering through the glass, smiling like long-lost kin and holding up a copy of Mountain Magic. They hadn't been face-to-face in at least ninety years, but the púca recognized the white hair and ember eyes immediately. She put down her bowl, gestured for her visitor to enter, and met her in an embrace before she was barely through the door.

"Tsula Stone, you old fox, I haven't seen you in literally ages. Where in the Two Worlds have you been keeping yourself?" she said when they stepped apart.

"I've been hanging loose among the Fallen," Tsula said, "where I don't have zealous clerics trying to convert me. You look like you've run away, too. Who are you hiding from?"

"Officially, I'm here on assignment from the Goodmother Wandalena," Wendl said as he morphed into his native form.

"You needn't do that just for me." Tsula smiled a tease. "We are púca, after all, I could go for a sweet old lady just as well."

Wendl laughed. "You haven't changed a bit, Tsula Stone. The last I heard of you, some were saying at the Abbey that you had taken up with some aged human, a writer of stories, I think they said."

"He didn't wear well," Tsula said. "So I let him go back to what he was. He wasn't any happier there. Humans can't be pleased. They only hunger for things, they can't have. Seriously, though, I've come about your ad for a shop assistant."

"Seriously? You want a job?"

"Quite."

"Hungry?" Wendl murmured, gesturing toward the table.

"Famished!" Tsula said sincerely.

"Let's make our breakfast then," Wendl said, taking up his bowl and spoon again. Once we've fed, we can talk about it."

"So, tell me, Tsula, how did you know I was here?" Wendl asked as they washed up their breakfast dishes.

"Your friends, Corvid and Hawke came to see me. They

were looking for Lugh, offered to split the bounty with me if they found him before you did."

"What did you tell those thieves?"

"I didn't know anything to tell them, Is he really here?"

Wendl, sensing the fox's surprise was genuine, shook his head. "The Goodmother says she's sent him among the Fallen. "Personally, I doubt he's married to a mission. I figure he just likes life better in Shadow."

Tsula teased a wry grin. "And how do you like life among the Fallen my púca friend?"

"I'm getting used to it," Wendl said. "There's always ample opportunity here in Shadow to practice the Rule."

"You must tell me sometime what in the Two Worlds possessed you to become a monk," Tsula said. "Surely in the Abbey, you were up to your neck in the Rule."

Wendl shrugged, began putting the cups away, slowly, one-by-one as he talked, "At Trier, everyone has enough to convince them they are filled. Any charity offered is taken as an offence. The Abbey may be the only place in the Two Worlds where one can successfully hide from their own poverty."

Tsula, surfeited with philosophical discourse, abruptly changed the subject. "I am serious about applying for this little job you are advertising. I can be a big help to you just now, and not only with the books."

"Sometimes the best help is not to help," Wendl murmured, "but why does a forest púca want a job in town?

Tsula laughed long enough to make Wendl wish she would stop. When she finally recovered from her mirth, she said, "Come on, now, good Brother, you're becoming as much a hypocrite as that old woman running your Abbey. I know this bookstore thing is just a cover for your púcaesque mischief. Well, I need a cover, too."

Feigning annoyance, Wendl said tersely, "You could go back to the woods with the other foxes."

"Coyotes are moving in. They make life precarious for foxes," Tsula said.

Wendl flickered for a moment, as if about to shift into another form, then steadied and said soft and serious, "If you live among people, you'll need to sleep under a roof."

Tsula waved her arms, "I thought Hemlock Cottage is a bed-and-breakfast. You do have a room vacant, don't you?"

"Well, until now I did," said the púca, looking for all the world like Abigail Trammell again.

It didn't take long for the two púca to settle into the routine of their new partnership. They took turns womaning the bookstore and herding the guests at Hemlock Cottage. Before winter had set in the locals were referring to the pair as "the Hemlock girls," it being understood by all that the two in question were old girls. Of course, none of their neighbors had any idea just how old they actually were. Where humans count years in decades, púca count in centuries.

Tsula lapsed into her vulpine form at night and ranged the woods and ridges under the hungry moon. Once, she was nearly shot by a hunter and twice had to outrun ravenous coyotes, but narrow escapes only served to whet her appetite for nocturnal adventures.

Halfway through Lent, reservation requests were coming in for the next tourist season at Hemlock Cottage, and it became clear that they would not be able to accommodate nearly all of them. AbiWendl said to her Other at breakfast on a raw March morning when a driving rain chased away last remnants of snow and drove against the windows like a snare of drums, "Dear, you know we could use another room or two here."

"You want to open a hotel now, do you?" Tsula murmured over her tea.

"I hadn't thought of it before, but it might be fun. There's two of us now." AbiWendl said. When Tsula just sat there, regarding her with an anticipatory gaze, she went on, "Seriously, several of our reservation inquiries are from Otherworld, and we have more Fallen wanting to stay than the house will hold."

"You'll need to find a builder, then." Tsula observed.

Wendl, electing to be Wendl for the moment, looked thoughtful, "If you think you can find somebody, go for it."

After Tsula opened the bookshop that morning, before any customers arrived, she sat down and made two copies of this note on spare envelopes.

Wanted: At Hemlock Cottage.
Housewright to add a room with a view.

One copy she posted at lunchtime on the bulletin board in the post office, and that night, she pinned the other to an old hemlock tree high up on a ridge south of town.

TEN

Neil Redding braced himself for the inevitable. "I need to talk to you," his father said one Sunday afternoon while his mother and sister were clearing the table after dinner.

"Yessir?" Neil said it like a question, although he had heard his parents talking late nights when they thought the rest of the world asleep.

"I've enrolled you at Orchard Hill Baptist Bible Institute," Lewis announced, as if all was settled and nothing remained to be questioned. "You can get a job this summer to start paying me back the tuition and start classes in the fall."

"But I haven't heard yet from my scholarship application to State's forestry program, Dad. If I was cut out to be a preacher, I got sewed up all wrong."

"Whom the Lord calls, he shapes and empowers," proclaimed Lewis.

"The Lord keeps telling me to be a forest ranger," murmured Neil.

"Your mother and I dedicated you to the Lord's service before you were born," his father said, his voice as hard as his face. "This has been decided, boy."

Then Neil committed the unpardonable sin. He shouted at his father, "God comes closer to me in the woods than ever in your church."

Saliva slicked Lewis' lips as his face purpled. Neil thought his father might spit on him. Instead, the preacher swung his fist. Neil ducked the blow and instinctively pushed Lewis away. The older man caught his foot on a chair, lost his balance and went down hard against the wall. Neil thought he might have been hurt, but before he could put out a hand to help him up, Lewis hissed at him like a snake, "You're none of mine, heathen. Be gone from this house."

Without a word, Neil went to his room, threw some clothes and his book from the Battered and Bartered table into his duffle, and snatched his coat from the closet on the way out. Coming down the stairs, he saw his mother and sister standing tightlipped and silent in the kitchen door. Neither uttered a word nor made a move toward him or his father, who still sat on the floor with his head in his hands when Neil closed the front door behind him.

Lewis Redding heard the door slam like an echo of judgement. He felt his wife's hand on his shoulder, and without looking up, brushed it away. It never occurred to Lewis that she might be seeking comfort as much as to give it. His own son was dead to him, as surely as if the boy had been coffined and buried in the mountain. The one he had counted on to get everything right in their life that he had got wrong in his own, had turned away from faith and obedience, and set off into the far country of apostasy and unbelief.

Lewis could not quite quell a nagging suspicion that his own unworthiness had damned his son. He thought of all the doubts and lusts and ill will and covetousness he had suppressed in his own heart down the years, denying even to himself his transgressions of intent and action gone unreckoned and unconfessed because he was the preacher, held by his congregants as above fault and flaw. He would have been astounded to know they recognized how partial and pathetic he was, and in spite of his innate meanness, trusted their God to speak and guide them through this broken man.

When Lewis finally hauled himself up from the floor, groaning, clinging to the overturned chair like a doddering ancient, he was alone in the house. "Have mercy. Have mercy," he begged the shadows, as if he were certain God lived and listened there. In truth, there was very little Lewis was certain of at that moment. He found enough coffee left in the pot to fill a cup, which he placed in the microwave and set for forty seconds. He carried it out onto his porch and by the time he had downed it, the heat and caffeine had restored enough edge that he could touch the tip of his anger, and he began to feel something like himself again. Wrath, he knew from repeated experience, could often substitute for certitude. He had been betrayed. He had good right to be angry. He was God's servant. Those who wronged him had wronged God and deserved their wretched futures.

Luke Armstrong lifted the battered sezve from the coals, held it to the cool morning breeze until the bubbles subsided. While he waited for the twigs to settle, he spied the hiker coming up the trail on the slope below. Male, young. Not much more than a boy, Luke judged. Although Luke's campsite could not be seen from the trail, the hiker would smell the smoke, and would look until he saw the faint ghost of Luke's fire spiraling up among the trees. Hospitality was not in Luke's plan for the day, but it was his own fault for not being gone at first light. He would not ignore the Rule. He poured the thick umber tea into his cup and prepared to make another.

Neil Redding stopped suddenly, listening, looking. His bones told him he was being watched. A bear most likely, but he didn't smell a bear. When the place had his full attention, he did smell burning wood. Only humans set fires in the woods on a bright sunshiny day. Moving only his head, Neil scanned the ridge above. No sign or sound of campers, but a thin blue haze rose lazily up from behind an upthrust of boulders until the morning's breeze shredded it in the treetops. A face appeared above the boulders, and a tangle of pale golden hair and beard called down, "Come up, Pilgrim, and break your fast, since we're both here with the food."

Food was all Neil needed to hear to be persuaded. He had walked out of his father's house and into the woods, spent the night on the mountain. Except for a couple of hours he had slept sitting against a tree, he had been walking. Not that he knew any place he should go, but he knew no place to go back to, either. He kept moving because to be still was to be defeated. He had just walked out of the only life he knew, and the only solution he could think of was to keep going until he walked into a life that belonged to him.

Where and when that might be, he hadn't a foggiest notion, other than that trees grew there. Trees were his passion and his friends. Trees had orphaned him and trees, he fervently believed against all logic to the contrary, would home and family him. He waved at the figure above, who returned the gesture before disappearing behind the boulders. Neil slipped the pack from his aching shoulders, and clutching the straps with one hand, began making his way up the pile toward breakfast.

"Drink some," Luke held out the steaming cup toward Neil as he dropped his pack and scanned the camp. Tent, fire, now mostly died to coals, and a blond giant, maybe the tallest man Neil had ever seen. No gear in sight. Neil supposed it was in the tent. He took the cup and lifted it to drink. "Careful, it's hot," the giant warned, and it was, but not too hot to sip. Neil could feel the heat flowing down through his throat and chest into his belly, immediately rendering him calm and grounded.

"Sit down and we'll partake some sustenance," Giant said. Neil, having outwalked his rebellion, did as he was told. A little pot sat among the embers, and within arm's reach, a couple of small wooden bowls, set out as if the big man had been expecting company. Neil hadn't noticed the bowls until Giant reached for them. He picked up the pot, poured something that looked like brown oatmeal into the bowls, and handed one to Neil. It smelled earthy, pungent with herbs. Looking closer, Neil saw vegetal bits and pieces he could not identify, but he decided the smell was delicious, an impression augmented by his hunger.

Giant broke a small pone of bread in half and handed one to Neil. "Don't have spoons. You can dip it up with this." Neil didn't see where the bread came from, either. Dark and crusty outside, porous and springy inside. When he dipped it into his potage, it sopped like a sponge. The giant lifted his own portion, dripping, to his mouth, and grinned across the fire. Neil did the same.

"Food for the gods," he said as he dipped what was left of his bread into what was left in his bowl.

"Perceptive," Giant said.

When the pot was empty, Giant stirred the ghost of their fire into the dirt, and while they waited for the embers to cool, refilled their mugs. He seemed in a mood to talk.

"You tourist or pilgrim?" he queried.

Neil gave question for question, "What's the difference?"

Giant released a low mirthful growl from deep within himself. "Tourists follow their map, pilgrims follow their dream. What are you following into the morning, young Friend?"

Neil thought for a moment. He didn't want to tell all he knew. He didn't want to admit all he didn't know. But he knew right now he needed to tell the truth. He took another sip of Giant's strange tea, swallowed, and said, "I guess I'm just walking away, Sir, looking for a sign to guide."

"You're a pilgrim for sure, then," Giant said. "You can call me Luke. After all, we're all gods in these woods."

Luke stood, began to rake the ashes from the fire with his boot, found no spark left in them. "I could use some company if we're headed the same way, Pilgrim," he said.

"I'm not following a map," Neil said. "I need to take care of a chore first, though."

Luke understood, nodded. "I'll gather up while you're at it then," he said.

Neil waded into the brush and found privacy behind an old poplar. He didn't see the paper pinned to the tree trunk until he was buckling his belt. "Hey, did you see this here?" he called.

When he turned, Luke stood right behind him, a canvas bag slung over one shoulder. "I figured it was close somewhere," he said. "Old Tsula's trying to draw me in."

"Why would somebody put an ad for a carpenter out here in the middle of the woods?" Neil asked.

"Because," Luke slapped Neil on the back hard enough to make the boy hope he wouldn't do it again, "they knew right here is where we'd be. You know anything about carpentering?"

"I know which end of a hammer drives the nail," Neil said.

"Then we have us a job to earn our keep among the Fallen," Luke said. "You do need a job, don't you?"

"I can't go home again," Neil answered.

Luke pointed at the ground. "Cover that good and come on, then."

When Neil caught up with him, the campsite was cleared and the tent was gone. "You get all your gear in that little bag?" he said.

Luke hoisted his bag as if it held only air. "That little bag will hold worlds of stuff if you fold it right," he said.

They walked away into the day, Neil brimming with more

questions than he could find words for, and Luke exuding confidence as if he'd done all this before.

"What if the job's taken by the time we get back to town?" Neil asked when they'd gone about a quarter mile back the way he'd come that morning.

Luke laughed. "Tsula wants us, Pilgrim. She won't settle for anybody less."

"Who's Tsula?" Neil ventured.

"A mangy little púca I used to know back on Otherworld. That kind usually pair up for their mischief. I wager Wendl VonTrier won't be far off when we get there."

"What's a púca?

"A fox. A crow. Anything you don't want them to be, usually. They are tricksters, but they keep their promises. Their righteousness is twisted, but it's real. They won't leave you worse off than they find you."

"Not like people then," Neil said it like experience.

"Not like humans at all." Luke's tone came out pensive. "Púca are not Fallen, understand."

"Like me?" Neil ventured.

Luke stopped, gazed at him as if measuring his soul, for a second, or an hour, or maybe days, then said softly, "In all the Two Worlds, there is only one such as you, Neil Redding. If you don't fill the only place that can find you, it will remain forever empty and creation will be that much incomplete."

Neil was afraid to ask anything after that, and they walked on in silence, listening to the birds and the wind and their own footfalls and breath, listening for the one word beyond all speaking.

ELEVEN

AbiWendl looked up from her book as the postmaster came through the door.

"Hello, Rhonda," she said. "Tired of reading stamps?"

Rhonda Shaw came straight to the counter of Drovers Gap's only independent bookstore and stared intently at the proprietor, "You okay, Abigail? You don't look quite yourself lately."

"I've been a bit scattered for a spell now, I admit," AbiWendl said. "Lot going on."

"I reckon," said Rhonda, nodding her head vigorously, as if testing its attachment to the rest of her. "Especially," she went on, "with your girlfriend moving in so sudden."

"Tsula Stone is not my girlfriend," AbiWendl retorted dryly. "She's just family."

"Must be a distant cousin," Rhonda mused aloud as she stared at some undefined interest across the street, "Youns don't look a thing alike."

AbiWendl closed her novel with an audible snap, "Rhonda Shaw, did you come into my store for something to read, or just to speculate in gossip?"

"If I'd come all this way just to gossip," Rhonda huffed, only pretending to be offended, "I'd be telling you how preacher Lewis run off his boy, Neil, and told the deacons at their meeting last night that he's planning to announce his resignation to the congregation at church tomorrow."

AbiWendl shook her head. "All this because his son left home?"

"That, and because Marcie took their girl and left the morning after. Oh, Abigail, it was purely awful. Preacher Lewis stood up in front of those men and cried like a little boy with a skint knee, said he wasn't worthy of his calling, that a man who couldn't govern his own family had no business to shepherd God's family."

"So, you were there at the meeting? I didn't know you were a deacon, Rhonda."

"I wasn't and I'm not. I'm just telling you what I heard."

"Well," murmured AbiWendl, "if ever I have any secret problems that require spiritual guidance, I'll confide in one of these upright deacons. They can tell you and before I know it, the whole town will be coming round to help me."

While Rhonda was trying to parse the full meaning of this declaration, AbiWendl said, "Do you need a book or do you just want to watch somebody read who knows how?"

Apparently, Rhonda actually wanted to buy a book. "Bernice Abner was telling me about a storybook she bought here. Dark in the Mountains, or something like that. She said it kept her awake all night reading. Said that writer fellow who lives up past the church wrote it and she was disappointed in him for writing such a thing because he'd always seemed to her like a very nice man."

AbiWendl nodded, stepped among her shelves and brought back the book and handed it to Rhonda. "It ain't dark yet," she said, quoting a song she'd heard on the radio, "but it's getting there."

Rhonda had hardly made off with her short stories tucked

into their Vintage Reads bag when Lewis Redding slunk in, head down, like a whipped puppy. He looked as if he'd been tossed out of a bar and slept it off in the rain. The púca gleaned enough of the preacher's disheveled thought to know he'd not been in a bar and hadn't been rained on but had stayed awake all night emptying a bottle of something he hadn't tasted in thirty years.

"You must've had to go all the way to Shelton Crossing to buy that poison from somebody who didn't know you," the bookseller said softly.

Lewis didn't try to deny what was apparently obvious to somebody he was barely acquainted with. He coughed, and before he coughed again, rasped, "I need a Bible." He didn't mention that the night before, at the depths of his drunken rage, he fed to his woodstove the Bible his wife Marcie had given him at his ordination.

"We have a good selection," AbiWendl said, "English, German, French, Japanese. I think we even have a couple of New Testaments in Greek and Cherokee back there somewhere."

Lewis groped within himself for his habitual anger but in his depleted state couldn't find it, "I mean a real Bible," he muttered. "You got King James?"

The Bible was in AbiWendl's hand before Lewis saw her reach for it. "This'll do for your need, Preacher," she said, placing the Bible on the counter in front of him. "Only this time, read it from your broken heart."

Lewis fumbled in his pocket, pushed his plastic across the counter. "I ain't a preacher any more," almost a whisper, "just an unwashed sinner like the rest of youns."

AbiWendl slid Lewis' credit card back across the counter, bagged his Bible and handed it to him, "That's a good start, brother Lewis," she said with a smile he would see again behind his eyes when he lay himself down to sleep that night.

The bookseller was tallying her receipts for the day when the door of Vintage Reads opened wide enough to accommodate his considerable girth and Ned Baskin walked in, wiping perspiration from his forehead with a checkered handkerchief although the day was far from hot.

"Hello, Mayor," AbiWendl said brightly. "What's up?"

Ignoring her question, Baskin said, "Drovers Gap is the only town I know where a body can walk uphill both ways."

"Would you rather do your mayoring in some big city down east where it's all flat?"

"Please, no," said the mayor. "Drovers Gap is big enough for me. Besides, I figure the Lord loved folk around here best."

"How do you figure that?" AbiWendll asked, though she knew what was coming.

"Down east, The Creator gave them just enough ground to cover the place, but here, He piled it up in great heaps."

"Generosity is where we find it, I suppose," murmured the bookseller. "Should I give you a book, or do you want to buy one?"

"I got more reading than I can do with reports and petitions," the mayor sighed. "No, Abigail, I came to tell you the commissioners met last night and voted to turn down your building application for an addition to Hemlock Cottage. You'll get a notice in the mail, but I wanted to tell you friendly."

"That hardly seems reasonable, considering they just approved a permit for that mess across the street from me."

"Well, that's the thing. Zoning that side of Main is going to be changed from mixed-use to commercial. Since your property will remain in the historic district . . ." Ned's voice trailed off. Abigail nodded, left the mayor dangling from his silence. She knew that two of the commissioners, a builder and a property developer applied to put up a mini-mall full of touristy shops and had spread around money and favors to facilitate the zoning change. "I reckon I'll have to make do as I am then, Mayor," she said.

Ned wiped his face again with his soggy handkerchief. "Well, my vote counted for you, Abigail," he said. "You could get approval for anything that doesn't change the footprint of the building or alter the outside appearance. I'm sorry." The mayor sounded mostly sincere. "I hope you don't blame me for this."

AbiWendl laughed. "Oh there's plenty of blame going around, Ned. I won't assign you more than your share."

"We're still friends, then?" Baskin ventured hopefully, extending his hand across the counter.

The púcawoman took it. "I'm a friend to the world," she said, with a smile that could rout an army.

After the Mayor fled the battlefield, AbiWendl finished her work, and sans customers, closed Vintage Reads a bit early, began walking toward Hemlock Cottage at the west end of Main Street. She looked like Abigail Trammell and talked like Abigail Trammell, and to all who knew her in Drovers Gap, was Abagail Trammell, but she wasn't thinking Abigail Trammell's thoughts. Under her skin, the púca Wendl VonTrier abided, as much he as she, and not entirely either, who might be here or there, or now or then, in this world or some other, or between the worlds, the only place a púca could rest entirely Púca.

As for Abigail Trammell, She was on Otherworld now, restored, according to Wandalena, to her true self, Gobnait of the bees, a middling deity. Wendl missed the woman she had been among the Fallen. The more the púca conformed to that persona, the more fraudulent the whole business felt. The gods and goddesses of the Otherworld pantheon were not rulers of their Stream. Selfish imaginations had rendered them tools of power and profit. The Fallen, on the other hand, were by their very finitude set free. If only they did not burden themselves with bartered expectations and needless wanting, they could be wiser and more potent than any of the lesser gods, even Lugh Long Arm, who, according to Tsula, had turned up at Hemlock Cottage today.

The púca figured Lugh would contrive to lengthen his sojourn among the Fallen. With that, at least, Wendl was in full sympathy. A world where everything was deemed perfect considered change anathema, allowed no need for makers and magic. Here among the Fallen, a wondrous fantastic wove through everything, though most of the Fallen rarely seemed to notice. Magic was in the very air of Shadow, crying out for embodiment. The more Wendl thought about it, the more certain the púca became. The Separation had not been set to protect Otherworld from the Fallen as the clerics taught. The Abbeys and their Superiors were afraid the vitality of Shadow might usurp and change established order. The Superiors, Wandalena being no exception, hoped, that left to their own devices, the Fallen would render their world desolate and impotent. If the broken deities were allowed to live unsupervised and unencumbered in the lesser world, they might awaken Gaia and loose her magic. The Separation would collapse, and Otherworld would begin to evolve again, perhaps until there remained no place there for Abbeys and Superiors.

TWELVE

Gobnait deftly replaced the lid on the hive, careful not to jostle the sixty thousand inhabitants. She handed off her bucket full of honeycomb to Callie, who would prepare it for storage. Callie, as usual, had her shawl wrapped around her face, leaving only one eye open to the day. She had been at the Abbey for centuries, according to Owl, and most in the community had never seen her face. She led a contingent of congregants who minded and dispensed the community's food stores. Gobnait supposed they were able at their tasks, as she'd never found any drink or sustenance lacking during her tenure here.

Indeed, the Abbey often shared their larder with folk in the town if a winter were long and a summer too wet or cool for a good crop. The Abbey fields and gardens, though, seemed to make their own weather, year after year. There were rumors and speculation among the cloistered, as well as without, that the hard seasons, when they came upon the land abroad, were the work of Callie and her cohort, directed by Goodmother Wandalena to keep the towns dependent upon the Abbey's good will. None of these conspiracy theories were ever repeated aloud by any of the Abbey faithful.

According to Owl, Callie's proper name was Cailleach Beira. "What kind of name is that?" Gobnait asked when he told her.

"An old name, from the One Tongue," he said, pleased to show his knowing. "She was here before us all. The Veiled One, Queen of Winter."

The old hag, who had seemed so vigorous when Gobnait arrived among the bees that spring, leaned now heavily upon her white staff of peeled holly, but lifted the honey with one hand, peered with her unblinking eye at Gobnait and whispered something before turning to hobble away toward the Abbey with her sweet burden. Callie said it so softly that Gobnait couldn't hear it clearly over the droning of the bees, but, as well as she could make it out, sounded like *Remember whence ye came.*

When Owl came by from the hives he'd been working to bid her to supper, she mentioned it to him. "What do you suppose she meant?" she said. In truth, Gobnait could scarcely remember anything beyond her life at the Abbey. The days passed. She might have been here a week, or all her life. The cloistered buildings and the attendant fields and orchards were all the world she needed.

Sometimes, on moonless nights, Gobnait would wake from dreams of a before, when she ruled a house and garden of her own, but the details slipped from her mind as she emerged from sleep. The dreams were not so frequent now, not so vivid. She forgot them before she was dressed and they surprised her all over again with each rare appearance.

Owl stared at her when she told him what the hag had said. "Whatever thee remembers," he growled quietly, tapping her forehead lightly with a gnarled finger, "speak of it to none. Not even me."

Gobnait was still pondering her elusive recollections when she lined up in the refectory to receive her evening ration. Where had she lived before the Abbey? Who had she been in the secular world? None of the congregants ever spoke of their past. Were their memories as blank as hers? Only once, she dared confess her curiosities to Mother Wandalena, who sternly admonished her, "You are here to practice peace for this world, that all may come to a good end, not to question origins, your own or any."

In her rush to change from her workdress, Gobnait dropped a spot of dirt on her wimple, and cleaning it made her late for supper. She came last in line. As she tried to catch her breath, Sister Brigit placed a thick slice of brown bread on her plate. She was hungry, hoped the soup would still be warm. When she reached Sister Gwen with her big caldron, the woman scraped her spoon loudly on the side of the empty vessel, shook her head. "You're late," she said.

Gobnait was about to pass on with her bit of dry bread when Gwen— Cerridwen as Owl called her, having his own strange names for them all—reached under her cloak and produced a bowl of something that smelled like soup but of a peculiar color, like liquid grass. "Eat it all yourself," she murmured under her breath, glancing around as if she was afraid somebody might be watching, "but don't share. It's the last I can give you."

Gobnait took her bowl and bread to the sisters' table and sat. She dipped her bread into the bowl and lifted it to her mouth, glanced toward the brothers who were seated at their own table along the opposite wall. That was not technically a transgression of a rule, but it was not in the manner of congregants to assess another's portion while eating. Had Mother Wandalena seen that errant look, it would have garnered a mild reprimand.

So, Gobnait was surprised to see brother Owl staring straight back at her. He gestured with his spoon toward his open mouth, then looked down to his own sustenance. Gobnait bit into her bit of sopping bread before it dripped onto her sleeve and tasted all the flavors of a garden growing in another world.

Goodmother Wandalena locked the door to her study, crossed the room and pulled aside the tapestry hanging behind her desk, revealing the only mirror in Trier Abbey, perhaps the only mirror in the province. Mirrors were instruments of vanity, and while not outlawed, would likely subject their owners to accusations of pride if found out. Pride was a vague offence, not specifically cited in the Red Rule, but people had been tribunaled and publicly flogged for it.

Wandalena gazed at her image for a moment, neither gratified nor disappointed, and only marginally assured of her own reality, then gestured at the glass, which dissolved into a stone-lined passage. Her minions Corvid and Hawke stood, eyes servilely downcast, hats in hand.

"You called us, Superior," said Orville Hawke, not a question.

"We are here to serve," said Wilbur Corvid, holding his hat before him like a beggar's bowl.

Wandalena took a bag from her desk drawer and dropped it into the hat. "You are here to get the Abbey's gold, and for that you will do my bidding."

"We will strive to please," said Hawke.

"We will spare no effort," said Corvid.

"You will do this thing I will tell you now," whispered Wandalena, smiling her sweetest smile which she had practiced in her mirror, "or you will forfeit to me more than what is in your hat. I assume we have an understanding."

"We are of one mind," said Hawke.

"We will not disappoint you, Goodmother," said Corvid.

"You may address me as your Superior," snapped Wandalena, "I would never mother the likes of you."

She sat behind her desk, gestured at the two chairs that suddenly materialized before her, "Quit bobbing there like a pair of felons ready to be hanged, and sit down. I'm about to tell you what you must do for me if you wish to stay intact long enough to spend your gold."

The moon set and the window and the wall became one darkness and Gobnait still lay in her cell wide awake. She heard the warder's footsteps in the hall outside her door, pacing fainter and farther toward silence. In ten minutes, she would hear them again in the opposite direction. Something in Gwen's soup had set her on edge. She hadn't slept, so wasn't dreaming, but her restless mind projected pictures on the dark. A garden. Vegetables and flowers. A whisper of breeze and a drone of bees. A book with words that swam off the page and strung across her room and out into the deep deep night. A flaming tendril of knowing that she could not quite read, but beckoning, buzzing in her head like the bees that she and Owl tended together.

She could hear them while she trimmed her poor drought-depleted beetle-infested roses. The voice behind her startling. The strange man who had reserved a room in her house. Strange name, he had, and spelled it that way. Wendl. She watched him turn into a big black bird as finally, she fell asleep.

In her dream, Gobnait got up, dressed and slipped out of the Abbey. She met the warder in the hall but passed by unseen. The warder walked the world awake, therefore blind to Gobnait's dreaming. The same with the warders at the big gate. Gobnait dreamed a noise outside, and the warders being half-drunk and half asleep, half-heard it and opened the gate to see what was going on. While they were curating the darkness she slipped through and dreamed herself away to the apiary.

The droning of the sleeping bees grew louder as she approached their yard. She could see their dreaming gathering like a cloud above the hives, glowing pale and blue against the night, like the first faint glint of dawn over the mountain. The humming and thrumming of their dream drew her in, carrying her on the sound until she was the sound, a vibration in the air, a spark upon the dark, as near as her next breath and as distant as a star. Gobnait became the word she heard and knew then what she must do. As she rose into the gathering light, she saw Owl dwindling away below, stretching his arms up into the air as he watched her go.

Thirteen

Neil Redding had been working with Luke Armstrong in Abigail's house for a week now. He had picked up some basic carpentry skills in the process and observed mysteries he never expected to master. The book lady wanted to add as many rooms as possible to her house without making it any larger, as the town commissioners had denied her zoning request to expand Hemlock Cottage. Luke apparently thought this a perfectly logical proposition and sent Neil off to Ponder's Lumber Yard with a list of materials.

The first puzzlement came when Luke began framing in a partition at the end of the upstairs hall about a foot in front of an existing window. They left an opening for a door aligned with the window. It took three days to construct the seven-paneled door, which Luke insisted had to be built by his hand alone without power tools or any assistance. He ordered the latch and hinges online at a website called Wildness Emporium. The day they finished the door, the hardware arrived. Luke opened the window that morning before they went down for breakfast and when they came back upstairs, the box was sitting on the windowsill, bearing assorted stamps printed with indecipherable characters, and a postmark declaring it wouldn't be sent for another week.

"That was quick," Neil said as Luke handed him a wicked-looking curved knife and told him to open the package.

"Their Stream flows faster." Luke said, as if that were sufficient answer. Neil opened the package, stared at the assorted objects, tarnished dark with age. "These aren't new," he said.

"I hope not." Luke answered, laconic as usual, and began demonstrating to Neil how to mortise the doorframe to receive the hinges and latchplate. When the door was in place, Luke closed it, pulled his carpenter's pencil from behind his ear, and sketched a symbol like a toppled *eight* on the top panel.

"What's that for?" Neil asked.

Putting his pencil away, Luke said, "It opens the door to wherever you need go. You'll paint over it tomorrow, but it will be there to make ways straight."

That night after supper, Neil walked down to Home Ground. His friend Ronan was playing his sax with a couple of guys Neil didn't know, a guitar player and a drummer who, according to Chloe Toibin, were "not from around here." The place was packed, and when the trio began to play, Neil understood why. "Magic music" was how Chloe described their playing, and before the first set was half-way through, Neil agreed with her assessment. The sax and guitar spiraled out into a wild, soaring dialog and the drummer's rhythmic insistence kept them tethered to earth. Without the drums, the music would have fallen flat, like a kite severed from its string.

Neil couldn't quite make up his mind just what sort of music he was hearing. It wasn't rock. It wasn't jazz. It wasn't blues. It wasn't anything he had ever heard the likes of, but it held him fast, conjuring images in his head of dark mountains and deep waters, stormy skies and lonesome winds. It felt like . . . the only word Neil could think of was *sex*, though his total experience of sex derived from movies and imagination.

Whatever sourced its magic, the music held the usually boisterous crowd rapt and silent, carrying each soul there away into some hidden inner place too deep for telling.

Chloe came by his table, her purple blaze of hair startling Neil out of his entrancement, "You want another beer, Neil?" she whispered.

Neil looked at his empty glass. "No thanks, Chloe. The second one is never quite as good as the first."

Chloe took his glass, stood there until he looked up at her. "It's a free concert, Neil, but you're supposed to buy stuff while you're here, you know."

Neil had money in his pocket. Luke had paid him before supper for the work he'd put in that week. "Then I'll take a double espresso and a slice of pie."

"What kind of pie you want?" Chloe said.

"You got pumpkin?"

She shook her purple cloud, "Not the season for pumpkin. We got squash. Tastes like pumpkin. Sorta."

"Sounds sorta nice, then," Neil murmured, gazing at Chloe, who had his attention now. It occurred to him that this girl he'd seen in class ever since first grade was something like a woman now, also something like an exotic purple flower he never expected to find blooming in Drovers Gap.

She left him to the music then, and Neil drowned in it. Five minutes or five years later, she returned with his pie and coffee, bent close enough that he could feel her breath tickling his ear when she whispered, "Don't look now, but your dad's here, in back by the door."

Of course, Neil had to look then, and sure enough, there was the elder Redding sitting at a table with two dark men in dark clothes, seemingly engrossed in conversation, oblivious to the music, immune to its spell as they pursued whatever obsessions held their minds. Lewis didn't look to catch his son's glance, and Neil didn't look that way again until the music was done. He was wondering how he would slip away without confronting his father when he saw the table by the door was empty. Lewis and his sinister cohorts had vacated the premises.

Neil didn't see Chloe anywhere, paid his check at the register. He left enough tip that she would be glad he'd been there. He threaded his way through all the party chatter and stepped out into the dark. The sky was full of stars and his head was full of Ronan's wild and otherworldly tunes.

Lewis Redding didn't feel quite himself as he walked out of Home Ground with the peculiar pair who showed up at his door as he was opening a can of sardines to sandwich between two slices of stale bread from which he'd carefully trimmed the blue mold. If Marcie didn't relent and come home soon, he'd have to go out and buy some groceries. He was trying hard to stay sober in case she did. He had a vague notion that the taste of sardines might lessen his craving for spirits. His hangover from his recent fall from grace had lingered long enough to convince him there was no future in lapsing into his pre-ministerial lifestyle from thirty years past.

He didn't ask God to forgive him for his sudden and precipitous backslide. He still believed in God's existence, but he'd no confidence at all that God cared what Lewis Redding did with his one futile and disappointing life. Everything Lewis had given to his Maker got thrown back in his face. His son hated him. His wife and daughter despised him. All the rules he'd told his congregation down the years would win God's favor had bought Lewis ingratitude and derision from those souls he valued above all others. He was a joke. His life was a lie. He'd been an honest drunk and the Lord had raised him up from the gutter to be a sober and sanctimonious fraud.

Then Orville Hawke and Wilbur Corvid knocked on his door to change his opinion of himself. "Brother Lewis," said

Mister Corvid, introducing himself and his sharp faced companion, "we've come representing the Restoration Fellowship."

"And our Mission Board has prayerfully considered and concluded that you are just the man to lead our ministry in Drovers Gap." announced Mister Hawke, beaming as if he expected Lewis to embrace the news as some sort of absolution and deliverance.

Lewis had never heard of the Restoration Fellowship, so figured they must be Mormons or Episcopalians. "I'm a Baptist," he said, supposing that would quell their interest in him. He had no desire to get ensnared in any further religious enterprising, Baptist or otherwise.

"Denominations don't do any harm as long as you don't inhale," Mister Corvid observed.

"We don't concern ourselves with labels," Mister Hawke said, placing a heavy hand on Lewis' shoulder and bending close to peer deeply into his eyes.

Lewis noticed that Hawke's eyes were golden as a cat's with huge black pupils that loomed like holes with no light or substance behind them, and his breath— Lewis wondered if the man, if he was a man, had been chewing burnt roadkill.

"The Cause needs a man like you," Mister Corvid interjected, "who can recognize the dark forces afoot that are striving to break up our families and lead our children into disobedience and rebellion."

Lewis reflected on the past couple of days and wondered if those were the same dark forces that had dismantled his own neat family and overthrown his patriarchal authority. "Of late, I've had some experience in that regard," he murmured.

Hawke and Corvid gently took his arms and guided him to his door. "Then come share a meal with us at our expense," said Mister Hawke.

"And we will enlighten you as to the wicked elements

intent on disrupting our town's spiritual serenity," said Mister Corvid.

Lewis didn't remember putting on his coat, or much of their discussion as they walked across town to Home Ground, but he was hungry by the time he spooned up his savory stew and the music began.

The details escaped him later, but he recalled that while he ate, Hawke and Corvid had briefed him at length on the nefarious plots underway to render Drovers Gap an iniquitous cesspool of unspeakable debauchery. It was the considered judgement of the Restoration Fellowship, that he, Lewis Redding, was the only man qualified to avert this disastrous dissolution. Why else had the forces of evil been arrayed against him and his family? The congregation turning on him that way proved his own flock had been infiltrated by these devils. There was no other word for such folk, Mister Corvid surmised. He spoke names of supposedly respectable citizens who were secretly serving as agents of this hellish insurrection. Lewis thought of every disagreement and conflict, however slight, he'd had with these particular people over the years, and nodded in agreement, realizing at last why they had refused to accept his righteous discernment.

"What did you think of the music tonight, Brother Lewis?" Mister Hawke queried as they came out onto the pavement at the end of the evening.

"It wasn't anything I'd hear in church," Lewis said. "But it was powerful. I was moved by it. I couldn't feel angry while I listened."

"That is why you must put a stop to it, Brother," said Mister Corvid, stabbing Lewis' sternum with a bony finger, igniting a heat that spread through his chest, leaving him feeling flushed and anxious.

"They use music's dark power to quell the virtuous wrath that you must rouse to defeat their insidious schemes," intoned Mister Hawke.

Lewis knew then that he alone was God's instrument to restore justice and bring judgement to Drovers Gap. He determined in his mind to use whatever means he could muster to fulfill his duty. He was still pondering what the first move in his campaign might be when he reached his front door and realized he had left Hawke and Corvid somewhere behind him in the night.

FOURTEEN

Stars flared like distant campfires in the inky sky as Neil Redding came in sight of Hemlock Cottage. The only light came from the front porch. Tsula or Abigail had left a light on for him. He hoped he could slip in quietly and not wake anyone. His father would have been livid had Neil been out at such an hour. No one here would scold or threaten punishment, but he was tired, and too full of his own troubled thoughts to participate in a late-night chat on any subject.

He envied Ronan, who had his talent and his instrument and had space in his life to do what he was born to do. Neil was pretending to be a carpenter when he really wanted to be growing trees, tending a forest somewhere, not assembling pieces of it into structures made to enclose and isolate. He wanted to spend his life under an open sky, walking spruce-clad mountains. He knew he was made for that, but how to get there from here? When he got caught up in Ronan's playing tonight, while the music was rolling out, everything seemed possible, every road straight and open for him to take. Now alone in the dark, he couldn't read his future in the stars. He figured he'd probably wrecked his life beyond repair. His father hated him, and Neil thought he might have given the old man good reason, but he knew one thing. He wouldn't go home again until he could go in his own time on his own terms. He would forgive, but he wouldn't beg forgiveness.

A pale glimmer at the corner of the house caught his eye as Neil was about to turn into Abigail's yard. He thought at first it was a dog lurking there, but when the animal crossed into the porchlight, he recognized it as a fox. A white fox. He'd heard the stories hunters told, but this was the first one he'd actually seen. The fox stopped and looked at him, eyes catching the light, flashes of cold fire, just for a second. Neil didn't think or hesitate, followed the fox around the corner into the shadow of the house. Down across Abigail's vegetable garden, past tall rows of okra and corn, by the verge of the woods beyond, in the scant light of a beclouded moon, he saw a white ghost, the fox, gazing at him with those burning unblinking eyes. When Neil began walking toward the animal, the fox yipped softly and disappeared among the trees.

At the other side of the garden, where the fox had been standing, a narrow path wound up a wooded slope into the dark throat of night. Neil stood for a time underneath a redbud tree, considering if he should go back to the house and sleep. Luke would have more work for him tomorrow and liked to start early while the day offered some cool. He had about decided to go to his rest when the clouds parted and the unveiled moon cast down its full glow. Away up the dim path, a blur of pale motion stirred a pool of moonlight beneath an opening in the tree canopy. The white fox yapped short and soft again and bled away into the deeper shadows ahead. Somewhere farther off in the woods an owl trilled a lonesome dirge. It might have been a warning but Neil heard an invitation, and stepped in among the trees.

Now and again he would catch sight of the fox, moving through a splash of moonlight. If he slowed, the fox would pause, piping sharply as if to urge the human on. If Neil walked faster, the fox would move ahead, maintaining their apartedness without increasing it. Time passed in a sequence of deep shadow and bright moon. Neil's cellphone went dark and dead, its battery spent. He might have been walking for minutes or hours. A mile or ten? There was only him and the white fox, always ahead and never nearer, and around them the trees and the night, the incessant whispered exchange between wind and leaves, and the constant scurry and rustle of small creatures finding their places in the nocturnal flow.

Neil expected moment to moment to cross a neighbor's yard or a familiar street, but the forest stretched on and on, up and up, until the faint sounds of the sleeping town below were swallowed whole by the night. Neil wondered if his walking were just a dream until a spiderweb feathered across his face. He lifted his hand to brush it away and concluded he trod the world awake.

Something rushed toward him out of the darkness. He felt more than saw it, threw up his hands, heard a flurry of wings and felt the wind of its passing, and the wood was silent and still again and ahead an opening in the trees onto what appeared to be a more-or-less level expanse of rock, mica flaked, glittering under the moon like grounded fireflies.

When Neil stepped out onto the ledge, the light wind chilled him to a shiver. A pale smudge of dawn limned the top of Hungry Mountain across the intervening valley and below he saw the lights of Drovers Gap illuminating beginnings. Just north of the town a flash of light flared into an angry glow that spread and brightened as he watched. It took him a minute to recognize his father's church, engulfed in flame.

Drovers Gap Police Chief Omar Longshadow stopped his pickup in front of Justice Fork Baptist Church. The town's police cruiser was in the shop. Across the yard, a scattered heap of ash and burnt timber was all that remained of the eighty-year-old sanctuary. The morning air still reeked of burning. A lone figure stooped among the debris, stirring the remains with what appeared to be a length of electrical conduit.

Omar sighed. He wasn't ready for this. In truth, he'd never wanted to be a policeman, but his father's sister, Wilma, had served for thirty-five years as sheriff of the county, and Warren Longshadow had been determined that one of his own would carry on the tradition. He saw law enforcement as an avenue for his son to escape marginalization and attain a position of respect and influence in the predominately anglo community, so he shamed and badgered Omar into following the profession. Warren named his only boy for a U. S. Army general he admired. Omar, fully cognizant of the irony, knew that motivation was lost on most people he met now. He was also aware that some folks addressed him as Chief without reference to his police rank.

He got out of the pickup. Slammed the door hard enough to attract the attention of the scavenger, who stood and watched him walking across the intervening tarmac.

"Morning, Preacher Redding," he said to the silent figure. "You looking for anything in particular?"

Lewis Redding shook his head. "Just looking for a meaning, I guess. There's nothing left to find."

"It was a hot fire," Omar said. He pointed to the yellow tape strung around the site. "You shouldn't be in here, you know. County Forensics hasn't gotten down to us yet."

Lewis dropped his piece of conduit, brushed his smudged hands against his jeans. "I'm sorry, Chief. It was just such a sorry sight. I hoped some small thing might be left from before."

Omar took the preacher's arm and led him back to the parking lot. "Let's go down to Home Ground and me buy you a cup of coffee, Preacher Lewis."

Lewis stepped away, tense. "This an interrogation, Chief?"

Omar laughed, lifted his hands. "No sir, not at all. But you are close to this. You know the people here. I just thought we might talk through what's happened and you can help me try to make sense of it."

For a second, Lewis looked like he might want to run away, then he attempted a smile that didn't quite jell, and said, "Well, I could use that coffee, for sure."

The policeman and the preacher settled into a corner booth at Home Ground Suds and Java. Purple-haired Chloe Toibin brought them menus and stood by, pencil at the ready.

Omar held up his menu, and looked at Lewis. "Hungry, Preacher?"

"No thanks, Chief," Lewis said. "I'd be spoiled for supper."

Omar handed the menus back to Chloe. "Just two coffees, I guess." As she started to turn, he said, "Wait." He looked at Lewis. "Preacher, I'm awfully dry. Would it offend you if I had a beer?"

Lewis found a genuine smile. "Not if I can have one, too."

Omar nodded to Chloe. "Two Green Man then. Hold the coffee."

Chloe left to fetch their beer. Omar said, "You not a Baptist anymore, Preacher?"

"I'm not a preacher anymore," Lewis said. "I reckon you've heard I resigned as pastor of Justice Fork. So you don't have to call me preacher."

Omar nodded. "You mad at the Justice Fork folk, Mister Redding?"

Lewis shook his head. "Unless you're about to arrest me, Lewis will do. No, Chief, I'm not mad at the congregation. I'm mad at myself. I'm not the virtuous soul I aspired to be. I'd rather be unemployed than a hypocrite."

"Lewis, you know I'll have to be asking this of everybody with connections to the church, because the fire does look suspicious, judging by our preliminary assessment of the scene. Can you tell me where you were last night?"

"I was at home all evening, Chief. I'd invited three of the Justice Fork Deacons over and I grilled us some steaks. I wanted to explain myself a bit more to them, about why I resigned so sudden, and I wanted to tell them about my vision. We were still discussing that when the town's emergency siren went off."

"Your vision?" Omar leaned forward, his interest piqued, "What about?"

"Chief, I agree with you the church fire was likely on purpose. I've seen the dark forces of blasphemous apostasy swirling about Drovers Gap like a swarm of voracious soul-eating locusts. The devil's minions move among us right here as we speak. If we don't rise up together to oppose them, they will render our town a desolation."

Before Omar had a chance to speak to that revelation, Chloe was back with their beers.

Chief Omar Longshadow was not an exceptionally astute policeman, but he was thorough. The next day, he knocked on the door at Marcie Lewis' sister's house. He'd gleaned from the wife of one of the Justice Fork Deacons that Marcy and her daughter were staying there for the time being.

"It was awful, Chief." Marcie said. "My husband and Neil had a terrible fight. Physical. Neil knocked his father down and left."

"What put them at such odds?" Omar queried.

"It was about Neil's schooling," she said. "Lewis had this conviction that Neil would become a minister. We . . . well, Lewis had dedicated our boy to the Lord when he was born, but Neil had never felt the call. Since he was small, all he'd ever talked about was wanting to be a forest ranger."

"Maybe the Lord was calling him to be a forest ranger," Omar said, wishing before it was out that he'd kept the thought to himself.

"I shared that possibility with Lewis once," Marcie murmured. "He got so mad he smashed one of my good china plates." She saw the expression on Omar's face, then added quickly, "Oh, he never raised a hand to me or our daughter, but Lewis had a temper. When he thought he was in the right, he couldn't abide being challenged."

"What about your son?" Omar said.

"Neil was the opposite. Always a quiet boy. He'd get really still and silent when he was angry. At least until the night he left."

"Do you think he might want to get back at his dad in some way?"

Marcie shook her head. "That wasn't Neil's way, Chief. When he walked out that door, I don't think he meant to ever see his father again."

"Have you seen Neil since he left home?" the policeman asked.

"No. We've talked on the phone a couple of times. He said he's working with a carpenter doing some renovation over at that tourist cottage, Abigail Trammell's."

"Do you know where he's staying?" Omar asked.

"Neil said that they are staying there until their project's finished."

Omar stood, put on his hat. "Thank you. You've been very helpful."

Marcie Lewis reached out and touched his sleeve. "Chief, my boy didn't set that fire."

"I don't have any reason to believe that he did," Omar said. "But if I'm going to find out what happened, I'll need to talk to him just like I'm talking to you and everybody else close to the church."

He could feel Marcie's eyes on his back as he walked to his car. He wondered if she would be on the phone to Hemlock Cottage before he was out of sight.

Fifteen

Neil Redding stood on his rock atop Warwoman Ridge for the best part of an hour, watching the smoke rising from the remains of Justice Fork Baptist Church in the valley below. The glow of the fire diminished as the new day began to brighten over Drovers Gap, until all that remained of the church was a gray smudge across the face of dawn. Neil cast about the woods for another hour searching for some sign of the white fox, who had disappeared with not a trace left behind.

He didn't know how he had managed to get so far from town, figured it would take him at least a couple of hours to walk down the mountain, assuming he didn't get lost on the way. Luke would have started work by now. Neil wondered if he would still have a job when he got back. He rubbed his empty stomach, mad at himself for missing a good breakfast at Hemlock Cottage. A thought crossed his mind, immediately dismissed, that his father might have something to do with the fire at the church.

Try as he might, he couldn't pick up the trail he'd followed through the darkness in pursuit of the fox. He couldn't find any sort of path or track at all. These woods were totally unfamiliar to him, improbable as that seemed, considering the time he'd spent wandering around this mountain growing up. He began working his way down along the wooded slope, reckoning downhill was in the general direction of town.

An incessant chatter of birds and squirrels echoed among the trees. Neil didn't hear the rowdy little stream until he was almost in it, as it chortled and snickered its way among mossed boulders. He had no trouble finding footing to cross, and as soon as he gained the far bank, he smelled smoke. Not smoke from a burning church, but a campfire. The smoke carried a message of coffee, and maybe ham or bacon. He spied a plume of hazy blue among the trees and made for it. If there were campers, there would be a trail.

In a small clearing just beyond sight of the stream, a fire crackled and popped. Two lanky figures shrouded in black ponchos sat on either side of the fire with metal plates in their laps, making their breakfast disappear.

A leathery face arranged about a huge sharp-tipped nose, looked up as Neil approached and a beakish mouth said, "I say, Mister Corvid, I do believe he has found us."

The other camper fixed his beady black eyes on Neil and said, "Lugh's pet, Mister Hawke, unless my old eyes deceive me. How fortuitous."

They stood, gawking, an ungainly vaguely avian pair of humanoids, like a coin showing both its sides at once. "You must be hungry, friend," said Wilbur Corvid.

"We saved you some," Orville Hawke said, gesturing at the pan sizzling among the coals.

Tired and spent, Neil considered it an offer he couldn't refuse.

When she met Owl at the apiary after Lauds, Gobnait told him about her dream.

He listened to her account in silence. When she finished, he turned away and gazed at the trees beyond the hives. "The bees want to tell you something," he said finally. "Whatever they have to say will not be safe for you to know or tell."

"Do the bees always tell the truth?" she asked him.

He laughed softly under his breath, but there was no cheer in it. "They do that," he said. "But the truth is dangerous to hold, a sword that is all blade, as likely to cut the wielder as the foe."

They worked through the morning and into the afternoon, cutting the laden combs from the hives. Callie came several times with her barrow to carry the sweet harvest back to the Abbey. Once, she stopped in front of Gobnait as she passed, peered from beneath her cowl. All Gobnait could see was one bright eye burning in that shadow, as if there were no face there at all, just that accusing eye.

"And did you dream?" the hag rasped.

"I so did," Gobnait said, bemused.

"Next time, come awake."

Callie turned and trundled away before Gobnait could speak. She looked at Owl, who had obviously been listening. He nodded and went back to his work. No words passed between them for the rest of the day, the silence broken only by birds in the surrounding wood, and the incessant drone and murmur of the bees.

At supper that evening, there was plenty of soup and bread for everybody, and she received her ration from the common pot. During the reading, Gobnait glanced across the room a couple of times at Owl among the brothers. Not once did he raise his head to return her gaze.

Neither sleep nor dreams found Gobnait that night. Sequestered in her cell, she prayed until she was tired, then lay awake waiting for something she didn't know. When she despaired of rest, she prayed some more. Twice in an hour she heard the Warder's staff tapping outside her door. She couldn't hear his soft steps as he passed, only the staff echoing off the stone floor, regular as a heartbeat and heartless as a clock marking seconds and minutes and hours unspent, yet forever lost to the insatiable past steadily devouring all their lives, erasing all loves not given.

Sometime near dawn, Gobnait roused and dressed, listened to the Warder approach and tap away into silence one more time, then slipped from her cell, and flowed quiet and fluid as a shadow among shadows, down the deserted hall and through the abbey gate, already opened in anticipation of the new day. A few congregants were stirring abroad early, wood gatherers, water carriers, stock tenders, gardeners. None spoke as they headed to their appointed tasks in the outer world. After Lauds, tongues would be loosed to greet and gossip.

As she neared the apiary, Gobnait heard the angry roar of the bees, swirling like a dark storm against the garish light flickering through the trees, a false dawn of flame and destruction. Acrid black smoke, dense and heavy, clung to the earth, refusing to rise into the chill morning air. It burned in her throat and stung her eyes as she rounded a barn and saw the hives all burning like funeral pyres.

Owl was there before her, on his knees in the dew-damped grass, hands in the air, keening what may have been either a prayer or a curse. She knelt beside the old monk, reached for his hand, felt the despair and rage trembling inside him.

"Who did this horror?" she whispered.

"None I would dare name aloud," he said, not turning his face from the conflagration before them.

"But you know?" she said.

"Owl knows," he murmured, still staring, the flames reflected in his eyes. "She's loose."

"What are we to do now?" Gobnait ventured, hardly hoping for an answer.

"Now we will follow the bees," Owl said, gazing at her

with a strange soul-chilling smile, "and hear them sing the
Two Worlds together again."

Neil Redding came awake in a fit of coughing. He gasped for
air and inhaled smoke. His eyes burned when he opened
them. He tried to shield his face with his hands and found he
was trussed up like a roasted pig. Then the wind shifted and
through tears he saw the campfire and two figures beyond
regarding him with inappropriate amusement.

"I say, Mister Hawke," exclaimed one, "it appears the pet
is awake."

"So he seems, Mister Corvid," the other said, "and
acquiring a flavor befitting his crime."

"I'm not a criminal," croaked Neil, spitting a mixture of
saliva, ashes and dirt. "Let me loose."

"You are, young friend, an arsonist." Mister Corvid said.
"Everyone in Drovers Gap says so."

"The pet reeks of burning, Mister Corvid," murmured
Orville Hawke. "If he looks like an arsonist and smells like an
arsonist . . ."

"I haven't set any fires," Neil sputtered. "You goons
drugged me. Let me go."

"Your father says you are an arsonist. He found your
watch at the scene of your crime," Corvid cawed gleefully.
"Do you think he might keep that disappointment to
himself?"

"The watch he gave his son to carry off to seminary,"
intoned Hawke. "You've broken your poor daddy's heart,
young man."

Neil was propped up against the trunk of a dying oak,
huge and hollow. He could see a dark opening beside him.
Something rustled unseen within. He tried to squirm away,
but his tight bonds permitted no leverage. "I didn't take the

watch when I left home," Neil protested. "It's still in my room at the house."

"It's on that policeman's desk right now, "said Mister Corvid.

"Everyone is going to be so disappointed in you now," Mister Hawke shook his head in mock dismay. "If you had only obeyed your father's wishes none of this ever need happen."

"You two crazies will never get away with this." Neil tried to shout, but only managed an angry whisper. "If you're smart, you'll let me loose and go hide under your rock."

"Wish we could," gloated Mister Corvid, practically jumping up and down. "But after you burned the church down, you came up here and set the woods afire."

"Unfortunately," said Mister Hawke, "you got caught in your own inflammatory manipulations . . ."

"And when they found you after the whole mountainside and half your little town burned down," cackled Corvid . . .

"You were cooked to a crispy brown like a plump little possum," finished Hawke.

While listening to this prophesy of his gruesome end, Neil felt the beginnings of a subtle vibration in the tree at his back. As the demented duo expounded on his projected demise, the vibration swelled into an audible roar. Corvid and Hawke stared open-mouthed as a dense roiling cumulus of bees exploded through the opening in the hollow oak.

In an instant, the air became thick with bees. The swarm ignored Neil but beset Corvid and Hawke in earnest. The devious duo swiped and flailed and yowled, whirled and danced for a futile moment then sprouted wings and feathers, assumed their native forms and flew away.

The bees calmed, gathered, settled into an immense rumbling mumbling humming ball on the low hanging limb of an old maple across the clearing. Neil struggled vainly to free himself as an old man, weathered and wrapped in a kilt the color of winterfallen leaves, stepped from the hollow tree, followed immediately by a similarly garbed woman. Neil recognized her immediately.

"Abigail Trammell," he blurted. "Am I glad to see you."

The old man regarded him coolly. The woman didn't seem to recognize him for a moment, then smiled. "Neil Redding? The preacher's son? I must be home at last."

Sixteen

Chief Omar Longshadow exited Drovers Gap's lone police cruiser outside Lewis Redding's house. The ex-preacher had called the office, left a message that he wanted to speak with the chief about an urgent matter connected with the burning of Justice Fork Baptist Church. He hadn't specified any details.

Omar already planned to have an additional chat with Redding. The man may have been deflocked but not quite defrocked it seemed. He had bought a big tent and gotten a permit from the town commissioners to pitch it on the vacant lot behind the post-office, and according to the posters he had put up around town, he was holding meetings he advertised as a Restoration Revival.

Omar hadn't attended the show, as he thought of it, but he'd heard from several who had. Constable Jolene Bear had been to a couple of the meetings and confirmed Omar's impression that Lewis Redding had launched a rabble-rousing enterprise on the premise that the church had been burned by a mysterious gang of evildoers intent on delivering the innocent souls of Drovers Gap into flaming perdition.

Lewis had assembled a following of disgruntled Baptists

from his former congregation, and a few fringe Methodists and Presbyterians who were always looking for a righteous fight to invigorate their lagging faith. As far as Omar had been informed, the Episcopalians were resisting Redding's invitation to holy war. As one of the vestry told Omar, "Lewis Redding gets more excited about Hell than he does about Jesus. That isn't our way."

Omar purposely didn't phone ahead, but when he stepped out of his car, he saw Redding sitting on his porch, waiting as if he'd been expecting a visit. Perched there in the shadows, out of the bright sunlight, he resembled a big black bird. The image of a vulture came to the policeman's mind.

Lewis didn't move or speak as Omar crossed the yard. Omar usually softened his approach with a snatch of small talk, maybe a remark about the weather. Today, he wasn't in the mood.

"I hear you've thought of something to tell me about the church fire, Preacher," he said.

Lewis didn't pause before he answered, "Yes, Chief, I can tell you who did it."

The sun had long set and a waxing gibbous moon argued with the dark by the time Omar parked his cruiser beside his house. The kitchen light was on. He figured his dad had made supper, no doubt cold by now. Warren would be irritated at having his good meal spoiled but would pretend not to be. Both men had in their turn been late for a lot of suppers, blessed with wives who forgave them for it, and then left them in the world alone. Omar's mother died of cancer while he was still in high school. His wife and daughter were driving to a basketball game he had been too busy to attend when a long-haul driver fell asleep at the wheel and ran his load of steel I-beams over the top of their SUV. Omar had arrived at the scene of an anonymous accident just in time to see their new Dodge explode in flames. Nine years later, two grieving men shared their sorrow and a house. As Warren remarked on occasion, "The only thing worse than being lonely is doing it by yourself."

Omar sat in his vehicle watching the moon dim behind a scrap of cloud, and while he waited for it to emerge on the far side of darkness, he replayed in his mind the visit with Lewis Redding.

The preacher had pulled a wristwatch from his jacket pocket and laid it on the porch railing in front of them. "I should have showed you this before, Chief," he said. "I found it at the church after the fire."

Omar bent and studied the watch without picking it up. "It doesn't look like it's been through fire," he said

"No," Lewis murmured, "It would have been dropped after."

"You think this belongs to whoever started the fire?"

"I'm sure of it, Chief," Lewis said.

"Then you've been withholding evidence, Lewis. Your handling of it has likely erased any forensic benefit it might give. Why didn't you show me this when we met out there?"

"Because it's my boy's watch, Chief. My own boy burned my church just to spite me."

Warren Longshadow looked up as his son came through the door. "You sat out there in your car a long time, Chief. Contemplating your sins?"

"Just wondering if I ought to arrest somebody, Dad. It's been a long day."

"I heated some stew back up," Warren said, sliding a bowl across the table. It steamed as it cooled.

Omar washed his hands in the kitchen sink, dried them on

a towel, sat in front of the bowl, took the cup of coffee his father handed him.

"Thanks, Dad. I'm glad one of us has kept out of trouble all day."

Warren laughed. "Who says I've kept out of trouble?"

Omar sipped his coffee tentatively, found it too hot to swallow. "Well, you didn't get caught, anyway. This stew smells good. What's in it?"

"Eat it first, and I'll tell you." Warren said, pouring a cup of coffee for himself before sitting down across from his son. "You're working too hard, boy. When are you going to put in for a vacation?"

Omar spooned his stew, savored his mouthful before he swallowed. "This stuff is delicious. Maybe I don't want to know what's in it."

"Well?" Warren said, waiting for an answer to his question.

Omar changed the subject. "Dad, tell me what you think of Lewis Redding."

"The preacher out at Justice Fork?"

"Yep, that's him. At least he was their preacher until last week when he resigned."

Warren smelled an interesting conversation. "You think he burned down his church?"

"He's on my list. You know people, Dad. What's your estimation of him?"

Warren dumped a heaping teaspoon of sugar into his coffee, stirred, gazed into the swirling dark as if he expected to find some clarity there. "I wouldn't peg him brave enough to be an arsonist, but Redding's a man convinced that God keeps score on us. That kind of conviction can make a man dangerous."

Omar put down his spoon and tried another sip of his coffee. "What kind of dangerous?"

"I don't mean violent, necessarily," Warren said, "although

I'd venture his wife's afraid of him. But any man who has unshakable faith in his own rightness can't be trusted to know the difference. That's all I'm saying."

Omar nodded, picked up his spoon. "Thanks, Dad. I value your opinion, especially when it agrees with mine. Now I'm going to eat my stew and we can talk about the weather or anything you like, except my day in uniform."

Owl pulled a wicked looking knife from his belt and began unfettering Neil Redding. The young man stared at the woman who had emerged from the tree with the beard and his bees. "You're not really the bookstore lady, are you?" he queried. He didn't know why he doubted his eyes, but as he took in her extrinsic garments, the question hung in his mind.

She looked puzzled for a moment, then nodded, and said amiably, "I didn't expect the Púca would allow me to be missed among the Fallen. What has Wendl been up to while I was on Otherworld?"

Owl helped him to his feet, and Neil stood rubbing his wrists, eyeing the big ball of bees humming in the maple across the clearing. "I reckon he's been pretty busy being you, Miss Trammell. He's been getting Hemlock Cottage ready for the tourist season. It's already booked full, thanks to Miss Tsula."

"Tsula who?" snapped Abigail, something resembling alarm in her tone.

Owl, looking very owlish at the moment, nodded as if this were no news to him. "The Daughter of the Stone, no doubt. Where there's one púca there's bound to be two."

"Abigail, Wendl, whoever," stammered Neil, "hired her to manage the bread and breakfast after they took over Gloria Proudfoot's bookstore."

"So Gloria sold Vintage Reads after all," mused Abigail.

"I'm not surprised Wendl would buy her out. He's a fool for books."

Owl, who was poking at the remnants of the campfire with the tip of his knife, suddenly raised it and pointed the blade at Neil. "How did you get involved with the púca?".

"They hired Luke Armstrong to do some renovations. He took me on as his helper."

Owl stabbed an ember with his knife, releasing a shower of sparks. "Lugh of the Long Arm," he said, standing and drawing a glowing glyph on the smoky air with his hot blade. "That might explain why the Goodmother's minions Hawke and Corvid are prowling among the Fallen. She'll need him to cage her dragon." He swallowed Neil's mind in his owlful gaze. "And what was their business with you?"

Neil shook his head. "I don't know. But I saw them talking with my father at Home Ground when I went to hear Ronan play."

Abigail looked at Owl. "His father is the local Baptist preacher," she informed.

Owl blinked his eyes dolefully, murmured, "If the Baptists are mixed up in this, it can't be good."

Seventeen

Barbara Battle counted the last of the receipts from the previous night's service and handed the talley to Lewis Redding. The Restoration Revival had been going on for three weeks now and the crowds were bigger than ever. He was no longer thinking about his next venue. He filled out the deposit slip, dropped it with the money into the zipper bag to deposit at Mountain Trust Bank.

Barbara showed up at the tent the third night of the Restoration Crusade and came back every night after that. After the first week, she volunteered to help. "Any way I can, Reverend Lewis," she said. "Whatever your need." Lewis never quite said yes to her offer, but she proceeded to make herself useful in ways he never anticipated. She found an office space, answered the phone, screened visitors, made appointments for counseling, ran errands, did his grocery shopping.

"You'd make a good wife," Lewis let slip one day, immediately added, "for somebody." He still had a wife, of course. She was living with her sister in Asheton. Their daughter was with her, transferred to the school there. Lewis didn't suppose she had any plans to come back. As for that worthless son of his, Lewis hoped he wouldn't .

Lewis thought Chief Longshadow was as convinced as he was that Neil had started the fire that burned Justice Fork Baptist Church. No blame had been proven yet. There was only the watch Lewis found, which Longshadow said merely indicated Neil might have been there sometime after the fire. If the policeman doubted Lewis's word about finding the watch, he never accused him of anything, and Lewis had been in company with three honest and godly men the evening of the fire, so could hardly be suspect. Still, he had the impression that Omar Longshadow just didn't like him. On reflection, Lewis concluded the feeling was mutual.

He glanced out the window, caught a glimpse of Barb Battle walking away to the bank. Although tonight's sermon awaited his attention, the glance extended into an attenuated gaze as he admired the fit of the woman's skirt, the way the material conformed to her movement. He thought she walked like a woman used to being watched. His hands tingled with unwarranted anticipation of impossibilities.

Lewis would have pursued this line of fruitless fantasy further, had not a big black Lincoln pulled to the curb in front of the office. Lewis sighed as Orville Hawke and Wilbur Corvid emerged, unfolding into the air like twin black and ungainly storks. Wilbur carried a large roll of papers under one arm. Lewis had on his preacher face by the time they came through the door.

"Brother Hawke, Brother Corvid," Lewis intoned in his pulpit voice, "What brings you out on this fine day?" He wasn't precisely happy to see them here, although he certainly had reason to pretend a welcome. They had, after all, funded his entire enterprise until the tithes and offerings began coming in. It didn't escape Lewis' attention that Justice Fork Baptist Church had not equaled the financial draw of his tent ministry. At street level, Restoration Crusade was more carnival than ministry, a contrived and carefully orchestrated performance, calculated to excite followers to recreational indignation and uncritical generosity.

Wilbur swept Lewis' sermon notes aside and spread his unrolled papers across the desk. "It's about time, don't you think, Brother Lewis? The Lord would not have us tarry before the harvest."

Lewis looked at Wilbur's papers, construction drawings for some enormous structure. He thought some of the lines might indicate a tower or maybe a steeple. Whatever it was, it was huge. Bigger, certainly, than Justice Fork Baptist Church. Bigger than his tent. Something glimmered on the edge of his bewilderment. "What am I looking at?" he whispered, as the lines and notations began to assume intelligible form.

"Restoration Cathedral," said Orville Hawke.

"And it's all yours," said Wilbur Corvid. "Or will be, when we're done with you."

———

Tsula Stone, Luke Armstrong, and Wendl VonTrier sat around the kitchen table at Hemlock Cottage, the remains of their breakfast between them. As Wendl poured another round of coffee, he said, "Would you have really foxed that poor boy, Tsula, having let him chase after you all night?"

Tsula laughed, poured a bit of her coffee into a saucer and lapped it up with her vulpesian tongue. For a second she seemed brinked on a shapeshift, then settled into her human form, took a ladylike sip from her cup, smiled demurely, said, "I would have changed him back in time for breakfast, but I would have loved to run with that beautiful boy. I would have, too, if those two dirty birds of Wandalena's hadn't grabbed him first."

"You mean Hawke and Corvid?" Luke queried.

"The very same, ugly as ever," Tsula said. "They got him

trussed up like a pig going to a barbecue, and while I was trying to figure out a rescue, who should pop in from Otherworld but our old buddy Owl, and Gobnait with her bees. The bees sent the ugly ducklings running. I figure I've left our young Redding in good hands. They should have him down here within the hour.

Wendl nearly spilt his coffee. "Gobnait? You're talking about Abigail here?"

Tsula, clearly enjoying herself. "She looked for all the world just like you, VonTrier. I wonder if Drovers Gap is big enough for two Abigails."

"It's hardly big enough for one," Luke said, shaking his head.

"I think VonTrier's back in town," Wendl said with a wry shrug.

"I want to know what the thugs meant to do with the boy," Luke put in. "Old Goodmother didn't send them out to collect Fallen."

"I heard most of their talk," Tsula said. "They went on and on about how Neil burned down his daddy's church."

"Except he was chasing you all night. He couldn't have done it," Luke said.

"Obviously, they intend he take the blame for the fire," Wendl said. "And if I know those scavengers, that's just part of their scheming. He looked at Tsula. "You up to a bit more shapeshifting, foxlady, or did you max out your spells luring your boy last night?"

"I'm with you," she said. "Let's find out what they're up to."

"Just like Púca to fly away and have fun and leave their betters to do the dishes," Luke said. "Our friends will come here first, I think. You two run along and play spy, and I'll try to keep the Redding lad out of Longshadow's clutches until you find out what's going on."

The two púca shimmered on the verge of gone as Luke queried, "What should I tell your Abigail, VonTrier?"

Wendl steadied for a moment. "Ask what took her so long," then became elsewhere.

Omar Longshadow stood on the porch at Hemlock Cottage waiting for someone to answer the bell. He was about to press it again when Trammell's hired carpenter opened the door.

"Morning, Chief," Luke Armstrong's tone sounded like he'd been expecting a visitor. "Miss Abigail isn't here right now. She had some errands to do down the street."

"Actually, I wanted to talk to you, Mister Armstrong," Omar said, trying to sound a pleasant and casual he didn't feel. Something about this Armstrong character rubbed him wrong. He couldn't quite pin it down, just didn't trust the man. He wondered how Abigail Trammell had come to hire Armstrong, who wasn't local, when there were several able housewrights in town she must have known better. Maybe there was some connection between the two that he didn't know about. And maybe, Omar conceded inwardly, the church fire had just made him more broadly suspicious than he needed to be.

"I hear you've hired young Redding as a helper," Omar said. "How's he working out?"

"Well enough to keep him on," Luke answered. "Not much experience, but he's a fast learner, knows how to use his hands, and gets his directions first time told."

"Neil's a smart boy," Omar said. "Could I talk to him?"

Luke didn't hesitate with his answer. "He isn't on the job today, Chief. I gave him a couple of days off. He'll be back in tomorrow."

"I'd like to chat with him today, if I could," Omar said. "I have something I think belongs to him."

Luke pointed up toward the mountains south of town. "He's up there somewhere, Chief. He and Tsula went off camping up by Warwoman."

"Tsula Stone? The woman Abigail has running her store?"

"That, too." If there was more to be said about Tsula, Luke chose not to.

"Not your average hiking companions," ventured Omar. "An old woman and a young man like that. She'll slow him down."

Luke laughed. "You don't know our Tsula, Chief. I doubt you could keep up with her in the woods."

Omar pulled out his notebook, scribbled something, clicked his pen, then dropped them back into his pocket. "You make her sound right formidable, Armstrong."

Luke looked dead serious as he said, "She is, but don't worry, Chief. She isn't a wicked witch. She won't turn your suspect into a bear or anything."

"I didn't say Neil Redding was a suspect," Omar said.

"No, Chief," agreed the carpenter. "You didn't."

Eighteen

Upon her return to Hemlock Cottage, Luke Armstrong and Neil Redding set to work building a dozen hives for Abigail's bees. In all, they had already added three guest rooms upstairs, spacious and cozy with arresting views of mountains and woods in another world and nary a glimpse of the town around, and, most importantly, invisible from outside the building. Luke's attempts to explain the logistics did little to alleviate Neil's mystification. When they were at work, joining timber, framing a wall, laying down a floor, everything appeared properly real, but when he stood in the street and looked back at the house, where he thought a window should be was the same blank wall as before, and where they had framed and shingled a dormer, he saw only the unbroken slope of a roof.

"It's all there," Luke assured him, "Just a little shy of the moment."

Inevitably, Chief Longshadow invited Neil to join him for coffee at Home Ground Suds and Java, seemingly the policeman's favorite venue for questioning potential suspects.

"I told Longshadow you and Tsula were up on the

mountain together the night of the fire," Luke said when Neil asked for time off work to meet with the policeman.

"You didn't need to lie for me, Luke," Neil protested. "I didn't burn the church down."

Luke shook his head, "I didn't lie. Tsula was watching you the whole time. If Abigail and Owl hadn't showed up when they did, she would have rescued you. She heard and saw everything."

Neil asked, "What am I supposed to tell the Chief?"

"Tell him the truth. He hears it seldom enough that he'll recognize it. Tell him everything you've told us, although you might leave the part out about Owl and Abigail and the bees coming out of a hollow tree."

It was a slow day at Vintage Reads, in part because Tsula Stone had hung a warding spell on the Battered and Bartered table when she opened that morning. Only two browsers had even stopped to scope the bargains; neither had ventured to come inside. Joyce Keller, the FedEx driver dropped off two boxes of books the previous afternoon just before closing. Opening the second one, Tsula sensed a purposeful approach and, with a copy of *Real Food* in her hand, looked up to see Chief Omar Longshadow cast his shadow across the entrance.

"Afternoon, Miss Stone," he said with his polite policeman voice. "If I'm not too much of an interruption, could we chat for a couple of minutes?"

Tsula responded with her bookseller smile. "Unless you've come to arrest me, Chief, you can call me Tsula."

Omar took off his hat, stood like a pupil arriving at the principal's office. Tsula recognized this as part of his protocol to soothe the contentious. "I'm just needing a bit of clarification about where everybody was the night Justice Fork Baptist Church burned."

Tsula adjusted her innocent face. "You think it was arson, then?"

"We don't have any evidence of that so far," Omar said, "but county forensics hasn't been able to rule it out. Meanwhile, I'm just trying to place everybody who might have some connection to the situation."

"And you figure I have some connection?"

"Well, young Redding might, and Luke Armstrong said you two were on the mountain together that evening."

"He told you right, Chief."

Omar turned his hat in his hand, as if inspecting it for a bug, then looked at Tsula. "Neil Redding said he was up there following a white fox. He said he was alone, got lost, until Abigail Trammell and Enoch Owl found him. He didn't mention you."

"Neil saw the fox, and I saw Neil, Chief. I assume he might have mentioned his encounter with his father's associates, Hawke and Corvid?"

"So you were there, then?" Omar said.

"How else would I know, Chief?" Tsula said, answering question for question.

<hr>

Owl carried a bag up the mountain to retrieve Abigail's bees. There were more bees in the swarm than Owl's bag could hold. After assessing the situation, he tried singing to them and they followed him back to Hemlock Cottage, where he and Abigail coaxed them into a hive. Over the next couple of weeks, several other swarms emerged from the hollow tree and found their way down the mountain to be homed in the other hives Luke and his helper had built and arranged along the verge of the wood behind Abigail's vegetable garden. The trees would shade them from the summer sun and shield them from the winter wind.

Abigail was delighted, but Owl's reactions were mixed. He speculated that if bees could fly between the Two Worlds, less welcome entities might find their way across the Separation. Luke and Tsula concurred, and Tsula's nocturnal traverses across the mountain became more regular as she watched for signs of intruders. Wendl VonTrier disappeared for several days into a search for the lair of Hawke and Corvid. When Chief Omar Longshadow came to question him, his unexplained absence insured Wendl's inclusion in the policeman's list of suspects.

Omar finally caught up with Hawke and Corvid in front of the office they had rented on Main Street. They were standing out front of the building directing a crew installing a sign that declared in a bright golden ecclesiastic font, *Restoration Crusade Ministries.*

"That's a nice sign, gentlemen," the Chief said.

"A sign for the times," said Orville Hawke.

"A harbinger of hope," added Wilbur Corvid.

"I'm hoping you can tell me where you were the night Justice Fork Baptist Church burned down." Omar said. "I hear you had a set to with Lewis Redding's son."

"Must've been somebody who looked like us, Chief. We were traveling away that night." Wilbur said.

"Up in the air," said Orville

"On the wing, as it were," chimed in Wilbur. "Returning from the mission field."

"What airline did you use?" queried Omar.

"It was a charter flight," said Orville Hawke.

Wilbur Corvid pulled a card from his vest and handed it to the policeman. "Here's our pilot, Chief," he said. "You can check with her."

Omar read the card, sky blue, with a drawing of what looked like an antique bi-plane above the text:

ICARUS AIR

Crop Dust and Spray
Scenic tour flights
Agrona Wells, licensed pilot

When Omar phoned Icarus Air, a maybe female voice said she was Agrona Wells; yes, a pilot; no, she was the whole operation; yes, she had flown Hawke and Corvid on the evening in question; no she couldn't tell him where they'd gone, but if he wanted to come to her airfield, she would show him. When Omar arrived the next morning, the airfield, as Agrona had called it, turned out to be a narrow strip of grass between two steep and wooded ridges twelve miles west of Asheton at the other end of Marshall County.

Omar parked in front of a large metal shed, presumably a hanger for Agrona's aircraft. He suspected the structure had a history as much bovine as aviatory. The only other vehicle in sight was a severely rusted and dented pickup, that may have been red or green or yellow at some earlier point in its tumultuous travels. Just beyond the hanger sat an open-cockpit biplane, that perhaps was airworthy during the first world war. As Omar got out of his car, a lean and weathered woman dressed for the lead role in a movie about Amelia Earhart came across the grass to meet him.

"Agrona Wells," she said, extending a hand that shook his with firm intention. "You the policeman who phoned yesterday?"

"Guilty as charged," he acknowledged. "Omar Longshadow, Chief of Police at Drovers Gap, down at the lower end of the county."

"And you came all this way yourself to see me," Agrona said. "How many on your force?"

"Just me, my sergeant, and a constable who mostly answers the office phone," Omar tried on a smile as he said it.

"Only three?" Agrona contrived to look surprised although Omar thought she likely already knew as much.

"What do they need a chief for?" she added, pretending there was a need to ask.

"Somebody has to take the blame if things go south," Omar said it like a joke.

The pilot anointed him with a sympathetic gaze. "Things go south in Drovers Gap very often, do they?" she murmured softly.

"Well, we've never had a church burned down before," Omar said. "Why couldn't you tell me over the phone where you took my two suspects the night of the fire?"

Agrona shrugged. "Because I don't know, Chief. I mean, they showed me how to get there but it isn't on a map. I checked. I'm not sure it's even in the world."

Omar gestured toward the decrepit plane. "That machine of yours doesn't look up to flying that far," he said dryly.

The pilot laughed. "Given a good tail wind, she might just fly forever. You up to a little ride, Chief Longshadow?"

Omar regarded the craft dubiously. "In that thing?"

"She may not be pretty, but she's beautiful in the air. Maybe a little rough on the landings sometimes, but Polly will get you there." Agrona handed Omar an antique aviator's helmet with goggles. "Here," she said, "climb aboard."

Omar clambered into one of the two passenger seats. "Let me down easy, Polly," he whispered under his breath as he secured his seat belt. Aloud, he said, "You fly this thing at night?"

"Only with a full moon," the pilot assured him.

Agrona leaned into the cockpit, set a couple of knobs on the control panel and stepped to the front of the plane. She pulled hard on the prop. The engine caught on her second pull. She jumped aboard, adjusted the throttle until the engine's rattle and chatter smoothed to a steady rumble. She looked back at Omar, yelled, "Keep your mouth closed so you won't get bugs in your teeth," then gave it gas. The engine revved, the prop grabbed air, and the plane called Polly with her mad pilot and terrified passenger bounded across the grass like a rabbit fleeing hounds.

Omar clung white-knuckled to his seat as Polly hopped and lunged down the narrow strip. The massed green of old-growth hardwoods at the end of the grass hurtled toward them at an alarming rate. The policeman was about to scream, *Abort! Stop!* When the wheels went silent, the nose of the plane lifted and the tops of hemlock and pines slipped by beneath, close enough, it seemed to Omar, that he might reach out and touch.

The airstrip fell away below and behind where Omar's stomach lay in the grass, awaiting his return. He fixed his gaze on a tiny silver cloud all alone in the deep deep blue and prayed as Agrona banked her craft over the woods and rose toward the crest of the nearest ridge. The ridge slipped below them, not quite so close as the trees had been, and Polly leveled, smooth as an arrow's flight. The engine seemed uncannily quiet, barely audible in the rush of their slipstream. Agrona looked back at him and pointed vaguely. He read her lips as much as he heard her voice, faint against the wind, "Not far."

Polly banked east, and before Omar was ready, distant mountains grew from a narrow blue undulation on the horizon to an imposing barrier of peaks and ridges, the highest of which married the clouds. Agrona deftly guided Polly through the gaps and valleys between summits looming dark above them like impending judgment. A steep ridge of fractured stone and stunted pine tumbled across the valley ahead of them. "Down there," Agrona yelled, pointing toward a tiny dot of bright blue just below the crest. She seemed to be aiming the plane directly toward it. As they approached, the circle grew to an opening that Omar thought might be almost wide enough for the plane to pass through. Almost.

"Climb," he shouted. It came out a scream.

"Close your eyes!" Agrona shouted back.

The policeman did as he was told. Through his closed lids, he sensed a brilliant flash like lightning without thunder. His ears popped loud in his skull as the craft plummeted like a raptor on her prey. An instant of shadow and roar and Omar opened his eyes to featureless gray. He had a momentary impression that they were flying upside down until the cloud thinned to a faint blue of sky above and mottled green of forest below.

Omar's stomach finally caught up with him as they emerged into clear daylight and around them loomed the close high mountains and beneath, rising gently to meet them a broad verdant field. A dirt track ran tan and straight ahead of them and Polly aligned with it. Agrona shouted, "The Mission Field," as the wheels touched earth lightly, once, twice, then rolling slower and slower to stop and still. Agrona cut the engine. Silence rang in their ears. Omar lifted his goggles and wiped tears from his eyes.

Nineteen

Wendl VonTrier sat on the back row, near the entrance. Up front, on a huge screen, Lewis Redding pointed out features of a projected image of the future Restoration Cathedral. According to Redding, this grandiose edifice would be the birthplace of a mighty moral movement to restore the nation to righteousness. The standing-room-only crowd was eating up his spiel.

Wendl, configured to resemble a tourist he passed on his way here, attracted no undue notice. He spied several people he knew among the throng, but none recognized him. He was just one more stranger among many attendees, some already converts, some attracted by this populist gospel of lost privilege regained, and some merely curious to see what the show was about.

Off to one side, Orville Hawke and Wilbur Corvid perched in a shadowy corner, constantly scanning the massed faces. Wendl thought they probably had a vague sense of his presence, which would account for their evident uneasiness, but in this maze of conflictant energies, they could not isolate his persona. He concentrated on damping his own aura, rendering his presence bland and dim.

Up on stage, Lewis began winding up his appeal, "They burned our church. They thought we would be silent in our loss. But they were merely clearing the ground for the sowing of a mighty harvest. We have been delivered of our lesser things so that we can build a true temple of righteousness and judgement where the wicked and destroyers cannot abide."

Across the congregation came shouts of *Amen* and *Praise* as people stood waving their arms and dancing in the aisles while the former Justice Fork deacons fanned out with buckets that shortly brimmed with cash. An organ boomed out a hymn about soldiers marching to war, and a thousand throats began singing the words, ready to march and war against any enemy encountered or imagined.

Hawke and Corvid wheeled front and center a cart piled with books. It looked just like the Battered and Bartered table from Vintage Reads. Lewis Redding pointed at the books as his amplified voice filled the tent. "And this, friends, is the poison they are using to foul the innocent minds of our youth."

A chorus of shouts became a roar. The congregation was morphing into a mob. Lewis held up his hands and silence fell immediate and absolute.

Into this stillness, the preacher spoke softly, almost gently, "And you all know where this came from." A single candle burned before an arrangement of flowers center stage. Lewis took it, held it high, then dropped it onto the books. The books, prepped for this event, instantly were enveloped in flames.

Wendl slipped from his seat and made for the entrance. He knew where this was going to end.

Abigail watched through her front window as the three crows landed on her walk. They cocked their heads and regarded

Hemlock Cottage as if sizing up accommodations. By now accustomed to the strange flock of seasonal guests Tsula had recruited this year, she wasn't greatly surprised when, after a bit of hopping about while exchanging a mutter of clucks and caws, the feathered trio morphed into three tall and dark women.

Abigail had been expecting them all morning. The Morrigan sisters, Bobbie, Mirabel and Nan, had reservations for a month, starting today. They were apparently old friends of Tsula, although Wendl had been less than enthusiastic at the prospect of their arrival. He said that on Otherworld, their presence was synonymous with trouble. "They love to foretell defeats and disasters," he confided to Abigail, "and delight in fulfilling their own prophesies."

"They sound like half the women in Drover's Gap," Abigail replied, her voice brimming with amused skepticism.

She thought they seemed nice enough in person. At least as agreeable as the typical run of tourist. Abigail turned on her best tourist smile and opened the door as they approached, "Welcome to Hemlock," she beamed.

"Such a lovely place you have," said Bobbie.

"Tsula Stone has told us so much about this house," cooed Mirabel, "It feels like coming home."

"Such a quiet and peaceful town," murmured Nan. "Ripe for excitement."

"Let me show you up to your room," Abigail said, gesturing for the sisters to follow. They had specifically asked to share one room. Neil had spent a morning helping Abigail rearrange a double and move in an extra bed. By the time they reached their room two flights up, the Morrigan sisters each carried a stuffed travel bag. Abigail no longer gave a second thought to the peculiar logistics of the alien guests her púca assistant had enticed to Drovers Gap. The sisters apparently deemed their quarters appropriate to their preferences. Nan hovered above her bed for an instant, as if she was about to become a crow again and fly away, then settled upon it as lightly as a flake of midnight snow.

"There's some drink and snacks downstairs when you're ready." Abigail said. "I'll be in the kitchen if you need anything. Dinner is at six." She closed the door and left the three mysteries to themselves.

Dinner had been Tsula's idea. She was convinced that the clientele she was bringing in would feel more at home if they didn't have to go out into the town for meals. When Abigail protested that she couldn't possibly handle all the extra work entailed in cooking an evening meal for a houseful of guests, Wendl had volunteered himself as chef and Owl as his sous, "just until we hire permanent staff." Luke and Neil refitted the kitchen and Luke one evening presented Abigail with a surprise, a carved and painted wooden sign to hang above the front porch. In the dark of a late-summer night, not long before the Morrigan sisters arrived, the Hemlock Cottage sign came down and the sun rose next morning on Hemlock House.

Abigail Trammell's guests were at least as entertaining to Drovers Gap residents as the town was to the "away people," as the locals referred to them. Since they all left money behind when they departed, they were not only tolerated, but more welcome than some of the natives were inclined to admit aloud. They were also easy targets for the rantings of Lewis Redding and his flock of culture vultures, who tended to regard anyone who might converse privately in some language other than English, as subversive and immoral individuals and anathema to pious and patriotic society.

Willie Graham couldn't remember when he first heard the voices. In the beginning, he didn't even recognize them as voices, just random sounds at odd quiet moments, like wind or rain or tinnitus. After some time, they evolved warm and modulated as human speech, though he could not identify words, or any particular language. The voices flowed like a small stream through the back of his mind, a barely perceptible murmuring behind the ordinary events happening on the surface of his days. Eventually, the voices began to shape words he could understand, but they never spoke to him, they floated around in his awareness like a conversation overheard from the next room. Willie decided the past was not gone after all, that the dead, however long since they last breathed, were never quite departed.

So, on a gentle September evening in Drovers Gap, the sort of end-of-summer night when half the people who speak to you on your walk home from the Wild Leek Pub are ghosts, Willy was only mildly surprised when he turned into his yard to see his mother sitting on his front porch, rocking gently in the soft breezy shadows.

"Hi Mom," said Willie, "It's been awhile."

Evelyn Graham kept changing form as she spoke. Willie couldn't decide if there were two of her becoming one, or one of her gaining multiplicity. *You've stayed out of trouble of late, son of mine. I've been content just to watch. Frankly, I didn't think you had it in you.* Her voice in his head kept wavering between singularity and a Greek chorus.

Willie sighed, sat on the steps, and stared down the hill toward Main Street. It made his head hurt to look at his mother when she got like this. "I'm getting old, Mom. Just like you did. I don't have a lot of energy to spare for naughtiness these days. But I must have done something amiss, or you wouldn't be here."

Don't talk to your mother like that. I'm only here to help, Willieboy, as any mother would. She sounded exactly like Evelyn when she was only human. Willie glanced around, and there she was, just an old lady, his mother, sitting in her rocking chair to catch the evening breeze.

"Don't recall asking for help," Willie mumbled.

Evelyn bit her words. *I'm not deaf anymore, Son. I can hear it even if you don't let it out of your mouth.* Willie opened his mouth to fire a retort, but couldn't think of anything to say, so just sat there staring at his mother.

You'll catch flies. Willie closed his mouth and she went on. *I thought, after what I told you about the place, you were going to make old Boyce Miller an offer on those acres up by Potter's Shoals he's been trying to sell for years. What changed your mind?"*

"Location, Mom. It's nowhere. Down in that holler, too steep to build on, no views, scrappy timber, bad road, no sun in winter. I'd be stuck with it just like Boyce has been. I can't run my business on your tall tales."

Evelyn flared up like a campfire then died back down into herself. *They're not tall tales. I heard them from those who were there. There's more in that ground than you'll find on your county maps, Willieboy.*

"Mom, I hated it when you called me Willieboy while you were breathing, and I don't like it any better now. I wish you wouldn't do that."

Willy didn't see his mother anymore, but imagined he felt her hand ruffling his hair as she passed, or maybe it was only the night breeze. A whisper in his ear, *Why Willy, you'll always be my very own boy.*

He wanted to tell Evelyn he wasn't her boy anymore, but before he could open his mouth to say it, she had flown away.

Willie was hungry after his encounter with the living dead, fancied he might like some pizza, but too tired to walk back down the hill to the Wild Leek, he stuffed his face with week-old cornbread and washed it down with buttermilk, gulping it from the carton. He almost passed on his evening shower, but he was cold. His knees ached. Thinking the hot water might ease him into himself, he proceeded with his nightly ritual, washing the detritus of a mildly frustrating day from his hide, and the clutter of vague discontents and ghostly dialogues from his brain. He pulled the covers up around his chin and, clean and empty as a newborn, let sleep swallow him whole.

Deep in the night, the moon shone down on Willie's pale face and dark open mouth and he dreamed frightening dreams about runaway trains and murderous strangers and blind justice, but he never stirred. Willie woke in the morning, dry-mouthed, but rested, dreams forgotten, buried in that deep dark among all the secrets he kept hidden from his waking self.

On the way to his office, he stopped by Home Ground, grabbed a sausage-and-egg biscuit with a cup of coffee from Doug, who was too busy to gossip. When Willie finally arrived at Mountain Realty, Betty was already there, and a customer from down the mountain in Pearis Falls was waiting, primed to find out if his dream retreat was still on the market.

Willie put his biscuit in his desk drawer, set his unopened coffee carefully beside it, and smiled at his prospect. "Why certainly, Mister Bonner. We can run up there right now and take a look, if you'd like." Frank Bonner liked the idea very much.

By late afternoon, Willie arrived back in town with a check in his jacket pocket. He waved as Frank drove away to a city thirty miles east and a thousand feet closer to sea level. Willie still wore his big smile when he came into the office and handed Betty the binder to lock away.

Getting ready to close that evening, Willie watched Betty tallying Bonner's check into the day's bank deposit. "Can I buy you dinner to celebrate?" he asked. "It's our biggest deal so far this year."

Betty sprinkled her little giggle across her desk. Willie couldn't decide if she was laughing at him or with him, and when she looked up, decided maybe she was just embarrassed.

"I'd love to Mister Graham, but I'm eating at the Smoke House with Brian tonight."

I could do better than barbecue. Instead, Willie said, "I'll ask you again at the closing."

Betty smiled, nodded, went back to her paperwork. Willie wondered what it was like to be Brian. As she tallied the figures, Betty paused suddenly, "Mister Graham, have you been behaving yourself lately?"

"I always behave myself, Betty. Why?"

She giggled nervously, perhaps afraid she'd overstepped some boundary. "Chief Longshadow was in while you were out. Said he wanted to ask you some questions."

While enamored of Bettys many and obvious charms, she irritated Willie the way she dribbled out information. "What about? Did he say?" straining the impatience out of his voice.

"Just said he wanted to ask some questions about the Miller property. I told him to call you in the morning."

Willie remembered what his dead mother said to him last night. He'd just taken a binder from Frank Bonner for that same piece of worthless ground.

TWENTY

Even on a day too warm for September, the sun set right on schedule. The day-trippers drifted away down the mountain toward home and the moon rose on the sort of late summer night when the stories come out in Drovers Gap and if you aren't careful, one of them might catch you unawares and swallow you whole.

If Willie Graham believed in ghosts, he didn't believe in stories. He didn't do much reading beyond his bank statement and would on no account read fiction. But on this September night, as he clicked off the light and locked the door on Mountain Realty, his departure did not go unnoticed.

He turned and watched his secretary walking away under the street lamp toward her car. Her four-inch heels clicked on the pavement. She didn't wear them to work, but tonight she had a date with a young man Willie wished was him.

"Don't stay out too late, Betty," he called after her. "We have an early day tomorrow."

"Don't you worry, Mister Graham. I'll be here on time," she answered, without turning around, bending to unlock her little vintage Miata. Willie admired the view. He kept trying to persuade her to call him Willie, but she steadfastly refused.

Betty's Miata came alive and purred away. Betty's boyfriend, who found the car for her, was an excellent mechanic.

Willie sighed, threw his jacket over his shoulder and began walking along the street. The shadow beneath his mailbox detached itself from the store front and slithered down the street after him. Willie had on rare occasions been afraid of his own shadow, but this one, he never saw coming.

Willie didn't want to eat by himself, so, Bettyless, he stopped at Wild Leek Pub, was grateful to find his preferred corner table in the back vacant. There he was less likely to be noticed observing and eavesdropping nearby patrons. Eventually the server did notice him, and since he was a faithful tipper, vectored in on his table.

"What are you having tonight, Willie Darlin'?" The words dripped off her tongue sweet and thick, like an invitation to some illicit activity. Willie knew she talked to all her customers like this.

He handed back the menu without opening it. "Shepherds Pie, and a glass of Forester Stout, thank you, Darnella."

"You always order pie and stout, Willie, and you always come in here by yourself. You need to change your routine, get more sociable."

"I might be more sociable if I weren't so hungry," Willie said through his smile.

"I'll bring your beer now," Darnella tossed over her shoulder, already turning to her errand.

Willie watched a woman he didn't know laugh at something the man at her table was saying. Willie wished he could make Betty laugh like that. He did make her laugh sometimes, but not like that. She always laughed at him, not with him. He wasn't a clown, just a klutz. He didn't elicit laughter, he was just the object of it. Nobody in Drover's Gap took him seriously. He thought that might be why he almost never sold property to anybody local. All his best deals were with people from away, people like Frank Bonner, who took nobody but themselves seriously, and never laughed at anything.

Darnella brought his beer, and by the time he drank half of it, she set his shepherds pie on the table.

"Youns want another beer, Willie Darlin?" somewhere between a whisper and a song.

"No thanks, Darnella. The second one is never quite as good as the first."

"You always say that," she cooed, tempting him almost to order a second stout just to defy prediction. But he didn't. Willie ate his pie like the good boy he was, all the while savoring in his mind the picture of Betty bending over her little car.

Willie skipped the strawberry cobbler for dessert. They made it with too much sugar for his taste. Sweet didn't sit well on his sensitive stomach. He paid his bill and on the way to the door stopped to chat with a couple of potential clients who were not quite friends. He nodded to old Coy Hendricks, sitting alone and unserved at his favorite table by the front window. Willie sold the Hendricks farm after Coy died five years ago. Coy's offspring were still squabbling over how to divide the proceeds. Willie didn't care. He got his commission, supposed the lawyers would eventually scarf up the biggest slice of the pie.

He stepped out into the gentle September evening that felt more like June, and began walking toward his house just a block up the hill. The shadow, having waited for him beneath a bench outside the pub, slid soundlessly in his wake.

Willie stopped at the post office on the corner just as Miss Coralie Havard came out with her mail. The shadow lurked underneath her big Buick parked in front. "Good evening Miss Coralie," Willie offered. "You're looking well."

"And you, Willie Graham, are a liar," she said.

Willie was taken aback, until he saw she was smiling. Willie had trouble recognizing jokes, especially when directed at him. "I hope you haven't been sick," he ventured gamely.

"Do I look sick to you, Willie?" Miss Havard wasn't smiling now.

To Willie, she did look sick. At least, she looked old. "No ma'am, I don't think so."

"Don't try to think, Willie," Coralie said, waving her bills and circulars at him as she headed for her car. "It's too much for you."

Willie stood and watched the old woman get into her big car and drive away. The shadow lay very still. Willie thought it was an oil puddle. He hoped it was from Miss Coralie's Buick and that she would be stranded somewhere too far for her to walk for help and that her cell phone would be dead. The shadow didn't move until Willie turned away and started walking up the hill to his house. A startled feline jumped a foot off the sidewalk as the shadow slid between her feet. Willie didn't see the cat. He was thinking about his mother, hoping she wouldn't come to visit tonight. He needed his rest.

Thankfully, the porch was vacant when Willy turned up his walk. The shadow, now barely discernable from the general dark, waited beneath the steps while he got out his keys, then darted deftly under the door as he was closing it.

Willie nearly fell asleep in the shower, eyes closed, leaning against the wet tiles, inhaling the steam, sweet as a song, hot water falling down on his body like an erotic dream, his hand moving down his belly, imagining it was Betty's hand. He came to himself in a flash of guilt, ashamed of his imagined therefore unconsented intimacy.

He fell into bed exhausted, was asleep before the quilt settled. The shadow waited patiently beneath his bed. When Willie began to snore, the shadow crept up and over the covers, slid across his neck and chin, and disappeared into the black hole of his mouth. Willie woke with a snort, scratched his neck, and instinctively swallowed his shadow.

He woke next morning feeling like he had a mouth full of straw. While he brushed his teeth he stared at the unfamiliar self in his mirror. Something was not right about his reflection. He couldn't pin it on anything in particular. Maybe his eyes, red and itching from his annual end-of-summer bout of hayfever. He decided that was the problem. He couldn't see the púca peering back at him from behind his pupils.

Shadowing was a relatively recent skill Wendl had learned from Tsula Stone. It wasn't proper possession, just a passive indwelling. Although he might give an intention or hesitation a gentle nudge, he couldn't compel any action not willed and initiated by his host. Wendl was here because he wanted a front-row seat at any negotiations between Willie Stone and the Evil Twins, Orville Hawke and Wilbur Corvid.

Although the symbiosis posed no real hindrance or inconvenience for Willie Graham, it did present an element of risk to the púca. The longer Wendl maintained as Willie's shadow, the more his darkness would become Willie's. If Wendl overstayed his welcome, his being might become so dispersed in Willie's aura that the púca would be unable to resubstantiate his own particularity, thus doomed to live out Willie's life as a persistent bad mood. Wendl figured he might safely spy for three or four days. If the Twins did not contact his host in that time, he would have to devise some other mode of surveillance.

When Willie finally came to terms with his true self and showed up at his office, Chief Omar Longshadow was already waiting for him, sitting on the bench outside, holding a cardboard tray with two cups emblazoned with the Home Ground logo.

"I've brought us some coffee," said the policeman, "I've already eaten both ham biscuits."

"Serves me right for making you wait," Willie said, unlocking the door. "Looks like Betty is running late this morning."

"She had a big night," Omar said dryly. "My sergeant reported he saw her Miata parked up on Justice Peak about two this morning. It wasn't the only car up there."

"Love is in the air this time of year," Willie murmured. He wanted to feel bad but a spark of amusement surprised him from someplace he couldn't scratch.

"Betty tells me you have questions about the Miller property," Willie said as soon as he swallowed a sip of the policeman's coffee. "Do you want to buy it, too?"

"I take it there's been some interest in it lately?"

"Like a parade. Those two away people backing Lewis Redding's Restoration Crusade were asking me about the property, wanting to know who owned it, asking directions how to get up there."

"You mean Orville Hawke and Wilbur Corvid?" Omar said.

"That's right. Them two. Then first thing yesterday morning, some guy from down the mountain at Pearis Falls shows up, wants to see it immediately. I take him up there and he writes a check for a binder on the spot."

"What's the draw?" Omar asked.

Willie shrugged, "Beats me. It's all just up-and-down mountainside. Laurel thickets and scrubby pine. It would be hell harvesting timber out of there. No paved road. No good building sites. There's a bold creek running through. Might be some good trout pools in it, but that doesn't make it worth what Boyce Miller's asking."

"What about the open field just below Warwoman Ridge?" queried Omar. "Is Boyce doing a little farming up there?"

"Boyce is too old and stove to farm anymore." Willie said. "I've never seen a field. Like I told you, it's just wooded mountainside, most of it too steep to tractor safely."

Omar pulled a still-green leafy branch from his pocket and

laid it on the desk between them. "I've seen a field, maybe about forty acres. Right against the ridge above Potters Shoals."

Willie picked up the branch, turned the stem slowly between his fingers. "How did you get there?" he asked.

"I flew in with Agrona Wells in her old crop duster."

Willie tried not to laugh, but he did, "That woman has a death wish. I wouldn't walk across the street with her." He was still laughing when he pulled a folder of maps from his filing cabinet and spread them on his desk. "Maybe you found the Lost Forty, Chief."

"Lost Forty?" Omar didn't see the joke.

"Local legend," said Willie, looking serious again, as he positioned two map sections showing the Miller property side by side. "At least, among realtors. The old survey maps before nineteen hundred show one hundred forty acres, including forty acres clear along the creek, belonging to Aengus McMinn. A hundred forty acres were transferred to Boyce's grandad for cash, but when Boyce's mother Lillian had it surveyed, there was only a hundred acres, all wooded. Nobody's ever explained what happened to the forty-acre field. The story goes that the McMinns were wicked strange, that the Devil took the forty acres as his tax."

"That's a good story, but it doesn't help me much." Omar said. "Could I have my leaf back? It might be evidence."

Willie handed it back, looking surprised that he still held it. "Chief, is that what it looks like?"

Omar nodded, carefully tucked away his botany bit. "It is that," he said.

TWENTY-ONE

Chief Longshadow had hardly cleared the door at Mountain Realty when Lewis Redding barged through, breathless and angry, his face an alarming shade of purple. "You've got to stop this, Willie," he shouted, spittle dribbling down his chin, before Willie even had a chance to voice his public hello.

"Stop what, Preacher Redding? I'm at a loss, here." Willie said, trying to look pleasant and sound calm. Lewis leaned with his hands on Willie's desk, head down, panting like a hound chased or chasing.

"You all right, Preacher?" Willie murmured, standing, concerned. As Betty came in Willie silently motioned for her to bring a cup of water. "Sit down here and tell me what's wrong," Willie said as Lewis was already slumping into the customer chair.

Betty handed the preacher his water. He nodded, presumably in thanks, took a sip, found his tongue again and said, hoarse and halting as a well-digger just pulled from a cave-in, "You . . . you own that building next door to us?"

"You mean next to Restoration Crusade, I reckon. Yessir, we rent to them just like we do to you."

Lewis took another swallow of his water. "You can't do that, Willie. They're the enemy."

"The Morrigan sisters? They just want to open a health spa there. The town's approved their application. I don't see how they could be a problem to you."

"They do devilish stuff, in there, Willie," Lewis croaked, his voice getting tight and loud again. "I can hear them through the walls, chanting and singing and stuff. Men moaning and women laughing. They're doing yoga and massages and they are foreigners. They don't even speak English to one another in there. Orville and Wilbur have been warring against evil a long time and they say these Morrigan women are the worst."

"Preacher, I think you need to think about this before you go talking it around." Willie said. "After all, Orville Hawke and Wilbur Corvid dropped in on us from who knows where. Maybe you ought to find out a little more about them before you take their word for good and bad."

The preacher left unconvinced and unsubdued. Willie reckoned Lewis counted him among the enemy now because he would not evict his new tenants. "Does he spew this stuff in that tent of his every night?" he said to Betty, who had sat through the diatribe silently shaking her head.

"I've never been to the meetings," she said, "and now I'll be sure not to." Willie thought there were tears in her eyes. "Brian has been trying to get me to go," she went on, "but I'm not much for preachers, especially one who's mean to his family."

"I didn't know Brian was interested in religion," Willie said.

"He wasn't," Betty said, rummaging her purse for a tissue. "Not until he started listening to the Restoration Crusade bunch. Brian's always resented outsiders who come in from away and make money off our town. He says that's who Lewis Redding is preaching against. Brian's changed, Mister

Graham. Everybody I know who goes to the Crusade has changed. You know what I think?"

Willie was tired. He wasn't sure he wanted to know anything else about Lewis Redding and Restoration Crusade, but he asked anyway, "What's that, Betty?"

Betty sighed, released her words like she was laying down a burden she had carried too long. "I think Lewis Redding is not preaching religion at all. I think he's just preaching pure hate."

Willie heard her, but all his attention was focused on the front window.

"Please. Not now," he whispered.

"What?" Betty sniffed, thinking he was reacting to her opinion of the preacher.

Willie pointed toward the window. A big black car had just pulled into the parking space out front, and Orville Hawke and Wilbur Corvid were unfolding onto the sidewalk, looking like a pair of hungry bats.

Barbara Battle looked up from the reception desk at the Restoration Crusade office as Chief Omar Longshadow opened the door. "Why hello, Chief," she cooed, launching her sweetest smile, a smile that she knew from experience could break the hearts of weak males and break the wills of strong ones. It disappointed her that she sensed no discernable effect on the policeman.

"Hello, Miss Battle," he said. "You holding down the fort all by yourself?"

"Helen's day off. Reverend Redding has gone to lunch and Mister Hawke and Mister Corvid are out taking care of some business for the Crusade," she said. "I'll be happy to help you any way I can, if you'll let me."

Omar gave her his policeman's smile, cultivated over the

years to calm the innocent and unsettle the guilty, "You can probably alleviate my curiosity, Miss Battle. I understand the Crusade is looking at a site for their new church."

"The Cathedral," she corrected. "Yes, Chief, The Crusade is considering the property up on Ravensbeak Ridge."

"So why are Hawke and Corvid interested in the Miller Property over by Potters Shoals?"

Barbara hesitated less than a second before she answered, but Omar noted it. "I'm not able to tell you about that," she said. Another pause. "It isn't for Restoration Crusade. It must be one of their personal projects. And please, Chief, call me Barbara."

"It's hard to keep a secret in Drovers Gap, Barbara. You surely have found that out by now. Anything you don't tell me, I'll hear from someone else before the day is out. I'd rather hear it from you, though. That way, I'll know I'm getting correct information."

"It isn't supposed to be public yet, Chief. Don't tell them I told you. They'd kill me if they found out. That's just a figure of speech, you understand."

"A good policeman never reveals his source, Barbara," Omar said, "and never forgets if he owes a favor."

"They want to build a conference center, Chief. It will be big. People from all over the world will come to train."

"What kind of training?"

Barbara glowed like a Byzantine saint as she said, "To restore righteousness, Chief," To cleanse the land of those who would hinder."

Barbara made up the conference center story. This was the first she'd heard of her associates wanting to buy the Miller property. She was livid. They were supposed to be working for her. *What are those little devils up to?* Whatever it was, she would be watching.

Frank Bonner should have been watching the road as he approached the high bridge over Green River George. The tiltycurvy road there had brought more than a few careless lives to abrupt terminations. But Frank had his mind on his deal. In his briefcase he had a signed receipt for his binder on the Miller property and seven hundred thousand dollars in cash. This buy would be off his company's ledger. He was certain that all Boyce Miller had to do was see Frank's money, and the old man would be jumping to sign away his family's history to insure the leisure and comfort of his last years. Frank would gain the access he needed for his sky-line spoiling development, and Boyce, if he didn't preserve his health unduly, would die with money left in the bank for his children to fight over. Frank took his eyes off the road for a split second to glance down at his stash before he looked back up to see two gangly figures in black suits, neat as Mormon missionaries, riding bicycles down the middle of the pavement, Frank hit his brakes too hard, felt, for a sickening two seconds, his Rover slide and swerve toward the railing. The two scarecrows on bicycles vanished. He caught a glimpse of startled faces, a uniformed figure, arms waving frantically. He closed his eyes and tried to remember how to pray. Eventually, Frank opened his eyes to see a patrol car sitting on the bridge, lights flashing and, just beyond it, the wrecker toiling cable up out of the gorge. The Rover had stopped barely short of running down the State Trooper in a yellow vest. The car that slid to a stop behind him halted inches from Frank's rear bumper. Expecting a lecture and likely a citation for driving too fast for conditions, Frank was surprised when the officer walked right past him as if he wasn't there, said something to the woman driving the car behind, then returned to stand with the road crew watching a mauled Rover, same color and model as Frank's, lurch up out of the gorge at the end of the wrecker cable.

If Frank had believed in anyone to thank for his own near

miss with oblivion, he would have. But, believing in nothing much beyond his money, Frank simply sat, cursing under his breath, while the dripping wreck inched aboard the wrecker. When one lane was finally clear, and the loaded wrecker sat in front of him, the crew began securing in place what was left of the Rover. The patrolman waved opposing traffic along, which by now, added up to several vehicles. Then, beckoned Bonner forward. His Rover stalled, and while he tried to get the engine started, the car behind somehow was suddenly ahead, moving away toward Drover's Gap. The engine caught, the wrecker pulled out, loaded with the smashed Rover, and Frank Bonner followed. He would be late for his appointment with Boyce Miller. Along the crooked road ahead, he'd not get another chance to pass the plodding wrecker.

Approaching the winding grade to Drovers Gap, Frank downshifted to take the steep incline. As he entered the first sharp turn, the road ahead of him narrowed inexplicably to a single lane. The Rover crowded in around him, fitting him as tightly as the cockpit of the fighter jet he had flown during the war. For a split second, in his mind he was back there, as the sky before him narrowed to a thin thread of brilliance, vertical and blinding. Then there was only formless night, and there was no Rover, no aircraft, and Frank was not flying but falling.

***

Orville Hawke and Wilbur Corvid stood in the mud and watched the Rover careen over the railing of the bridge above, and tumble end over end nearly two-hundred feet to the Green River. Before it hit the water, they joined wills to slip the driver from his doomed vehicle and sent him to a better place. Frank Bonner would not be happy upon his arrival there, but Hawke and Corvid Associates had faith that he would consider his condition an improvement over being drowned.

Go fetch it, Orville thought to his associate. Wilbur thought back, *Why is it always me?* and waded into the river, undeterred by the swift current, kept walking as the water closed over his head. He was breathing the air from another world, the same place where Frank Bonner had flown. When he reached the submerged Rover, lying on its side in the middle of the river, Wilbur peered through the windshield and saw, floating just inside the glass, the brief case containing Frank Bonner's money. Bonner had meant for it to buy Boyce Miller's steep farm, and Hawke and Corvid Associates intended it to fulfil that purpose. By the time the river filled the Rover's interior, Wilbur had appropriated the briefcase and stood holding it on shore.

"Good Lord, it's gone. Can't see it at all," someone shouted from the bridge. They didn't see Orville and Wilbur. They were staring at the spot where the Rover had been swallowed by the flood. They wouldn't have spied the bedraggled duo with the briefcase, in any case. Nobody saw Hawke and Corvid when they didn't want to be seen.

Not far down the river, an old fishermen's shack teetered on the brink of collapse, but the patched roof held out most of the rain. In the relative dry, Orville opened the case. He counted out enough of the money inside to pay for two new suits, and closed the case on the rest, handed it back for Wilbur to carry. When the rain slacked, They began climbing the slippery path up toward the parking area beside the highway. They could hear sirens behind them, wailing down toward Green River Bridge.

Boyce Miller showed up bright and early to sign over his farm and collect Frank Bonner's money. Willie was still unlocking the front door at Mountain Realty while Betty stood by, arms loaded with the morning mail, as Boyce parked his ancient International pickup beside Betty's sleek and shiny Miata.

"Morning, children," Boyce called as Willie opened the door and stepped aside for Betty and his client to enter.

"Morning, Mister Miller," Betty said as she disappeared inside.

"Morning, Boyce," Willie said as lights began coming on, the fluorescents buzzing and flickering in the cool, settling into a pale shimmer as Willie ushered the old man into his office.

"Coffee, youns?" Betty asked, pouring water into the Bunn.

"You're a good girl, Betty," said Boyce, slumping into a chair in front of Willie's desk. She interpreted his appraisal of her virtue as a *yes*.

"Thanks, Betty," Willie said. "You've saved my life." He set a cardboard box in front of Boyce and opened it to reveal the sticky buns he'd picked up at the Feral Flour Bake Shop on his way to work.

"Don't mind at all," said Boyce, as he took two of them, one with carob icing and set them on the napkin Willie provided, to await union with his coffee and person.

Willie retrieved a fat folder from a file cabinet and sat behind his desk, opened the folder and arranged the papers between them. Little pink tabs peeked out on all the appropriate pages. Betty, whatever her shortcomings might be in the real world, was competent and thorough in the office. Willie thought that Boyce was right. Betty was a good girl indeed. He feared Brian wouldn't recognize her worth.

Willie beamed at the old farmer. "Well, sir, today's the day. Bonner should be pulling in any time now."

Boyce nodded, speechless. His mouth was full of chocolate covered sticky bun. Even if his mouth had been free, he wouldn't have told Willie that he'd been expecting Frank Bonner at Potters Shoals two hours before. Bonner had come to see Boyce the same day he wrote the check in Willie's office for his binder, offered to pay Boyce in hard cash if he'd consent to cut the realtor out of the deal and spare the commission. Bonner didn't show, though. Boyce had kept his appointment in hopes that at the end of the day, he would have gained something more than coffee and sticky buns.

Twenty-Two

Nearly two hours beyond their appointment time, after repeated calls by Willie and Betty to Frank Bonner's mobile number went unanswered, Boyce Miller stood up to leave. "Can I keep his binder fee if he backs out of the deal?" Boyce queried as he slipped on his jacket.

"It's all yours, in that case," Willie assured. "We'll keep calling. Something must have happened to hold Bonner up." Boyce stopped half-way through the door. stood pointing as the big wrecker from Hyatt's Road Service and Repair rumbled up the street with a mangled Rover lashed to its back.

"Is that . . ." murmured Betty.

"Could be. Hard to say," said Boyce.

"I do hope not," said Willie, seeing his big commission evaporating into the brisk autumn air.

A familiar black Lincoln with tinted windows followed close behind the wrecker and pulled into the parking area in front of Mountain Realty. The Devious Duo got out and flashed their dangerous smiles at the trio standing in the door. Orville Hawke led the way with Wilbur Corvid at his heels carrying a fat briefcase that looked like someone had left it out in the rain.

"Don't leave on our account," Orville Hawke waved as if they were all good friends. "We've come bearing grist for the Miller."

Willie and Betty stepped aside and Boyce backed through the door as Hawke and Corvid strode into the office. Betty hastily retrieved the splattered papers as Wilbur set the briefcase, still dripping river water, on the desk. Orville opened the case, revealing bundles of fresh green currency. Willie's eyes widened. Betty gasped. Boyce grinned like a man just saved from hanging as Orville said, "We've come to buy your property, Mister Miller, for as much money as this bag holds."

"We have a binder on this property from Frank Bonner," Willie said, "We're trying to contact him now to close the sale."

"You're not likely to get through to him where he is now," said Wilbur Corvid.

"Mister Bonner is no longer resident in our story," Orville Hawke announced, still casting his toxic smile upon them all, "If I were you, Mister Graham, I'd cash his check before his bank is informed of his current status."

"Count it first," growled Boyce Miller.

Chief Longshadow had barely sat to supper with his father when the phone rang. Warren, poised to beg a blessing, waited while he listened to his son's side of the ensuing conversation, "Yes, it was Bonner's Rover that went off the bridge, according to State Patrol . . . No, they haven't found the driver. There will be divers on the river first thing in the morning . . . It's nearly a two hundred foot drop down there, Willie. If Bonner was in the vehicle, he's out of this world . . . Yes, if I hear anything, I'll let you know. Why this urgent interest? You have another buyer . . . What? Who? . . . No, I won't spread it around, but I'm glad to know. Thanks for calling . . . Bye."

Omar sat back to table, stared at his coffee, muttered to himself more than to Warren, "Well."

"Well?" said Warren, after another silence.

"Ask the blessing Dad, and I'll tell you." Omar said, adding, "And say a prayer for all the bad people in our town."

Warren closed his eyes, lifted his face and raised his arms. "Great God of Heaven, teach us to be thankful for the love at this table and the food on our plates. Strengthen our wills and wash clean our hearts, and steer those who mean hurt or ill far from our door until such time they be changed and reconciled."

When he opened his eyes, his son gazed at him with a quizzical expression. "You sure, Dad, all those apostate souls will be reconciled?" Omar wore a half-smile, for he'd already heard his father's answer.

"Nothing is ever lost to God, Son. Not us. Not them. Not any. The Maker of all is in all and will claim His own in each and every world He's wrought."

"Amen," said Omar, half convinced and hoping against experience to see it come true. He lifted his cup and sipped at his coffee which was still hot enough to startle.

Wilbur Hawke produced from one of the voluminous pockets in his black coat a contract covering a straight transfer between two parties with no mention of a realtor. Willie opened his mouth to protest but before he could speak, Orville speared him with a devastating smile and handed him a bundle of currency equivalent to his commission, as he and Betty discovered later when they counted it alone. Willie returned his own smile, much less convincing and persuasive than Hawke's, and he and his secretary sat by mute and still while Boyce Miller signed away his farm and his family's legacy and departed happily with a damp briefcase full of soggy cash. By the time he got it home and opened it to gloat, he would find the green paper all fuzzy with blue and pink mold.

Hawke and Corvid left shortly afterward, making courtly bows to Betty and clapping Willie on the back heartily as they departed. "Welcome to our little entrepreneurial family, Willieboy," Hawke crowed, squeezing Willie's thin shoulder hard enough to make him wince. "The world is finally turning your way. Stick with us and it will continue in that direction."

Willie rubbed his sore shoulder and would have told them he was not their relation, even in business, but they were away before he could gather his thought, much less the words to say it. He and Betty sat down and counted the money three times. Betty stared at the stack of one-hundred-dollar bills on the table between them and said softly, "How should I enter this on the ledger?"

"I'll do it later, Betty," Willie said, and took three bills from the top of the stack and put them in her hand. "You've worked as hard for this deal as I have," he murmured. "You deserve to share the reward for our labors together."

Betty smiled at Willie the kind of smile Willie had been longing to see longer than long, tucked her three hundred dollars into her purse, then accepted Willie's invitation to dinner, sending him into such a paroxysm of ecstasy that he tripped over his words, "We'll cebrelate," he piped like a birthday child.

"Yes, we will," Betty beamed back, apparently as unaware of his tangled syllables as Willie.

Willie didn't have reservations, but he checked his Apple Grove app and found they had a table open, which he promptly claimed. His luck was changing, his Shadow assured him. As they drove the short mile to Apple Grove Restaurant, Willie thought Betty seemed different somehow, more at ease in his company. Perhaps it was just that this was the first time they had shared space on a social basis. She kept up a constant stream of chatter, walked closer to him than she would have at the office. Crossing the Apple Grove parking lot, she reached up and took hold of his arm, although when he placed his hand over hers, she turned him loose. Willie didn't want to be turned loose.

Entering the restaurant, Chloe Toibin stood smiling to usher them to their table. To Willie's great relief, she didn't act surprised to see him in female company. Her hair was still purple, but a darker, muted shade, that complemented her dress. Willie tried not to show his surprise at the dress.

"You're not working at Home Ground now, Chloe?" he asked as they sat and she handed them menus.

"I'm just there mornings, now, Mister Graham. Evenings, I move up in the world."

"Don't we all," murmured Betty. Willie marveled silently at his promotion to Mister Graham.

Chloe flawlessly recited her well-rehearsed spiel regarding dinner specials. She seemed to be genuinely enjoying it. Willie had a hard time reconciling this engaging, borderline elegant young woman with the Chloe he knew at Home Ground Suds and Java. *Context is everything,* whispered his Shadow, *Flow with it.*

Chloe interrupted his inner dialogue. "What would you like to drink while you peruse your menus?" she said smoothly, her highlander accent calibrated to charm city ears. Betty ordered a chardonnay and Willie, though he wanted coffee, ordered an oatmeal stout. He'd read somewhere that coffee made for unpleasant breath. "Leon will be your server," Chloe lilted and was away to place their drink orders, leaving Willie helpless in Betty's gaze.

Willie was terrified he wouldn't be able to maintain entertaining conversation during dinner, having never talked much to Betty apart from work details. He could hardly tell her about his infrequent discussions with his dead mother, which up until now had been major points of interest in his exceeding dull and predictable personal life. His fears turned out to be unwarranted. Betty sustained a non-stop monologue about Brian and his exploits in the automotive realm. An occasional smile and nod or monosyllabic response sufficed to get Willie unscathed through Betty's puttanesca and wine and his steak and salad to dessert.

For dessert, Willie settled for a double espresso, as it was way past his bedtime now and he was already feeling overfed and sleepy. Betty was three spoons into her chocolate mousse when she suddenly stared open-mouthed past Willie's shoulder, as if she'd been confronted by a ghost. Willie was turning to see what had startled her, but she put out her hand and hissed, "Don't look."

So he looked at Betty instead, watched her open mouth morph to a grim clinch as her pale face cycled past pink to mauve. The effect was unnerving. Willie had eaten and drunk way too much. He thought his stomach might be about to overthrow him. He had never been so close to someone who appeared to be losing their mind.

Betty prodded his hand with her spoon, a not entirely painless gesture. "Look and see who is that woman,"

"You told me not to look," Willie whispered back, though there was no need to whisper in the chatterful restaurant.

"Who's that woman with Bryan," she hissed, stabbing him again with her spoon. "Look and tell me." Willie was glad she hadn't ordered pie for dessert and been wielding a fork.

He turned enough to glance around the room, saw Betty's boyfriend and his apparent date as they were being seated near the door.

"It's Helen Troy," he informed Betty, "She used to be the church secretary at Justice Fork Baptist Church before it burned down. She works for Restoration Crusade now."

Betty stood, gathered her purse and jacket, "Thanks for

the lovely dinner, Willie. She said sweetly. "You're a good man." Then she picked up her full waterglass and walked toward the door. If Brian saw her coming, he pretended not to, until with a graceful flourish, she emptied the glass over his head as she swept past his table.

Willie sat where he was, relishing the spectacle as he finished his espresso, both disappointed and relieved that he had been spared the potential ritual of a good-night kiss. His bladder was full and his stomach was upset and he wasn't at all sure that tonight he would have been up to the task.

Once relative tranquility had been restored to his environs, Willie's Shadow persuaded him, subtly, of course, that he wanted another shot of espresso. When Leon Ogle came by his table again, Willie ordered it, along with a slice of key lime pie, just because he could, though his Shadow cringed inside his head. Leon headed for the kitchen and Willie fled to the men's necessary.

By the time he returned to his table, he was in a state to enjoy his pie at leisure and wonder about his sudden craving for caffeine. Brian and Helen never once glanced in his direction. He guessed they hadn't spied Betty before the dousing. Leon was a watchful waiter, returned with the check as soon as the last bite of pie disappeared. Willie gladly handed off his plastic, figured the evening had been a worthy investment.

The crowd was thinning as he left the restaurant. Chloe smiled at him at the door. "Your girlfriend is right fierce," she whispered as he passed. Willie stopped, returned her smile. "Betty isn't my girlfriend, Chloe. I wouldn't want to be drowned in public. We were just celebrating closing on a big deal."

Chloe's smile didn't look convinced. "Have a good evening, Mister Graham. Thanks for coming by." Willie figured she appreciated the evening's entertainment he'd provided as much as his business. He stepped out into the cool evening, looked up as a scrap of cloud slid across the face of the moon. It appeared to Willie that the moon winked at him. He was definitely on a roll, he thought. For the first time, he found himself wishing that his mother would come visiting. Tonight, he would have lots to tell her.

Not if I can help it, thought the Shadow behind his eyes, *She knows too much already.*

"On the other hand," whispered Willie to the dark, "Maybe I'll just keep Betty to myself for now."

Before he came in sight of his house, Willie knew his mother was waiting for him. Her acrid presence simmered on the edge of his awareness like a salty stew forgotten and left too long on the fire. The air reeked of her anger. It seemed to Willie that his mother had always been angry, in her life as well as in death. Angry at his father for being hard. Angry at Willie for being soft. He wished he might have had siblings to absorb some of Evelyn's scathing rebuke. Perhaps if she had daughters to disappoint her, she might have found some quality in her son to like.

As Willie walked across his yard, he felt his Shadow stir and rise into a dark wall behind his eyes, opaque, featurless. All his secrets would be safe from his mother's disapproval tonight. He climbed the porch steps and there she was, but not quite as formidable as he remembered, a bit more transparent than usual, not as heavy and oppressive on his perception. The old rocker she sat in was still tonight, as if Evelyn couldn't quite raise enough breeze to set it in motion.

Willie . . . she wheezed and he tensed and braced himself for the inevitable *Willieboy*, which this time never quite emerged. Instead, she paused, flickered in the dim light, gathered herself and sighed, *William, you're not yourself tonight. What have you gotten into?*

The Shadow slid smoothly into the foreground of his awareness until the Shadow was speaking as much as Willie.

"Nothing that requires your permission, Mom. How have you been?"

A slight breeze swept up the hill and across the yard, setting Evelyn's form rippling like bit of laundry hung on a line to dry, Willie had to concentrate to catch her words, which seemed to be coming from an increasing distance, *I'm dead, William. I can't be anywhere except in your mind, and now you're shutting me out. It isn't fair, after all I've suffered for you and there's no one but you left to remember me.*

For the first time in his life, Willie saw his mother as a broken and diminished soul, felt something akin to pity for what she had made of herself in life and what remained of her in death. "I'm not trying to shut you out, Mom," he said, believing in the moment that it was the truth, "I've just had a lot on my mind lately. I've been busy."

Evelyn's body frayed at the edges, thinned and paled on the verge of disappearing, rank and smoky against the gathering dark as she gathered all her remaining will into words. She wanted to scream at her son, but her voice came as a hiss in the air, like a kettle without enough heat under it to bring it to a boil, *William. You've been too busy to spare one thought for your mother. You've become a hard and unyielding man just like your father, unbending to my will. Very well, if you refuse to bend, I can break you yet.*

Willie's mouth opened, but it was the Shadow's speech that billowed out into the evening as a dark cloud enveloping the wraith that had been Evelyn Graham. The words astonished Willie as much as they did the ghost, "Evelyn Graham, I bid your shade to burn as hot as your viperous tongue."

Willie watched, transfixed, as his mother rose from her chair, took a step toward him, then stared down at the flames devouring her feet. She stretched out toward her son arms that became fire and smoked away to nothing in the night. Willie gazed into her terrified eyes as her face and head unfurled into a fiery flower upon the dark, and Evelyn Graham was gone, leaving a faint scent of burnt almonds in her wake. Willie realized the Shadow had gone, too. He stood alone, emptied of expectations and condemnations, full of his own possibilities. Willie Graham was free at last.

TWENTY-THREE

Lewis Redding looked out over the massed faces upturned toward him like flowers to the sun. Beside him, a bonfire spewed sparks and embers into the night air where sparks masqueraded briefly as stars. For nearly an hour, people had been coming in an unbroken line to toss their heretical volumes into the flames. Behind Lewis loomed the big tent where he held his burn rallies until last week, when the fire had gotten out of hand and threatened a conflagration. Hawke and Corvid suggested then that it might be prudent to hold their book burnings under the sky weather permitting, and to preach on other subjects on inclement evenings.

On this particular night, the stars blazed down mercilessly, undimmed by cloud or fog, and the moon was just emerging from behind Ravensbeak Ridge, as Barbara Battle, garbed in a white flowing dress that covered her from neck to ankle, a parody of modesty that managed to inform the audience of her contours short of blatant revelation, fed the last of the evening's offensive documents to the coals.

"Little Children," Lewis intoned, spreading his arms like an inviting embrace, "we will never be rid of these devilish lies, no matter how many we destroy, until we have eliminated their source. We must kill the viper in her nest, before she can spread her poison."

A chorus of *say-it-preacher*'s and *amen*'s resounded in the night. Wilbur Corvid brought a glass-fronted box on stage and held it up so the people could see the snake coiled inside. Orville Hawke opened the lid and Lewis thrust his hand into the box. The serpent latched on to his fist immediately, and Lewis pulled it out of the box and held the viper, still clinging to his hand, over the fire. "The only way to kill the evil is with fire," he shouted, and shook the copperhead loose into the flames. The fire popped and sizzled and the crowd leaped from their seats in a cathartic frenzy.

Lewis held up his hands, one of them dripping blood from the wound he'd just received. The crowd fell silent and still as if he'd turned a switch.

"Tomorrow night, my friends, we will meet here again, and go to confront evil in its lair." He spoke softly, but in the sudden quiet all of them heard his words clearly and not one missed the fire in his eyes. Lewis spoke a benediction over them and repeated, louder, "Tomorrow."

"Tomorrow!" shouted six hundred throats like a single voice. And without another word, the crowd departed to homes and beds.

Inside the tent, while Barbara and the Associates counted the money, Lewis peeled the latex glove with its fake and bloodied wound and threw it in the trash. "That thing sure looked real, boys," he said. "Where do you get this stuff?"

"We have our sources," murmured Orville Hawke. "For operating expenses," he said, stuffing a bundle of bills into his coat pocket.

"A snake is as real as people see it," added Wilbur Corvid.

Next morning as Tsula Stone walked to Vintage Reads in a misty rain, she saw flyers posted on every post and corner, *Rally for Decency – Tonight!* Among the inflammatory slogans, a photograph of Vintage Reads remained clearly identifiable though partially obscured by a big red *X*. A cluster of the posters adorned the windows of the bookstore when she arrived. She tore them down before she unlocked the door.

Customers that morning were mostly day-trippers and tourists. An hour after she opened the bookstore, a wan sun glimmered through the clouds and she put the Battered and Bartered table out front. Before noon, a straggly crew of teenaged males galloped down the sidewalk, turning over the book display as they passed, scattering volumes across the still damp sidewalk. Two would-be customers helped her retrieve them. She brought the table, piled with the jumbled books, inside for rest of the day.

The afternoon passed without incident. A few customers, all out-of-towners, came in to browse and drink the free coffee. Several actually purchased books. The UPS driver stopped by shortly before she closed, delivered two heavy boxes, and carried away the day's mail orders. These days, there were more sales through the Vintage Reads website than over the counter.

Tsula closed a few minutes early. The air seemed burdened with ill-will. She wanted to get back to Hemlock House, share a meal with kindred spirits, then assume her own familiar shape and run under the moon until dawn, or until she grew tired enough to sleep, whichever came first.

The "Hemlock Tribe," as they had come to be called by the contingent of Lewis Redding's followers, who by now comprised half the population of Drovers Gap, were still at table when a throng of torch-bearing, hymn-singing crusaders surged down the street on their way downtown. A few gestured and yelled epithets toward the house, but most seemed intent on their pre-ordained mission.

"The Peasants are restless tonight," Luke said. Nobody laughed.

The Reverend Lewis Redding had roused his tented hoard to optimum frenzy by the time he wrapped up his harangue. "And now we will process like orderly and concerned citizens across town to that storehouse of satanic scribblings called Vintage Reads, and we will make known to the town of Drovers Gap our soulful opposition to those obscene and oppressive writings infecting the impressionable young minds of our future generation. Our expressions will be circumspect, but as forcible as is required to acquire the attention of our Commissioners. We will not be silent and we will not stand idle until our town is cleansed of this scourge." Lewis paused to relish the acclamations and exultations of his followers, then declared, "We will go with you, Brothers Hawke and Corvid and I, and together we will ignite the restoration of the soul health of Drovers Gap and all her people."

Lewis and the Evil Twins strode down the aisle and out of the tent and the chanting, jeering crowd spilled out behind them. Some sang. Some shouted. Some raised signs and banners, some lit torches. Amid all the passion and pandemonium, none seemed to notice when Orville Hawke and Wilbur Corvid drew the preacher aside and watched until the mob had passed them by. It might be safer, the associates advised Lewis, if they beheld the spectacle from a distance.

As the protesters thronged past Hemlock House, Abigail Trammell phoned Omar Longshadow, and by the time the milling multitude had traversed the length of Main Street, the chief and his two officers stood in front of Vintage Reads bookstore, looking serious and as determined as the situation might require. As the first wave of book-banners approached, Mayor Ned, who had been hastily summoned via Omar's cell phone, rounded the corner, breathless after trotting down the hill from his house two blocks away, and took his stand with the three uniformed police.

The mayor raised his hands for quiet, but the gathering crowd answered the gesture with more loud and unintelligible shouting until Constable Jolene Bear handed him a bullhorn and he startled himself as much as any in the mob with his blast of reason. "People, this is not how we do protests in Drovers Gap. You will have ample opportunity to voice your concerns at the Commissioner's meeting tomorrow night. We will stay there all night if need be to hear everything you have to say."

"Shut it down, tonight," somebody shouted. "Drive out the sinners!" a woman's voice, shrill and strident. More shouts, as the crowd surged forward. Mayor Ned slipped behind the constabulary, his back against the door. The constable and sergeant looked at their chief, their faces all question, their hands on their holsters. In one quick instinctive move, Omar stepped forward and brought his baton cracking behind the knees of the nearest rioter, spilling the burly man backward into the two behind him, staggering them as well. Someone a bit farther back into the crowd heaved his torch at the window of the bookshop. The torch extinguished as it struck, but shattered the glass, releasing a black roiling roaring nimbus of angry bees.

At first, the marauders didn't realize what afflicted them. They swore and swatted as bees stung their arms and faces, tangled in their hair, got inside their clothes. The crowd panicked and scattered, yelling and screaming, pulling off shirts and skirts as they ran, trying to get at the sources of their pain while four figures remained outside Vintage Reads, unscathed and wondering at the bizarre spectacle unfolding before them.

"Bosch," murmured Constable Jolene.

"Bosch?" Mayor Ned questioned.

"It looks like a painting by Hironimus Bosch," she explained.

On a hill a block above Vintage Reads, Lewis Redding watched unbelieving as his damaged and demoralized followers straggled slinking and hobbling up Main Street, anxious to put some distance between their bespotted hides and the scene of their debacle. The bees had dispersed into the night as quickly as they appeared, their droning roar now superseded by the faint groans and curses of the miscreant humans.

In contrast to the forlorn and dejected instigator of the night's entertainment, Orville Hawke and Wilbur Corvid seemed upbeat, bordering on euphoric. "Don't you worry, Reverend Lewis," said Orville, patting the crestfallen preacher on his shoulder. "Your tent will be doubly full tomorrow night."

"Not after this," Lewis protested. "They will think I sent them on a fool's mission."

"Then you must convince them they were holy fools on a righteous crusade," Wilbur cajoled.

"Point out to them that the forces of evil marshalled against them out of fear of the virtuous powers," Orville added.

"Joshua's army marched around Jericho seven times," said Wilbur,

"And not until the seventh circuit," admonished Orville, punching Lewis in the chest with a taloned finger to impress his point in the preacher's tender flesh.

"You're just getting started," whispered Wilbur, laying his hand upon the sore spot Hawke's finger had left behind.

"You can count on us, fellow soldier," Orville said heartily, slapping Lewis on the shoulders again hard enough to send his glasses sliding down his nose.

Not precisely convinced, either of ultimate victory, or the tenacity of friendship, Lewis walked home alone with his confusion. He wasn't surprised, when he turned into his yard, to see Chief Omar Longshadow's pickup parked in the drive. A light shone through a window from inside, but the porch was in shadow, dark as the night around. Lewis went up the steps and was taking out his keys when he heard the creak of his old rocking chair and made out the faint form of the police chief sitting there.

"What happened tonight was a riot, Preacher," Omar said quietly.

"I wasn't there," Lewis said, at least a literal truth.

"That doesn't render you blameless," countered Omar. "Your influence was there and active. We are awfully lucky nobody was killed."

"The just are shielded by righteousness," said Lewis, wishing he had a chapter and verse to quote but lacking imagination to invent a reference. Nevertheless, he managed to dredge up a hint of his sermon voice.

"There's nothing right about crowd violence and attempted arson, Preacher," the policeman said, his voice calm and even as if issuing a traffic citation. "There will be some accounting called for from all responsible for what happened this evening, the instigators as well as the perpetrators. Meanwhile, I strongly urge you to preach calm and restraint to your congregation in that tent of yours."

"I can only preach what is given me to say," Lewis intoned, finding his public voice again. "I can only be faithful to my message."

"If your message incites folk to endanger their neighbors and vandalize their property," Omar's words came out now as hard as quiet, "the town Commissioners can revoke your permit to hold meetings."

"If the town had revoked that witch's permit to pander her wicked books, none of this need have happened, Chief." Lewis was braced for a sharp retort, but Omar didn't answer, just stood and gazed into the preacher's eyes, as if trying to sort the darkness he saw behind them, then stepped off the porch and walked away toward his vehicle.

Lewis was unlocking his door when he heard the voice behind him, "Just one more question for you tonight, Reverend Lewis."

Lewis turned. He couldn't see the policeman's face, only his dark silhouette against the pickup's headlights. "What's that, Chief Longshadow?"

"Where did you buy that Bible you have tucked under your arm?"

Lewis watched the pickup back out into the street and pull away toward town. He watched until night wrapped tight around the taillights and swallowed them whole. He opened the door and stepped into his house. A light came from the kitchen. He left it on when he went out for the Crusade service. Another light glimmered in the hall from farther back in the house. He reckoned he had missed that one somehow. It was not Lewis' habit to leave lights on when he didn't need them. Though his income from the Restoration Crusade far exceeded his extremely modest salary from Justice Fork Baptist Church, such economies endured more out of habit than necessity.

He dropped his Bible onto the table with a sigh like a convict being unburdened of his shackles. He headed down the hall toward his bathroom, pulling off his tie, peeling his shirt, leaving them in the floor behind him like the shed skin of a snake. He would pick them up when he was clean. None but God were left in this house to observe his housekeeping lapse, and in truth, Lewis had never thought of God as a persnickety housekeeper. His wife had been, but Marcie was gone now. She wouldn't have protested, but meekly picked up after him, and perhaps, over the supper she had prepared and served, she might let him overhear her lecturing their offspring about having enough work to do without gathering up carelessly discarded clothing. She would expect him to feel mildly guilty, and he would be magnanimous and not inform her that he only felt slightly annoyed. She was his wife, after all, and it was her duty to render all his paths straight and uncluttered.

He stood in the shower a long time, with the water as hot as he could stand it, steam wrapping around him like a warm and silky cloak. He soaped his body down with a big chunk of his favorite pine tar soap, surprised as always, that the black waxy stuff could produce such white and generous lather. He scrubbed and rubbed himself all over with the soap, paying special attention to those parts where it felt the best, and was rinsing down when he saw a vaguely human form, pale and bright, through the shower curtain.

Lewis turned off the water, with a dripping arm reached and pulled the curtain aside, braced for fight or flight, and there stood Barbara Battle, wearing the same flowing white dress she had during the Crusade meeting. Obviously, she too, had foregone the rigors of the march on the bookstore.

Lewis gasped, scrambled for enough shower curtain to cover his embarrassment. Barbara smiled, slipped her dress from her shoulders and let it fall around her feet, like a cedar dropping snow at spring thaw. The sight both gratified and terrified Lewis. He couldn't move until Barbara reached out and took his hand and placed it against her bare breast. Lewis struggled to keep his legs straight and his feet beneath him.

"Oh, Barbara," he whispered, "Oh, Barbara." He knew he was lost now and he didn't care. She knelt before him like a communicant at a chancel rail and when he felt her hot and wet around him, Lewis Redding relinquished whatever tattered remnants of his soul remained to him.

Twenty-Four

Willie Graham finally summoned courage to invite Betty for an overnight excursion to take in dinner and a play in Asheton. To his astonishment, she accepted, and while Betty totally altered Willie's view of life, they missed the street theatre in front of Vintage Reads. As he approached the bookstore the morning after, Willie was surprised to see Luke Armstrong nailing up a sheet of plywood over the shattered glass storefront.

"What's happened?" He queried. "Is everyone alright?"

"None suffered but them who did it," Luke returned dryly. "If you want to buy a book, store's open."

In fact, Willie did want to buy a book. He had recently developed a consuming interest in local history, especially events pertaining to Warwoman Ridge. He found Wendl VonTrier inside, tending store for the day.

"What sparked your interest in our Civil War history?" the birdman asked as Willie came through the door, before he could even offer greeting or question.

How did you know? Instead, Willie answered, "Something my mother told me once."

"About the railroad," Wendl said, looking more like a bird than a man for a second.

"Was there ever a railway tunnel on the grade below Warwoman Ridge around Potters Shoals?" Willie asked, assuming at this point no explanation of his motives was required.

"That was the plan," Wendl confirmed. "But, according to historical accounts, it never quite happened. They got it completed halfway through before the war stopped construction, and afterward, the railroad company, being short of funding, chose a route longer but less costly to build."

"I can't find any records in the county archives as to where the old line ran, or where the tunnel entrance was located," Willie said.

"I have something that might help you there," Wendl scurried away among his shelves and emerged momentarily clutching a beat-up leather-bound folio which he opened and spread on the counter between them. "This is an old engineering reference from Carolina Rail's construction division." Wendl flipped through a few sheets then stabbed one with a finger, "See, here is where the old line ran up through the Miller property that you just sold to Hawke and Corvid." He traced the line of the railway to a place where the map's contour lines crowded close together. "Here's where the tunnel began."

"Ah," sighed Willie, "That would be rough getting to,"

"The entrance has collapsed. Some say it was blown up intentionally. So you can't access the tunnel from there." Wendl pointed to a series of tiny squares farther up the slope, "These are ventilation shafts, drilled down from above. If there's still a tunnel under that mountain, you would have to enter it there."

"You know a lot about this," Willie said. Wendl just smiled. "How much for the book?" Willie asked.

"It's a rare volume," Wendl said, still smiling, "But I'll loan it to you for free. Just don't lose it or you'll have to pay double."

Willie smiled back, not sure if it was a joke or not. "Thanks muchly," he said sincerely as Wendl wrapped the folio. "Thank you," again as Willie took the package and turned to go.

"It's there." Wendl said, as Willie reached the door.

"What?" Willie stopped and looked back.

"The gold you're after. It's there under the mountain, where they parked the engine." Wendl said cheerfully.

"If you know that, why haven't you taken it yourself?" Willie asked.

"Money is only attractive to those who want things they can't have," Wendl said. As Willie closed the door behind him, he thought he glimpsed a black and glistening raven perched atop the counter.

Willie sat at his desk at Mountain Realty, pouring over his mapbook as Betty finished up her paperwork for the day. She walked up behind him, put a hand on his shoulder. It felt good. Willie looked up from his book, kissed the hand.

"Whatcha reading, Willie?" she asked, peering at the map.

"It's an old map of where the railway ran before the civil war." Willie said, tracing the line with his finger. "Here's where they started to build a tunnel but never finished."

"Isn't that the Miller property Hawke and Corvid bought?" Betty said.

"Yep, but there's something there I'd like to get hold of before the deed's recorded. Something not even old Boyce knows he has up there."

Betty was interested now. "What could that be, Willie?"

"In that tunnel. There's over four hundred pounds of Confederate gold. When they fled Richmond, the rebels put the gold on a train and drove it as far south as Carolina. Union forces had already seized the line farther south, so they brought the stash west to here, pulled it into that tunnel and dynamited the entrance."

"That's just an old folk tale, Willie. Nobody even knows where the old railroad was."

"This map shows us where it was," Willie said.

"How do you know the map is accurate?"

"The man who loaned me this map says it is. He says the gold is there, just waiting for somebody to come bring it out."

"So why didn't the man who had this map get it for himself?"

Willie shrugged. "Good question, Betty. I asked him that."

"And what did he say?"

"He just said he didn't need the money."

"And you believe him?" Betty said.

"I believe he told the truth about the gold still being there. The only trouble is, we'd have to bring it up one of these ventilation shafts, see these little squares?" Willie said, pointing. "I'd have to get some equipment and some help, and there's nobody I can trust for that."

"Could two people do it?" Betty asked.

"I suppose so, if they had a hoist of some kind. One to go down into the tunnel and one to operate the hoist on the surface."

"I could ask Brian," Betty said. "He has all kind of equipment and doesn't tell everything he knows."

"I thought you and Brian were done since we've been close," Willie said, surprised.

"Brian would do anything to please me, if he thought it would give him a chance to get me back. I can manage Brian, if you're sure the gold is there. We'd have to give him a cut, of course."

"Of course, we would," murmured Willie, more to himself than Betty. "Let me think on it."

Contrary to Lewis Redding's expectations, as Hawke and Corvid predicted, the tent was filled to overflowing at the next Restoration Crusade Meeting. Big screens were set up outside to provide an inside view for those followers who did not arrive early enough to claim seating under cover. Even the weather was cooperative, the night mild and calm, although away on the horizon, lightning flickered unheard from thunderstorms westward.

Barbara Battle, garbed in the flowing white gown that had become her uniform, explained the projected architect's renderings of the Restoration Cathedral that was to be built on Ravensbeak Ridge. The spectacular and otherworldly façade would have been at home on the cover of an Isaac Asimov novel. Hawke and Corvid passed an extra round of buckets among the enthusiastic crowd and all returned overflowing with cash and checks, although checks were not encouraged, being a tool of wicked and exploitive bankers of mostly alien descent.

A paid and practiced band struck up the first praise song of the evening. Words flashed on a screen and the assembled disciples sang them out with one voice. There was a lot of repetition as most of the songs averaged about three lines total, but there were a lot of songs, and the congregation was well winded by the time Lewis stepped forward and raised his Bible over his head like a weapon. He continued brandishing it throughout his sermon, though he never actually read from it. Apparently, he considered his exhortations had gained sufficient authority that they no longer required girding with chapter and verse to stand against scrutiny and inquiry.

In reality, Lewis' preaching encountered little critical headwind at this point, for to the die-hard converts still in his camp, whatever Reverend Lewis Redding pronounced was Gospel, pure and simple.

Lewis ranted for over an hour, buoyed by the rabid adoration of his fans. When the last song had been sung and the last buckets had been passed and returned full of cash and the crowd filtered away into the night to imagine future mayhem they might inflict upon their town in the name of righteous restoration, Lewis was exhausted. He left Barbara Battle and the Bird Boys, as he privately called Hawke and Corvid, to count the money, and drove home in his new Tesla.

Pulling into his drive, he pressed the button on the dash and watched as the door opened and lights came on in his new garage. Lewis sat for a couple of minutes, still as a corpse, pondering his situation. He had a lot of new stuff now, but Restoration Crusade was no longer his ministry. He belonged to the Cause, which was, he reflected, to restore Drovers Gap to something it had never been. He remembered a story in one of the gospels about a man who built bigger and bigger barns to hold his ever-increasing possessions, until one night, death informed him that he had exchanged his soul for all this stuff he was about to leave behind.

Lewis remembered a time when he had a family who may have loved him. At least they had taken pains to please him without getting paid for it. The Tesla slid into the garage smoothly and quietly, like a knife into a wound. Lewis got out of the car, closed the door, opened it again, and retrieved his Bible. The Bible he bought at Vintage Reads. He thought he ought to buy a new one somewhere with a more agreeable history, and he wished, not for the first time, that he had back the old Bible he fed to his stove during his alcoholic apocalypse.

Lewis pressed the icon on his phone and the door to the garage closed and the light inside went out. There was nothing to do now but go into his house and find something cold and dead to eat. He would have a new house soon. Hawke and Corvid had shown him the plans for the mansion that would be part of the Restoration Cathedral complex at

Ravensbeak Ridge. They told him that there he would not even need to press buttons for light and heat and cool and music. He could just speak, and his will would be executed by his intelligent house.

Lewis was glad for a moment, when he stepped up onto his porch, that this house wasn't that smart. He inserted his metal key into a metal lock, twisted his hand, heard a satisfying click, and opened the door. The light switch was deaf. He had to grope the dark wall to find it. That wasn't a problem. His hand remembered where it was.

The light blinded him at first. "I'm glad the sun doesn't come up that sudden," he said aloud to the house. He shaded his eyes with his hand, and was so startled when he saw her, he dropped his keys. It was a second before he recognized his estranged wife. Another second before he remembered to reach down and pick up his keys. A second after that before he remembered how to speak.

"What on God's green earth are you doing here, woman?" Lewis said. He felt unaccountably guilty. He wondered how long she had been waiting for him. If she had looked through the house. If she had seen Barbara Battle's clothes in the bedroom closet. What other incriminating objects might have been lying about? Lewis stared, frozen and mute. He was afraid to ask the questions crowding his mind.

"You are a wicked man, Lewis Redding," Marcie said quietly, as if commenting on the weather.

"Yes, I suppose I must be," Lewis whispered, realizing it was true.

"Someone needs to put a stop to you." She said, in the same tone she once used when the trash needed taking out.

"Everybody is afraid of me now," Lewis said. "Nobody would dare try." While he was saying the words, Marcie took something out of her purse. Lewis saw it was a gun, with unwarranted calm, watched her point it at him and pull the trigger.

He never heard the shot. He became aware that he was lying on his back in his open doorway. He didn't feel the hard floor under him. His consciousness was concentrated on the pain in his chest. He put his hand where it hurt. It felt sticky and warm. Dimly he saw Marcie's legs as she stepped over him and out the door. He heard the gun hit the floor somewhere close beside his head. Then the whole world was black and silent for a while.

The next thing Lewis heard was the rattling gurgle of his own attempted breathing. Instead of air, he seemed to be inhaling hot bitter syrup. Barbara Battle stood over him, gazing down curiously.

"I've been shot," he tried to say, but he choked on the words before he could get them out. Pain exploded in his chest.

Barbara knelt beside him. Her white gown had been exchanged for a red one. She put her face close to his. Her breath was hot and smelled of death. He saw the flash of her teeth as she growled, "I could just eat you up."

Lewis was barely aware of the hurt in his throat, the pull of tearing flesh. It seemed to be happening to somebody else far far away. Lewis Redding was no longer resident in his body by the time she began to feed.

Twenty-Five

Omar Longshadow put his book aside and reached to turn out the lamp. It was after two in the morning, and although he should have been tired, he lay in his bed wakeful and on edge, an hour after he had suppered and showered and retreated to his room to avoid further rehashing his frustrating day for his father.

Omar didn't get home until after midnight. The Drovers Gap Police Department had kept vigil at Vintage Reads after the Restoration Crusade meeting dispersed, hoping to forestall any recurrence of the mayhem precipitated by the previous rally. This night, thankfully, the performance had produced a lot of noise but no organized foray into town to vandalize apostate shopkeepers.

As soon as Drovers Gap was quiet and mostly asleep, Omar bid his two officers goodnight and came home to his cold supper, which Warren re-heated in the microwave, then sat by attentively in case his son had any exciting intelligence to divulge.

After a bowl of pretty-good wadihad and a couple of beers, when Omar related only the ordinary nuisances of a policeman's day, he couldn't be sure if his father was relieved or disappointed that their village had been spared another spectacular uprising. Two hours later, Omar thought the darkness might turn out to be his old friend after all and nudge him to sleep, when his phone lit up and bugled a text. It was from Constable Jolene Bear, who had drawn the graveyard shift: *House fire at Lewis Redding's. FD en route. Chuck alerted. Will meet you there.*

"Shit," Omar muttered to his phone, realized as he scrambled for his clothes that this was why sleep had been so fugitive. He had been waiting for just this sort of thing to happen. By the time he laced his boots, Omar was thinking possible arson, already drawing up a list of suspects in his head. They included most of the current residents at Abigail Trammell's Hemlock House.

The overcast glowed a dull mauve as Chief Omar Longshadow started his pickup. He could hear sirens in the distance, falling silent as they converged on the site of the fire. Driving through town, he saw people out on Main Street, pointing, walking, some of them running, drawn toward the disaster like flies to a corpse. Crowd control might be a problem, he surmised. He hoped County would send some bodies to augment the lawful presence of the Drovers Gap Police Department.

Omar pulled to a stop behind the Department cruiser that his constable was driving tonight. His two subordinates were already engaged in herding away from the fire a scattering of spectators who had accumulated on the scene. They didn't require much encouragement to keep their distance. The fire was hot. The house, a great orange flower blossoming in the night. As the chief walked to join his colleagues, he felt a sprinkle of wet against his face. He hoped it would rain enough to help.

"Where's Redding?" Omar asked.

Sergeant Priestley shrugged. Constable Bear pointed to the burning house, "In there, maybe. Nobody's seen him."

Cars with faces pressed against windows now jammed the street behind them. Two highway patrol units stopped at the corner, and troopers dispersed among the gawkers, began urging departures, threatening arrest to the slow and uncooperative, clearing a way for what needed to come next. Hardly had a lane been opened than a black-and-white emblazoned with a Sheriff's star crept in among the assorted emergency vehicles parked on Lewis Redding's demolished lawn. Two deputies donned their orange slickers as they walked across the mutilated grass. "Morning, Chief," the one Omar knew said cheerfully. "It is morning, isn't it?"

"Hard to say, Ken," Omar said. "Looks an awfully lot like last night."

"Doesn't look good for anybody in that house," said the other deputy.

"Anybody was in there is a crispy critter now," said Sergeant Priestley, his grin in his voice.

"That's not funny," said Constable Bear. She handed her colleagues their rain slickers. While the males had been flirting with dominance, she had gone to their vehicles and fetched their dry.

Chief Omar Longshadow watched the hint of dawn brightening over the nearest ridge and shivered inside his raincoat as he sat in the county's forensics van with Doctor Rita Fleming. He had been well on his way to soaked before his constable delivered his rain gear, and underneath his slicker, his clothes clung damply to his hide. He felt stiff and cold, suspected he might be developing a sore throat.

Am I going to be sick from this? Omar thought as the medical examiner described her crew's gleanings from the ashes. "We found bones. Human. There wasn't a lot else left of the victim. I've never seen a house fire burn so hot and consume so thoroughly. This was no ordinary burn. I'm thinking the crime scene analysis people will find this blaze had a lot of help."

Omar coughed, tried to smother it in his sleeve. "Sorry," he said, "Were the remains Lewis Redding's"

Rita poured hot coffee from a thermos into a plastic foam cup and handed it to the policeman. She seemed to have an ample supply of cups. Omar suspected she used them for more than coffee. "Dental records might confirm that, but we haven't found the head. Whoever it was, I can tell you didn't die from the fire. We'll check DNA, of course"

"Natural causes?" Omar queried, though he guessed that was the least likely possibility.

Rita poured a cup of coffee for herself, added something to it from a flask that she held out to Omar. He waved it away.

"Whatever the cause, before the victim, probably male, burned, the body was dismembered. Bones were retrieved from various areas of the burn site. As if limbs had been severed and left in different rooms. The bones were clean, more than just burned clean, as if they had been stripped of flesh and muscle. Some bore marks like cuts from a sharp knife or cleaver. Or teeth. A few looked as if they had been gnawed. A femur was split neatly in half, as would be done to extract marrow."

Omar wished he'd taken some of Rita's whiskey. "What are you telling me here?"

Softly, almost a whisper, as if she were divulging a secret, "I'm telling you the victim was dissected. Butchered like an animal by someone who had practice at the procedure."

"You said some of the bones had tooth marks on them."

"Yes," Rita said. "We'll examine the remains more thoroughly when we get them back to the morgue, but my strong impression is that your victim was at least partially eaten at the scene."

"Hell," muttered the policeman.

"Right here in Drovers Gap," confirmed the medical examiner.

A week after Lewis Redding's house burned down, Marcie Redding left her daughter with her sister Beth Coggins and drove into Drovers Gap and parked in front of Town Hall. She had not come to pay her taxes or her water bill. The Police Station occupied two rooms on the first floor. Marcie hadn't told anyone what she planned to do. It was overhearing Barbara Battle at the post office that decided her. According to Battle, expounding to Rhonda Fleming about Chief Longshadow's failure to arrest a suspect. "Everybody knows that Abigail Trammell and her wicked minions are behind it. They wanted to shut Preacher Lewis up, and started the fire to cover his murder."

Marcie felt that Lewis had gotten pretty much as he deserved. She had shut him up and felt small guilt over it. She had done what was necessary for everybody's good. But she was not about to let someone else take the blame for a crime she had committed. As it was, speculation ran rampant, and consistently in wrong directions. Official news stated only that Reverend Lewis Redding's remains had been found in his burned house. The public remained hungry for details and filled them in from their own imaginations. Some said Lewis was a victim of an accidental fire. A few questioned whether the preacher was sober at the time. It appeared that more people were coming to believe Battle's tale of murder and arson. The Police said information would be forthcoming upon completion of their investigation. Marcie wasn't sure the town could wait that long. She knew too many people who were always eager to believe the worst and act upon it.

Constable Jolene was busily shuffling papers on her desk

when Marcie came through the door. "Can I help you Mrs. Redding?"

"Is Chief Longshadow in?" Marcie asked, trying to keep her nerves out of her voice.

"He's out meeting with the crime scene people at . . ." Jolene seemed undecided how to finish her sentence, after an awkward silent second, settled for "I'm sorry for your loss, Mrs. Redding."

"I lost Lewis a long time ago," murmured Marcie. "It's important I talk with the Chief as soon as possible."

"He won't be long," Jolene assured. "He's coming back here after the meeting. What did you need to talk to him about?"

The officer visibly paled as Marcie said, "I need to confess to killing my husband."

Constable Bear stood behind her desk, gestured to a chair. "Sit down. Don't go anywhere. Don't talk to anybody. "I'll call him right now." As she left the room, presumably to talk to her chief in private, she turned and said, "Can I get you some coffee or anything?"

"The crime scene team found no trace of accelerants, but the fire burned unaccountably hot. What little was left doesn't tell us much. I was hoping the bones might have given you something," Chief Omar Longshadow said to Rita Fleming as they sat in her office in Asheton.

"The bones are keeping most of their secrets, Chief," she said as she poured another cup of her exceptional coffee, this time, fresh-brewed. "There is one thing new," she added, and held up a plastic bag containing what appeared to be charred fragments of a rib. "This rib was broken by some inflicted trauma, maybe he was stabbed, perhaps shot. Something pierced a rib, though."

"More likely shot," Omar said. "We found what was left of a gun at the scene. No condition for a ballistics test, though."

"We can at least confirm our victim is Lewis Redding," Rita said. "DNA samples yielded a conclusive match."

Omar was on his way to the parking lot when the call came through from Jolene. "Chief, Marcie Redding is here in the office waiting to talk to you."

"I'm on my way in now. Saves me a trip. I needed to interview her today. Did she say what she wants?"

"You won't believe this, Chief."

"I might, if you ever get around to telling me."

"She says she wants to confess to murdering her husband."

"Oh, I believe you," Omar said because he did. "Don't let her leave until I get there."

"You mean arrest her?" Constable Bear didn't sound as if she was quite ready for the undertaking.

"Not unless you have to," Omar said. He thought he heard a sigh, maybe of relief, over the phone. "I'd rather she talk to me voluntarily if she will. If we have to arrest her, you can read the charge."

"I've never charged anyone," Jolene murmured.

"It's easy," Omar said. "I won't let her hit you or anything."

———

Marcie Redding stood when Omar walked into his office. "Sit down, Marcie, please," he said, "You're not in official custody yet. We're just going to talk and clarify your situation." She sat, tried on a smile that didn't take. They had known one another since childhood, dated in high school. Omar thought she was pretty then and realized he thought of her the same now. "Tell me what happened, Marcie."

Marcie coughed on her first word. Started again, "I shot him, Omar. You know what he had become, what he was doing to people. Somebody had to put a stop to it. It seemed like it was up to me. I was his wife. I should have led him to do better."

You were his spouse, not his parent. You're not responsible for your husband's meanness. Aloud, Omar asked, "Do you still have the weapon, Marcie?"

"I dropped it on the floor when I left. It was an old pistol he kept in the garage to shoot rats, he said."

"We found a gun at the scene. The fire half melted it. Was Lewis dead when you left the house?"

"He was lying on the floor, moaning. Tried to say something. I couldn't tell what. I just left him there."

"Did you start the fire, Marcie?" By now Omar was fairly convinced she hadn't.

"No, Omar. I don't know anything about the fire. There was nothing burning when I was there."

Omar leaned forward, reached to put his hand on hers to stop her trembling, rested it on the arm of her chair instead. "Did you see anyone else there? Did you do anything to Lewis after you shot him?"

Marcie shook her head. "I don't think anyone else was around. I didn't touch him after he fell. I was still afraid of him. I just went."

Omar sighed, stood, wanted to put a hand on her shoulder, reach an arm around her for comfort, but the Drovers Gap Chief of Police couldn't do that. Instead, he said, "Go home to your girl Marcie. I don't need to tell you to remain in the area. We will have to discuss this more, you understand. But don't talk about it to anyone else before this is all settled."

Marcie nodded. "Thank you," she whispered. He helped her on with her coat, and she left. Jolene, whom Omar knew had been listening, said, "You think she did it, Chief?"

"I think she shot him," Omar said, "but sure as hell she didn't cut him apart and eat him for supper."

"We're in big trouble if it gets out we have a confession and didn't make an arrest," Jolene said.

Omar shook his head. "No, I'm in big trouble. You don't know anything about it."

Twenty-Six

Simon woke to darkness, aware that another thousand years had passed. Would this be his last waking, he wondered. Would the next sleep be forever?

He coughed into the echoing blackness. His breath illumined the cave for a moment. Simon had time to see that everything was undisturbed, just as he had arranged them before he bedded down on a winter night after slaughtering three hundred Norman archers. The wound he had taken during that encounter, severe enough to have killed a lesser dragon, had healed long before Simon woke, probably during the first hundred years of his sleep.

Awake and aware, Simon lay for several days listening to his own breathing, watching his exhalations trace glowing tendrils against the dark. As he gathered himself, his three hearts beat by the hour with increasing force until they found their common rhythm and drummed the black air with a singular cadence vibrating through the stony matrix of the mountain. In the forest on the surface, a hundred feet above Simon's lair, the creatures of the wood felt in the ground and the trees and the air the dragon's driving triune pulse and began to consider other places to be.

When he finally felt fully himself, the dragon named Simon let free a flaming roar that shook the mountain for a mile around, putting birds to flight and deer on the run, and released the spell that concealed the entrance to the dragoncave. The fire of his voice faded down to dark and Simon saw a faint light coming through the opening from outside. The light was bluish and smelled like morning. A new day was beginning somewhere in the world and this dragon was present in the midst of it. Alert now, drawing his powers, the Dragon was hungry.

Far away, across miles and years, at the very edge of the world, Goodmother Wandalena did not notice the dawn breaking above Trier Abbey. She sat, wrapped in a blanket, at her desk where she had been all night, scrying, searching. The hearth was cold, the unattended fire long gone out. The warming pan at her feet now held more ash than heat. Someone was knocking timidly at her door, but Wandalena didn't hear. Intent on the water in her seerbowl, she saw a cleft in a rocky cliff, and saw a flare of light within. "It's awake," she said aloud, her breath visible as smoke in the frigid air. As the knocking at the door continued, Wandalena breathed her summons into her bowl.

"Enter," Wandalena shouted at the door. The word emerged something like a snarl, startling even the speaker. The door opened only enough for a cowed novice to put her head around it.

"Goodmother, the High Sheriff is here to see you. Shall I send him in?"

"He will be in, sent or not," sighed Wandalena. "While you're here, see to my fire."

The High Sheriff of Trier, Marcus Starr, was probably the tallest male in the province. He had to bow his head to walk through the door. The novice came in behind him, glanced at the hearth, and scurried away to find firewood.

"Shut the door, girl," the Superior shouted after her.

The sheriff stepped to the door and closed it quietly. "Damnation, it's cold in here. Do you religious deem it a sin to be comfortable at your work?"

Wandalena's grimace barely intensified her habitual expression. "You're in a holy house, lawman. You should govern your speech accordingly."

"I've used no word your flock wouldn't hear in one of your sermons, Goodmother." Marcus retorted, not bothering to suppress his smile. "I'm here to report we've investigated the arson of your apiary, and it is as we suspected."

"You mean our hives were burned by dragonfire, as I told you at the time," Wandalena said.

"As you speculated, Goodmother," Marcus corrected, "Since you never bothered to go out and see for yourself, you could hardly be certain."

"As Superior of this house, I'm under a vow of stability, lawman. You know that. But from these walls I see things you cannot imagine." Wandalena measured her words and tone but her rising pique flickered on her face.

"If you see the dragon that committed this atrocity, we might catch it sooner, before it torches something like a church," the sheriff said.

"That I know for certain, lawman," Wandalena announced, "It was Babd Catha."

"That old demon?" Marcus said, sounding as surprised as he looked. "The Battle Crow hasn't been seen in Trier for generations. It is assumed she died long ago."

"Dragons don't die very often," murmured Wandalena, "She was a prisoner in our catacombs for the past four hundred years."

"Was?" It was the sheriff's turn now to be irritated.

"She escaped the night of the apiary fire."

"On her own?" The sheriff queried.

"She was secured by an old spell," said Wandalena. "Spells wear thin over time, and in this case, those with knowledge to renew the binding had all died. We knew it was just a matter of time."

"Then you should have killed it," Marcus said sharply.

"We don't kill here." Wandalena growled.

"No, you just find others to do it for you."

"We thought we had time yet," Wandalena said, "We would have done what was necessary."

"But you didn't," said the sheriff. "Where is it now?"

"Gone over to Shadow," answered the Superior. "Among the Fallen now, no threat to us."

"Shadow is ever a threat, Goodmother," Marcus admonished. "If dragons can pass the Separation, what safety is left?

"Powers don't endure long in that environment," Wandalena said blandly. "If the Battle Crow comes back at all, it will be as a sparrow."

"Where are your beekeepers, Goodmother? Nobody seems to have seen them since the burning."

"Neither have I, lawman," Wandalena confessed. "They have gone after their bees, I imagine."

* * *

Simon Ryder scented Goodmother Wandalena's summons the moment he emerged from the dragoncave, but it was three days before the dragon arrived at Trier Abbey. The first thing on Simon's agenda was to find a blooded meal to restore his depleted reserves. A herd of fat beef cattle halfway down Simon's mountain tempted mightily, but he passed them by, not prepared to alert the local human population to his presence. Humans were clever beasts, Simon knew from experience. At the end of each dragonsleep, they seemed to have devised some more potent and efficient means for dispatching dragons.

Bears were also emerging from hibernation, and it took

only half a day to find one still slow and drowsy, not so corpulent as he had been in the fall, but meaty enough to restore adequate earthlight to renew the concealing spell at the dragoncave entrance and allow Simon to morph into a passably human form and begin the trek to the Abbey at Trier. He followed a somewhat circuitous route, avoiding large settlements, keeping close to forested areas where wild game was accessible. Simon was still hungry and somewhat diminished after his sleep.

Along the way, the dragon avoided commerce with humans as much as possible, although his guise as a monk drew little interest for the most part. A wave and a comment on the weather sufficed for most encounters. One old man asked if he were bound for the Abbey and needed a guide. Simon assured that the way was known fortunately, for there was no money to pay a guide.

On the morning of the second day Simon came nearest to having a real conversation when he met a young girl, maybe eight years old, walking to her school.

"Good morning, Sir," she said, gazing at Simon curiously as they approached.

"Good morning, Miss," said Simon, "Have a good day at school."

They passed, and Simon felt the child's attention behind. The dragon stopped and turned. The child stood in the middle of the road, watching him intently. "Are you a dragon?" she queried.

"Do I look like a dragon?" Simon said.

"You look like a monk," the girl answered, "but you smell like a dragon."

"I'll work on that," Simon murmured, and they turned and went on their ways. Simon didn't ask the child how she knew what a dragon smelled like, but thought that with such discerning children in it, there might be hope for this world.

The dragon arrived at Trier in the waning afternoon,

when the dun walls of the houses were yet warm in the sun, and the blue shadows along the street were already chill. Simon had been soaking up Sol's heat all day and was by now immune to the cool. A pig, fugitive from a nearby farm, had been grubbing roots in a woodland about two miles this side of the previous village, and roasted on the spot with breath to spare, had provided a tasty lunch. Approaching the gate of Trier Abbey, Simon felt fully regained of all his powers. By far the largest and grandest building in town, the spire of its chapel had been visible for most of the last hour before the dragon spied the first of the shabby shops and dwellings clustered around the abbey enclosure.

The Dragon could have flown from his cave, of course, made three hours of a three-day walk, but walking consumed far less energy, and gave Simon time to acquaint with this new era he had awakened in, while he gathered sustenance from the land and the light. Now fully restored to himself, he accosted the officious young monk manning the main gate.

"Brother, I'm here in answer to your Goodmother's summons. She has been awaiting my arrival these three long days and need wait no longer," said the dragon.

The monk pulled a pair of spectacles from the pocket of his robe and perched them on his thin nose. He peered at his list, "And you are?" he intoned, glancing over the top of his spectacles.

"Ryder," answered the dragon, amused, sensing the monk's pride in his new glasses, which, in the young man's mind, imbued him with as much authority as a bishop's mitre, at least regarding supplicant laity.

"Simon?" queried the monk, peering at his list, avoiding the gaze that had uneased him.

"Is there another Ryder on your roll, Brother Laurus?" the dragon asked.

"How did you . . ." then, abandoning his question for fear of the answer, Laurus called into the shadows at his back,

"Sister Miriam, escort this Simon Ryder to Goodmother Wandalena. She wills to grant him audience immediately upon his arrival."

After several turns, the young novice knocked at a low narrow door at the end of a long narrow corridor, in a quavering contralto announced his arrival, and the instant he entered, closed the door behind him and scurried away down the hall. Simon sensed she did not lurk at the keyhole to eavesdrop.

Good girl, he sent after her. She felt it as a subtle lift in her mood. Soundless praise also has its power.

Behind the desk centered in the room, a woman. All black, except for a crinkled caramel face and a silver trefoil. Smaller than might be expected from her powerful aura. Better an ally than an adversary, Simon judged. Never, at best, a friend. The dragon could see that this human had no friends. The Goodmother saw two kinds of people in her world, the many who were obligated to do her bidding and the few whose will she was bound to honor. Simon suspected that in practice, she answered to no one but herself, and to her God, of course, in whom, Simon saw, she did, at least sometimes, believe.

Parhaps Wandalena sensed the dragon's probing, for her voice manifested more strident than usual to cloak her unease. "I hope you had a good sleep, Dragon. As you have answered my summons, I assume you are prepared to honor my request."

Simon went to the fireplace, piled with wet wood that smouldered feebly, producing more smoke than heat. He breathed a whiff of dragonfire upon it, igniting it to sustaining flame. Then he faced Wandalena, said amiably, "Do you request or command, Goodmother?"

Wandalena surprised the dragon by finding a smile among her store of rarely used expressions. "A dragon follows no directive not its own. If I commanded, you would ignore it. I would rather share with you a common desire."

"Then among the many, we are one," Simon said, bowing slightly. "What does the Goodmother Wandalena want of me?"

"Do you know of Badb Catha?" Wandalena said. She knew he did.

Simon held fast to his human face, allowing only a faint wisp of smoke to escape his right nostril. "You are a typical religious, Goodmother, always answering question for question. I do know of that old Battle Crow. She is the oldest of our kind. I saw her once in my youth, and that was enough. I've sensed no trace of her presence in our world since my last sleep. I would like to imagine she is cold."

"If by cold, you mean dead, I must disappoint you, Dragon. The Crow is very much alive, but not in this world. She has gone among the Fallen."

"Then we must mourn for the Fallen," Simon said solemnly, "For they have no means whereby to contain her evil."

Goodmother Wandalena stood with an alacrity at odds with her obvious age, stretched out a gnarled and parchmental hand toward the dragon. "No, Simon Ryder, but you do," she said, dropping into his upturned palm a small sphere the size of a robin's egg and clear as water.

TWENTY-SEVEN

At the first Restoration Crusade meeting since Lewis Redding's incineration, Orville Hawke and Wilbur Corvid were not in public view. Barbara Battle had insisted they remain behind the scenes. "You were part of Redding's show," she told them, "But I need a smoother brand. Besides," she added, "You two need to devote your energies to getting the Cathedral built. Tents are not really my style." Henceforth, the Evil Twins majored on their construction project and Barbara manipulated the smoke and mirrors before the gullible fans.

A packed house belted out the words projected on the gigantic screen behind a choir and the former Justice Fork Baptist Praise Band as the assembly revved up for Barbara's appearance. They sang a dozen songs, each consisting of two or three lines repeated twenty times. This performance generated more adrenalin spike than any increase in spiritual fervor. The crowd considered them synonymous.

By the time Barbara stepped onto the stage, the congregation was at a low simmer ready to boil. Spotlights followed her to the lectern as the house band worked into a cacophonic frenzy. The big screen behind her projected luminous radiations intended to approximate a halo. Garbed in white from head to toe, her hair teased round her head in a glittering cloud, Barbara smiled upon her subjects and raised her arms. Nine hundred and eighty-seven voices erupted as one thundering ovation that could have been described with equal accuracy as a roar or a cheer or a scream.

Barbara Battle lowered her arms, and the voices of her congregation went suddenly silent as if she'd turned off a radio. Their minds were hers now. If she told them the world was a cube, they would believe her. She stretched out her hands toward their hungry faces and began, "We are here, sisters and brothers, to carry on the work our beloved Lewis Redding began, and together we will finish it. Together, we will free Drovers Gap from the dark forces he rallied us against. Together, we will restore our town to its rightful order."

A few shouted *yes*'s sprinkled from the crowd, like the first dry kernels of corn that pop over a fire.

Barbara went on, "Our dear Brother Lewis looked in the face that darkness that besets us, and shown the light of truth upon it. The darkness feared his light and rose up in vain to destroy him. They burned his church, and when he would not be silent, they torched his house and took his life."

More shouts now from the crowd, some of them just wordless growls and shrieks, dripping hate and fear and suspicion on surrounding heads.

"But Lewis Redding is not silenced," Barbara shouting now, her voice not quite a woman's voice any longer, not quite human, "We are his voice."

"Yes," like thunder from the crowd.

"We will seek them out one by one and expose them all."

"Yes!"

"We will reveal their faces and call them by name."

"Yes!"

"We will bid them to confession and repentance,"

"Yes!"

"Those who refuse to repent, we will cast out from among us."

"Yes!

"Those who remain in our midst, obstinate in their darkness, we will purge."

"Yes!"

"We will be cleansed of the wicked ones, every one of them," thundered Barbara Battle, her eyes glowing like live coals, her face shining like iron in the forge.

"Yes, we will," the mob thundered back, in this moment no longer people, melded by their own paranoia into a single beast possessed, chanting, "Yes, we will! Yes, we will! Yes, we will!"

Hemlock House stood quietly in the night, a shadow within shadows. No lights in her windows. All the souls within sequestered in their beds at this hour, some asleep, some watching the dark, listening for the light. Not all the resident souls were within, however. One roamed out high on a wooded ridge above the town, chasing a blooded meal. One stood tall and still, like a tree trunk, or the shadow of one, at the edge of the wood beyond the garden, as if awaiting some sign or portent from the heavens, watching the clouds obscure and reveal stars in their turn. The figure didn't move as the back door of the house opened and Abigail Trammell slipped out onto her deck and began walking down toward the end of her garden where her bees droned and mumbled in their hives. While individual bees might nap and doze, the hive never sleeps. There is always movement, connections, communal intentions being executed. The needs of the many ever prioritized to serve the need of the hive. Individual lives terminate but the hive lives on. Even the

Queen is banished if a younger would serve better the urge for increase.

Abigail stepped past rows of weary okra, weighed down with pods too large and tough to eat (they would be saved for next year's seed), down through wilted squash vines and tottering corn stalks, until she was close enough to the hives, pale squares under the moon, to hear the low sweet music of her bees, as constant and as variable as her own heartbeat. On nights when some ache or worry kept sleep at bay, she would come down to her little apiary and stand among the bees until their nocturnal murmuring, measured and mellowed as the chanting of monks, became the shape of words in her head that released her from the tensions and strivings of her day.

On a midsummer evening, she would have been tempted to lie down and sleep there on the sweet grass between the hives, but tonight the cold wet might be frosted before sunrise, so she just stood in her nightdress and robe, arms wrapped around to conserve her warmth and postpone her retreat to her house as long as it took for the night's chill to seep through her defenses, and she closed her eyes and listened to the bees droning revelations until she became aware of that other presence among the shadows.

"Wendl VonTrier," she said softly, as if speaking to a lover or a frightened child, "I know it is you there."

The tall thin shadow among the other shadows shed its shape like water and flowed toward her. She opened her eyes and turned and Wendl stood beside her, close enough that she could see the moon's reflection in his deepdark eyes.

"Yes," said the púca, "we are awake with the bees, alive in their music."

They stood unspeaking for a long moment, gazing out above the roofs of the town toward Ravensbeak Ridge where between the waves of fog drifting across the mountain's face, lights flickered and flared as crews worked around the clock to finish Barbara Battle's Restoration Cathedral. The wind swept away the sound of their striving before it reached Drovers Gap. From that distance, they toiled silent as stars. Above them, a billowing of lightning-laced clouds gathered toward a storm.

"Where did so much hate and pure meanness come from, Wendl?" Abigail asked.

"I fear it has always been among us," Wendl sighed. "These intruders did not bring it here. It festered like a stagnant pool in greedy and fearful hearts until the Battle Crow and her minions provided a channel through which it could flow out into the world."

"Battle Crow?" said Abigail. "You mean Barbara Battle?"

"The same," Wendl replied. "Babd Catha is her true name and dragon is her nature. She is nourished by death and sustained by fear. She farms despair and pain like a farmer his corn and potatoes."

As he spoke, a bright burst of green light exploded in the sky eastward and trailed westerly until it disappeared into the dark beyond Warwoman Ridge. A shuddering rumble like distant thunder or a sonic boom sounded a few seconds later.

"What on earth was that?" Abigail exclaimed.

"It's what this púca has been watching for," murmured Wendl, "A thing beyond hate or affection that may prove our death or our salvation. We'd best go in before we're wet upon."

Willie pointed to the tiny squares on his topographical map. "These are ventilation shafts. This is how we get into the tunnel where the gold is."

Brian shook his head. "I doubt it, Willie. I've heard those tales, too, but with all the people who went looking for it over the years, if there was a trainload of gold under that

mountain, somebody would have gotten to it long before now
and brought it out."

"Not a trainload, Brian," Willie corrected, "Just four
hundred pounds."

"Four hundred pounds of rock, more likely," Brian
snorted. "How come you know so much about this? Where
did you get that map?"

"I got it from that VonTrier guy at Vintage Reads."

"Did he sell you the railroad to go with it?" Brian asked
with a smirk.

"I didn't buy it, Brian," Willie said. "He loaned it to me.
It's his map."

"So why hasn't he got the gold for himself, then?"

Willie shrugged. "He claims he has all the money he wants
already."

"Nobody has all the money they want, Willie. You're crazy
as that old man if you believe any of this."

"All I'm asking, Brian," Willie pleading now, sensing
Brian's waning interest, "is that you go up there with me to
take a look. Even if there's no gold, we might find some
Confederate relics that would be worth something. I've
checked this against the old maps at the Land Registry. There
really was an old railroad up through there, abandoned after
the Civil War. Boyce Miller says he found traces of the railbed
on his property."

Brian peered at the map again, as if waiting for it to show
him more than he saw. "I tell you what, Willie," he said finally,
"I go up there with you and if we find one of those ventilation
shafts, we'll get a hoist and help you go down for a looksee.
You pay me thirty dollars an hour, including driving time, if
we don't find anything. If there's any valuables under that
mountain, we split three ways, you, me, and Betty."

"I agreed with Betty to split it even, Brian. Two ways. If
Betty wants to share her part with you, that between you two."

Brian stared at Willie for a moment, then smiled and held

out a hand. "You drive a hard bargain, Sir. You must be a millionaire already." Willie shook the offered paw. Brian still looked uneasy. "You really think you can trust this Wendl character?"

"About as much as I trust you, "Willie said solemnly.

"Barbara Battle says Wendl VonTrier is the devil," Brian said.

"My mother says Barbara Battle is the devil," Willie countered.

"Your mother's dead," Brian said, trying to laugh but not sure if he should. "You're weird as shit, Willie Graham."

Twenty-Eight

"You wanted to see me, Mayor," Omar Longshadow said as he stood in the open door of Ned Baskin's office.

"Yup, Chief, thanks for coming by," the corpulent mayor pushed back his chair, pulled open a desk drawer, and hauled out a bottle of single malt and a couple of glasses. He gestured toward a chair with the bottle. "You still on duty, Chief?"

"Just did my shift and turned the town over to Sergeant Priestley. I'm on my way to supper after this." Omar said, settling into the indicated chair.

"Care to join me then?" the mayor said, pushing a glass toward the policeman and preparing to pour.

Omar held up a hand. "No thanks, it's early for me yet. I need to eat something first."

Ned put the glass back into his desk drawer and filled his own. "Well, don't mind me, then. It's been a long day." He took a slow sip of his whiskey and held the glass to the light while he sorted the words he was about to loose.

Omar waited in silence, listening to the big man's

wheezing breath, thinking to himself, *There's old men and there's drunks, but there's not many old drunks.*

Two swallows later, Baskin set down his empty glass, gazed at his Chief of Police and said, "How's it going with our big crime spree, Omar?"

The fact that Ned used his first name meant he was headed into some rough water, Omar figured. "We don't have any firm leads yet on the arson cases, either the church or the preacher's house. County has been helping our investigation. Redding's death is murder, we're certain of that, and I have one suspect that I'm not ready to pull in yet, as that might hamper our other inquiries."

"Don't suppose you'd tell me who your suspect is," murmured Ned.

"As I said, just a suspect. Nothing hard at all. We're a small town, Mayor, wouldn't do to sow unwarranted suspicions about. You know that."

The mayor leaned forward, rested his elbows on his desk, pushed his florid face toward Omar. "Wellsir, unwarranted suspicions are proliferating all over the place. The commissioners are hot on my ass. Your contract is up next month, and town elections the month after that. There's two jobs in jeopardy here. I'm not going to be in a position to recommend your contract be renewed unless, mighty soon, you can lay some blame where it sticks."

"I understand that, Mayor."

Ned raised his hands. "Nothing personal, Omar. I like you. You've done us a good job up until now, just like your dad did, but this is where we are."

"I'll keep you informed," Omar said, stood, picked up his hat, and walked to the door.

"Close that, if you will," Ned called as Omar passed through. Soon as the door shut, Ned opened the bottle and refilled his glass.

As Omar passed his own office, he saw Jolene Bear, also on her way to the exit.

"Calling it a day, Constable Bear?" he said, as he stopped and held the door for her to catch up.

"I am, Chief," she said, looking tired but cheerful. "It's Sarge's turn to do night patrol, and he's welcome to it. Did you talk Ned Baskin into pushing the commission for another hand?"

Omar allowed himself a rueful laugh. "Far from it. If anything, you might be looking for another Chief real soon."

Jolene stopped, open-mouthed as they reached her car. "What?" she stammered, "You didn't quit us, did you?"

Omar shook his head. "No, nothing like that. But the commissioners have lit a fire under Ned about the arsons and Lewis's murder. They are afraid all our unsolved crime will scare off the tourists. Ned is afraid for his job. He thinks if I'm afraid for mine, it will make us catch criminals faster."

Jolene leaned against her vehicle and folded her arms. "The mayor's no fool. He should know we're doing everything we can."

"He knows, but if blame falls down, he'd rather it land in my pocket than his."

"Do you think this is the end of it?" Jolene said. "I mean, Lewis Redding stirred up all this bad feeling going around, and he's dead now. Maybe it will all just die down once we catch the perp."

"I think there's a lot more to this than we know yet," Omar said. I don't think it's a safe assumption that the arsons and murder were all committed by the same person."

"Do you still think Marcie Lewis didn't kill her husband?" Jolene asked.

"I think she shot him, but I don't think she dismembered his body and burned down his house. Marcie isn't going to run off and leave her daughter. I'll have a nice long talk with her again tomorrow."

"Well, her secret's safe with me," Jolene said. "Preacher or not, Lewis Redding was a mean man. My guess is he had it coming."

"Not our job," said Omar. "We just catch the bad guys when we can, we don't judge 'em. Goodnight, Constable Bear."

"Good night, Chief."

Omar turned away to get to his own vehicle, and heard Jolene's voice behind him. "Chief?"

"Yup," he said turning around to her smile.

"You want to get a drink before we go home?" she said.

Omar found a smile of his own, felt something heavy lift away from his shoulders, "Why, Constable Bear, that's the nicest thing anybody's said to me all day"

At Wild Leek Pub, Darnella Pace approached two thirds of the Drover's Gap Police Department, She pulled a pencil from her apron pocket and poised it over her pad. "What youns having?"

"A Forester Stout for me," Jolene Bear said, and looked at her chief.

"I'll have a Trixter," said Omar. "I'm buying."

"No you're not," Jolene said. "I'm holding out for dinner sometime." She looked at Darnella. "Can you bring us an order of sweet potato fries to go with that?" She nodded to Omar. "You'll share it, won't you?"

Omar laughed. "How can I refuse an offer like that, even though it will spoil my supper."

"You're a big man. You can handle it," murmured Darnella. She glanced from one to the other. "Anything else I can bring youns?"

"We're good, I think," from Jolene, turning to Omar.

"That's all for me, thanks," Omar said.

Darnella's pen disappeared back into her apron, and she was away. Omar put up a hand to hide a yawn. It had been a long day. He hadn't slept well for weeks. He was tired and almost wishing he had not been so quick to accept Jolene's invitation to be here.

"You seriously think they might let you go, Chief?" she asked.

"I'd say it's a distinct possibility," Omar folded his hands on the table, which Jolene knew was a sign he was engaging in earnest conversation. "Half the commission thinks I haven't been doing my job and the other half's mad at me because I have. Unless we get a break in this Lewis Redding business, I wouldn't make any bets on my contract being renewed."

"You wouldn't be easy to replace," Jolene said. "You're better than they pay you for."

"Low pay, in this case, Constable Bear, is tantamount to job security. That might just save my hide, when they find out what real talent will cost."

"What made you want to become a policeman, anyway? I never figured you for that in school when we were growing up."

Omar sighed, unfolded his hands, left them flat on the table, palms down in front of him, "I never wanted to be a policeman, exactly, but it was expected of me. My dad, as you know, was chief here close to forever. His big sister, my aunt Wilma, was county sheriff for over thirty years, and their daddy was on the Asheton force before them. There wasn't much of a choice to make."

"What did you really want to be, then?" Jolene said, playing with the utensils Darnella had left behind.

"You'll laugh," Omar said.

Jolene turned on her serious face. "I would never laugh at somebody's dream."

"I wanted to be a forest ranger," Omar confessed.

Jolene nodded, didn't look at all surprised. "Like Lewis Redding's boy."

"What?"

"Neil Redding wants to be a forest ranger. Lewis was hellbent on him being a preacher he was. I guess the pressure's off now and Neil can grow his own set of wings."

"Unless he turns out to be our killer," Omar said, wishing immediately he hadn't.

Jolene nodded, "Marcie's sudden confession could be to protect her son," she said.

"Just what I was thinking," agreed her boss.

Darnella appeared with brews and fries, and as soon as she retreated, Omar took a sip of his beer and said, "What about you, then?"

Jolene set down her stout. "What about me?"

"What made you want to be a cop?"

She took a long swallow of her Forester, then, "It's complicated, you want the long version or the short?"

TWENTY-NINE

The sun dropped down behind the mountain as Brian's jeep churned and jostled up the old logging road in the deep shadow along a creek. They saw no sign of the abandoned civil-war era railroad. Previous generations had taken up the rails and sold them off for scrap and the forest had long ago recycled the wooden cross ties. The gravel railbed had over a century and a half washed away toward the creek below. A vague ledge meandering up the mountainside was all that remained of the great endeavor.

The road ended abruptly against a towering tumble of boulders and earth that had fallen long enough in the past that mature trees with trunks two feet or more in diameter thrust skyward among the rubble. There was barely clearance for the jeep to turn around.

"Shit," growled Brian, "this is as far as we get in this thing."

Betty, sitting beside him, looked as if she might cry. "Do we have to climb up that?" she asked.

"No, Darling," said Brian. "You can sit right here and let the mosquitos drain your blood until me and Willie get back." He turned and looked at Willie sitting behind them, bruised and battered among jostled equipment. "Where the hell are we now, map expert?"

Willie pushed his map across the back of the seat so Brian could see, traced the line of the old railway with his finger until it terminated. "If I read correctly, it looks like we're about here where the tunnel began."

"Well, if I read correctly, it looks like half the mountain's done fell atop it." Brian sneered, staring out the window toward the piled boulders.

Willie was unperturbed, he moved his finger an inch on the map. "And up here these little squares are supposed to be ventilation shafts. That's how we get down into the tunnel. There's five or six marked on the map. One of them's bound to be open."

"You hope it is," growled Brian.

While Betty and Brian stared skeptically at the tip of Willie's finger, he added, "The nearest is only about a quarter mile from here."

"A quarter mile straight up," Brian said.

"What do we do now?" Betty pleaded, wanting to hear they were going home.

"Now we break out the gear and lug it up to one of Willie's black holes," said Brian, before it gets pitch dark on us."

It took three trips to get the hoist and all associated gear up the tangled and thorny slope to where they thought the ventilator shaft should be. Betty went ahead with the lantern after the first ascent, with Brian all the while yelling at her that she wasn't shining it where he needed it. It was full dark by the time they hauled up their last load. Brian was mad and Willie felt like a man who'd been beaten and Betty was on the brink of tears. Tempers weren't improved when after close to an hour of casting about among rhododendron and windfall pines they had turned up no sign of the elusive shaft.

"Dammit, Willie," Brian shouted. "You got us up here on

this benighted knob for some fairytale. We won't be able to see shit before morning."

Willie waved his map like a flag. "It can't be that far away. We're right on it, according to my GPS."

Brian snatched the map away and peered at it in the light of his lantern. "If we find that damned hole in the ground, I might just throw you down it, you crazy coot."

Betty, sobbing audibly, "Don't be like that, Brian. You're such a bully." Brian aimed his lantern at her face. Tears gleamed in the light. He snickered, threw the map at Willie. Betty bleated, "Please, Brian, I gotta go."

"We're going no place, girl," Brian barked. We got sleeping bags in the jeep. We'll stay right here until there's light enough to see by, and Willieboy's gonna pay us by the hour for our time, just like he promised."

Betty, struggling not to weep, whined, "No Brian, I gotta go now. I gotta pee."

"Well, go to it, then," Brian snapped.

"I need privacy, Brian," Betty whispered.

"Well, go squat behind a tree or something," Brian said, "There's plenty of 'em out here."

Willie seemed unaware of the exchange as he scrambled through the brush trying to collect his map. Betty took her lantern and moved off into the general dark until her light flickered uncertainly through a maze of laurel.

Brian glared at Willie. "A fine mess you've gotten us into this time, Ollie," he sneered. Willie concentrated on refolding his map until they heard Betty's scream. Her light had disappeared entirely. Lanterns in hand, the men plunged and staggered through the thicket in the direction they supposed she had taken.

"Betty, where are you?" Willie called, on the verge of crying himself.

"Over here," Betty's voice wavery with exhaustion and terror, "Help me, quick." Brian aimed his lantern into the

Laurel thicket. Betty called again, "I see your light. Oh, please hurry."

Following the voice, the men cast their lights amongst the tangle of laurel and rhododendron and saw Betty's face and arms, her hands clinging to a gnarled branch. The rest of her had vanished into the mountain. Willie reached her first. Brian was bigger, stronger, but Willie, being smaller was able to squirm his way faster. Willie thought the locals called the thickets laurel hells with good reason. He set down his light, reached under Betty's arms and pulled with strength he never knew he possessed. She did her part and by the time Brian reached the scene, she had her feet on solid ground.

They peered into the hole she had just vacated. Too far below, they saw her lantern still alight. The three stood for a long moment, listening to their heartbeats and ragged breaths, staring at that lone light way down under. Somewhere off in the night, an owl called.

"I'll be damned," Brian said at last.

You just might be, Willie thought in his mother's voice.

"It's that shaft thing, Willie, just like you said," Betty murmured wonderingly.

The old woman was desperate if she called for him, Simon Ryder concluded as the novice closed the Superior's door behind them, then trotted ahead to shepherd him down the hallway. She kept glancing back furtively as they proceeded toward the Abbey gates, as if she feared he might burst into flames any second and cremate them all. She didn't know Simon was a dragon, of course. A light scan of her mind revealed as much. She wasn't even aware of his gentle probe. Simon considered a religious colony similar in constitution to a beehive in an apiary. What the queen knew, the minions sensed untold. The body was the collective will of the head.

When the abbey gates swung ponderously shut at his back, Simon stood in the town square, watching the people of Trier go about their daily business. Yes, like bees, he thought, each one believing their small task was the most important endeavor in the world, never more than vaguely aware of the pattern into which they were woven, never to delight or wonder at the larger purpose that moved them all toward resolution.

In an instant when no soul was watching, Simon shifted just enough from the moment to be rendered invisible to human eyes. Resolving into his habitual form, he lifted his wings and took flight. People were startled at the sudden burst of wind that swirled across the square and looking up when the swift shadow swept over them, they beheld the dragon aloft and rising, and they were afraid.

Simon circled once above the town, just for fun. He wasn't hungry yet. Away on the western horizon a storm was gathering. The dragon wheeled and flew after it. The storm was energy and fire. He would ride that power through the Separation into Shadow. If he found Badb Catha among the fallen, he might attempt to contain her, or he might not. She was, after all the first of their kind, gathering herself for eons. She might be too strong even for Simon to subdue. He would watch, keep to himself, secure his place, steep himself in Earthlight, which surely burned even in Shadow, if one sought deep enough below the surface. When he was ready, he would see what to do, what was possible, what would weaken, and what would sustain.

The distant storm waned and dissipated before the dragon reached it but sensing a stronger tempest just beyond the nearest range of mountains, he turned in pursuit of that turmoil. As the intervening miles diminished, the storm, as if responding to the dragon's proximity, intensified, raking the trees with leaf-stripping, branch-splintering hail, blasting the summits with volleys of lightning. The dragon, ever nearer, shapeshifting, morphing into a cumulous of fire and darkness, a rush and a wind, an annihilation that met the storm and became the storm, gathering the spin of it, the lightning and the hail of it into a tightening spiral, concentrating the power and the force of it into one blazing searing point of heaven's fire that pierced the boundary of the world and disappeared, leaving only stillness and stars in its wake.

And on a winter's night, high above Drovers Gap, the worst thunderstorm in anyone's memory is flooding the creeks, toppling trees, drowning the fallow fields, downing powerlines, loosing shingles, and driving every human in the county to seek dry and shelter. Nobody is abroad to see a deeper dark emerge from the center of the storm, resolving into enormous pinioned wings bearing aloft on the gale a squamatacious body, scales glistening in the lightning's glare, trailing a serpentine tail flickering with latent charge. A relatively slender neck almost as long as the body supports a reptilian head, small compared to the body, but with a mouth that might swallow a man whole. The head glances earthward with eyes that glow like molten iron. The mouth opens with a roar that dwarfs the thunder, and spews not lightning but dragonfire down the dark. In spite of the deluge, a string of fires springs up in the forest below. By tomorrow, the fires will be extinguished by the driving rains and assumed to have been started by downed electrical lines.

Just west of Warwoman Ridge, not far from where Willie Graham, Betty, and her once and maybe boyfriend huddle miserable in Brian's jeep, the dragon named Simon senses a void within the earth, settles to an opening in a place that is not drawn on any map, cools and dwindles to something resembling human form, and walks inside the mountain.

THIRTY

illie, Betty and Brian clambered down the mountain to the logging road as squalls of rain began crossing the ridge above in sufficient quantity to wet them thoroughly before they regained the shelter of their Jeep.

"I'm cold, Brian," Betty said, "Can't we go home and come back tomorrow?"

Brian reached into the back and hauled out one of the sleeping bags, "Here," he growled, dumping it into her lap. "If you're cold, put this around you. We're not going to drive out of here in this shit."

By now the rain had become a steady deluge. The old logging road had turned into a raging creek. Brian secretly wondered if there would be any road left for them by morning. Lightning strobed the landscape continually. Thunder and rain, at times mixed with hail or sleet made a steady roar. The humans had to shout at one another to be heard over the din. They soon tired of shouting and retreated into a sulky silence. Willie, cramped and folded among the gear, hardly said a word. He was worried what Wendl would say when he got his maps back soaked and muddy. He fell into an uneasy drowse while pondering Brian's severely limited stock of descriptive nouns.

The storm raged on unabated while the exhausted adventurers slept. Brian roused from his stupor sometime near dawn. He heard Betty's muffled whimpering from her sleeping bag. He reached out a hand to touch her shoulder, but she pushed it away, tried to squirm as far away from him as the confines of the jeep would allow.

"Bitch," Brian muttered, and retreated into oblivion.

Behind them, among all the tools and gear, his head resting on a duffel, his unzipped sleeping bag folded around him like a blanket, Willie murmured softly in his sleep. He was dreaming. It wasn't a pleasant dream. He dreamed about his mother.

Eventually, morning came as morning always does. Stiff and sore, the three seekers clambered out of the jeep just as a hazy sun peeped over the nearest ridge. It clung to the treetops for a few minutes as they staggered and stomped to regain acquaintance with their lower limbs. Brian wandered off among the rhododendron to satisfy some unspoken need. Betty stared away among the woods, her shoulders trembling slightly as if she were cold.

Willie wanted to touch, stepped up close behind her, raised his hand to reach for her shoulder but, perhaps recalling her response to Brian the night before, found himself too timid to risk contact. Instead, he murmured softly, "You alright, Betty?"

Betty turned, startled, as if she had forgotten he was there. Willie thought he saw tears glistening in the early light. Without a word, she pressed her hands against his arms and rested her forehead on his chest. This made Willie, who had assumed Brian had reestablished his boyfriend claim, indescribably happy. They stood just this way while the sun, a bright balloon, loosed her hold on the trees and floated upward above the mountain. They didn't move or speak until Brian emerged from his thicket.

Betty stepped away, looked up at Willie, wiped her face with her fingers, whispered, "I'm sorry," and turned to Brian. "Don't I get coffee, at least?"

Brian apparently traveled prepared for all contingences. From his stash in the rear of the jeep, he hauled out a little primus stove and a plastic milk jug filled with water, and from his backpack, produced a small jar of instant coffee. For breakfast, they had to make do with a half-full box of decidedly stale donuts, and a few strips of turkey jerky shrink-sealed in plastic. The donuts had the consistency of cardboard and the jerky tasted more plastic than fowl, but the fare served to muffle complaint from their empty guts. The coffee was worse than church coffee, but rendered them awake, and to a degree, grounded.

They expected to meet numbing cold when they left the shelter of Brian's jeep, had waited for some glimpse of sun before they finally emerged to grapple with their day. Instead, they met a morning unseasonably warm. Cool enough, but far from frigid. Brian took off his jacket and worked in his shirtsleeves as he handed out the few items they had not wrangled up the mountain the evening before.

He set a chainsaw on the ground in front of Willie. "Don't trip on a root and cut your leg off with this thing, Willieboy. Your watered-down blood would likely rust the chain."

Betty carried a half-empty five-gallon red plastic can with a label that promised *GAS*. Brian hoisted a light canvas backpack and started up the way they traversed the day before.

Willie followed next and Betty trailed last, looking at every step as if she might decide to run the other way. An inconclusive meandering line of broken twigs and bent branches marked their previous evening's passage, but Brian in his eagerness, missed the sign and twice they had to retrace their steps to find the right path. According to Brian, this occurrence was the result of his being distracted by Betty's and Willie's continual whining. He claimed this even though Betty had swallowed all her whines and Willie had said nothing aloud, being engrossed in an interior conversation with his dead mother. The sun climbed overhead, and the morning continued to warm. Before they reached the rhododendron thicket surrounding the shaft opening, all three were drenched with sweat.

Brian took the chainsaw and waded and wormed his way into Betty's infamous "laurel hell," where he cut enough of the tangle around the shaft opening to set up the tripod for the hoist. Then he sat on the ground and shouted, "Betty girl, bring me my pack." As soon as she handed it over, he pulled out a can of warm lager, opened it, and reclining on one elbow, sipped his beer while directing Betty and Willie dragging aside all the cut limbs and lugging the tripod and hoist to the *drop-site*, as Brian called it. "I shouldn't have to do all the work here," he said, grinning like a mule eating briars.

When it was finally time to assemble the tripod, Brian looked at Willie and said, "Where's my socket wrench?"

"Why should I know?" Willie said.

"Because I told you to bring the wrench and sockets, Willyboy"

"No, you didn't."

"I handed 'em to you, Mister Map Expert. You go back down there and find 'em or I'll throw you in this shitting hole and leave you there."

Willie looked to Betty for support. Betty just looked miserable until she looked the other way.

Without further protest or defense, Willie clambered back down the mountain and did a thorough search of the jeep and its surroundings. Once during his search, he thought somebody shouted or screamed from the mountain above. He stopped and listened, and only heard the clamor of quarrelling crows. Failing to turn up the socket kit, he made his way back up the slope. Unlike Brian, he didn't miss their trail.

"I couldn't find anything," he said. "There's no socket wrench in the jeep or thereabouts, I'm sure."

Brian grinned at him, looking proud of himself. Betty sat on the ground a few feet away. Her hair was loose, and she had dirt on her face. Willie had never seen her in such a state.

"That's okay, Willieboy," Brian drawled. "We found it."

It was nearly noon by the time the tripod was set in place over the shaft opening, and the hoist was secured to it. Brian affixed an eighty-foot nylon rope to the reel, then wound it on. He attached to the other end a lineman's harness he had stolen from the tv cable company when they fired him. He handed the harness to a surprised Willie. "Down you go now, Willie boy."

"Why me," sputtered Willie.

"Because, old son," beamed Brian, "ditsy Betty here would probably fall out on her soft head and you two weaklings don't have enough muscle to haul me back to the surface, much less the gold, if there is any."

"Will that knot hold?" Willie asked.

"Don't you worry, Willieboy," Brian drawled through his discomfiting grin. "I know how to tie a knot. You ain't getting loose from this, I promise you."

Reluctantly, Willie put on the headlamp Brian shoved at him, slipped the harness under his shoulders and hips and leaned back into it, his feet planted against the rim of the opening. Brian released the brake and began lowering him into the ground a little faster than Willie found comfortable. He listened to the whir of gears from the hoist until the earth blocked the sound, then he listened to the rattle of an occasional clod or pebble clattering down the shaft. He watched the circle of sky above him getting progressively smaller. He wondered what would happen if the rope broke or the tripod collapsed, and he fell to the bottom of the shaft and the hoist plummeted down on top of him. He thought about snakes and other creepy things that lurked in dark places. He profoundly wished Brian was a man he could trust.

Willie thought it would be cool in the hole, but it verged on hot. He was sweating again. Thirsty. Now and then the wall of the shaft brushed against him, and he instinctively pushed himself away with his feet. He went creeping down under the world forever until he switched on his headlamp and looked below him and saw red earth, glistening in his light like damp clay. When his feet touched it and did not sink and felt his own weight, he shouted, "I'm here!" The line stopped spooling. Willie looked up then. The opening was alarmingly tiny and far. He could barely make out Brian's and Betty's faces peering down at him.

"Do you see the gold?" Brian's voice floated down.

Willie looked around. All he saw was darkness, until, yes, something, a glint of metal. He played his light across the object. Big. He realized it was the front of an old railroad locomotive, sitting in a layer of dried mud a foot or two deep. The rails, he figured, ran right under his feet, buried over time in sediment from seeping or flowing water. "I see the train," he shouted.

"Find the gold," Brian again, faint and far away.

Willie didn't want to do it, but he wriggled free of the harness and trudged toward the locomotive. There was barely room in the tunnel for him to squeeze along the side and climb aboard the cab. His headlamp revealed nothing but blackness beyond the tender behind. Disappointment was setting in before he discerned the two crates, one against each side of the cab. Willie knelt down, coughing on the dust he raised. He hadn't brought any tools, but the wood of the crate was rotten, and gave way when he jerked on it. He saw the yellow shine from inside the box.

"Yes!" he yelled, scrambled down from the cab and ran

back to the shaft opening. His harness and line were gone. He looked up to see Brian still watching. "I found the gold!" he shouted. "Let down the harness."

"Good boy," Willie," Brian called down. "See you later."

Betty's face reappeared for an instant, "I'm sorry, Willie," she cried, then disappeared as if she had been pulled away.

After that, Willie could see only that tiny disk of sky. He sat in the dust staring at it until it dimmed away to a dark where a single star shown down on his misery.

Thirty-One

Chief Omar Longshadow and Constable Jolene Bear sat side-by side across a table from Marcie Redding during a second interview regarding her husband's death. Omar had advised Marcie that her attorney should be present, but she remained adamant that she didn't need a lawyer.

"All I know is, I shot him. I left him to burn up in that house. It was horrible. I have dreams about it," Marcie said, voice trembling, eyes brimming.

"What did you do with the gun?" Jolene queried.

"I told you. I dropped it on the floor as I left."

"Inside?" Omar asked.

"Yes. Before I went out the door," Marcie said. Noting the dubious expressions on the faces across the table, she added. "I'm sure."

"Are you sure Lewis was alive then?" Omar persisted.

"Yes, he was lying on the floor, moaning, looking like he wanted to kill me."

"And there was nothing burning when you left?" Jolene asked. "No smoke, no sign of a fire?"

"Nothing like that." Marcie said, clearly exasperated that

two dense cops didn't seem willing to accept her guilt. "I've told you what happened. I shot Lewis and left him to burn in that fire. Whether he was alive or not when I drove off, I killed him. Why won't you believe me?"

"Our problem is," Omar said, "You really need to be telling us this with your attorney present. Otherwise, everything you've said is suspect, could have been stated under duress. Any good lawyer could get it thrown out of court."

Marcie, sounding angry now, "I don't need a lawyer, Omar. I'm guilty, dammit."

Omar shrugged. "We don't have any evidence of the crime. No identifiable weapon has been found. The Medical examiner couldn't rule out him being shot but found indications something else might have killed him."

"Something else?" Marcie stammered. "What do you mean?"

"It isn't pretty, Marcie." Constable Bear said.

"I don't care. I want to know."

Omar spoke quietly, slowly, "The bones that survived the fire had marks on them. They had been chewed, gnawed at, by some sort of animal. Something big. That might be how the fire got started."

Marcie sat silent, pale, absolutely still, holding her breath.

Jolene asked, almost gently, "Is there anything else you can tell us, Marcie? Anything you saw? Any detail at all you haven't told us?"

Marcie released a long shuddering sigh. "Well, there is one thing. I thought I was dreaming it, or hallucinating, I was distraught. It was crazy."

"Tell us, Marcie," Omar murmured.

Marcie's voice, all calm now, detached, as if reading a story from a book, "As I backed the car out of the drive, I thought I saw her on top of the house."

"On top of the house?" Omar asked, "Who?"

"Well, not on it, above it a little in the air, like a bird

coming down to roost. She had wings. Big wings. They were like flames."

"Who had wings, Marcie?" Constable Jolene whispered, trying not to break the spell.

"It was the Restoration Crusade woman, the preacher."

"Barbara Battle?" prompted Omar.

"Yes. That one." Marcie said.

Wendl VonTrier saw the three jittery young men lurking across the street, leaning on their dented and rusty Jeep, as if it were a shield, staring at the front of Vintage Reads. He pretended not to notice them as he attended the woman herding two scampering children, a brightly present girl and a translucent boy. She wanted one of them to buy a book. The children wanted to explore, touch every title in the store, as if by osmosis, they could absorb all the accumulated wisdom and nonsense populating the shelves.

"We have to go, now," fretted the woman. "Your parents are meeting us for dinner. Pick your book, so this nice man can help somebody else."

She shot a pleading glance at Wendl. He reached down by the boy, pulled a book from the shelf, and said, "What about this one?"

The boy looked at Wendl, who was projecting a rather fox-like face at the moment. "I already looked at that one," the boy said, and turned away to attack another shelf.

"Look again," Wendl murmured softly. The boy turned back to him to behold a bear holding a book. The picture on the cover was strange, and it was moving, like in a video.

"What's it about?" queried the boy, interested now, stepping closer, reaching for it.

"Huge dragons and small boys," Wendl said, holding the

book back just beyond the child's reach. "Together they make the best stories."

"I want that one," said the boy.

"But," said Wendl, who was beginning to look to the boy as if he might be a dragon, albeit a spindly and wrinkled one. "Does the book want you?"

"How do I know?" said the boy. "What do books want, anyway?"

"They want to be read," said Wendl. "They want to be known and understood, just like you do. Can you read it?"

"Does it have big words?" asked the boy.

"Open it and see," said Wendl, who still looked like a skinny old man to the woman, whose name was Cora, but the boy was definitely seeing a small dragon.

The boy took the book, somewhat timidly from the dragon's talons, and when he tried to open it, the book did not resist. Nobody but the boy saw what he saw inside, but his face was alight with joy, when he shouted with all his boy voice, "Yes!"

The little girl stood beside him, turned away, pretending not to overhear as she gazed at a big book with an eagle on the cover, titled *Birds Around the World.*

Wendl bent over and asked, "Is that your book?"

"Close, but I don't think so," obviously, a precocious child. "Do you have any books on how to fly?"

"You can't learn to fly from books," Wendl said, "It's all in here." He tapped her lightly on the head.

"Really?" asked the girl.

"Really," said Wendl, looking something like a large fuzzy dog. "Close your eyes."

"Okay," said the girl who wanted to fly, and closed her eyes.

"Now think about how light you are," said Wendl.

"I'm almost light enough to float away," the girl said.

"You are light enough. You are floating away right now," whispered the púca.

The little girl, lighter than a feather, felt herself rising into the air.

"Oh," she squeeled. "How do I get down?"

"Just open your eyes," Wendl said.

She opened her eyes and found herself firmly planted on the floor again.

"I'll take the eagle book," she said, full of delight at her newly discovered ability.

"This is a special edition," Wendl said as they walked toward the counter. "Just for you, Millicent."

"How do you know my name?"

"Your brother told me," Wendl said. "He wants to be a dragon, you know."

"I know," said Millicent. "But he isn't my brother; he's my imaginary friend. Nobody can see him but me."

"I saw him." Wendl said, with a wink. For an instant, the girl saw an incredibly old tortoise blinking an eye.

"Are you imaginary, too?" asked the girl as Wendl wrapped her book.

He handed her the parcel. "All of us are thought up somewhere," he said with a special smile only Millicent could see.

Cora had barely herded her charge and the invisible dragon boy out the door before the three goons attached to the jeep parked across the street launched themselves at Vintage Reads. The largest goon carried a baseball bat, the middle one sported a red beard. The smallest looked as if he might be wishing he were somewhere else.

Wendl watched their swagger, gathered his powers. He knew what would happen next.

The big reiver in the lead pushed the door open with enough force to send it banging against the store front. He swung his bat against a display pylon just inside, scattering multihued children's books across the floor. Red Beard pointed at Wendl, shouting, "Heads up, Old Man. We're about to clean up your act."

Wendl looked at the smallest of the trio, more a boy than a man, and smiled. The wannabe terrorist's face began leaking tears. Big Man brought his bat down across the counter, spilling papers, books and the POS terminal over the side. "There's no place in Drovers Gap for such grinning filth as you," he roared, reaching his beefy hand across the counter to grab the púca by the throat, only to realize he had hold of a thick-bodied serpent the size of his arm. Before he could turn loose, the snake twined about his arm and the scaly triangular head poised inches from his face. Golden eyes slitted with midnight peered into his soul and he screamed when the forked tongue flicked the tip of his nose with a touch too brief to distinguish between ice or fire.

Big Man dropped his bat and swung his arm wildly, as if trying to rid himself of his limb as well as the offending snake. His arm remained attached but the snake hurtled across the room to smack Redbeard square in the chest. Before he could lift a hand in defense, the snake was wound tightly around his torso, pinning his arms to his side. Redbeard then commenced a manic strathspey, whooping and moaning, "Lord, Lord, Somebody get it off."

Big Man stood in front of him, waving his arms at the snake but not daring to get close enough to touch. When he realized he was no longer connected to his bat, he bolted for the door.

The serpent dropped to the floor and slithered away, silently and swiftly, behind the counter. Redbeard, bawling like a babe, hugged himself and followed his leader, whimpering, "Thank you Jesus Thank you Jesus" as he fled.

Through all this chaos and confusion, the least of them stood mute, unmoving, transfixed, in the middle of the puddle spreading at his feet. Wendl came around the counter, picked up the bat, and handed it to the last man standing. "Play ball, son," he said gently.

Whosever son he was apparently chose to play with some other team on a field far away. Wordless, he fled, flinging his bat onto the street as he ran. By the time he reached the opposite curb, the Jeep and his two friends had vanished.

He looked back toward the scene of the crime once. Wendl waved at him cheerfully through the glass before he ran away out of sight, his urine making squishy sounds in his shoes.

THIRTY-TWO

After repeated attempts to contact Barbara Battle by phone, Chief Omar Longshadow had no real expectation of finding her on the premises when he walked into the Restoration Crusade offices the morning after his interview with Marcie Redding. Barbara styled herself now as the Reverend Barbara Battle, and when he told the striking woman with deep-set eyes at the reception desk that he wanted to speak to the Reverend, she surprised him by announcing, "Of Course, Chief Longshadow. I'll tell her you're here. She's expecting you."

Omar sat in a wide uncomfortable chair, too low and soft for him, and was about to check in with his office when the evangelist appeared, striding toward him with outstretched hand and a too-good-to-be-true smile that dazzled without enlightening. "It's so good to see you again, Chief," she purred, her voice deeper, more resonant than he remembered. She looked younger, too, than he'd thought.

"Reverend," he acknowledged, feeling as if the temperature in the room had gone up five degrees. Before he could declare his purpose, Barbara went on, "You've been talking to everyone in town about Brother Lewis' awful demise. Everyone except me. I was beginning to feel left out."

"I do have some questions, Reverend Battle," Omar said, wondering why he felt subtly intimidated by this woman. "We haven't been able to find out much about that night or the events leading up to the fire. You were a close associate of Lewis and I'm hopeful you might be able to shed some light on this tragedy."

"I'll be happy to share all I have to offer, Chief," she said. Her smile brightened even more and Omar's hair stiffened as if he were standing too close to a microwave. "Let's go to my office where we can unburden our minds without interruption."

Omar followed Barbara Battle through a maze of corridors that seemed far longer than the extents of the building would allow. Eventually, she opened an ornate door into a room that resembled more an audience chamber than a working office. Omar thought of the baroque sets on the televangelist programs he had glimpsed on TV. Barbara sat at her desk and gestured the policeman to a chair. Her gargantuan desk stood on a low dias so that when he sat, she was slightly above him. The whole room was subtly arranged to make a visitor feel at a disadvantage without actually sensing why.

The desk was not so tall as to block Omar's view of Barbara's startling cleavage, which he hadn't observed until now and instantly chose to ignore. It was not the first time possibly guilty females had sought to distract his vision from questions at hand.

The room was uncomfortably warm, although Barbara seemed unaware of it. Omar tried to ignore the sweat trickling underneath his uniform shirt as he opened his interview, "Reverend, can you remember where you were the night Lewis Redding's house burned?"

Barbara leaned forward over her desk, like a judge in a

courtroom, lifted an eyebrow as she said. "Am I one of your suspects, Chief Longshadow?" Omar thought, *What doesn't she want me to see?* He said, "We haven't identified any suspects yet, Reverend. If we can determine what all the people associated with Redding were doing that night, it will narrow our search considerably."

Barbara sat back in her tall chair, looking serious and attentive, "Of course, Chief," she said, "I was at the Crusade meeting, obviously. Half the town can verify that. Afterward, Lewis- Brother Lewis and I were with our board members Orville Hawke and Wilbur Corvid counting and securing the offerings for deposit. After that, we discussed the plans for the Restoration Cathedral. Lewis wasn't quite himself, seemed preoccupied. He said he wasn't feeling well and left for home around nine-thirty or ten. Orville and Wilbur and I went over architectural drawings and cost estimates until midnight, or a little after. That's when we heard the siren and saw the firetrucks go by."

"Will you ask Mister Hawke and Mister Corvid to get in touch with me at earliest convenience, Reverend? I'll need to talk with them, too."

Barbara smiled a prim and proper smile, at odds with the piercing lights in her eyes as she answered, "I'll tell them, Chief. Actually, they are up on Ravensbeak at the construction site all afternoon. You can probably catch them there."

"I'll do that, Reverend." Omar said, anxious to be at a distance. "Thank you for taking time to talk with me."

"I hope we'll talk more again soon, Chief Longshadow," looking as if she meant it.

"That seems likely," Omar said, grateful to be going. After Barbara closed her door behind him, he had to retrace his steps three times in the maze of corridors before he found his way to reception.

It was dark forever and Willie heard rustlings and slitherings around him and made himself as small as he could. Nothing alive and dreadful touched him during that long night and sometimes he slept and sometimes he was awake and afraid. He dared not turn on his headlamp for fear of being seen and of what he might see. When he felt water dripping on his head and shoulders, he looked up to see rain falling down from a dim gray circle too far above. Morning had come in the world aloft.

Willie thought he should be cold, but it was like sitting in a sauna in his deep dark hole. He watched several gray leaves flittering down the shaft and realized they were bats coming home to sleep the day away. He turned on his lamp, swept its feeble beam across the roof of the tunnel. It swarmed with the creatures. He had been sitting in their dung all night long. Willie looked at his hands and legs, resisted an impulse to retch, and turned off his light.

Something moved down the tunnel opposite the engine. Something big. Something hungry, likely. Willie wondered if he would be safer inside the cab of the engine, but he was afraid to leave his little window on the real world, the world he had no logical expectation of entering again.

He listened, trying to hear if the big whatever-it-was had come any nearer, but it was quiet in the tunnel except for the sibilant shifting of the bats massed over his head, and the faint whisper of the updraft in the ventilation shaft, almost like a song, almost words.

Willie stood, stared up at the portal above, gradually brightening with the coming day. The rain had stopped. He wished he'd had a container of some sort to collect some of it. More than terrified, he was thirsty. In mindless desperation, Willie reached up as far as he could toward the light and shouted, "Help me. Please, somebody help me." Down under the ground nobody answered him, not even his mother. He wondered if she would talk to him when he was dead like her.

Willie yelled and screamed and cried until his raw throat would tolerate nothing beyond a whisper. He shined his lamp up the shaft into the misty morning of the world above until the battery was spent, then threw the useless device up the shaft with all his strength. It narrowly missed hitting him in the head on the way back down. Willie would have thrown it again but he was too tired.

He slumped back to the ground and sat in the mud and filth and wondered how long it would take for him to perish without food or water. He guessed that Brian and Betty would be back when they thought him properly deceased and take all the gold for themselves. His mother was right. He was a fool. Betty would never have feelings for a nothing man like him. Now she would have the money without having to pretend. She would have Brian. He hoped Brian would give her all she deserved.

That thought provoked a chuckle. The chuckle escalated without volition into a laugh. Willie laughed and laughed. It made his throat hurt to laugh. That struck him as funny so he laughed some more until his stomach and sides were sore and he realized he was wetting himself. Willie got very quiet then and wished he'd sat still and quiet all along. Something farther down the tunnel had heard him and was moving again. He could hear the thud and drag of its progress as the tunnel became stifling hot and a dull red glow began to eat away at the shadows around him. Willie would have pulled that dark around him like a blanket to hide in, but it was melting away before the glowing haze that began filling the tunnel now. He could see the front of the old locomotive clearly, and scrambled toward it on all fours, wailing like a crippled hound.

As he crawled, Willie could feel pulses of hot air on his neck and back, like from an open furnace. The ground under him vibrated with footfalls that sounded like trees falling. Willie rolled onto his back and put his hands over his face.

Between his bleeding fingers he looked into the face of his childhood nightmare.

The dragon stood huge above Willie, it's head almost brushing the roof of the tunnel. The bats squeaked and fled like a cloud of burnt leaves up the ventilator shaft. The apparition's breath, like steam from a boiler, hot to pain. Willie closed his eyes, whimpering, curled into a fetal ball, waited to die, praying it would be swift.

The air cooled precipitously. The tunnel was quiet. No talons tore his flesh, No teeth dismembered him. No superheated breath seared his skin. Willie, without lifting his head, opened one eye. Here and there across the floor of the tunnel, small fires burned where some bit of debris had been ignited. Willie moved a hand. Nothing bit it off or crushed it to a pulp. He turned his head and looked up at the man standing beside him.

A tall man, with steam or smoke streaming from his clothes, as if he'd been walking through fire, but a man all the same. Not a dragon. Just a man. "What happened to you?" the man asked, his voice deep and quiet.

Willie tried to speak, couldn't find enough air in him to force out the words. He coughed, inhaled, and tried again, barely a whisper, "I fell."

The man appeared to think that was funny. His laugh, much too loud to be just a man's laugh, but in this dark place, nothing seemed to Willie the way it should.

"Then I'm in the right place," said Tall Man. "Among the Fallen, as Goodmother wished." He watched silently as Willie struggled to sit upright. "What is your name, fallen one?" he said when Willie accomplished the maneuver.

"Willie. Willie Graham."

"What are you doing in this place down under, Willie Graham?"

"I was looking for that," Willie said, pointing to the locomotive.

Tall Man laughed again, shook his head. For a second, a trick of the light made his eyes look full of flames. "I think you were looking for what it carried here."

"You saw the gold?" Willie stammered.

Another laugh, booming, too loud for just a laugh, like thunder before a deluge, "I can smell it, Willie Graham, and now you've told me. It smells more appetizing than you, be assured. I have some good news for you."

"What's that?" Willie asked.

"I'm not going to eat you today." Simon Ryder replied.

THIRTY-THREE

On her way to the post office to check her mailbox, Abigail Trammell met Bernice Abner coming out of Dolf's Market. "Good morning, Bernice, lovely weather for this time of year, isn't it?"

Bernice passed by without so much as a glance or reply in Abigail's direction. Bernice wasn't the only person who had been acting strangely toward her lately, Abigail thought. Their friendly little town wasn't so friendly anymore.

Apart from a couple of advertisements, her mailbox held a notice to pick up a package. She carried it to the lobby and found herself the only customer. Rhonda Shaw sat behind the counter gazing at a sheet of postage stamps bearing the portrait of a deceased rock musician. Rhonda looked up as Abigail came in, waved the stamps in the air, "I preferred it when they used flowers," she said, "I never heard of any of these people."

Abigail laid her notice on the counter. "Says I have a package, Rhonda. I hope it's the book I ordered."

Rhonda disappeared for a moment to fetch the package and left Abigail to ponder the strange encounter with her neighbor. When Rhonda reappeared, it seemed the right size and shape for a book.

"What's wrong with Bernice, today?" Abigail asked, wondering if she should take her neighbor's snub personally.

Rhonda handed over the package. "You mean apart from being Bernice?"

"Thanks," Abigail said, taking possession of her book. "I mean I spoke to her just as I was coming in and she wouldn't even look at me, steamed on down the street as if I were a ghost or something."

Rhonda shook her head. "Bernice has been going to that Crusade thing. She's let that preacher woman get in her head. I wish she were the only one. Half the town has swallowed Barbara Battle's lies."

"What's she telling folks in that tent of hers, beside 'Give me your money'?"

Rhonda glanced around to make sure they were still alone, seemed glad for a chance to vent, "Well, for one thing, she's saying that you are a witch bound for hell."

"That's ridiculous, Rhonda." Abigail couldn't quite swallow her laugh. "There are a half dozen other souls in this town who'd wear that label better than me."

Rhonda kept her stern face, "It isn't funny, Abigail. She's stirring folk up. Not just about you, but those foreigners staying at your place. She says they are the devil's imps come among us to do his bidding. Souleaters, she calls them."

Abigail shook her head in disbelief. "I'm not the only B&B in town. All of us have our share of eccentric guests. Goodness, Rhonda, I'm just running a boarding house, not some kind of coven. Why is Battle singling me out?"

"I don't know," Rhonda said. "You're not from around here. You have your own ways. Some thought you a bit peculiar before all this Crusade nonsense started. You're just an easy target, I suppose."

"What does she need a target for?" Abigail murmured, though she thought she knew.

The Postmaster confirmed her suspicion. "Because it is easier to rouse people to be against something than for something. Because love is harder to come by than hate. Because people will pay money quicker to see something torn down that to watch something built."

"You don't have a very high opinion of our fellow townfolk, do you, Rhonda?"

Rhonda leaned across the counter, lowered her voice to a whisper, as if the walls might hear. "I've seen these people come and go since before you were here, Abigail Trammell. I've seen their mail. I know what they read when nobody's looking over their shoulder. I can tell you that most of them have a mean streak, deep down, and are always and ever looking for an opportunity to express it. Barbara Battle makes vindictiveness look to them like a righteous cause."

Another customer came in and put an end to Rhonda Shaw's confessional. Nobody spoke while Abigail retreated with her package. She was unnerved by the exchange. The sun did not warm the chill she felt inside. The familiar street loomed before her alien and foreboding. Her more-or-less comfortable world was hers no longer.

On the way home, she stopped in Dolf's Market to pick up a quart of half-and-half and two dozen eggs. Dolf was his usual friendly self, but the three other customers in the store managed to find other directions to look as Abigail collected her items. She felt like a ghost, imagined she might actually be invisible to them. The thought occurred that we really don't see the other people around us. We only recognize our own notion of who they are, and if anything breaks that illusion, we have no connection at all.

Dolf took her plastic happily. In the current climate, Abigail wondered if he would have smiled so broadly had she not been spending money in his store.

Leaving the market, she saw the three young hoodlums sitting on a bench across the street. They watched her approaching and as she went by, they laughed at something and one of them sent his empty beer can clattering across the pavement in her direction. A passing truck flattened it before it reached the near curb. She didn't look back to see the three men get up and follow her as she passed Vintage Reads and Town Hall and neared Hemlock House. She didn't see the one with the red beard take a running step into the street and throw the bottle. She felt it strike the back of her head. No pain, just a vast echo somewhere behind her eyes as the world turned to water and night. She didn't see the ground rising to catch her.

Above or below, a light wavered, flickered, flared and ebbed, waxed and waned, but always there, gradually nearing. Abigail didn't know if she were flying or falling toward it, but the light drew her out of her darkness like a swimmer down deep rising toward the surface of a sunlit sea. The dark paled to a dappled glow, like sunlight veiled by leaves, buoying her onward toward the shimmering brightness beckoning, reaching, pulling her until she was there, bursting through into air and breath.

Water. A lake, apparently, where she floated, gazing across the glare at a tree-bound shore. The water was warm. She looked down into it, past her treading arms and saw she was naked. Somehow she didn't think that strange or alarming. She started swimming for the nearest shore, steady smooth strokes with a strength she hadn't felt within herself for years. An unaccustomed joy took hold of her, like coming home. Where the water shallowed, she stood and walked ashore. Sunlight tingled her drying skin. Abigail looked down at her glistening breasts and belly and legs and saw a young body.

Her body. As if every best she had ever been in her life, she still was.

At water's edge, a narrow beach of smooth bronze pebbles sloped gently upward. Underfoot, they felt pleasantly cool, all perfectly round, like all the cannonballs from all the wars ever fought in the Two Worlds come aground on this peaceful shore. When she looked up at the trees beyond, a figure of indeterminate gender stood just within the forest shade, smiling at her.

Abigail felt no shame being seen as she was. The figure held out some sort of robe, the colors of leaf and shadow. The colors changed hue and tone, shifting as the light breeze rippled the garment. Abigail stepped forward and the mysterious bearer slipped the robe over her shoulders and wrapped it close around her, kneeling before her to tie it with a sash that shared its blue with the sky. One by one, her feet were lifted, gently, deftly, and she wore slippers, the color of the pebbles, but infinitely softer.

She looked at the stranger's bird-like face, searched her mind for a question to ask, found too many for her to know which she should speak first. An arm that seemed too long for the body that bore it, stretched out, pointing into the forest. The figure flowed on ahead, losing definition, dissolving into shadow as Abigail followed, becoming more forest with every step.

The apparition led her ever deeper among the trees, now striding, now hardly touching the ground at all, now airborne, one instant womanly in form, the next angular and masculine, next a wispy cloud of going, a glow one moment and a shadow the instant after on the moss-bound path of pebbles, as uniform in form and hue as those on the beach, hardly disturbed by passages light and infrequent. As Abigail hurried after her Guide, unseen birds sang to her music melodious and unfamiliar. Once, not too far off the path, an animal with big ears like a deer lifted her head from browsing to watch as

Abigail passed. Not a deer, though, too light and lean even for a deer, and too tall, with big round eyes that bulged from the thin furred head. As the creature turned, it almost disappeared into the shadows, like a knife blade seen on edge.

After a mile, or perhaps twice that, but not a tiring distance, she lost sight of her guide at a sharp bend in the path, and coming round it, the trees suddenly parted to reveal a clearing of maybe a half-acre, sloping gently up toward more trees, and a green round-topped mountain beyond.

In the center of the clearing, a tree rose taller than the trees of the surrounding forest, broad and spreading as it was tall, with multihued leaves sparkling like gems in the sunlight. In the shade of the tree stood a small house, one or two rooms, stone walled, roofed with wooden shakes. The structure appeared recently built, although the doors and windows were weathered gray, perhaps salvaged from some earlier dwelling that once occupied the site.

A woman stood in the shade of the porch, as if she had been waiting for Abigail's arrival. A moment passed before Abigail recognized her as the same soul who had led her through the wood. As Abigail crossed the yard, the woman stepped down to meet her and held out a hand. "Welcome, to my home," she said, her eyes reflecting all the lights in her guardian tree. "Come in, Sister. We have some time now to talk about why you are here."

Inside the cabin was as bright as out. A single window opened into the shade of the yard. Centering the room, a small table with an irregularly shaped top, apparently sliced from a tree trunk, polished to a satin sheen. The woman set two sky-hued yunomi on the table, gestured for Abigail to sit in one of two cushioned chairs fashioned from sections of twisted rhododendron and vines.

Abigail settled. The woman filled their cups with a dark tea from a bronze teapot. Then she sat, drinking from her little cup, gazing at Abigail with merry green eyes.

Abigail sipped her tea. The taste was none she knew but pleasant, earthy, rich. "None of this is real, is it?" she ventured into the silence.

The woman's voice came musical, almost singing, "Life is as real as we allow it to be, Abigail. We are the dreams that stuff is made of. If we remembered our dreams when we wake, they would change our world beyond recognition. We shouldn't fear that, but we do. That is why we forget, to protect our precious illusions."

"How do you know my name?" Abigail hoped a simple question might draw a simple answer.

The woman smiled, took another sip of her tea before she answered, "You've been reading my book."

"That book talked to me," Abigail murmured, remembering from the world she'd left.

"And it talked to me of you," said the woman. "That book, any book is a window, a door between author and reader. While we are in the book, both of us experience the same time, the same place. A book is a miracle, a joining, a drawing in and a release into other worlds. That book is why you are here now."

"Something hit me," Abigail said.

"Something did," responded the woman, "and loosed you from your world, but the way of the book was still open within you, and brought you to me."

"You wrote Forest Soul?" queried Abigail. "You're Millicent McTeer?"

"I'm Millicent," the woman said lightly, brinking laughter, "McTeer no longer. In this Stream, they call me Flyer."

Abigail remembered her tea, expected it to be cold, but the cup was warm and full when she picked it up. Steam rose from it as she sipped, tickling her nose. "Why here?" she said, "Why am I here?"

"Passing the little while before our Mentor calls you back to your own Stream," Millicent answered, looking more serious now, "and also to receive a gift I'm to share with you."

"Mentor?" Abgail questioned, "Like a teacher?"

"Like the púca," the Flyer laughed, "Like Wendl VonTrier."

"Him," Abigail exclaimed. "I should have known. Everything changed when he showed up."

"It always does," the Flyer said, "Our time's about up. There's something I must give you before you go. Come with me."

The Flyer lead Abigail back out onto the porch where a branch of the jeweled tree by the house extended within reach. "Take a leaf, Abigail. She won't mind."

Abigail reached up and plucked a leaf that changed color when she touched it. The leaf felt cool and hard, but came away readily in her hand, kept shifting color as she held it, wondering.

"Eat it," the Flyer said.

"What?"

"Down the hatch, girl," the Flyer laughed, gesturing toward her mouth.

Tentatively, Abagail tucked it between her lips, laid it gently on her tongue where it instantly melted away to a sweet and spicy infusion, warm, full of voices, whisperings, tiny bells ringing. The Flyer smiled at Abigail through a green haze as the world faded to black.

Thirty-Four

Big Brian Tompkins and his partners in malicious mischief, Red Johnson and Tater Campbell, slipped furtively inside the back door of the Restoration Crusade offices in Drovers Gap. Their faltering jeep had run out of gas before they were out of town. Although nobody was looking for them yet, having not found a witness to their bottling of Abigail Trammell, they were already fugitive from their guilt, and convinced the combined assets of Drovers Gap law enforcement were hot on their heels. Orville Hawk and Wilbur Corvid intercepted them just inside the door.

"We thought you boys might be in another state by now," said Orville.

"Reverend Barbara will not be pleased to see you here," added Wilbur.

"Damned old crate quit on us," mumbled Big Brian. "You've got to hide us."

"We need some money to make it go," offered Red.

Tater just inspected his shoes in silence, as if looking helpless and miserable might inspire someone to deliver him from his mess.

"We don't have to do anything," said Orville.

"You three just need to disappear," added Wilbur

Before the truant trio could summon a reply, Barbara Battle herself came down the hall, like a frigate steaming into battle. "And so they shall," she cheerfully assured all concerned parties. She thrust a fat manila envelope into Big Brian's hands, startling him so that he nearly dropped it.

"There's ten thousand dollars in there, little ones. You've been a great embarrassment to me and I want you to go as far and as fast as that will take you. Your faces will not be seen anywhere near Drover's Gap again."

"We won't get far in that old jeep of Brian's," mumbled Tater, finally finding his voice.

Barbara looked at Wilbur, "Give them the keys to the van." Wilbur looked surprised, then nodded, smiled, and surrendered the keys.

"I promise, we won't come back until everything's died down," assured Red.

"As I said," Barbara repeated with exaggerated patience, "you will not be seen again in this town. We will remember you fondly."

"Can we keep the van, then?" Brian asked, his hope in his voice.

"To the very end, I promise," Barbara said. "Now go."

The miscreants fled, as if there were a prize for whoever cleared the door first.

Barbara and her henchmen watched as the van coughed to life and lurched away down the alley. "Now, she said, "One of you go visit our good friend Omar Longshadow and inform the constabulary that three of our part-time construction workers have robbed our safe and absconded with our van. The other can have some flowers sent to the hospital for Abigail Trammell, bless her apostate heart. Meanwhile, I will see our departed ne'er-do-wells on their way and ensure their disappearance is permanent."

Brian drove, Red sat beside him, and Tater, on his knees behind them, draped his arms over the seat backs. "Sit down back there," Brian barked, "Quit breathing your wet on me like a sick puppy."

Tater obeyed reluctantly. "I can't see back here," he protested.

"You don't need to see, Tatertot." Brian said. "You don't know where we're going."

"Where are we going, Big Brian?" Red ventured.

"Someplace we can spend this money in peace," Brian replied.

"You don't know where we're going," accused Tater, rolling among bundles of Restoration Crusade newsletters as the van rounded a sharp curve.

"I'm going away from Drovers Gap and the law with a bundle of cash in my pocket. If youns don't like that direction, I'll stop and you can walk off to wherever you want to go." After that, Brian concentrated on his driving and his passengers hung on grimly and silent as Quakers in meeting.

A mile outside Drovers Gap the highway began to writhe like a snake, twisting and dropping a thousand feet over the next five miles. On one side of the unshouldered pavement, the mountain loomed steep as a castle wall, and on the other dropped away to a raging, pent-up river. Brian kept glancing in the rear-view mirror, expecting to see the Drover's Gap police cruiser rounding the bend behind them. This morning, the road remained peculiarly devoid of traffic. The only vehicle they met was a Gray Eagle bus that honked as the van crowded the centerline on a curve.

Half-way down the grade, a shadow passed over the road, too close and dark for a cloud. The fugitives paid no attention until a moment later the shadow eclipsed them again.

"What's that?" Brian asked, taking a curve too fast, the van leaning like a ship in a gale.

Red craned his face against the glass and squinted up into the sun. "I see wings. Biguns," he said quietly, as if in church.

"Plane? Helicopter?" said Brian. Behind them Tater scrambled to gain a view.

"I told you to sit down, Tater," Brian yelled again.

"Lord, it's huge," Red said, rolling down his window and putting his head outside, "It ain't no helicopter. It's . . ."

Something banged hard against the side of the van, almost wresting the wheel from Brian's hands. Red slumped back into his seat. A sickly odor filled the van, reminded Brian of when he worked at the slaughterhouse in Macedonia. Tater was screaming in his ear. He looked over at Red. Red didn't say a word. He had no head.

Brian looked back to his road just in time to see a steel guardrail arcing around another curve. The van shuddered with the impact, screamed against the metal barrier until Brian managed to pull away. Too hard, over-compensating as the van lurched across the pavement to carom off the sheer rockface bordering the opposite side of the road. Something came loose and went rattling on the road behind as the van swerved right again. This time, there was no barrier ahead and an instant later, no ground beneath.

Everything that happened next happened very quickly over what seemed to Brian a long time. The nose of the van went down, he saw treetops, the river below coming up fast. More rocks and trees growing upside down, then sky, blue as his mother's eyes, a blur of something with wings like a bat, much too big to be a bat. What was left of Red went flying toward the back of the van and Tater screaming like a banshee. Treetops again and Red smashing into the windshield. Awful noise, like the end of the world, just for an instant, until nothing at all.

After a while that might have been minutes or hours or

years, Brian slowly came alive to mind-shredding pain. Something in his eyes made it hard to see. His right arm wouldn't work. He wiped his face with his left hand which slowly shifted into focus as he looked at it. He wondered where all the blood came from. He couldn't see Tater but at least the boy was quiet. The van rested at an unaccustomed angle. Red was hanging halfway out the passenger window. All Brian could see of him was feet and legs. There was something peculiar about Red that he couldn't quite remember.

More than anything in the world, Brian wanted to get out of that van. It was going to be difficult because he couldn't find his legs. They were hidden from view beneath the crumpled dash. The steering wheel was bent into his belly, which he supposed was why he hurt so much. He wondered if his legs were gone like, yes, he remembered now, like Red's head.

Brian would have called for help, but his mouth was full of something. He could feel it drooling warm down his front beneath his vest. Through the windshield he saw a tangle of pine limbs and branches. The driver's-side window was missing its glass. When Brian turned to look out he could feel a cool breeze and hear the river tumbling somewhere a lot closer than he had meant for it to be today. He could see trees and boulders and Barbara Battle standing a few feet away, looking very pleased with herself.

"Help me," he tried to say, a sputtering mutter that didn't sound at all like words.

"Don't worry, I'll be quick," Barbara said, stepping close, reaching in, patting him gently on the chest. She took the envelope from his vest pocket and stepped back again. "Goodbye, Big Brian," she said sweetly.

He watched like in a dream as Barbara Battle's face grew long and scaley like a lizard's and she opened her mouth and there was fire everywhere. Brian felt the down of his vest melting into his ribs as his eyes went blind from the heat and light. He drew a breath to scream and inhaled flames.

Willie Graham stepped out of the shower and looked at the stranger in his bathroom mirror. He hadn't shaved in three days. He wondered if it might be easier just to grow a beard. Brian had a beard. Betty must like it. Maybe if Willie grew a beard, she might . . . *No. Enough of that.* Willie didn't need his mother to tell him that Betty was only interested in the gold in that buried train. He figured that as soon as they thought him sufficiently dead, she and Brian would be back there to get it.

Willie laughed at his own foolishness and his growing delight at being still alive. Heaven looks after fools and children, his mother used to say. Evelyn hadn't been to visit since his night in the dragon's lair. He should have known. Every treasure hidden in a cave, or in this case, a tunnel, has a dragon to guard it. This one, as far as Willie was concerned, was welcome to keep his gold.

Willie plugged in his razor and commenced to mow his face. He didn't need to hide behind his hair. Willie thought he was done with hiding now. He was a special case. He guessed not many people had seen a dragon face to face. He figured even fewer had come home to tell about it. Not that Willie would be telling anybody. That was one of the conditions the dragon had insisted on when it lifted Willie out of that deep dark hole. Simon Ryder was on a mission and Willie, in gratitude for not being dismembered and devoured, would be Simon's spy and accomplice among the Fallen. That's what Willie had promised, being in no position at the time to argue terms, and now he intended to do no less. Unlike some he could name in Drovers Gap, Willie was a man of his word.

He still wondered how much of what had happened down in the ground was a dream. He was fairly certain the dragon had picked him up and flown him through the dark to deposit him at his own house. He didn't think he could have walked the distance in his condition and was sure nobody would have offered such a filthy specimen a ride.

"You're a dragon-rider now, Willie," Simon said while Willie sat on his front steps gathering his wits and strength to climb up to his door.

"What's a dragon-rider?" Willie asked.

Simon, answering question for question, "Don't you read fantasy novels?"

Willie confessed, "I don't read fiction."

"You live in a small world, then," the dragon said before he flew away, a darkness into darkness.

Clean and dressed, looking like a real realtor again, Willie tucked his wallet into his jacket pocket and prepared to treat himself to breakfast at Home Ground. Betty and Brian would be mighty surprised to see him if they met. On the other hand, if they went back to retrieve the gold without him, an even bigger surprise awaited. He was still trying to decide if he ought to tell Chief Longshadow about the whole business and let justice prevail. But that would involve telling about the dragon, which Willie had vowed not to do, not that any sane and reasonable policeman would believe him. First things first. Maybe coffee and some bacon and eggs and a couple of Doug's good biscuits would inspire him with a plan.

Willie pocketed his keys and was on his way to the front door when he heard the knock. He stopped. Held his breath. He was still trying to decide whether to answer or pretend he was elsewhere when, "Willie? You in there?"

He recognized the voice, opened the door to a distraught and mud-splattered Betty. "Oh, Willie," she gasped, and hugged him like a long-lost lover.

"Hello Betty," he said. "Where's Brian?" He wanted mightily to hug her back.

"I don't know," she said, turning her tear-streaked face up

at him. "Brian's fallen in with that Crusade bunch and we broke up again. He said he'd kill me if I told anybody about the gold or what we done to you, so I went up there to get you out of that hole. That man who lives up around there, I think he said his name was Simon, told me he got you out already and brought you home. I got the Miata stuck on that road and here I am. You may not want to see me but I am purely glad to see you, Willie."

She said all this in one breath without a pause. Willie was impressed with the performance. "You saw Simon?" he queried.

"Yes, he helped me get the Miata unstuck. He's one strong man."

"You don't know the half of it, Betty," Willie said. "You want to have breakfast with me?"

"I'm a mess," she said, looking down at her muddy legs.

"Does that keep you from being hungry?" Willie said, laughing until Betty smiled back at him.

THIRTY-FIVE

Constable Jolene Bear had already made a dozen stops along Main Street, questioning shopkeepers, the old men who manned the benches on the sidewalk in front of Dolf's grocery, any passerby recognizably local who might have witnessed the assault on Abigail Trammell. It was a fool's errand, she figured. Anyone not part of the Crusade coven would have come forward immediately. Not everybody in town was gullible enough to swallow Barbara Battle's vitriol against all associated with Vintage Reads bookstore. Abigail was not the devil's disciple, but a kind and generous citizen of the community, whose only sins were a somewhat pricky disposition, and a bed-and-breakfast inhabited by souls not from around here, which was typical of any of the several boarding houses in town. Battle needed to give her followers an enemy, an accessible target for their war against imaginary evil, and Wendl VonTrier and Abigail Trammell were the most likely candidates she could come up with in Drovers Gap.

Jolene almost passed by Walt Goodwin, his head and arms hidden in a trash bin, a bucket half-full of aluminum drink cans sitting at his feet. Walt was the town's self-appointed watcher. He was on the street at all hours in all weathers. Walt protested that he wasn't homeless, but she had been called to pick him up on several occasions when the altar guild ladies at Saint John in the Wilderness had been startled to find him fast asleep on a pew. A couple of times complaints had come in when Walt was caught watching interactions that were not intended to be public knowledge. Walt, in short, knew most of the untold secrets in Drovers Gap. He just might have seen something, if he could be persuaded to tell it.

She waited until Walt came up from his dive, a crumpled Green Man can in each fist. He smiled triumphantly at her and dropped the cans into his bucket. "Walt, how're youns doing today?" she ventured.

Walt was near-sighted, stood right in her face as he answered, "Ganny I'm right pert, Constable Jolene, to be old and broke down as I am. Who would hear me complain if I wasn't?" Walt seemed to think this funny. Jolene wished he had laughed down wind.

Jolene took a step back, hoped Walt wouldn't follow. "I reckon you've heard about Abigail Trammell getting hurt. We're trying to find out what happened to her, so I'm asking around town if anybody saw anything."

Walt chewed on his beard while he made up his mind about answering. Finally, "I didn't see aught, Constable Jolene, but ganny I know who done it."

"That would be a big help to me, Walt." Jolene said sincerely.

"You won't tell I told ye? That'n would kill me if he found out."

"It's between us and God, Walt," she said, "A cop is as good as a priest to keep a secret. What do you know?"

Walt shook his head like he didn't quite believe her, but he leaned close and whispered, "I didn't see, but I got ears. I heard 'em talking about what they'd done. They was already wishing they hadn't. Figured you bunch would be coming atter 'em.

"Who did you hear, Walt?

"There was three. Didn't see 'em, like I said, but I knowed the voices. Red Johnson said he throwed that bottle. Big Brian said he shoulda throwed it harder or not at all."

"Brian?"

"Brian, you know, that mechanical feller what's sweet on Betty down to Mountain Realty."

Constable Jolene Bear and Sergeant Chuck Priestley crossed Doris Thompkin's muddy yard, stepped up onto the porch, as an unseen canine presence beneath the floor growled a half-hearted warning. The beast knew it was outnumbered and chose discretion as the better part of valor. Sergeant pounded on the door, shouted, "Police. We need to talk to Brian."

After a prolonged silence, during which the emaciated hound appeared from beneath the porch and slunk out-of-sight around the corner of the house, the officers heard muffled stir and shuffle from within. Jolene knocked more gently and called, not so loud as her partner, "Doris? It's Jolene. Sergeant Priestley is with me. Is Brian here?"

A click of the lock, and the door parted a crack. The hurt and haggard face of Brian's mother appeared in the opening. "He ain't been home since day afore yestiddy, Jolene. What's that boy got hisself into now?"

The door opened a bit wider. Jolene saw the black eye and bruised cheek. "Doris, did Brian hit you?" she queried.

Doris lifted a hand to her battered face, as if surprised to find it injured. "We settle our difference at home, don't you know. I'd not want the Law into it."

"Doris," Jolene said, speaking more softly yet, "We could give you some protection from him, if you'd let us."

"Brian'd find a way to get me back. You know that. Besides, it was my fault. He wanted my gummit check and I wouldn't tell him where I put it. He's gone now. He'll be all repenting and kind when he comes back."

Until the next time, Jolene thought. Chuck, who had been standing respectfully silent during the exchange between the women, ventured in a more conciliatory tone, "Where is your son now, Ma'am?"

"Half-way to hell by now, if I'm lucky," Doris retorted, unable to damp her rage any longer. "He's gone with a pair of that Barbara Battle's tribe. They won't bring him home until they've hurt somebody."

Chief Omar Longshadow was in a bad mood when he exited the Restoration Crusade offices and headed for his pickup. He asked himself if he would have found the robbery victims more believable if anybody but Barbara Battle and her deplorable duo had been robbed. How had three extraordinarily incompetent thieves managed to gain such easy access to the company safe and vehicle? According to Battle, the safe had been open because they were preparing a cash deposit to cover the payroll on the construction site. She had been called out of the office just for a few moments to talk to a supporter in reception, and when she returned, the cash was missing. She couldn't recall the supporter's name, there were so many of them these days, but the receptionist would know, and she had gone home early. Omar wrote down her name and address. He would certainly follow up.

Either Hawke or Corvid had inadvertently left keys in the van; they couldn't decide which of them might have been negligent there. Brian's much-abused jeep was parked just around the corner. The fuel gauge rested on empty. Omar was just settling into the diver's seat when the call came from his officers.

"Brian isn't at home. His mother says he left two days ago with a couple of Battle's minions. She hasn't heard from him since," Jolene reported. "You think they might be our thieves?"

"According to Battle and her henchmen, they are indeed," Omar said. "Something's not right about this, though. It all went too easy. Almost like they had a helping hand."

"You think it's a set-up?" Jolene asked.

"More like a cover-up," Omar said, but all I have now is notions. We need to find those lads and have a little heart-to-heart."

"We'll come on back in, then," Jolene answered. Chuck said something to her. Omar couldn't make out the words, then Jolene again, "Unless you want us to keep looking for them."

"We'll let the Sheriff and Highway Patrol do the looking for us. They'll be running now, already a long way from Drovers Gap if they're smart. The Crusade van will be easy to spot if they're on the road. Come back to town. We'll compare notes and decide what next."

Jolene's voice garbled a bit. "Then . . . out."

Omar was about to pull out into the street when the other call came in from Fire and Rescue that totally rearranged the rest of his day.

"We've found your stolen van, what's left of it," a state trooper told him over the radio.

"What about the occupants?" Omar asked.

"Not so much left of them," came the curt response.

When Omar arrived at the accident scene, on a narrow twisting highway hung on the side of a mountain that was wasn't designed to host a road, he found one of the two lanes closed and troopers directing alternating traffic on the other. Two ambulances, a firetruck, and several state and county government vehicles were aligned along the guardrail in the closed lane. A sheriff's deputy directed him to park behind a Forest Service truck full of fire-fighting equipment.

"Afternoon, Chief," the deputy said as Omar disengaged from his pickup. "Somebody's contrived to make our day interesting."

"Tell me about it," Omar said.

"A trucker reported a wildfire. The woods are soaked after last night's rain, and the fire had pretty much died down by the time a crew got here. The wreck's down there by the river. That's where the fire was." The deputy pointed at the muddy tracks just beyond the far end of the guard rail, "Looks like there's where they went over."

"They?" How many occupants were there?"

"Two or three maybe, according to the medical examiner. It's hard to tell under the circumstances. She's got a forensics team working down there now."

Omar peered over the guard rail to the river below. He could see eight or ten individuals in hazmat suits moving among the trees. Smoke was still rising from the blackened area around the residue of the van. Blue tarps, more than three, were stretched on the ground at various points nearby. Omar supposed they sheltered human remains.

Before he spoke, the deputy read his question on his face. "Everything scattered, Chief. Bones stripped and gnawed, like some big animal's been at them. I hope they was killed before they got eaten." Omar didn't answer. He was watching the activity below and remembering. The deputy paused, kept talking, "What do you reckon it was that would just gobble a body up like that, Chief? Maybe a big cat, do you think?"

"I don't think it was any kind of animal that belongs around here," Omar said, "But this isn't its first kill in our neighborhood."

"You've got a big problem, then," the deputy murmured.

Behind them traffic moved slowly past, uphill for a few

minutes, then down. Passengers in the cars pressed curious faces against glass, trying to see what disaster they had avoided. All they saw was a row of orange jackets and vests ranged along the guard rail, their wearers staring down the sheer drop at the evening news.

An hour passed that seemed to Omar like a day. His mind asked him questions he didn't want to answer. A light rain misted down by the time black bags were hoisted slowly up the slope and loaded into the ambulances. It took longer yet for the rescue and investigation personnel to make their way up the treacherous mountainside, now slicked with renewed rain.

Omar found the medical examiner in the process of stowing her equipment and gear into her car. "Rita, can you give me anything here?" he said.

She turned, showed him a bleak face. "I can tell you there were three people went down the mountain in that van, although the remains were all strewn about outside the vehicle. It was an unnaturally hot fire. Who knows what they were carrying that was so volatile. Forensics didn't find any traces of an accelerant, but those bones were cooked, striated. By all appearances the victims had been dismembered and eaten. Does any of this sound familiar to you?"

"I'm afraid it does," Omar murmured.

"Here's the clincher," Jill continued, "We found no skulls. Apparently, all three victims were decapitated."

"So no chance of dental records," Omar said.

"We'll get DNA analysis. That should give us something. Right now, I'd say it's safe to assume they were male adults, probably under fifty years of age. Ask me tomorrow, and I can tell you more."

Thirty-Six

Abigail floated in the dark that felt like water, warm, buoyant. It didn't seem to hinder her breathing, but she wasn't sure she was breathing. She watched the tree dimming, fading into night above her, and felt the light from below, like sunlight, on her back. A drum beat softly in her head, slow, steady. After a time, Abigail realized she was listening to her own pulse as the water or air or whatever she floated in began to pale gradually until the sky above was bright again, coalescing around a shadow that became a face that, as she watched with detached fascination, became Wendl VonTrier.

"Ah, you have returned to us at last," he murmured and took her cold hand in his warm one. She could feel the heat of his life in her stiff fingers, flowing from her hand up through her arms into her chest, expanding, ringing in her head and through her whole body until she was brimmed with awakening like a glass slowly becoming full of rich red wine with not one drop spilled over.

When the words finally filtered down from her brain to her mouth, Abigail whispered, "How long?" her dry lips shaping the words with slow hesitant care, as if she spoke them for the first time.

"Three days," Wendl said cheerfully. "You needed the rest."

She gazed at the question lying unsaid down in her mind. While she considered how to bring it up to the level of speech, Wendl answered, "Your assailants are no longer with us. They were consumed in their spite."

"Dancing in the dragon's mouth," Abigail said quietly, as words began to come with more natural ease.

"You saw, then?" queried the púca.

"I saw the Flyer," said Abigail, inhabiting herself fully now, "I ate of her tree, and dreamed the dragon. We have met the enemy and she is Barbara Battle."

Wendl pulled up a chair and sat beside the bed, "Chief Longshadow will be wanting to talk to you shortly," he said. "Will you tell him your dream?"

"I shall tell him what I know," Abigail declared.

Wendl stood, smiled, squeezed her hand, and again she slept.

Barbara Battle stood in the empty Restoration Cathedral, gazing at the stars' refracted gleam through the vaulted glass above her head. Tomorrow night the space would be thronged by her followers. Here, she would seal her spell over their minds and own their very souls, she had no doubt. Those she deemed worthy, she would send abroad to search out her enemies, expose any who opposed her purpose, and spread her message to the desperate and deluded. Any among her flock who did not meet her measure would feed her hunger more directly, like those three rubes in the van down by the river. There was nothing unsuitable about this lesser world that fire and burning could not remedy.

And when all Shadow was hers, and she had tired of the taste of Fallen blood, perhaps she would return to Trier and bury that witch Wandalena beneath the stones of her cursed abbey. Musing thus on the fate of worlds and dragons, she loosed her inner fire and expanded her substance to manifest her true form and Badb Catha, Battle Crow, the first dragon, towered high and mighty in the trembling air, as two dark figures rushed forward between the pews.

"Careful!" cried Orville Hawke.

"Don't," shouted Wilbur Corvid.

But it was too late. The dragon threw back her head and roared her exultation. The vaulted glass shattered and rained down around her like broken stars.

The devious duo cowered under their brief cases until the thunderous descent trailed into an occasional clink and tinkle. When they looked up, Barbara Battle stood before them, her fire confined behind her eyes.

"You will fix this," she said evenly.

"It can't be done in a day," said Orville.

"We will need more money," said Wilbur.

"We will meet tomorrow as planned," Barbara said pleasantly. "We will show the people what desecration our enemies have wrought upon our holy space. Those who love us will gladly sell their houses and children if need be to give us the funds we need."

"But without a roof?" murmured Wilbur.

"It might rain," ventured Orville.

"I am the Dragon," Barbara said. "It wouldn't dare."

Everyone within five miles of Drovers Gap heard the roar like a low-flying jet that ruptured the silence of an otherwise clear and pleasant evening. The more curious and excitable residents abandoned their supper tables and ran outside into their yards in anticipation of some disaster worthy of a televised Special Report. Up on the ridge, clearly visible from the town, the lights in the Restoration Cathedral, which had been illuminating the mountaintop for the past three evenings, were extinguished, although several minor flickers, small brush fires, perhaps, scattered about the site. Warren and Omar Longshadow stood on their front porch, hands in pockets, gazing up at Ravensbeak Ridge.

"Reckon an armed drone crashed into Battle's basilica?" Warren mused, glancing wryly at his son.

Omar, still watching the lights fluttering about the cathedral site, shook his head. "This town couldn't be that lucky," he whispered to himself. He reached for the cell phone on his belt, but the device came to life before he had it in his hand. He swiped the screen and barked, "Longshadow."

"Chief?" Jolene's voice, "Chuck just got a call from the Restoration people. Trouble up there."

"What else from that crew?" Omar said. "We could see it from here."

He could hear Jolene take a breath before she spoke, "Nobody hurt, apparently, but they claim somebody set off a bomb in the building."

"Call the sheriff," Omar said. "County will want this one. "I'll meet you two up there." He stepped inside the house, took his hat and jacket from the rack beside the door. Hesitated, retrieved his side arm before he emerged again into the night. Over his shoulder, he called to his father, who still stood on the porch, staring at the mountain, "Save me some stew, Dad."

"I ain't that hungry, son," Warren called back as Omar unlocked his pickup and slid behind the steering wheel, "You be careful, now."

"I'll so be," Omar hollered back before he slammed the door and put his keys to the ignition. He had the truck on the road before it registered that it was the first time in a long while his father had told him to be careful in his duties.

Omar found the town's two fire trucks and the EMC van ahead of him as he left town. He drove close behind along the twisting road up Ravensbeak Ridge. The Restoration Cathedral grounds were lit like a sports stadium, but the Cathedral itself loomed dark against the night sky, the remaining shards of the transparent roof flaring and flickering in the lights from below. Barbara Battle and her doleful duo stood out front like royalty receiving guests. Omar's sergeant and constable pulled in just behind him as he parked his pickup. He supposed the Sheriff's crew wouldn't be far behind.

The fire brigade commenced pulling out hoses and arraying their equipment, but it quickly became apparent there was little in the way of fire to engage, apart from a scatter of small blazes among the shrubbery, apparently ignited by falling debris.

"It doesn't smell like a bomb," Omar observed to his collegues as they approached Battle and her cohorts. He had done his military service with a demolitions crew, and was well acquainted with explosions.

"Something smells peculiar, though," Constable Jolene said, wrinkling her nose.

"Sulfur," said the sergeant.

"What's that?" Omar said.

"Sulfur," repeated Chuck. "My dad kept bees when I was a kid. We'd stack the empty hives and burn sulfur to cleanse them after a mite infestation."

"Hello, Sheriff," said Barbara, as they reached the door. They could see hand-held lights flashing against the walls inside as the fire personnel searched for a spark to justify their presence. "Shouldn't you be out there arresting the people who did this?" she added with a sardonic smirk. Omar thought she seemed to be enjoying the show, not playing the part of a victim at all.

"First," said Omar, "we need to determine precisely what's been done."

"A bomb, obviously," said Orville Hawke.

"We could have all been killed," added Wilbur Corvid.

Figures in bulky hazmat suits began trooping out of the building. Omar spoke to their chief, a friend of his, "Can I get in there tonight to take a look?"

"Sorry, Omar, It ain't safe for you. We don't know how unstable the remains of the roof could be. It might come down anytime. We'll cordon the site and assess it in the morning. Come back then and we'll take a look together."

Omar was inclined to argue but county law enforcement and emergency vehicles began pulling into the parking lot, ending the conversation. It was, after all, their jurisdiction, and the thought crossed Omar's mind that his future might be simpler if he allowed them their own headaches.

In the early hours of the following day, before the first hint of dawn outlined the ridgetops east of Drovers Gap, Badb Catha, aka Barbara Battle prowled restlessly about her lair deep inside Ravensbeak Ridge, blasted out of the mountain by her own breath and will. Not even the Associates knew of this place. Hawke and Corvid were not the only ones who kept secrets. As soon as the fiasco at the Cathedral died down, she had dispatched her two familiars to fetch more gold from their stash. Time and again, she had tried to pry the location from them, but they claimed it was a place sequestered in some obscure dimensional fold attuned only to their perceptions, so impossible to take her there. She often considered roasting the mystery out of them, but if they were, as they claimed, the embodied lock and key, she wouldn't risk spoiling the spell.

Once she tried to follow them, wrapped in a cloaking spell, hovering silently above the treetops as they made their way through the forest around Potters Shoals just west of Warwoman Ridge. She thought they were getting near the place, could feel the tension in the air that always tugged at her senses near a Threshold, when they passed behind a large tree that blocked them from view for a second . . . two seconds . . . three . . . and they were simply gone. They had disclosed the existence of their hoard voluntarily one day when she railed at her lack of funds, and they had never denied her demands for cash, so she had allowed them their secret. But one day soon, she meant to force a revelation. They were useful to her now, but less than irreplaceable as time went by. Other more powerful allies would be drawn to her forces as she revealed her true nature to these fallen creatures who possessed no powers they had not stolen from nature, who fouled their world with their insatiable desires for things that were burdensome and unnourishing to them. In the end, these Fallen would nourish her. They would be dragonbread.

She looked around her sanctum. In the wall opposite, each displayed in its own niche, were the heads she had collected so far. Lewis Redding. He was special. He was her first kill among the Fallen. The other three had names of their own, she supposed. She hadn't bothered to find out. They hadn't even tasted good.

Wendl Von Trier was busy with a pair of daytripper customers, suggesting titles informative of local ghosts, when Willie Graham opened the door to Vintage Reads and slipped inside, his briefcase clutched in front of him with both hands as if he were bearing treasure. Wendl nodded at him over the haunt hunters' shoulders. Willie detached one hand from his burden long enough to raise a timid wave, then immediately seized the briefcase again. He pretended to browse books he looked at without seeing until Wendl had dispatched his customers with three books by local authors who specialized in tales of Drovers Gap's dead and fled.

"Hello, Friend Willie," said Wendl. "You look like you're carrying the weight of the world there."

Willie set his briefcase down and opened it. "I've brought your maps back." Almost in a whisper, he added, "Not in pristine condition, I'm afraid." Wendl lifted the folio from the case and laid it on the counter. Willie, watching Wendl's face as the púca leafed slowly through the sheets, confessed "I had . . . difficulties."

Wendl gazed at each creased and mud-stained map until it shown clear and fresh again, before turning to the next. Willie waited silently, his hands clasped before him like a contrite sinner until Wendl closed the cover and smiled. "No harm done, Willie Graham. Did you find your treasure among your difficulties?"

"I found . . ." Willie began, then stood, mouth agape, searching his brain for some completing word that wouldn't compromise his vow of secrecy.

"Well, you've been found, at least," Wendl said, slipping the map folio out of sight beneath his counter. "I'm grateful I could assist you."

Willie closed his briefcase, considered for a moment whether to flee back into the ordinary world or to continue his quest. Finally, he summoned up a timid query, "Do you have any books on dragons?"

"You mean fairytales," Wendl said, prolonging Willie's agony.

"No, I mean for real," Willie whispered from a face rapidly shading toward crimson.

"Dragons don't exist in the for real world, I'm told by all

who think they know," Wendl said, keeping his laugh behind his face.

"What about the really-real world?" Willie said, finding a level of persistence he hadn't known he possessed.

Wendl gazed at him for a long moment, as if reading his mind. "In that context," he said after the silence, "I believe there are at least two of them presently among the Fallen."

THIRTY-SEVEN

Rain. Falling from the sky in swirling murmurations of misty drops. Dripping from needles and branches, landing on last autumn's curled untrodden leaves with percussive clicks and splats. Music unheard by any human ear, but not unheard. Heaven's tears, gathering in rivulets to fill the singing creeks, brimming the air with conversations between water and stone and the everlistening and everwatchful trees.

A single tree, bound to its place, sees little, hears little, knows little, but a forest, tall and broad as the mountain, hears all, sees deep, and knows everything. The message the falling rain has gleaned from the weeping air, gets taken in by leaf and spine and bark, transmitted through twig and branch, limb and trunk down to labyrinthine root and fungi laced among rock and soil, tree to tree across that deeply dark where words don't go. A single tree is just a thought. A forest is a mind.

Eventually, the intelligence delivered by the rain filters down to Simon Ryder in his sequestery, where he has been waiting and listening now for weeks, a span of infinitesimal duration to a creature for whom youth lasts a thousand years.

The rain has washed from the night air the faintest touch of the forests' oldest nemesis, the unmistakable sulfuric trace of dragonbreath.

The dragon stirs, casts about until he finds a seep-fed puddle of water, breathes gently into it. The water boils and roils briefly then settles and clears and Simon sees the inscrutable visage of Goodmother Wandalena reflected in its surface.

The Old One is here and near and has shown her true form among the Fallen, Simon projects at the makeshift seerbowl.

After a moment, her thought returns to him from Otherworld, *Will you be able to take her?*

He replies immediately, *I can but try, Goodmother. In this Shadow, there can be only one dragon.*

The Goodmother's reflection actually smiles, *Then I will pray Simon Rider proves the one.* The smile fades. *Lugh is there to help, have you need,* she adds. A draft ripples the surface of the puddle and it is mere water again, troubled to faint fluorescence by its briefly simultaneous existence in both the worlds.

Orville Hawke and Wilbur Corvid stood in extended argument before the gaping mouth of the abandoned railway tunnel that opened into the Lost Forty, that phantom plot of ground between the mountains hidden for generations behind a spell woven by some anonymous Confederate charm spinner. Though unseen and barely remembered, stories persisted, told by few and believed by none who heard them, about a Confederate cabinet member's wife from New Orleans, a woman of unverifiable ancestry, who had disappeared the acreage to protect the hiding place of the last of the Confederate treasury. In variations of the tale, it was not the wife, but the unwilling mistress of the cabinet official who had bought her freedom with the spell.

Whether any of the legends spoke to historical fact, the guardian enchantment had held fast for a century and a half, not because it was a particularly good spell- Hawke judged it the work of a marginally adept amateur -but simply because none had ventured to test it. The surrounding land being too steep to farm or log, nobody knew precisely where to look for the forty acres, or even missed them. Over time, stories about vanished land and hidden treasure began to filter through the coves and along the creeks, but they were counted by all hearers as just tales to shorten long winter nights around a fire.

Recently, though, the barrier had been breached with some regularity by Orville and Wilbur, and the spell had begun to fray around the edges. They had discovered several entry portals on their commutes and no longer required the services of Mountain Air to gain access. But now that at least three humans knew of this place, the conjuration was in tatters and very soon the Lost Forty would be lost to none who happened upon it.

"Let's leave now," Wilbur Corvid complained. "The whole place stinks of dragonbreath."

"Not our dragon, either," murmured Orville Hawke, staring into the black void resembling an open mouth in the face of the amazed mountain.

"Can there be two?" Wilbur speculated. "Where would it have come from?"

Orville rustled his feathers into a shrug, "The Goodmother must have sent it. She thinks we are not doing our job."

"Well," Wilbur said, not quite meeting his associate's gaze. "We haven't exactly."

Orville bristled further, "No, Mister Corvid, we are not quite exactly in the service of the Abbey. In truth, we never have been. We pursue our missions as means to secure our fortune, but along the way to enriching ourselves, we contrive to accomplish the Abbey's ends. As long as the Goodmother sees the results she sought, she doesn't enquire about our activities or our profits."

"She wants Badb Catha contained," replied Wilbur. "But the Battle Crow is too strong for us."

"Then, my friend," Orville said, pointing to the tunnel entrance, we'd best grab our gold in there and scurry away before Wandalena finds out."

"I'm going to the post office, Willie," Betty said as she slipped into her coat and reached for her purse. "I'll stop by Home Ground and grab a carry-out for lunch. Can I get you anything?"

Willie Graham, engrossed in the tax returns just received from his accountant, mumbled without looking up from his desk, "What are you having?"

"Today's special. Bacon and spinach quiche."

Willie finally lifted his gaze from his figures, launched a genuine smile, "Sounds delicious," he said. "I'll take one of those, too. Get some money from petty cash. I'm buying."

He sat watching her as she crossed the street. He wondered if the time was ripe to confess that he loved her. Betty had never quite become his girlfriend, but their shared misadventures had made them friends. Willie wanted Betty in his life for the duration. He suspected the feeling was mutual. Maybe, he thought, today, while they were eating quiche together, he might ask her to marry him.

Betty disappeared into the post office, and Willie was still staring at the scene she had just occupied, when a figure came walking purposefully down Main Street. Willie recognized the man immediately. He held his breath, watched with some trepidation as Simon Ryder came straight to his door. Willie was standing behind his desk, wishing he were somewhere else, when the dragon stepped inside.

"Hello, Willie Graham," Simon said pleasantly. "How are you doing since last we met?"

"Pretty well, thanks to you," Willie said. "Nobody's thrown me down a hole lately." Remembering, he queried, "Did you . . .?"

Ryder shook his head. "That wasn't me. I'm here to ask a favor, though."

"If I can," Willie replied, caution in his voice. He had a feeling that any request from a dragon was likely to be highly inconvenient. This dragon, however, he was indebted to. He would not refuse.

"Fed Ex will deliver a package to you. I need you to put it in a safe place for me. Don't open it. Don't tell anyone you have it. At the proper time, I will instruct you what to do with it."

"That's all?" queried Willie, mystified, intrigued.

"If it isn't an inconvenience," Ryder said. "Another small favor, if I may. Can you tell me if there's a qualified cabinetmaker in town?"

Willie thought for a moment. "There's Luke Armstrong. He just opened up a shop. He's been doing some work for Abigail Trammell up at Hemlock House. She swears by him. He does general carpentry, too. Abigail says he can make anything."

"Then he's just the man I need for my job," Ryder said. "Where's his shop?

Neil Redding scarcely heard the voice over the wail of the electric planer. He turned off the machine and looked up at the dark figure standing in the doorway of the shop. The man repeated, "Is Lugh about?"

"Luke's out on an installation," Neil informed the stranger. He glanced at the big clock on the wall above the door. "He should be back any time now. You can come back in about half an hour, or you can maybe catch him down at Vintage Reads, or just call him on his cell." Neil recited the phone number. "There's a card on the desk there," he added, pointing to a rack of cards and brochures.

The tall man stepped closer. His coat, made of some heavy rough-woven material, was almost as dark as his face, and smelled like the man had been standing close to a fire. "What are you working on there?"

"Making a door for a new room at Hemlock House," Neil said, standing back to give the stranger a view. Neil was proud of his work.

The stranger stretched out a hand and swept it palm down over the door, without quite touching. A flash of surprise flickered across his face, "That's a Throughdoor," the stranger said, leaning down for a closer inspection. "Did your boss teach you this?

Neil, himself surprised at the man's perception, replied, "I can't spell the wood yet. Luke does that, but he taught me how to do the joinery." The stranger nodded, still gazing at the nearly completed door. Unsettled by the scrutiny, Neil confessed, "I still have a lot to learn."

"About joinery or conjuring?" the dark man said, glancing up and tossing a smile.

"About joinery," Luke responded. "Luke hasn't trusted me to learn spells and charms."

Dark Man looked back at the door-in-progress. "From the looks of this, you've been a good student so far. Keep it up and one day soon you will shape weirdings as well as you do wood."

Wondering at the strange turn of conversation, Neil gazed

silently at his project. When he looked up again, he was alone. A thin swirl of smoke hung in the air that smelled slightly of sage and sulfur.

***

Abigail Trammell considered she felt remarkably well after her ordeal, except for a headache nagging at nuisance level on the outskirts of her day. Her neighbor, Bernice Abner, insisted on driving her home from the hospital, which was a nuisance of another kind. Abigail reckoned a good walk might have done her head more good.

As she expected, her gossipy neighbor plied her with questions non-stop the whole way, trolling for details in hopes of being the first to hear and tell.

"No, I didn't see who threw the bottle," Abigail replied to the repeated query after pretending three times not to hear, "I didn't even know it was a bottle until I woke up in the hospital and Chief Longshadow told me what had happened."

Bernice stopped to let a family cross the street in front of Dolf's Market, waved to the mother, whom she knew, and drove on. "Ain't it awful, though, what happened to them poor boys what done it?" she said without taking her eyes from the road ahead.

"I didn't know it was settled who attacked me," Abigail responded, her annoyance creeping into her voice as she wearied of the interrogation.

"Well, Walt Goodwin heard 'em talking of it," Bernice babbled on oblivious, tickled to be able to inform one so close to the event. "He's been telling it around to everybody since they stole that van and got burned up alive in it. I know they was bad boys, but I wouldn't wish such a demise on the wickedest person I know." Bernice so caught up in her speech that she almost drove right past Hemlock House.

Abigail braced her hands on the dash against the sudden

stop. She manufactured a smile, reached to open the door, murmured, "Thanks for the ride, Bernice."

As she stepped from the car, Bernice called after her, "Some are saying it wasn't an accident."

Abigail turned, peered back at Bernice's shadowed form, "I never thought it was an accident. They meant to hit me, Bernice."

"I meant, no accident that them boys got burnt up," Bernice clarified, clutching the steering wheel as if she might need to flee for her life, "Some are saying there was a curse put on the three of 'em."

Disbelief on her face and in her voice, Abigail exclaimed, "Bernice Abner, surely you don't believe in such as that."

Bernice wouldn't look at her neighbor, continued clinging to her steering wheel as if the car was all that held her to the world, "There be more than a few who do believe. That's what Battle's teaching 'em up at the Cathedral. You just be careful, Abigail Trammell."

Abigail shut the door and walked toward her house without a word or backward glance. She heard gravel crunch as Bernice's Prius pulled away and was glad to be alone.

THIRTY-EIGHT

Simon Ryder walked along Main Street, past the bank with a sign on the door that promised this branch would be closed in three weeks, but that banking services would be conveniently offered at a branch eight miles distant in the county seat. Just beyond a new restaurant with a fancy sign, a bistro with pretensions, he came to Vintage Reads. Wendl VonTrier looked up from his counter, waved through the glass as if expecting him. Ryder opened the door and stepped inside.

"Hello, púca," he said cheerfully. "This little town seems populated with as many morphons as humans. You probably know already whom I've come seeking."

"I would rather hear you say it," Wendl replied, smiling as if they were friends. "We already have our resident dragon, so I assume you've come for a fight."

"Not with you, VonTrier, unless you've taken old Battle Crow's side. I need converse with Lugh."

"You know which side we're on, Simon, or we'd have felt your fire before we beheld your face," Wendl said. "Luke Armstrong is building some shelves on the Otherworld side of our store, in case Babd Catha decides to burn the place down." He pointed toward the ranks of shelves. "Go down the third aisle. You'll see the seam just past the travel section."

"Is the Separation so far unraveled," queried Ryder, "That one can open way through wherever?"

"We're in the Thin here," Wendl said. "And we have a galère. That makes it easier."

"Too easy," retorted Ryder, "Especially for wickeds like the Crow."

"Can you take her back over?" queried the púca.

"So the Goodmother wills," answered the dragon. "Need be, can I count on your aid?"

"So Goodmother wills," responded Wendl. "Why else are we here?"

Midway past a section of guides for hiking trails and assorted Appalachian tourist destinations, Ryder spied the seam between the worlds, a line in the air so fine that any eye not trained to transitions would never have seen it. No other customers were in the store to note his transference, so he simply flattened, turned himself on edge and slipped through.

The view on this side of the Separation looked pretty much as the other. Two rows of bookshelves, so far empty of books. One set of shelves was still a work in progress.

A door at the end of the row, which in the lesser world would have opened into a Drover's Gap alley paralleling Main Street, here gave a view of a yard bounded by green conifers and steep mountains rising close beyond to a sky blue enough to taste. Ryder didn't see Lugh, but he could hear his hammer pounding. Even in this true realm, making required work.

The hammer fell silent and Lugh was watching expectantly as Simon stepped outside.

"So you decided to come visit our little hamlet among the Fallen. Word of your arrival preceded you. We wondered how long you would stay hidden under your mountain. I trust you veiled your presence from the Battle Crow more effectively than you have from us."

Simon laughed, convincingly human, "If she detected my presence, she has been too timid to acknowledge it."

"She hasn't been shy with Drover's Gap, I'm afraid." Luke said, laying aside his hammer. "Goodmother told us you might effect a remedy. What do you need from me in that cause?"

"I need you to make for me a bindingbox," Simon said.

Luke lifted a brow. "Is that all, then?"

"Simple enough, it would seem," Simon said. "That talented youngster at your shop could make a box."

"He could make the box, if I gave him the joinery," said Luke, spreading his hands, "but a binding spell, especially one strong enough to contain the first dragon, hasn't been tried on this world, and has obviously been broken in the other."

Simon stretched out his arm and pointed away above the trees. "Time enough will wear away those mountains and the strongest spell. Can you do it?"

"I will if I can," Luke said, "But I'll need a key to lock it."

"I have it here, from Goodmother's own hand," Simon reached into his jacket pocket and held out a small leather bag. Luke took it and emptied into his upturned palm a shiny object the size and shape of a robin's egg, but transparent as water and smooth and cool as glass. The scene around reflected in its depths as clean and sharp as on the retina of an eye.

"Don't admire it too long, or you'll be taken in," Simon said as Luke regarded the stone in his hand.

Luke swept it back into the bag and dropped it into his vest pocket. "When do you need it?" he asked, all levity aside now.

"I would not rush you in such work, but the need is dire. Could I have it in five days?" Simon said.

"The Crow is ready to devour this whole town," Luke said solemnly, "by all the gods, you shall have it in three."

After considerable argument and speculation, with much trepidation, Orville Hawke and Wilbur Corvid gestured their cellphone lights on and entered the tunnel. An acrid sulfurous haze lingered in the air as they followed the abandoned rails. Wilbur kept glancing back at the half circle of sunlight retreating behind them.

"Dragon's been in here. What if it comes back?" he whined. "We won't be Hawke and Corvid, we'll be roast turkey."

"Stop your moaning and hurry up," Orville snapped. "A few minutes is all we need. Don't slow us down."

Wilbur coughed as they shuffled along. The lights from their phones were dimmed by the fog thickening as they progressed. Not soon enough, the abandoned locomotive glinted faintly in the gloom.

Orville played his light over the machine, surprised. "It's all cleaned it up like new. as if the dragon planned to drive it away."

"Maybe the thief needs it to carry off what's left of our gold." Wilbur murmured.

"I doubt it," Orville said. "It would have a lifting charm as good as ours. Only three bars left. Under spell they wouldn't weigh more than five or six pounds. We could fly out of here with that."

Wilbur swept his light across the roof of the tunnel. "I don't see any opening up there. It's blocked up the ventilator shaft. It means to trap us."

Orville climbed up into the cab of the locomotive. "Not if we grab and go."

Wilbur peered after his cohort, "Hand it down then and let's be out of here."

Wilbur could hear Hawke scrambling about in the engine cab for too long. "It's gone." Orville said finally. "The gold's been moved."

"I think we should move ourselves, then," Wilbur

whispered.

"Not until we find the gold," Orville hissed. "A dragon wouldn't stash its hoard outside its lair. The gold is here someplace."

"You find it, then," Wilbur shouted as he turned to flee. "I'm leaving."

A shape loomed out of the darkness, blocking the tunnel. Wilbur could feel the heat emanating from it. A voice rolled and volleyed like thunder inside the mountain, "Don't leave now. It's dinnertime." Then there was fire all around.

Barbara Battle was in a foul mood as she gazed out upon the crowd gathering in the Restoration Cathedral parking lot. She had not slept at all well the night before. Dreams of a dragon come to usurp her place had left her tired and on edge. She kept telling herself she needn't worry. The only Elderdragon left with power to challenge her was Simon Ryder, and he would be sleeping on Otherworld for years yet. Barbara figured if Goodmother Wandalena had discovered his lair, he would likely awaken in the dungeon beneath Trier Abbey.

Yet, all day long, an ominous sense of presence had flickered on the edge of her awareness. Something was not right. Something had come among the Fallen that did not belong here. She was wary. Adding to her unease, Hawke and Corvid had not returned. She cast about for their trace but caught no scent of them. As a result, instead of focusing on her proclamation, she had been forced to direct the staff herself as they prepared for the rally tonight.

The weather, at least, had proven cooperative. Under a full moon, a throng was assembling in the stands that had been erected in front of the Cathedral. On a stage before the entrance, a praise choir and band were already rousing the crowd to chants and choruses. Lights played over the shattered cathedral dome, evidence, as she would point out in her proclamation, of the enemies of truth who would go to any length of destruction to forestall the coming Restoration.

The gathering crowd surpassed her expectations. Barbara reckoned half the town and county were there to hear her. The bleachers were filled, and people had spread blankets and folding chairs over the grounds. As far as she could see to the limits of the floodlights, a sea of expectant faces awaited her appearance. They would drink her words as she would drink warm blood, and they would become the instruments of her vengeance on their kind. They would commence the slaughter and destruction that she would consummate.

Barbara straightened the folds of her robe, adjusted the golden chain draped across her chest, and stepped into the lights. Nine thousand voices rose into the gathering night with a roar like a tempest-roused ocean.

Constable Jolene Bear sat on the farthest fringe of the throng, away from the bright lights around the stage. She saw several people in the crowd she knew by sight, but none who knew her well. If any recognized her, they gave no sign. People around Drovers Gap were used to seeing her in uniform, with her hair tucked away beneath her campaign hat, not in jeans and a flannel shirt with her auburn locks flaming down around her shoulders.

She made a point of singing along with the songs. They were all familiar to her from childhood church and her enthusiasm was not forced. She did not join in the vocal responses from the crowd as Barbara Battle launched into her harangue, until the whole assembly fell quiet as the speaker began to recount the horrific events surrounding the wreck of the Restoration Crusade van.

"Evil will always exact its price," Barbara intoned, speaking almost softly, as if confiding a confidence, relying on the sound system to amplify and convey her intimacy to her subjects. "The wickedness that prowls our home of Drovers

Gap is ever met with righteous fire. The three young hoodlums who stole our van betrayed our trust and paid dearly for it. Our cause endures and they are but ash and bone, scattered on the earth to be stirred and trampled under foot of beast and human."

A low murmur began pulsing through the crowd, like the approach of a distant storm.

"Those enemies to us who attempted to destroy our cathedral will also be found in the flames of justice."

A few shouted *amen*'s and *truth*'s sprinkled the night.

"It is our task, our sacred duty to discover and reveal the vile heretics that infect our community, and purge ourselves of their presence with fires of judgment,"

Battle was shouting now, raising a clinched fist toward the indifferent and unblinking stars. The crowd came to their feet like a rising tsunami, one great howl beneath the moon. Jolene tightened herself around the knot in her stomach and began to make her way to her car. She didn't want to hear or see what she knew was coming next.

Thirty-Nine

As she drove down the twisting descending road back to Drovers Gap, Constable Jolene Bear thought she had left the Restoration Cathedral campus unnoticed. She had driven up in her personal vehicle, a vintage Gremlin on most days parked in a shed attached to her barn. Apparently, nobody had recognized her as one of the Drovers Gap constabulary. She punched her cell phone to life.

"Call Chief Longshadow," she instructed the device.

"Calling Omar Longshadow now," her phone assured her.

She listened to the pulsing purr until a familiar voice affirmed connection, "Omar Longshadow."

"Chief, I'm on my way back from the Restoration rally at the Cathedral. Doesn't look good up there."

Omar's irritation came as clear as his words, "I told you to stay away from there. Those people are dangerous."

"They never knew I was there," Jolene assured her boss. "Battle's trying to incite another riot. We need to get ready."

"I'm not happy with you disobeying my order," Omar said. "Come on by here and tell me all about it."

"I'm on my way," Jolene said, was about to close her phone when Omar's voice came through, "You had supper?"

"No, Chief. I didn't have time to eat before the rally."

"I'll tell Dad to set another plate. Venison stew," the sternness gone from his voice now.

"Sounds like a plan," Jolene said.

The next thing Omar heard from his subordinate was a startled, "Shit!"

"What?" he queried.

"No brakes," frantic. Omar heard scraping and crunching of a vehicle offroad, plowing through trees and brush, terminating in a sickening thud. Then silence.

"Jolene?" He shouted into his phone. "Jolene, are you all right?"

Warren Longshadow looked up to see his son grab his jacket off the rack and start for the door. "What's up, Son?" he said, noting that Omar was taking his weapon.

"Jolene Bear's had an accident up on Ravensbeak Road. I'm headed up there."

"You want me to go with you?" the old man asked.

"No, she's fine, but her Gremlin's off the road. I'm going up to bring her home." Omar said, already half-way through the door.

"You need a gun for that?" Warren queried, but the door was already closed. A few seconds later, he heard Omar's pickup start and pull out of the yard. He stood by the window and watched the headlights slide away across the dark. He shook his head in frustration. Omar was trying to be protective, not telling him things, but Warren had walked this road himself, and he could smell trouble coming to his town when it was still a long way off. Right now, the air reeked of it.

There were some distinct advantages to getting old, Warren thought. Chief among them was that nobody had any expectations of an old man, and left him free to do pretty much as he pleased. Among the disadvantages was that, like an old car, he got left parked in the garage while the real business of the world went on outside, and if he was lucky, got taken out now and then for a Sunday drive.

He figured the stew would be cold by the time Omar came home, so he filled a bowl and sat himself down to eat some of it. The stew was good, even if he had cooked it himself. Salty enough, but Warren added a sprinkle more just to spite his cardiologist and cut off a slice of lassy bread to sop it with.

"Brakes failed," Jolene said over the phone. Omar couldn't shake the feeling that there was more to it than that. Jolene was all right, she told him, but as he drove out of Drovers Gap and started up the grade to Ravensbeak Ridge, images of the burned out van crumpled beside a mountain river filled his head. He drove faster than caution dictated.

When he figured he was near the place where Jolene said her Gremlin had left the road, he slowed, scanning the shoulder for some sign of an accident. Rounding a bend, the headlights revealed Jolene standing beside the pavement and waving. As he exited his vehicle, she tossed him a smile as irritating as it was reassuring.

"I told you to wait off the road, out of sight," he said, playing his flashlight over her figure to assure himself she was as undamaged as she claimed.

"I did," Jolene said, almost cheerfully. "But that heap you drive makes a racket I'd recognize anywhere. I didn't want you to miss me."

"At least it stays on the road," Omar growled.

He aimed his light down the wooded slope, picked up the glint of the Gremlin, tilted almost on its side atop a tangle of limber pine saplings, bent nearly to the ground beneath the weight.

"You were lucky," he said, trying to sound stern and keep the relief out of his voice. He didn't entirely succeed.

"Somebody will be disappointed, I imagine," Jolene said lightly. It occurred to Omar that she was enjoying her adventure. It bothered him considerably that she seemed to take her safety so lightly.

He scowled at his Constable. "How do you figure that?"

"Come on down here and I'll show you," she said, leading him off through the broken brush below the road. He followed, musing that Jolene Bear's disposition was particularly suited for their line of work.

Once beside the Gremlin, Jolene played her light across the upturned vehicle's underbody until she found what she was looking for. "See that, now," she said, pointing like a school child at show-and-tell.

Omar looked, nodded gravely. "Appears your brake line's been cut," he murmured.

"There's a whiskey bottle, half full, behind the driver's seat." Jolene added.

"Never knew you favored hard drink, Constable," Omar said, stretching up to peer into the Gremlin's open door.

"Never have," Jolene said, but somebody wanted you to think so, and figured I would be in no condition to deny it."

One of the bowed saplings snapped suddenly and startled, they stepped back as the Gremlin settled closer to ground.

"Listen, Jolene," Omar said, putting a hand on her shoulder to gain full attention. "I don't want you anywhere around Barbara Battle or any of her people. Until we find out who did this, you stay in the office. No more playing spy or snooping about. You hear me now?"

Jolene removed his hand from her shoulder, held on to it as she grinned up at him, "We got 'em scared now, don't we, Chief?"

The next morning, a wrecker chugged up the grade, winched Jolene's Gremlin clear of the pine thicket and hauled it back to town. One of the mechanics at the garage noted the clean cut brake line and pointed it out to Omar, who instructed him not to communicate his observations to the public, "On-going investigation," he pronounced.

The mechanic nodded knowingly, keeping to himself his speculations that a jealous boyfriend might be involved. He reckoned that, even in uniform, Jolene Bear was a striking woman, equipped to incite deadly passion in unwary males.

Omar called a de-briefing of sorts the same day at his office. Jolene outlined her impressions from the rally. "That woman was whipping the crowd into a frenzy, like she had a spell on them, declaring the whole town to be the devil's disciples, set on destroying the Restoration ministry, and calling down fiery retribution on all who don't swallow her swill and fall in behind her. We'll be facing a crazed mob before long if something isn't done to cool her down."

Sergeant Priestley appeared unperturbed by her report. "Don't you think you're exaggerating a mite here, Missy?" he said with a condescending smirk. "Maybe you're just upset because you trashed your daddy's old Gremlin."

"Somebody sabotaged it," Omar snapped. "It might have been an attempt at intimidation. More likely it was attempted murder."

Chuck, raising his voice, waving a hand in the air. "That brake line could've broke while she was piloting down through the woods."

"So, Sarge, you really don't think there might be a connection with my showing up at the rally?" Jolene queried.

Chuck stood, braced his hand on the table, leaned toward her like a guard dog straining at his leash. "I think there's been a lot of wicked stuff going on in Drovers Gap, and Reverend Battle is the only person in this town with gumption enough to face down the devil. Instead of trying to fault her for Jolene's careless driving, we ought to be helping Restoration Crusade clean up our community." He appeared about to sit down and shut up, then, seized by a further burst of inspiration, pointed at Jolene and sneered, "What about that whiskey bottle in your Gremlin? You saying that ain't yourn? Got prints on it?"

"We're checking," Omar said.

"None of mine," Jolene put in, "I had sense not to pick it up."

"Who told you about the bottle, Sergeant?' Omar asked.

Chuck sat, staring at his hands for a moment, finally looked up and barked, "If you wanted your mechanic to keep his mouth shut, you should've paid him better."

A tense silence reigned until Omar said, "Why don't you go issue some illegal parking citations, Sergeant, while you cool down and reassess your future with this department."

Priestley got up from the table and left without any further speculation or accusation. When the door closed behind him, Jolene turned to Omar, "You don't think . . .?"

Omar completed her question for her, "That he planted the whisky in your car? No, he was on duty here in town all evening. I've checked around already. Too many people saw him here for him to have been up on Ravensbeak during the rally. I talked with him a couple of times myself that evening.

"So how did he know about the bottle?" Jolene asked, frustration in her voice.

"Well, I don't think Ed Long told him," Omar said, "Chuck heard it from somebody directly involved, somebody who is definitely not on our side."

"You make it sound like some sort of war," Jolene murmured.

Omar stared out the window at his town. "Oh, I think it is that," he said quietly.

FORTY

Sergeant Priestley did not ticket any parking violations. Instead, he went straight down Main Street to the offices of Restoration Crusade, where he found Ben Murkan, former chairman of deacons at Justice Fork Baptist Church, directing a crew packing up the contents and loading everything into a large van parked out front.

Surprised, he asked Murkan, "You moving out?"

"We're relocating our offices to the Restoration Cathedral campus. Drovers Gap is no longer a safe place for the righteous," Murkan said, eying Sergeant's uniform. "Those who are charged with maintaining the public's safety are bringing the town to perdition. True Believers should not abide in this town until it is cleansed and restored."

"That's what I came to talk about," Sergeant said. "I want to be part of the cleansing."

"You wear the enemy's livery," Murkan said, tapping Sergeant's badge. "Is that your heart under there?"

"I took this badge swearing to protect this town for good people. People like me. I still want to do that. I never made a promise to coddle foreigners who come in here wanting to take over and change everything."

"And what if it took destroying some things to restore the town to its former contentments?" Murkan queried. "Would you be able to lock your Chief in that jail he rules? Would you tend the fires of restoration if they consumed your friends and kin? Could you do that to cleanse your town?"

Sergeant's pulse pounded in his head as if he had received a jolt of amphetamine. His voice trembled as he said, "I would do whatever it takes."

Abigail Trammell strolled through her winter's garden, stopping now and then to pull up a sere stalk of corn or okra remaining from the year past. It would soon be time to turn some earth, spread compost, set out onions and sow early greens. Amid all the change and turmoil in the town, the regular rhythms of the seasons provided comfort, a sense of stability and continuance. She thought more often lately of the time she had spent at Trier Abbey. She reckoned she did miss it somewhat. The regular progression of days, the patterns of work and rest and praise, repeating and renewing. How long had she been there? Weeks, months, years? Who could say? In Drovers Gap, it had been no time at all. Nobody here had even missed her.

The day was warm for late winter. Her bees were flying already. The steady drone of their commutes did not impress her as a murmuring multitude, but like one voice, speaking to her particularly, almost words. What secrets did the hive hold that were forbidden to humans to know? It occurred to her as she listened that a colony manifest essentially as one mind, with a hundred thousand wings, a hundred thousand eyes, as united as the cells in her body, tethered but not fettered. What breadth of vision, what depth and range of thought might a hive mind be capable of? Would it be any less perceptive and intelligent than her own skull-bound brain, or would that understanding be vastly beyond anything a single human could conceive?

Abigail sighed, stopped beside one of the hives, careful not to stand in the flight path of the bees as they steadily went and returned. She lay her hand lightly on the top of the hive and felt in her fingertips the throbbing life within. Like the beating of a heart, she thought, like the turning of a world.

Owl had gone up on the mountain at first light, declaring his intention to traverse the Separation to Trier, and secure a stock of queens to maintain the lineage of their bee colonies. He maintained that the bees of Shadow were frail and depleted of magic, their honey less nourishing, its healing power diminished. When he returned, he and Abigail would check each hive, and if their queen were faltering, replace her with a strong new sovereign.

A voice from across the yard interrupted her musing. Wendl VonTrier stood on her back porch, waving a package over his head. "Dear Miss Trammell," he called. "At long last, it has arrived."

Abigail hurried across her garden as Wendl disappeared inside her house. She came through the door to find him already unwrapping his parcel on the kitchen table. By now she was accustomed to the esoteric books and artifacts the púca seemed to accumulate from all over this and other worlds. She had long since given up speculating about the routes and means by which his treasures came to him.

"What on God's good earth have you brought to us now, Mister VonTrier?" she huffed, still trying to catch her breath after her dash through the garden.

"For you, Dear Miss Trammell," Wendl murmured, his eyes alight. "A present from afar."

"Mercy." Abigail exclaimed as he lifted a small wooden box from the wrappings and set it before her. "And it isn't even my birthday," she lilted like a delighted child.

Wendl chuckled from deep in his chest, looking and sounding like a bemused lion. "Every morning, we are born again in the dawn. Every day is your birthday, and every day brings a gift, dear Miss Trammell. This one is extra, just because Wendl likes you especially. Aren't you going to open it?"

Abigail ran a hand lightly over the top of the box, made of some sort of close-grained tropical wood, dovetailed at the corners, polished smooth except for an intaglio image of a gryphon inscribed on the top. As she reached to trace the lineaments of the mythical creature with her fingertip, something like an electric spark leapt from the image to her hand.

Startled, Abigail suppressed a little yelp, glanced up to see Wendl's satisfied smile as he nodded encouragingly. Abigail gingerly picked up the box, lifted the lid and gazed at the transparent sphere, the size of an orange, nestled inside. She set the box back on the table, stood with one hand in the air, trying to decide if she dared touch the pristine orb, when it rose out of the box like a gas-filled balloon until it hovered before her face.

"Oh my," she murmured, spellbound. As she peered into its crystalline depths, shapes and colors began to swirl and coalesce within it until she beheld the image of a village surrounded by mountains. A moment passed before she recognized her own little town, seen from above as in a drone's view.

"It's Drovers Gap," she whispered. "It's us." Tiny people walked up and down Main Street. Minute vehicles trundled through the town. "It's marvelous, Mister VonTrier," she said. "Thank you. But what am I to do with such a remarkable thing?"

"The Gryphon will see the good or evil that wants to come your way, and will welcome or ward as your need requires," Wendl said, as if explaining the operation of a cell phone.

"Keep it close and consult it often. We are entering unsettling times."

As he spoke, the sphere became just a transparent ball again, and slowly sank like an oversize soap bubble back into its box.

Abigail replaced the lid. Tears glistened in her eyes as she said, "It's a beautiful thing, whatever it is for, and I will cherish it."

Wendl nodded. "Your Gryphon will cherish you, if you will allow it, dear Miss Trammell. It will keep you safe when Wendl is not among the Fallen."

"Surely you're not leaving us now," Abigail retorted.

"Fear not," dear Miss Trammell," Wendl said, laughing. There is a time to go, but now is my time to stay. We have much yet to learn and do together."

Barbara Battle paced restlessly around her office, released the spell concealing the cabinet behind her desk to count her trophies. She had a growing desire to increase their number. Then she closed it and walked across the room to gaze out the window at the work on the Cathedral roof. Lights were rigged so workmen could labor around the clock. At night, the glare could be seen clearly from down in Drovers Gap. She had plans to install a permanent beacon atop the structure to remind all the souls in the village that she was there above them, watching them all from Ravensbeak.

The damaged roof had turned out to be fortuitous. Her followers were convinced now that it was wanton destruction perpetrated by the Crusade's enemies. The zeal was building to cleanse the town of all who opposed her. One spark would suffice to unleash a purging conflagration.

The intercom at her desk interrupted her reverie. Her

secretary informed, "Reverend Battle, the police sergeant is here to see you."

"Send him in," Barbara instructed, and settled herself into a regal pose behind her desk. The desk was raised so that when Sergeant Priestley came in, even standing, he had to look up to meet her gaze.

"Sit down, Sergeant, and tell me why you're here," she said, gesturing toward a chair that would elevate her even more in her visitor's view.

Chuck obeyed, though obviously discomfited at having to look up to a woman of power. It made him feel like a little boy. "Didn't Ben Murkan tell you why I've come?" he said, stress pitching his voice upward.

"He told me," she said, enlarging herself subtly. Sergeant would sense it without seeing it. "I want to hear it from you."

"I . . . I want to offer my services to the Crusade," he mumbled, so soft she could barely hear his voice though she read his thought clearly.

"How do you suppose you could help Restoration Crusade, Sergeant?" she said, her speech echoing inside Chuck's head as if she spoke to him from all directions. Suddenly, he wasn't sure he knew the answer to her query. Chuck wilted before her gaze until he found some words, "I want to help you clean up our town, to drive out the evil doers in our midst."

"Is this the official view of the Drovers Gap police department?" Barbara asked in a tone that implied she knew the answer.

"No, Reverend," They think you are the evil here."

"Do you deny you have ever entertained such thoughts?" she queried, her mischief in her voice.

Chuck shrugged, "I had doubts at first, but I'm sorry for them now."

"An honest answer, Sergeant," she said. "Thoughts do not always come invited, but in any case, one must choose whether to starve them of attention or nurture them into deed."

Chuck nodded mutely, not lifting his gaze from his shoes.

"But you are deeply conflicted, Sergeant," she went on. "How can I trust you?"

"I own my darkness but I crave the light," he replied, earnest and sincere.

"In that case, come pray with me," she said, tying her spell behind her back.

FORTY-ONE

"Where's Chuck?" Omar asked as he came into the office, "We need to have a serious chat."

"He hasn't checked in, Chief," Constable Jolene said. "Did he do patrol last night?"

"I couldn't raise him on the radio or on his phone." Omar said. "Nobody I've talked to this morning recalls seeing him. Call his house and see if he's there."

Omar scanned his email messages while Jolene navigated her phone call with Sergeant Priestley's wife. When she hung up the phone, she reported, "Wilma says he left around midnight in their car. The police cruiser is sitting in the yard there. They had a big argument, she says. Chuck told her he's not working for the town anymore, that Barbara Battle has hired him to head Crusade security."

Omar shook his head. "I reckon that means he's Battle's disappointment now. We'd better go out there and pick up the town's property. Get some keys in case he took his with him."

Fifteen minutes later, Wilma Priestley teetered on the brink of tears as she told about the confrontation with her husband the evening before. "He's been listening to that hateful Battle

Woman, swallowing her lies, turning against our friends and neighbors that we've known all our lives. He says we're the devil's children now. I told him the only devil in this town is Barbara Battle." She touched the bruise on her cheek. "He hit me, Omar, when I said that. He's never hardly raised his voice to me afore. He wouldn't've done this in his right mind."

"Will you be safe here when he comes home?" Omar asked. "We can take you to town with us. Abigail Trammell would put you up at her place until things get settled for you."

"I'm alright here, thanks," Wilma said. "My sister's coming to pick me up. I can stay with her. He wouldn't dare show his face there."

Chuck had left the keys to the cruiser in the vehicle. Jolene drove it back to Drovers Gap. Omar waited with Wilma until her sister arrived. A gusty wind was lifting dust from the road when he started his pickup. He intended to visit the Resurrection Cathedral and officially terminate Sergeant's career with the Drovers Gap Police Department. Before he turned onto the road up Ravensbeak Ridge, however, he saw an ominous plume of smoke, and an urgent call changed his itinerary.

"Chief, that you?"

"You got me. What's up?"

"This is Will Donavan with the Forestry Service. We got our hands full with wildfire coming down from Justice Peak. The wind is agin' us and we're getting dense smoke on the Hendo highway. Could you divert any traffic coming this way from Drovers Gap until we get the situation in hand?"

"Roger, Will," Omar said as he passed the turn-off and headed toward town. "Keep me posted."

Omar called Jolene. "I got the alert already, Chief. We're on it," she affirmed when he told her about the fire. By the time he reached Drovers Gap, the police cruiser was in position to block access to the Hendo road and a town streets crew was erecting barriers. Jolene, busy directing traffic, threw a wave as he eased his pickup to a stop on the shoulder. A bank of ugly brown smoke was gathering over the ridge west of town as Omar emerged from his vehicle. Already, the air was tainted with the sharp odor of burning forest.

"Any problems?" he asked his Constable.

"Not really," Jolene said. "Most are being cooperative. I've been letting people through who live this side of the burn zone, to go check on their homes and stock, but advising them to stay alert for a possible evacuation order. Do you think there will be need for evacuation?"

"I'd say that's likely," Omar said, casting his gaze at the darkening horizon. "It's awfully dry out there, and with this wind . . ." He decided not to voice his pessimistic speculation.

"This could be the big one the Forestry people have been warning . . ." Jolene began, then broke off the conversation to lean toward the open window of a stopped car and explain the emergency to a family, obviously tourists, with two children in the back seat. The driver thanked her and obediently turned around and drove back along Main Street the way he had come.

By the time Omar reached his office, a highway department crew had erected a barricade east of town with a sign directing through traffic toward the interstate highway north of Drovers Gap. Jolene returned with the cruiser shortly after, having been relieved of her traffic duties by state troopers. Omar bid her call all the local bed-and-breakfast owners to determine how many vacancies might be in town in event of evacuations, Abigail Trammell said feel free to send as many as need be to her place. Hemlock House wasn't the biggest hospitality operation in town. Omar wondered how she would make room but didn't ask. He suspected there were many things about Abigail and her friends at Hemlock that the good people of Drovers Gap were not prepared to know.

As the afternoon waned, the only traffic coming through town and up the Hendo road was forest service vehicles towing trailers hauling bulldozers, tractors and other firefighting equipment. In all the shops and stores along Main Street, radios blared the latest news updates about the fire. People gathered in little clusters on the sidewalks to whisper their apprehensions, taking pains not to upset their children. The children, of course, overheard everything, and in their innocence, gleaned a stronger sense of adventure than of danger or disaster.

Toward nightfall, the gusty winds persisted unabated. The smoky haze had become uncomfortable to breathe and the Evening News broadcast featured reports that two homes had burned out on the mountain and a mandatory evacuation order was now in effect for the Marshall County highlands east of Ravensbeak Ridge.

It was after midnight when Chief Omar Longshadow finally got to bed. He was hardly asleep, it seemed to him, before his phone chimed and he roused to read a text that the Ravensbeak fire, as the news outlets called it, had jumped the fireline along Hendo road and was leapfrogging over containment efforts past Roundtop and Justice Fork north of town.

Warren was frying bacon for their breakfast and glanced out their kitchen window. What he'd mistaken for the first tint of dawn revealed itself to be the glint of flames as trees began to burn along the crest of the ridge above their farm.

"Dad, you'd better lock up and come to town with me until they get this under control." Omar said, grimacing as he burned his lips on the fresh-poured coffee. Even as he spoke, they heard Forestry Service trucks rumbling past on the county road.

"I've got to take care of my stock, son," Warren protested.

Omar broke a couple of biscuits, layered fried egg and bacon inside, wrapped them up and dropped them in his jacket pocket to eat when he had time. "One old cow, a half-blind mule and two sheep. Not an investment worth risking your life for."

"They're lives I'm responsible for. If the fire starts getting too close, or if I'm told to evacuate, I'll loose them to make their way and come on down. I promise," Warren said, watching as trees exploded into fireballs on the ridgetop a mile distant.

"Don't wait until the last second," Omar admonished. "I'm not ready yet to be an orphan." Without waiting for a response, he was out the door and into his pickup. His eyes burned from the smog. The air felt chill in spite of the encroaching fire on the hills beyond. He thought he saw a flurry of snow whirling by. It wasn't that cold, though. Then he realized the pale flakes were ashes on the wind.

He turned back to the house, saw Warren in the doorway, pulling on his jacket. "Dad, get out of here now," he shouted, got into his pickup and drove away toward his responsibilities.

As Omar turned onto Main Street, a white Restoration Crusade van headed out of town roared past him. He slowed, watched the vehicle diminishing in his rearview mirror, considered briefly enforcing the town's speed limit, then drove on, reckoning Drovers Gap was a better place with Battle's minions away from it. Besides, he had weightier matters on his mind. His town was under threat.

When he entered his office he found Dolf Thomas sitting in a chair, holding a bloody towel in his hand. Jolene was bent over him affixing a bandage to his scalp.

"What's going on?" Omar asked, and before anyone answered, "Dolf, you alright?"

Dolf winced as he tried to nod. Jolene grabbed his head with both hands, "Hold still, Dolf. I'm not done yet," she said, sounding like a mother scolding a recalcitrant child. Dolf lapsed into an obedient silence and Jolene answered for him, "Some of the Crusader goons attacked him, Chief. Made off with some goods from the Market."

She straightened, inspected her work. Satisfied she'd done all needful for the moment, "Okay, Dolf," she said, "I'm finished with you."

The old man seemed about to stand, thought better of it and settled back into his chair, continued the narration, "They come into my store, Chief, two of 'em, and started putting up some of those Restoration Crusade posters on my door. I told 'em I didn't want that stuff all over my place, and one of 'em, big feller, he was, pushed me down and I hit my head. Then there was a bunch of 'em coming through the door, kicking at me and knocking stuff in the floor. I crawled up under a counter and they grobbed up all they could carry and carted it off. I didn't budge airy they be all gone, then I called Jolene and she come down and brought me here."

"All this because of a poster?" Omar queried.

"Poster was just an excuse to get in my store, Chief," Dolf said, gingerly touching his bandaged head. "They was there to rob my goods. You going to arrest them?"

"Can you identify the parties?" Omar asked.

"For sure that big one that pushed me down. Great bushy black beard. Beady-eyed as a pig. Came at me like a big old bear. I'd know him, and maybe the scrawny little turnip head with the posters. Not sure about the rest. Mostly I just saw their feet from under that counter."

"You wait here, Dolf, and rest," Omar said. "We'll talk more when I get back. Did you lock up the store when you left?"

Dolf rubbed a shoulder tentatively, flexed his arm, somewhat stiffly, "Jolene did. I lost my glasses and was a bit unsituated." Jolene silently held up Dolf's keys.

"We're going down to scope over the scene," Omar said. "Don't you go anywhere until I come back. You need anything, Mayor Ned's secretary is right across the hall. You ask her."

"Yessir, Chief," murmured the storekeeper, slumping in his chair, no spit and vinegar left in him.

Omar and Jolene found half the stores on Main Street closed and dark as they walked toward Dolf's Market. The few people they met along the way bore luggage, backpacks, assorted traveling gear, apparently intent on being some place other than Drovers Gap. Posters flaunting the Restoration Crusade logo were plastered on the storefronts they passed. When they reached Dolf's Market, they found one centered on the door. Beneath the peculiar image of a dragon entwined around a cross, they read-

RETRIBUTION OR RESTORATION?
Drovers Gap will be cleansed by fire.
The faithless and apostate will be consumed.
Believe, belong, and be spared.
Find safety with Mother Barbara
At Restoration Cathedral.

"So it's Mother Barbara now is it?" Jolene said as she took Dolf's keys and unlocked the door. "Next, she will be claiming to be the Pope."

"Or God," murmured Omar as he followed her inside.

The shelves had been ransacked, some of them overturned. What hadn't been carried away lay scattered across the floor. Broken glass crunched underfoot. Puddles, sticky and pungent, stuck to their shoes. There seemed no pattern to the plunder. The thieves had grabbed whatever was closest at hand, groceries, clothes, tools, anything convenient to carry. The looters apparently were bent mainly on destruction. Thievery had been an afterthought.

A momentary gleam beneath a counter caught Omar's eye. He stooped, retrieved something, and held it up for Jolene to see. Dolf's eyeglasses, miraculously unscathed.

FORTY-TWO

"Are we going to take a ride up Ravensbeak now?" Jolene asked.

"Later, we'll have to," Omar said. "But for now, we have our plate full here in town. There will be folk coming in ahead of the fire with no place to stay. And there may be some more Restoration goons wandering about up to no good. The law is getting stretched pretty thin around here."

When they got back to town hall, somebody had posted a sign out front promising *HOUSING INFO* and a dozen people were inside at reception waiting hopefully if not patiently for direction.

Jolene joined in phoning to find accommodations for the refugees, and Omar headed for the mayor's office. When he knocked on the open door, Ned Baskin's phone was already ringing. Ned answered, "Just a moment, I'll be right with you," and cupped his palm over the receiver, looked a question at his chief of police.

"Ned, I need some temporary personnel for public safety," Omar said, "Without Priestley, there's just Jolene and me to cope with our emergency situation."

Ned shook his head, whispered, "I've got nobody, Omar.

All my people that ain't fled down the mountain are out on the fireline. County's talked to the governor. We may have some Guard in here by tomorrow."

"Today would be nice," Omar said dryly, and left the mayor at the mercy of his phone. When he crossed the hall to his own office, he found Jolene on the phone while a family of four stood waiting expectantly. Warren leaned against Omar's desk talking to Dolf as they stared at the county map on the opposite wall.

"Hello, Dad," Omar said. "What brings you to town?" It was a question he didn't want answered.

Warren answered anyway. "Fire people ordered me out. We still had a house when I left, but the fire's down to the upper pasture. I don't expect they can stop it there."

"The wind's ag'in us," Dolf murmured.

"Not just the wind," Warren said. "According to the fire crew up by our place, they think somebody's starting fresh fires behind their lines. A couple of crews nearly got trapped in there this morning."

Omar shook his head, unable to find words for his anger and dismay. When he could control his voice, he said, "Dad, you interested in coming out of retirement?"

An hour later, Warren had recruited, in addition to Dolf, two other friends, both retired public safety officers, to join what they dubbed the "geezer patrol." Omar instructed them to be helpful where they could, and to keep an eye out for potential trouble, but not to engage any miscreants they encountered, rather call him or Jolene and beat a prompt retreat.

"We don't want anybody else getting pounded on like Dolf," he said. He pulled a pair of glasses from his jacket pocket and handed them to the storekeeper, "Thought you might need these," he said. "Reckon you dropped them in all the excitement down at your place."

Chuck Priestley unconsciously assumed a military posture as he gazed up at his employer enthroned on her dais. She studied him for a long moment, adding to his discomfort. Instinctively, he was afraid of Mother Barbara, as she preferred her staff and followers address her. Chuck's only comfort in this situation was the knowledge that as head of security for Restoration Crusade, he elicited a measure of fear and trepidation from those further down the corporate ladder.

"How many people do we have here now, Guardian?" Mother Barbara asked at the precise second the silence became unbearable. Chuck suspected that, as with most of her queries, she already knew the answer before she spoke the question.

"We're past twenty-three hundred now. Fifty-six more, with six children among them, have come in so far today," Chuck answered. "We're running out of shelter. We'll need more tents, at least."

"We have enough for now," Mother Barbara said. "It is time to close the road."

"People are desperate down there," Chuck noted. "We'll have to post armed guards to keep them out."

"The woods are dry," Barbara stating an obvious. "The fire will make the road impassible."

"The winds have kept the fire on the other side of the ridge, Mother Barbara," Chuck said. "There's no fire within five miles of the road."

"There will be tonight," Barbara assured him. "You will see to that for me, won't you, Guardian Priestley?" Her tone wasn't questioning.

"Of course, Mother," Chuck murmured, bowed, and went to do as he was told. It bothered him, though. Since boyhood, he had hunted these woods. He had always felt more sympathy for the creatures there than for the people in his life.

It twisted him against himself to set aflame the only places where he had ever felt at home in his world.

No one refused Mother Barbara more than once, though. Only those who consistently answered *yes* ever told anyone about their experiences in her presence. Now and again on their arson missions out in the woods, Chuck Priestley and his crew had come upon skeletal remains that appeared human. Mostly, they kept to themselves any speculations they might entertain about whose bones they might be. However, the Fire Brigade, as they called themselves, shared an unspoken impression that the mysterious predator responsible for the kills was not entirely unfamiliar to them all. And though each of them pictured in his mind the same face, none would have dared breathe the name aloud.

A caravan of vehicles full of diehard tourists and displaced locals left town that afternoon only to begin returning an hour after their departure. "The highway's blocked," they reported. Omar's phone call to the Highway Department confirmed there had been a landslide blocking the highway. He informed those intent on departure of an alternate route, a tortuous gravel road that twisted alongside a creek down a narrow valley to rejoin the highway below the landslide. So far, at least, it remained clear of the fire zone.

All the inns and bed-and-breakfast establishments were booked. Somehow, when requested, Abigail Trammell still found "room for one more" at Hemlock House. Families were pitching tents in the town park and local residents found their yards turning into villages. Some who had sought refuge at Restoration Cathedral, which, by a seeming miracle, remained unscathed, reported that during the night a new blaze had broken out and now blocked access to the Ravensbeak Ridge road.

Jolene attempted to reach the Cathedral by phone but her calls went unanswered, until finally, an unidentified individual responded with a terse, "It's too late. You will all burn down there." As night fell, the air was thick with smoke. The oppressive overcast glowed a dull red from the reflected flames that now raged on three sides of the town. Fire exploded along the ridgetops as trees burst like flares and the fire began burning down the slopes toward the town.

The wildfire now threatened the series of wells that sourced the town's water supply. The mayor's office advised residents to fill their bathtubs and any available container with water. Toward ten o'clock that evening, Omar reluctantly issued a directive to begin a mandatory evacuation of the town as soon as it was light. He knew there would be some who would refuse to go. He also knew that any who stayed would likely burn with the town. He had never thought of himself as a particularly religious man, but he was learning now to pray.

Daybreak brought not so much a dawn but a murky twilight gradually paling into a choking smog that seeped under doors and through walls until everything, quilts and clothes and skin, smelled of smoke and ash. By mid-morning, even the gravel track that snaked down the mountain along Joe's Creek was overrun by the conflagration, rendering Drovers Gap surrounded by raging forestfire, cut off from the outside world.

Plans were made to begin evacuating the town by helicopter, then canceled as the billowing smoke and high winds rendered the operation untenable.

Warren Longshadow proposed a desperate tactic of setting backfires around the perimeter of the village to burn up the surrounding slopes to meet the larger blaze encroaching from above. This was argued and debated until the winds began dropping live embers onto Main Street, sending the few pedestrians who braved the open air scurrying frantically for shelter. A coterie of stalwart volunteers was then dispatched to begin setting back fires.

Sometime around noon, phone lines went dead, and shortly after, electricity failed. People cursed and wept and prayed for deliverance from the inferno seemingly about to consume them all.

When Abigail glimpsed the first flames through the woods beyond her garden, she and Owl began carrying water from her house to pour over their hives. Several of her guests joined in to help. She knew it was a futile effort, but the alternative was to do nothing, and to stand by and watch her beloved bees burn Abigail judged unthinkable. However, they had hardly begun the task when the stream from her garden hose slowed to a trickle of drops, then ceased altogether.

"It's time to go home, Sister Gobnait," Owl announced quietly. Abigail nodded her understanding and they retreated to her house. She dashed upstairs with Owl right behind and ran down the hall to Wendl's room, breathed a prayer and threw open the door. For a long moment she gazed down the tree bound path she had followed to Trier Abbey, breathed in the clear pungent air of a moist spruce forest after a night's rain. She propped the door open with a chair before she and Owl began herding her guests up the stair and through the door to Otherworld. She feared to close the door again lest the way to salvation be closed with it.

Some resisted direction, unable to believe what their eyes told them. Two or three preferred to take their chances in the world they knew, even as it burned around them. Finally, though, the majority trooped obediently after Owl into a brighter day.

Abigail turned and started down her stairs. Owl stood in the door, looking his question after her.

"Go," she shouted and waved him on. "I must tell the others." She found her cellphone on her dresser in her room and tapped in Wendl's number. To her immense relief, he answered promptly.

When she explained her intention, the púca answered as calmly as if they were discussing plans for a picnic, "Fear not, Dear Miss Trammell. There is also a Threshold here at Vintage Reads. Wendl has alerted the constabulary and they are gathering as many as are left in town. Do not leave your gift behind."

"My gift?" Abigail stammered.

"The globe," Wendl said. "It holds the town within." She thought he might say more, but either he ended the call or their connection was broken.

A shudder went through the house, as if a violent wind had shaken it. Abigail raced up the stairs to find the door to Wendl's room closed, the chair that had stayed it lying overturned in the hallway. When she opened the door, she saw only Wendl's impossibly neat bedroom. The light through the window bathed the room in a dirty orange glow. Smoke billowing past outside veiled any view of the town beyond.

A deep calm settled over Abigail as she closed the door, the sort of lucid stillness one feels when a last hope has faded or when they reconcile with death. She thought she still might join the exodus from the bookstore, but even as the thought came to her, she knew with certainty she would not. On her way through the house she passed her own bedroom and remembered Wendl's last words to her, *Don't leave your gift behind.*

The globe waited where she had left it, on a shelf beside her bathtub, now filled with water per Mayor Ned's instructions. The sphere gleamed with a ruddy light, like the sky outside her window. She peered into its depths at the tiny people streaming like a column of ants down the wee Main Street toward a lilliputian Vintage Reads. A miniscule Wendl

VonTrier standing by the door looked out at her and beckoned, as if he felt her watching.

When she lifted the globe in her hands, it felt hot to the touch. Her hands, slippery with sweat and anxiety, fumbled the object, it slid from her grasp and splashed into the tub. It floated there for a moment and as she reached out to retrieve it, sank beneath the surface. Abigail watched in dismay as Wendl's magical gift dissolved and disappeared before her eyes.

FORTY-THREE

endl VonTrier had just carried the last of his irreplacable Otherworldish volumes into his refuge and was preparing to lock up Vintage Reads and head to Hemlock House when his front door flung open and a dozen people burst into the store. Behind them, ash and bits of burning foliage rained down onto Main Street. They began brushing smoky bits from clothes and hair, inspecting one another for damage. The bookstore smelled like fire and panic.

As the little clutch of refugees stood staring through the glass storefront at the end of their world, the púca called gently, "Follow Wendl. There is a safe place here." They turned as one, and having no place else to go, followed him through the maze of bookshelves, up one row and down another until they had passed more shelves than the little store could possibly contain, and at the end of an aisle, a door, which Wendl opened for them and they stepped out into a grassy meadow with wooded hills beyond, and birdsong and fresh air and blue sky populated with blindingly white clouds and sunshine warm on the skin and no smoke nor fire anywhere.

"Don't wander off and get yourselves lost," he admonished. "Stay here. I'll be back." He closed the door on their astonishment and went back to his desk in the front of the store. The phone line was dead, but he keyed the police number on his cell and Jolene answered.

"Bring all the people you can find to Vintage Reads," he said. "They will be safe with Wendl."

"Wendl? What do you mean?" she stammered, uncomprehending.

"Believe, or come and be convinced," Wendl said, accustomed by now to human skepticism.

Jolene must have alerted her chief, for five minutes later, Omar Longshadow, looking parched and exhausted, came in from the street. "What's all this?" he demanded. Wendl escorted him to the far side of the store that existed in Otherworld. Omar, astonished as any would be, grasped the reality of the situation, greeted the survivors, fielded questions about loved ones left behind. "Don't worry," he said, pretending he didn't. "We'll bring everybody through."

Two women and a man volunteered to go with him back into Drovers Gap and assist with herding survivors. He hesitated, until Wendl's encouraging nod overwhelmed his training, "Come on then," he said. "Time's running out."

Soon after, a steady stream of scorched and bedraggled souls began making their way through town to the bookstore.

Abigail stood a long time after any trace of Wendl's globe had vanished, staring at the water in her bathtub. She might still be able to join the exodus through Vintage Reads, but that way was already closed to her in her mind. She had been to the Abbey once in her memory and perhaps before that. If she had been at home there, she would not have returned among the Fallen. Drovers Gap was her place. This was her house and home. If it was to burn, she would burn with it.

She went to her kitchen, poured a generous glass of elderberry wine, carried it along with her much loved and reread copy of *The Forest Soul* back to her bedroom, took off her shoes, lay down on her bed and pulled up the quilt, took a sip of the dark astringent contents of her glass, opened her book and closed her eyes, listening as the book began to recite one of her favorite passages.

There remained nothing to be done now, she thought, but surrender to the situation, to read and to pray until the fire either took her with her house or passed her by. She would remain in her place. Belonging was her last defense. She listened to Millicent McTeer's voice in the book, the same voice who spoke to her when a tossed bottle had lifted her out of herself and baptized her in a mountain lake, dissolving her like Wendl's globe in her bath, until she had been formed again under another sun.

Abigail heard the now familiar voice of her Otherworldly mentor say, *A tree must grow where it is planted, while the soul makes her own weather…*and while she listened, she slept and while she slept, Abigail dreamed words that may have been from the book or may have been her own. She woke suddenly to a roaring sound, like a great wind, or a stormy sea. Her window was dark. She thought at first she was hearing the fire eating her house, then realized it was only rain driving against her roof.

Abigail lay still as a stone, hardly daring to breath, fearing any movement, any thought might break the spell. The house was cool, the rain drumming on walls and shingles like a vast applause at the end of an opera. Not just a shower, this, no ordinary storm. A deluge. A flood. Water ran in rippling sheets down the windowpanes. No gusty winds. No lightning lacing the clouds. Just a mighty inundation of heaven's tears pulling down from the sky peace and healing for the beleaguered town.

Mercy, she breathed. "Mercy. Mercy," Abigail repeated aloud. It was the only word she could call to her lips. Mercy drenched her mind like the rain streaming down upon her garden. It left no room for fear or anger. While she sheltered warm and dry beneath her quilt, within her house preserved and unscathed amid so much destruction, Mercy was her only reality. God or Christ or Mother Earth or Father Sky had looked upon their peril and noted their helplessness and poured out upon them all, irrespective of merit or blame, the saving mercy of the rain.

After a time that might have been an hour or might have been several, Abigail realized she was hungry and got out of bed and put on her shoes. She stood before her mirror, surprised. She had not felt the tears streaming down her face. She wiped her cheeks and brushed her hair, pulled on a sweater for the room was almost chill now, and went off to her kitchen to begin her new life.

"Surely, it is morning," Abigail thought aloud to herself. It felt like morning, as if she had awakened from a night's sound sleep. The twilight from her kitchen window gave no clue. It might have been morning or dusk, or even high noon on the other side of the dense clouds that hung low in the sky, dropping rain and more rain, in wreaths and veils and curtains that obliterated any long view of the town or the mountains beyond. She could barely make out the pale squares of her beehives beyond the garden. As far as she could see, the trees still stood dark and close around her yard. She saw no sign of fire, smelled no scent of burning in the air.

She crushed a couple spoonfuls of toasted barley and put on water to boil. Wendl had taught her that. All the comfort of coffee without unsettling her stomach. Abigail wished he were here, wondered if he had gone with the others. The house was too quiet, especially so after the crowd of refugees it had briefly homed. She had always thought of herself as a loner, a solitary person, but now in the silence and the stillness, she longed for her connections, for Wendl, and faithful Owl, for Luke and Neil and Tsula and all the rest. She wanted somebody to talk to her, to recognize her face, to acknowledge and affirm her place and presence upon the earth.

The kettle's whistling interrupted her lonesome. She poured water into her cup and watched the steam rising like a promise or a prayer. Suddenly, Abigail didn't feel alone or lonely at all. She had trusted herself to whatever or whoever upheld the world, and she had been seen and delivered. Why her, of all people, when so many had suffered and perished? There was no answer. She only knew she was here by no doing of her own. She had been shown a great and holy mercy. She had the rest of her life to discover why.

In her refrigerator, Abigail found the final slice of her fruitcake. If she had been saving it for a special occasion, she figured now was it. She stood at her front door, sipping her mugicha and munching the bit of cake she held in her fingers, and listened to the rain. The street in front of Hemlock House, submerged in runoff from the storm, resembled a small river flowing past. The deluge continued unabated as rain drove through the town in sheets and waves. She opened the door and let the cool mist-laden air swirl in around her. It smelled of spruce and spring. No fire could sustain in such a downpour.

Abigail imagined that if she had Wendl's globe, she might see weary firefighters out on the ridges surrounding the town, standing with their helmets in their hands, faces turned up to the blessed rain, drinking in Heaven's deliverance. What she envisioned was in reality being repeated in a hundred sites on the wooded mountainsides and along the roads that wound through the coves and hollows between. The great fire, that had afflicted the land like a hungry dragon seeking whom it might devour, was dead, washing down the slopes in a slurry of mud and ash. For many springs to come, the hills and valleys around Drovers Gap would be greener for it.

Abigail swallowed her last crumb of cake, set her empty cup on the table by her door, and stepped out onto her porch. Raindrops splattered on her feet and the mist blowing in sparkled in her hair. She fought a mad girlish impulse to dash out into the torrent and run through the storm-drenched town to find her star boarder. She was still considering this when through the rain and fog she saw a solitary figure walking up Main Street toward her house. Before she could see face or feature, she knew who it was. There was no mistaking that impossibly thin and agile being who strode through the maelstrom as if it were a balmy sunshiney day. She flew across her yard, immediately soaked through, her clothes clinging to her like a second skin as she ran toward arms that opened to lift and hold her when she leaped, and they laughed and whirled together in a wild púca-ish dance under the rain.

Rain fell without break or diminishment for three days and three nights. Omar Longshadow, his father Warren, and Constable Jolene slept at City Hall, bunking in the jail cells in the police department. After the first night, Warren remarked, "Now I know why we have so few repeat offenders in this town. After a night on one of those cots, nobody would want to do anything to cause him having to sleep in there again."

Dolf braved the rain to scavenge them provisions from his wrecked store. "At least ye'll have plenty of water to drink," he said dryly upon his return, his words being the only dry thing about him.

The fourth morning brought a spectacular dawn as the last of the clouds fled a true blue sky and the air smelled sweet and the mountains all around looked close enough to touch. The solar panels atop Town Hall began to recharge battery banks and cell phones and they had lights again. The Forestry Service declared the fire extinct and the Highway Department informed that crews were at work clearing the roads east and west of town. It was expected that within a day or so Drovers Gap would rejoin civilization.

Stepping out into the glare of the bright new day, the Drovers Gap constabulary found streets swept clean and pavements sparkling in the sun. An occasional drift of debris against a building or beside a curb provided the only clues of the flood that had ensued. The stores they passed appeared undamaged without and for the most part dry within. Drovers Gap was a town cleansed, and strangely empty. They called out, heard their voices echo in the still air, but no answer, no sight of other living souls.

At Vintage Reads, they found the door shut, but unlocked. Omar opened the door and called, "VonTrier? Anybody here?" Wherever Wendl had taken their neighbors, they were apparently still there. Back along Main Street, they traversed the three blocks to the other end of town, where they met Wendl Von Trier and Abigail Trammell coming out of Hemlock House.

"What did you do with all my people?" Omar asked when his surprise had settled.

"You sure you want them back?" Wendl retorted, "They were a lot of trouble to you."

"I don't have a job without them," Omar said.

At that point, they heard voices in the distance and turned to see Owl leading a raggle taggle procession up the middle of Main Street. Drovers Gap had come home.

FORTY-FOUR

Abigail was delighted to have Hemlock House full of guests again, although within a couple of days, those who still had homes left to go to, departed to their own. She hired Chloe Toibin to help with serving meals but still insisted on doing most of the cooking herself. Wendl, when he wasn't busy at Vintage Reads, gently imposed his presence in the kitchen, suggesting some new recipes he claimed to have picked up during his travels among the worlds. Word got out around town about the delicious and adventurous menu at Hemlock House and before long, dinner guests outnumbered the roomers.

It was Luke Armstrong who one morning over breakfast finally spoke aloud what had been growing in Abigail's own mind. "Miss Trammell," he said over his second cup of coffee, "You need to open a full restaurant here. Nowhere else in the county can one find the sort of food you serve."

"I doubt that," she said. "I run a boarding house here. I just cook on the side."

"Which side is the most fun?" put in Chloe.

"Well, I do like to cook," admitted Abigail.

"How many did you seat for dinner last night?" Wendl asked.

"As many as we have room for. Forty and a few," she answered.

"And how many did you turn away?"

Abigail hesitated, trying to recall. "More than that," she said.

Owl spoke up, "We have the garden and the bees. We already grow most of the vegetables we serve. We could expand the garden and I could raise enough to feed an army."

Abigail tried to swallow her excitement. "We'd have to build an addition. I mean, in this world. I'd have to get a permit. The commissioners turned down my last application."

"Dear Miss Trammell," Wendl murmured, "Let me persuade the commissioners for you."

It was never quite clear what Wendl said to Mayor Ned and the commissioners. There were rumors later that some secrets had been barely kept within that room. In any case, Luke Armstrong drew up plans, permits were issued with due deliberation, and Luke assembled a crew and construction commenced before summer set in.

In the aftermath of the fire, everyone's mind was consumed with recovery and reconstruction. Former crimes and sufferings, if still remembered, were not paramount preoccupations. Nobody pestered Chief Omar Longshadow about Lewis Redding's mysterious demise. Omar had not forgotten, though. With no evidence beyond the widow's hysterical hallucination, his gut instinct told him that Barbara Battle was involved, if not solely responsible for the death. He did, however, have a solid connection to the assault at Dolf Thomas' store.

So on a bright blue-eyed morning, armed with Dolf's

description of his assailants, the policeman threw his chainsaw into the bed of his pickup and drove out of town up the Ravensbeak Ridge road toward Restoration Cathedral. He found it slow going. The heat of the fire had left the pavement buckled and crumbling in places. Remains of trees littered the road. He had to stop several times and drag limbs aside, and once, he needed to retrieve his chainsaw and cut a section from a charred tree trunk in order to pass.

Approaching the Cathedral campus, he rounded a bend to be confronted by a steel gate barring the road. The sharp demarcation between the green forest stretching unscathed away up the mountain beyond the gate and the fire-ravaged slopes below, startled, as if some invisible barrier had limited the progress of the blaze. Beside the gate stood a small guardhouse, gleaming pristine and new in the sunlight. Two burly men wearing military style uniforms emerged and approached Omar's pickup. He recognized the larger of the pair from previous encounters in the course of his duties. The man bent and peered into the cab, his sanguineous face shaded by his cap.

"You're a bit out of your jurisdiction, ain't you, Chief?" he rumbled, flashing a not-quite-friendly smile.

"I can come back with the sheriff, if need be," Omar replied, undeterred. "I need to talk to Barbara Battle. I'm trying to identify three suspects in an altercation that took place in my town. They left the scene driving a Crusade van."

"Mother Battle is not available today, Chief. You can talk to the Guardians Commander, if you like. He can tell you if your suspects are among us," purred the guard, obviously pleased to be issuing permissions to a former nemesis.

"I'll start with your commander, then," Omar said.

The guard disappeared into his hut for a long moment, returned bearing a clipboard in his beefy hand. He gestured for his comrade to open the gate, pushed the clipboard through the window of Omar's truck. "First building on the left," he said. "Sign here."

As Omar drove on, he glanced in his rearview mirror, saw the guard swing the gate closed behind him. As the gate shut, the scene appeared to ripple as if viewed through troubled water. Along the road, he passed people at work in garden plots that had been cleared among the trees. A few sheep browsed in a little paddock along the way. Just off the road, three men worked on a small tractor. Omar judged that Battle and her followers were setting up an off-grid community. The woods on either side opened up ahead to reveal the Restoration Cathedral, somewhat altered now from its original state. The shattered dome had been removed completely, and the outer walls opened up into a portico of columns and arches, more like an amphitheater. Omar was surprised to see so much work accomplished in so little time. Apparently while the rest of the county had been fighting fire, the Restoration Crusade had been tearing down their barns and building them bigger.

The first building on the left was a refurbished farmhouse that Omar remembered from before the property was purchased by Restoration Crusade. A sign in front of the house declared *GUARDIANS*. Omar parked his pickup beside a utility vehicle with the Restoration Crusade logo painted on the door, took a long look around before entering the house. A crisp young woman seated behind a desk just inside the door was talking on her intercom when he entered, said a few words more, hung up and greeted him, "Chief Longshadow. The Commander is expecting you." Omar recognized her from the former Crusade office in town, as she smiled and led him across the room, opened a door and ushered him through.

The high-ceilinged office was unexpectedly large, too large to fit the apparent size of the modest house it occupied. The dark walls and floor merged into shadow as the door closed behind Omar. The only bright light in the windowless room illuminated a large desk with a polished stone top. Behind it sat a uniformed man Omar recognized as his former sergeant.

"Sergeant, you've grown up," Omar said. The man behind the desk seemed fit, but noticeably older than the sergeant he remembered.

"Commander now, Chief," the guardian corrected, launched a smile not intended to comfort, and gestured for Omar to sit. "What need has brought you among us Believers today?"

Omar remained standing. "Three men, driving one of your vehicles, assaulted Dolf Thomas in his store when they were in Drovers Gap posting Crusade flyers not long after the wildfires started. I'm trying to identify them so we can file charges."

"The Restoration isn't in your jurisdiction is it, Chief?" The commander's tone more statement than question.

"I'm not here to arrest anybody. I just need to know who they are so I can inform the sheriff," Omar said.

"Do you have names, descriptions?" the Guardian asked.

"I have a description from the victim." Omar said, holding out a copy of Dolf's statement.

Sergeant pretended to study the document. "You say they were posting fliers and driving our van?"

"Yes. The date is on that statement." Omar said.

Sergeant shook his head, reprised his dangerous smile. "Then I'm afraid, Chief, you are too late."

"How so?" Omar queried.

"These three were a grave disappointment to us," Chuck said solemnly. "I can give you their names." He paused to write on a sheet of paper and slipped it across the desk to the policeman before continuing. "We learned of their misbehaviors and dismissed them from our assembly. They joined the Forest Service volunteers after they left us and were unfortunately among those lost fighting the fire."

"I'd like to confirm this with your employer, Commander," Omar said.

"If you mean our Mother Barbara, Chief, she is away presently. She will no doubt return in a few days. You can call the Crusade office and arrange an appointment. I'm sure she will be happy to entertain any question you have."

"I'll do that," Omar said. "You never talked this fancy, Commander, when you were a lowly police sergeant."

"Chief Longshadow, you would be amazed at the graces we have acquired under Mother Barbara's tutelage. You might want to join us one day soon."

Fat Chance. Omar swallowed this remark and turned to go. The crisp young woman opened the door for him before he reached it. When the gate finally closed behind him, Omar glanced at his watch, which apparently had stopped. He checked his cell. Although he figured he'd been on Cathedral property the better part of an hour, his phone insisted he had signed in at the gate only five minutes ago.

FORTY-FIVE

ommander Chuck Priestley stood mute and still, waiting to be addressed. Mother Barbara was particular about protocol. None of her underlings, not even the commander of her Guardians, was allowed to speak to her until she had acknowledged their presence. Chuck resisted the impulse to raise a hand to shield his eyes from the dazzling spotlight overhead. Deep shadow ruled the rest of the room. He had only the vaguest impression of Barbara Battle's form behind her desk, looming above him like a throne in the semi-dark. Something about her wasn't quite right, although when he tried to focus on her figure his vision blurred and his brain fuzzed to the point he was not at all sure what he saw, and an instant after was uncertain if he saw anything at all.

"Yes, Commander. Sit down and talk to me." It was her voice, but strained, with a gravely edge. He wondered if she were quite well but dared not inquire. No one questioned the Mother about anything and all trembled to offer answer.

Chuck sat, though it discomfited him more than standing on his feet. The Mother's invitations were tantamount to command. He offered his report, "Omar Longshadow, was here, inquiring about the three of your sheep who transgressed at the market in Drovers Gap."

"And you told him they are no longer known by us."

"I so did, Mother. I told the Chief they had been burnt in the fire."

"You always tell more than is required of you, Commander," the voice in the shadows admonished. "Be careful that flaw doesn't precipitate your unraveling."

Chuck stared at his hands clinched in his lap, tried to relax them, looked up and peered into the dark with what he prayed was a neutral expression, "Forgive my lapse, Mother. I will measure my words in the future."

"Guard your mouth, then, Commander," said the voice that was not quite the voice he knew. "Nothing that passes your lips is ever forgotten here. Your silence may shield you when words fail."

"The policeman requested audience with you, Mother," Chuck said, risking a few words.

"And?"

"I told him you were away, and he should make an appointment on your return."

"Again, you said more than you should, and an untruth besides," Battle said. "You are a habitual liar, Commander. And you are fortunate indeed that I still have some need of you. Pray I do not find your replacement soon."

The room was stifling hot. Chuck felt sweat running down his chest beneath his uniform. His breath short, catching in his throat, as if he were about to drown. He coughed, murmured, "Yes, Mother, I will pray."

"Then for the time being, you may keep your tongue. You will need it presently to issue my invitation to Omar Longshadow. Now leave me and address your duties. Another cull is due tonight."

Chuck stood on trembling legs, bowed low and, his dignity

in shreds, stumbled toward the door that would release him to air and light.

Badb Catha a.k.a. Battle Crow a.k.a. Barbara Battle a.k.a. Mother Barbara relaxed in her darkness, released her long body to twine out into the shadows. She had expended herself to a dangerous minimum attempting to maintain her fire against the rain that just kept on falling until, depleted, she had let it go, without enough power left even to hold her human form properly. One spell she might have defeated, but the deluge was born of a compound magic that reeked of dragon and púca and who-knew-what entities besides. Even among the Fallen, Wandalena apparently had allies, and now they were arrayed against her.

The First Dragon, however, had every intention of being the last. She would rest and feed until she had regathered her strength, hone her cunning, grow her powers and cast her plans. In the end this world would be hers, and that would be only the beginning.

That idiot guardian's fear had been refreshing, nourishing. Battle felt better already, her appetite whetted for the culling tonight. All those screams. All that blood. So much death and terror to feed her fire with. She could hardly wait. It was a pity, she thought, she had not been quite up to facing the policeman today. Soon she would be in condition to entertain him properly. He was a fool like all humans, but he was a fool with principles, the most dangerous kind. A holy fool, he might have been called on another world in an earlier age. She imagined he would be quite tasty. His head would be a prize item in her growing collection.

Barbara turned up the lights, gathered herself, and studied her reflection in the mirror. To all appearances she looked properly human. She was definitely getting stronger, more stable. She would be able to hold her shape long enough to preach to her congregation tonight, rouse them to a proper frenzy where they would delight in pointing out the apostates to be culled from the fellowship, those who asked awkward questions, or sounded too soft and hesitant in their praise of the Mother, or expressed pity or compassion for the lost souls who didn't serve the Restoration, or any who might in a moment's weakness breathe aloud a wish that they could return among the Fallen.

The Restored were not allowed doubt or regret. None looked back. None of them looked to anyone but Mother Barbara for their life and being. Any who might falter or stray aside from the way simply ceased to exist, vanished in the Cull, forgotten, never again to be spoken of by the living.

On his way back to Drovers Gap, Chief Omar Longshadow phoned his office, "Jolene, get in touch with the Forest Service, and see what they have on these people." He read off to her the names Chuck Priestley had given him. "They are supposed to be on the list of firefighter casualties."

Before he reached town, Constable Jolene called back, "Chief, the Forestry Service has no record of these three ever working for them, either as paid staff or volunteers. They are not on the casualty list."

"Thanks. I thought that might be the case," Omar said. "According to our old friend Chuck up at Restoration Cathedral, these are the birds who attacked Dolf at his store. I'm going to call the sheriff and tell him what we have. Maybe County can get a warrant, rattle Mother Barbara's cage and shake something loose."

"Oh, Chief," Jolene said before he tapped off, "There was a guy here who filled out an application for Priestley's old job."

Omar had already decided to promote Constable Bear to Sergeant but he didn't tell her that. "Any training or experience?" he said instead.

"Says he was military," Jolene said. "Gave a long list of references."

"Anybody we know?"

"Several agencies I never heard of," Jolene said, "And a bunch of individuals. Only one local name that I recognized, the old guy who runs Vintage Reads.

"You mean VonTrier?"

"Wendl VonTrier," she confirmed. "Weird ain't it?"

"Curiouser and curiouser," Omar agreed. "I'll stop and have a chat with Wendl on my way. Who is our applicant? What's your impression?"

"He's a hunk," reported Jolene enthusiastically.

"That isn't what I meant, Constable,"

"Big man. Dark. Seems foreign but does English like a native. Sure of himself. Says he travels a lot. Is staying at Hemlock with Abigail Trammell. Looking for a place to settle down, he says. Would like to contribute to the community."

Omar couldn't prevent a chuckle, "That's what they all say looking for a job. What did you say his name was?"

"I didn't," confessed Constable Jolene. "It's right here. Simon Ryder,"

After he quit the call, Omar went straight to Vintage Reads. Wendl's name among the references on Ryder's employment application came as a surprise, the only name on the list Jolene recognized, and the last name among all the town's residents Omar would have expected to see there.

Omar judged VonTrier the strangest character in a town full of them. He found the bookseller likeable, approachable, had no reason to consider him any other than a trustworthy citizen, yet there was something vaguely alien about Wendl, apart from his peculiar name. His unnaturally lean frame, amber eyes that looked right through anyone who gained his attention, the low voice, almost a growl but more like the purring of a big cat, that set up a buzzing behind your eyes as he spoke to you, this and a host of other marked peculiarities, seemed to Omar abnormal to the point of being not quite human.

Stepping out of the bright morning into the shadowy sanctum of the bookstore, The policeman felt, as he did every time he entered the place, as if he had walked into another world that looked very much the same world he'd been born into, but belonged to a reality very much other. As the door closed behind Omar, his sundazzled eyes couldn't be certain if Wendl's spidery form emerged soundless from behind a row of shelves, or maybe just materialized in the air.

"A Good afternoon, Chief Longshadow," the spiderman buzzed at him, "Are you in search of a story or merely seeking factual enlightenment?"

"I haven't finished my own story yet, Mister Wendl," Omar said, "And facts lately have been contradictory and confounding. I reckon I'm after enlightment."

"My mind is an open book to you, Chief," Wendl purred. "We are seekers on the same path."

"I have such hopes," Omar affirmed, "Tell me about your friend Simon Ryder. He's applied to join our little constabulary and listed you as a reference."

"I can tell you that Ryder and I have served the same institutions in the past. He doubtless possesses some talents that might prove useful in your work, and I have never known him to tell an untruth or betray a trust, although he is not always precisely what he appears." Wendl paused before adding, "You should meet him and form your own assessment of his nature."

"I'd like to do that," Omar said. "He gave Abigail Trammell's boarding house as his local address. You think I might catch him there?"

"Very likely you can," Wendl said. "He'll certainly be

there for dinner tonight. Simon never misses a meal. Come share table with us this evening and you can discuss at length while you enjoy dear Miss Trammell's delicious fare." Wendl punctuated this invitation with a guttural rumble that rose up out of his chest and apparently, he intended to approximate a friendly chuckle.

"I might just do that," Omar said. "Abigail can concoct a feast out of bread and water."

Forty-Six

"Constable Bear, would you be free to join me for dinner tonight?" queried Omar Longshadow as they prepared to close the police office for the day.

"Is this a date, Chief?" she said, pushing a sheaf of papers from her desktop into a drawer.

"You can call it work if that makes you feel better," Omar answered. "I'm meeting your hunk, Simon Ryder at Hemlock House during dinner. Thought you might want to ask him some personal questions."

Jolene laughed, recognizing the tease, "I already know he isn't married," she said. "It's on his application. But yes, if you're serious, I would like to be in on the interview, and a meal from Abigail Trammell's kitchen has considerable appeal all its own."

"Well. I'm ready when you are, then," Omar murmured, pulling on his hat and jacket." It's a nice day. We can walk over there and scope out the town on the way. Call it patrol duty and count you on the clock."

"Chief, does that mean the department is paying for the meal?" Jolene said as they set out down Main Street.

Omar smiled, shook his head. "If it isn't, I'd still like to buy you dinner if you'd let me."

Jolene gave him back the smile, "You know, I think I'd like that even better."

Arriving at Hemlock House not long before dinner service closed, they passed a half-dozen cars parked out front. "Abigail's business has been picking up lately, with all these new folk coming in since the fire," Jolene observed.

Omar said, "Maybe I should have made reservations."

The dining room was still crowded when they came in, but Chloe Toibin showed them to the lone vacant table in a far corner with a view of Abigail's garden. "We saved you a place, Chief," she said as she seated them.

"How did you know we'd be here?" Omar asked.

"Wendl told us," she said. "He knows stuff." She handed them menus. "Drinks?

"I'm fine with this water for now," Omar said.

"I'll have a Forester," answered Jolene.

Chloe bustled away to fetch Jolene's beer.

"I never pegged you as a stout drinker," Omar observed, taking a sip of his spring water.

"I worked through lunch," Jolene said. "It'll take the edge off my appetite and keep me from wolfing down Abigail's delicious food."

Omar peered at her over his menu. "Do you always plan your life so carefully?"

Jolene allowed a little laugh into the air between them. "If I'd planned my life, do you think I'd be working for you?"

While Omar pondered that question, Chloe returned with Jolene's Forester. "Youns ready to order?"

"I'll have the shrimp and grits," Jolene said, gesturing her menu in Omar's direction. "He's buying."

"What's the special?" Omar queried.

"Meatloaf," Chloe informed with apparent satisfaction. "Always meatloaf on Wednesdays."

"I'll have meatloaf," Omar said.

Jolene testified later that Abigail's shrimp and grits surpassed her greatest expectations, redolent of the sea and with the creamy earthiness of highland corn. Omar told her then she should write for a cooking magazine. His meatloaf was rich and moist, more and other than any meatloaf he could recall, with a taste and texture that was at once familiar and quite new to him. He offered a bite to Jolene, who savored it for a moment then identified the mystery ingredient. "Flax seed," She pronounced with assurance.

"You sure?" quizzed Omar.

She nodded, forked another bite of Omar's meatloaf. "Flax seed," she said again.

By the time dessert arrived the other diners had gradually filtered away and Omar looked around surprised to find they were the only patrons left. He'd already decided his interview with Simon Ryder would happen some other day, an eventuality that discomfited him not the least, and was concentrating on his espresso and fig tart when Jolene looked up suddenly and exclaimed, "Here comes our hunk now."

Omar followed her gaze, reckoned her epithet was not inaccurate. A very tall, very dark, man approached their table, exuding a luminous presence that rendered previous company a dim and unconvincing approximation of intelligent human life.

"May I join you, Officers?" he inquired with stage politeness, like an actor in a play. His voice, almost two, at once through the ear and in the mind.

Omar detected something unsettlingly familiar about the intonations. *Who else do I know who talks like this?* But he smiled, pointed to a chair, "Have a seat Mister Ryder, and tell us about yourself."

"That would be a boring story, Chief," Ryder said, pulling out a chair and sitting, "I'd rather tell you about Barbara Battle."

"Barbara Battle isn't applying for a job in my

department," Omar said.

Ryder laughed a soft little bark, flashing a startling array of gleaming white teeth. His mirth hung in the air around him, more a feeling than a scent, but cloying as incense. "I'm afraid I'm not either, Chief, though the notion is tempting. The application was to get your attention. I can't stay in your town much longer, but while I am among the Fallen, I want to be helpful."

Before Omar could inquire about just who the Fallen might be, Jolene asked, "Helpful how?"

Ryder leaned forward, gathered them into his smouldering gaze, and made his pitch. "Barbara Battle presents a grave threat to your community. You will have to deal with her soon rather than late, and I've been sent here to assist you in that endeavour."

"And just who has sent you on this mission of mercy?" Omar demanded.

"For now, let's just say I'm an agent for another jurisdiction where Battle escaped custody. My job is to get her back where she can do no more harm." Ryder said

Jolene spoke up, "What jurisdiction? State? National? Another country?"

"Not any country you've heard of, certainly," Ryder said quietly. "The point is, I can help you protect your people from her depredations."

Omar stared at the stranger across the table, wondering why, contrary to all reason and logic, his gut instinct was telling him to trust this mysterious stranger. "I think Barbara Battle has murdered at least one person since she's been here, maybe more," he said before the silence thickened to uncomfortable, "But I can't prove any of it. Like my colleague said, just what kind of help are you offering us Mister Ryder, and at what cost?"

Ryder spread his hands suddenly, rippling the air visibly, as if it were liquid. "I'm not here to take anything from you at all, Chief Longshadow, except to rid you of that evil on the mountain out there. She has powers you can't match. She won't let you arrest her, even if you find proof of her crimes. You have no idea of the dark force you are dealing with here, Chief. I can make her gone for you."

Omar regarded his dessert, his cold espresso and his half-eaten, slumped and deflated tart. A lunatic had spoiled what promised to be a rare pleasant evening with a woman he needed to know better. He cleared his throat, tried and failed to match the calm ferocity of Ryder's gaze, "And you can match Battle's supposed powers, Ryder? You can just waltz up Ravensbeak Ridge and disappear her for us, is that it? You some kind of assassin, are you? Maybe I should be arresting you."

"That would be mighty inconvenient for both of us, Chief," Ryder murmured. Only one of her own kind can deal with her."

"What kind is that?" Jolene asked.

"She isn't human," Simon said. "She isn't of your world. She was born outside your Stream. Her real name is Badb Catha and she is the oldest of us all. She is the Battle Crow, the First Dragon."

"I'm glad we had a good meal first, Mister Ryder," Omar said, "Just so the evening wasn't wasted, but I'm too old for fairy tales."

"Every fairytale is real somewhere." Ryder spoke softly, his voice a subtle rumble down in his throat, "And Badb Catha is your reality here and now. That's a fact."

Fairytale or not, Jolene found herself half believing. "How do you know Battle is a dragon?"

"Because I share her lineage," Ryder said. "I am dragon myself."

"Show me," Omar said.

Later, Omar and Jolene would wonder if all they saw next really happened, or if they hallucinated. When Omar voiced his challenge, the lights were suddenly dimmed by a sulfurous haze and Simon Ryder's eyes flared like livid coals in a face morphing into an elongated reptilian head with a mouth that opened to disclose a fiery maw belching flames like a crematorium. They heard a roar that didn't tremor the air but rose up from the depths of their terrified souls. Jolene opened her mouth to scream but found no breath within her to push it past her throat. Instinctively, Omar reached for his sidearm, only to recall he'd left his weapon locked in his desk at town hall. "I can't digest my food properly if I'm weaponized," He'd joked to Jolene.

The dragon towered over them, impossibly large, more than a room twice the size could contain. The two police officers stared blankly at their death and dismemberment, paralyzed, unvoiced. The terror that filled them left no space in their minds for any prayer or thought or will to flee. They could not summon even the motivation to close their eyes to their impending unbecoming as the dragon's great taloned claws reached out about to seize and crush their life.

Then it was over. Not a cessation exactly, more an instantaneous shift, like a splice in a videotape. One second they were on the brink of being devoured by an unspeakable horror, and before they could even comprehend what was happening to them, the room was normal, the air clear, their unfinished desserts still on their plates, Simon Ryder sitting opposite them at the table, his apparently human hands folded in front of him as he gazed on them with a sad and cryptic little smile.

When Omar heard his heart still beating behind his ribs and finally remembered to breathe again, He glanced at Jolene, who was staring not at Ryder but toward the kitchen door. Abigail Trammell and Wendl VonTrier were standing there together, Wendl with a towel draped over an arm, striking a waiter's pose.

"I love it when he does that," he said.

FORTY-SEVEN

Abigail brought tea made from a blend of herbs harvested from her garden, and poured cups for everyone. "This will calm our nerves and settle our minds," she said as Wendl brought chairs and they joined the Tischgespräch.

"How did you make us see that just now?" Jolene asked, staring awestruck at Simon, as if she expected any moment he might revert to dragonshape.

He shrugged. "You saw me as I am," he said. "That was my true form. This human appearance is a mental construct, projected for your peace-of-mind. It requires considerable expenditure of energy to maintain. There is a reason dragon love to hide in caves and forests, away from human eyes." He gestured toward Wendl, "On the other hand, entities like my púca friend here, are true shape-shifters. With Von Trier, what you see is what you get."

Wendl laughed, "Would you like me to demonstrate?"

Omar took a sip of his tea, surprised at the tastiness, took another before he said, "I don't think I'm up to another transformation." He turned back to Simon, "So you say Barbara Battle is a dragon we just imagine is human."

"She imagines she is human," Simon clarified, "And projects her fantasy into your minds. Dragon be telepaths. After all the effort she expended trying to burn down the county, she's probably hard put to keep up appearances about now."

"That explains this morning," Omar said.

"You've seen her today?" Abigail asked?

"I tried. I went to ask her about her goons who attacked Dolf Thomas at his store. Priestly told me she was away. Yet I'm pretty sure I overheard the receptionist at the Guardian headquarters talking to 'Mother Barbara' on the intercom."

"That's good," Wendl observed. "The old Battle Crow is still weak. We should make our move to remove her now rather than later."

"We are ready, as well prepared as can be, at any rate," Simon said

"So what happens next?" Omar asked. "You going to put on your dragon suit and fly up to Ravensbeak and take her out?"

"I would enjoy that enormously," Simon answered. "Unfortunately, even if I could overcome her, a dragonduel would be terrible, scorching the earth and fouling the air for a hundred miles around. No, your need requires a more subtle magic than I can perform."

"But you said you were prepared," Jolene said.

"I so did," Simon nodded. "The weapon is shaped, charged and in good hands."

"Who's hands?" Omar asked.

"Go see your realtor." Simon said. "Tell him Simon Ryder sent you."

"Willie Graham?" said Jolene, wanting to laugh but afraid to.

"You're kidding," Omar said to a suddenly empty chair. If the dragon Simon Ryder was still in the room, he had blinded the humans to his presence.

Barbara Battle was in a bad mood as she summoned the commander of her Guardians. Dreams and visions had troubled her rest. In her dreams she was imprisoned again beneath the Abbey at Trier. Her visions were of a dragon, old and powerful, not as ancient as she, the First, but old, and possessed of a strength to match her own. There were yet a few of her kind left in the Two Worlds. Most of them slept in the mountains around Trier on Otherworld. The one in her vision was here among the Fallen, near enough to challenge. The rain that extinguished her fire and spared the town could have been dragonwork. The more she considered the possibility, the more likely it seemed.

She cast her presence out into the air, scanning for some scent or sense of another of her kind, but as far as she could reach, she encountered no dragonessence. There were púca about, meddlesome, but no threat to her. A dragon might be cloaked, she supposed. Earthlight was dim among the Fallen. Truelife might be veiled in the unreality of this place. Most of the Fallen never found their life, fed on illusion and deception their entire span of being. It was easy to make them see what you wanted, and to blind them to what you wished concealed. But dragonsight could pierce the fog of unknowing. If there were another dragon on this world, she should know it. Still, the dreams persisted. Something was not right. What had she missed, overlooked? Uncertainty gnawed, a tiny mindmouse, never quite seen, never loud, but never still nor silent.

The intercom on her desk buzzed like a guilty conscience and she heard the voice of her secretary, "Mother Barbara, the Commander is here."

What a sweet-voiced child she is. Smells delicious. Perhaps I'll have her culled when I've found a better secretary. She'd be a breakfast delight. Aloud, Barbara responded, "Send him in, Helen."

"Mother Barbara will see you now Commander," Helen

Troy said in her duty voice. As Chuck Priestley followed her to the office door, he leaned close and whispered, "How about tonight?"

"I can't. I have to attend seminary tonight," she whispered back.

"Can't you skip it, say you're sick?" Chuck murmured as Helen reached to knock.

"You know I can't," she hissed back, knocked gently three times, opened the door and addressed the shadows beyond, "Commander Priestly is here, Mother Barbara."

"Show him through," responded a voice, resonant, sounding almost feminine, almost human, almost kind.

Chuck stepped past Helen, stood stiffly, hands folded in front of him, speechless, immobile, not even breathing until he heard the door close behind him.

"Sit down and relax, Commander," Barbara Battle intoned from behind her desk. "I'm not going to eat you. Not today."

Chuck sat as commanded. He did not relax. He had not considered the possibility of being devoured by his employer, but now that she had planted the notion in his head, he reckoned such an eventuality as more than hypothetical. He'd never actually seen the Greatmother dismember and eat a human being, but he heard rumors from the cleaning crew. Members who were culled from the Body supposedly returned down the mountain among the Fallen, but not all of them were seen to leave. Most were simply no longer seen.

"How are your eyes working?" Mother Barbara inquired, gently, as if he'd been sick.

"My eyes?" Chuck stammered. *What is she asking?* His vision was fine except when in the Mother's proximity where he could never be sure precisely what he was seeing, nor later remember exactly what he had seen.

"Your spies in town," Barbara clarified. "Have they been keeping track of the policeman as I requested?"

"Oh, yes, Mother Barbara. I have their reports here," Chuck replied, scrolling the notes on his phone. "After he left the Restoration, he returned to Drovers Gap where he went to Vintage Reads and talked to Wendl Von Trier. From there, he went to Town Hall, and stayed at the Police Department until six p.m. when he and Constable Jolene Bear went to Hemlock House where they had dinner and talked with Abigail Trammell, VonTrier, and a man we don't know, not one of the local residents."

"How long were they there?" Barbara asked.

Chuck consulted his phone again. "Three hours. Two hours after the dining room service closed."

"Obviously, they weren't just savoring their dessert," Barbara said. "Do we know what this big discussion was about?"

"I'm afraid we don't, Mother." Our informant is a dishwasher. He asked their server, Chloe Toibin, what they were talking about so long. She said she didn't know, but they seemed serious. Toibin left shortly after that. At one point, our guy heard a big commotion in the dining room, but when he looked out, the group was still sitting around the table talking too quietly for him to hear."

Barbara looked thoughtful, "Is this Toibin one of your informants?"

"Not really." Chuck shook his head. "But she likes to talk and our dishwasher likes to ask."

"Cultivate her, however you can," Barbara said. "We can always use somebody with social access and people skills. What happened after they left Trammell's place?"

"Longshadow and Bear returned on foot to their office, collected their vehicles and presumably went home for the night."

"You sure they went straight home?"

Chuck wasn't sure. "They went in that direction. They

weren't followed, but they were at their homes an hour later when they answered 'wrong-number' calls on their land lines."

"What about the stranger they met at Trammell's nest? Do we see any more of him?" The stranger stirred a vague sense of alarm far back in Battle's mind, like a persistent unscratchable itch.

Chuck consulted his phone again. "The stranger left Hemlock House right before Longshadow and Bear, and walked over to Mountain Realty, which was closed, but Willie Graham met him there and they went inside. About thirty minutes later, Graham came out alone and walked to his house about a block away. Our man waited for an hour, but didn't see the stranger leave. He scoped out the building then and was pretty sure it was empty."

"Pretty sure is not certain," Barbara snapped. "I expected better from you, Commander."

Chuck had better sense than to offer excuses. "Yes, Mother Barbara," he said. "Understood."

"When Mister Graham arrives at his office first thing in the morning, I want you there, Commander Priestley, to personally offer him an invitation he can't refuse, and to provide transportation enabling him to accept immediately."

FORTY-EIGHT

Willie Graham had a sleepless night full of waking dreams and hallucinations his mind projected against the dark. It all started with the phone call at the end of a near perfect day. Betty had come to his place after work and he had made a supper for them. Asparagus and grilled trout. He thought she might stay the night this time, but her sister called while they were eating and when they finished their meal, Betty left to aid in some family crisis. Willie was still musing about how cell phones hinder one's social life when he got the other call.

"Willie Graham here," he answered. He didn't recognize the caller ID.

"Willie, this is Simon Ryder. You still have my box?"

"Yes, it's down at my office,"

"You haven't opened it?" the dragonman queried.

"You told me not to," Willie said.

"Very important you don't." Simon said, "Go down and get it. I'll meet you there and tell you what to do with it."

"Now?" Willie had just put on his pajamas and was about to brush his teeth.

"Now or never," said the dragon.

"I'm on my way," Willie said. He put on his jeans, tucked his pajama top into the waist and pulled on a sweater. He was out his front door before his feet settled into his new loafers that Betty had bought for him. As he trotted down the street toward Mountain Realty, he could make out the dark figure already waiting for him in the shadows by the door. Willie Graham, small town realtor, stereotypical average guy, had been summoned by a dragon, figured his life was taking one more turn toward interesting and recalled an ancient Chinese curse.

Willie wasn't surprised when he stepped out his door to go to work next morning and saw the black SUV with the Restoration Crusade logo on the door sitting in his drive with the motor running. In his pocket, Willie carried the mysterious wooden box Ryder had sent him.

"She will want this," Ryder said. "And you are going to give it to her."

"Why can't you just take it to her then?" Willie asked. "It's your box after all."

"Because she would know what I am," Ryder's tone sounded like it was obvious. "There can't be but one dragon in the room."

"What's in the box?" Willie asked. He had been tempted, but had honored Ryder's admonition never to open it.

"The key to the world," Ryder said. "She will ask you that, and when she opens it, close your eyes."

So when the burly Guardian got out of the vehicle and opened a door, Willie got in, as if it had all been arranged. He was surprised to see Commander Chuck Priestley waiting for him inside. "Mother Barbara wants to have a little chat," Chuck said politely.

"I know," Willie responded, trying to sound like the spy

character he saw once on tv. "I have something that belongs to her."

Chuck, sensing there was more to this business than he knew, directed a hostile stare at his passenger, seemed about to speak, then apparently deciding that in this case, ignorance was his best defense, tapped the shoulder of the uniformed driver, and the vehicle moved off through the waking town toward Ravensbeak Ridge.

When Betty arrived at the Mountain Realty office next morning, she was disappointed to find her employer not there before her. She wanted to apologize for having to leave in the middle of their supper to go tend her distraught sibling. She had hoped the evening might come to a more gratifying conclusion, and was fairly confident Willie had shared her expectation. She wished sometimes Willie Graham were not so shy toward her, that he would be more assertive about their perhaps relationship, but that was part of his charm. He never presumed. In any situation, he always left her room to declare her own way.

But after an hour, there was no sign of Willie. Two prospective clients called and she took messages. When she left the notes on Willie's desk, she found a cryptic scrawl on his notepad, *Badb Catha*. Foreign, it looked like. Somebody's name?

A couple of prospective buyers, recently retired, from down the mountain at Pearis Falls, came for their nine-thirty appointment. Willie wasn't answering his phone so Betty closed the office and took them to view the property they had inquired about. At first they were somewhat put-off by Willie's absence, but Betty invented and assigned to him a sudden illness, and exuded sufficient charm to return to the office an hour later to take their binder check and signature on a commitment to purchase. Willie would be proud of her, she was certain, as soon as she could find him.

More phone calls came in. Betty took messages, rescheduled appointments, placated and made excuses regarding matters she couldn't resolve on her own. Noon arrived and she still had not been able to contact her absent boss. She phoned Feral Flour Bakeshop and ordered a pizza for her lunch, and while she waited for it to arrive, she googled Badb Catha. The world-wide web informed her that Badb Catha was a Celtic deity, a goddess, or maybe three of them, of war and destruction. The name translated into English as *Battle Crow*. Weird, but someway familiar. *Battle*, she thought. What about Battle? Of course, that was it. Willie had gone to see Barbara Battle, the old crow. But why hadn't he called in? What could be taking him so long?

———

Willie watched the trees slip past as the road began winding up the east side of Ravensbeak Ridge. The bulky driver concentrated on his road. Chuck Priestly sat watching him as if studying some sort of exotic specimen in a zoo. Willie pretended not to notice, pretended to be calm and confident and self-contained. To his own surprise, he almost was.

Before he left Ryder at Mountain Realty the previous evening, the dragon had reached out suddenly and laid a palm against his chest. Willie recoiled from the jolt, like an electric shock, that the touch precipitated.

"Just a wee bit of dragonfire," Ryder said, laughing softly. It will calm you tomorrow when they come for you. It will guide you if you call on it. Don't resist. Just rest in that little fire. Trust where it leads you. It will fade when you don't need it anymore."

Willie could feel it now. A warmth beneath his ribs. A presence. Like a second heart. It was comforting. He felt enabled by it. He reckoned he was in no hurry to be rid of this dragonfire, as Ryder had called it. The van stopped at a gate. Priestly spoke to his phone and the gate opened. Willie saw the Cathedral up ahead brilliant under the morning sun as the gate closed behind. The gleaming façade towered into the air, reflecting the sunlight like a column of fire. *Dragonfire*, Willie thought.

Contrasting sharply with the burnt slopes below, the Restoration Crusade campus was greening into summer, like another world. The van stopped beside the rear entrance on the cathedral's west side. In the building's shadow, the air felt almost chill. The driver got out and opened the door as if Willie were an honored dignitary. Priestly got out and walked into the building beside him and the big driver followed behind. Willie wondered what would happen if he decided to leave just then, if the big man would beat him senseless, or if Priestly would just grab him and drag him wherever they wanted him to go.

Omar Longshadow was making his morning coffee when he saw the Restoration Crusade SUV pass the window at Town Hall. *There goes trouble*, he thought. He was still pondering his attempt to interview Barbara Battle at the Cathedral when Constable Bear came in. "You want to hold down the office while I go up the street and talk to Willie Graham?" he said. Omar habitually phrased his directives as questions. Mountain pride would always embrace a request more readily than an order.

"Sure, Chief," Jolene answered, dropping a box from Feral Flour Bake Shop on the desk. "I brought donuts."

Omar drove straight to Mountain Realty. The morning was bright and beautiful. Any other day he would have walked, but the sight of Battle's wagon had instilled a vague nagging urgency. He wanted to enlighten himself regarding Ryder's cryptic reference to the realtor. It was hard to imagine Willie Graham as being a force to be reckoned with in their conflict with the Crusade gang.

Betty was at her desk when Omar came through the door. Her worried face found a smile when she looked up from the paper in her hand.

"Morning, Chief," she said. "Have you seen anything of my boss this morning?"

"I was hoping to find Willie here," Omar said. "I need to talk to him about something."

"He isn't here, Chief." Betty looked on the verge of tears. "I've tried calling him at home and on his mobile, but he doesn't answer." She waved her sheet of paper at him, "Oh, Chief," her voice catching in her throat. "I'm afraid Willie's gotten into some trouble." She pushed the paper at him, "Do you know what this means?"

Omar took the sheet, read *Badb Catha*. He remembered the SUV with the intertwined RC on the side. "It's Gaelic for Battle Crow, Betty, and I think you may be right about Willie."

"Wait here," Commander Priestly said, gesturing at a row of chairs opposite the reception desk. He murmured some words to the dark-haired young woman behind the desk, whose name tag declared her to be Helen, then disappeared behind a farther door. Willie sat, unsettled as he was, not entirely oblivious to Helen's tastefully displayed charms, while the burly driver sat beside him exuding menace. Willie could feel a noticeable warmth emanating from Simon's little box in his pocket. He took a curious comfort from the presence and felt a growing reluctance to be parted from it.

Helen's intercom buzzed softly. She gave it her attention, then looked up at Willie, "Mister Graham?" in a soft and sultry voice that might sell blue pills in a TV commercial, "Mother Barbara will see you now."

Helen stood and Willie followed her to the door, while Driver remained glaring and immobile in his chair. Helen opened the door and ushered him through, wafting a not quite natural sweetness that might have been perfume. In the dimly lit room beyond, Barbara Battle sat at a huge desk, raised above the floor where Chuck Priestley stood beside a single chair, like a soldier at attention.

Battle looked to Willie more regal than he remembered. Perhaps it was the surroundings, but she seemed to be smoldering with pent-up power, a tangible fierceness, almost beautiful, almost frightening.

"You may leave us, Commander," she murmured, gazing at Chuck, then turned her attention to Willie, "Mister Graham and I wish to engage in private."

"Are you sure, Mother Barbara? I . . ." Chuck began with evident unease.

"I will not repeat myself to you, Priestly," Battle responded, so softly Willie could barely hear, though Chuck recoiled as if he'd been struck, turned and fled the room without a word.

"Sit down, sir, please" she said pleasantly to Willie when they were alone. Willie wilted under her thunderous smile and did as he was told.

Badb Catha gazed down at the puny human male seated before her. Pale and soft and weak. Tasteless, not even fit for a snack. Confused. He didn't even have mind to be properly afraid of her. Yet, she sensed a danger in him. He carried power, though he did not seem to be aware of it. An aura not his own clung to his person. Something alien to this fallen world, yet familiar to her. Something from her deep past. She could almost name it . . . No, impossible. Or was it?

"You reek of Dragon, Willie Graham," she said in her human voice, but not quite so friendly now. "Anyone I know?"

"Do you know Simon Ryder?" the human asked.

You're either very brave, or just the fool you appear to be. Instead, she said, "I knew him on another world. He would have done well to stay there."

"That is his intention," the human said, as if reciting a message from memory, "He only came here to bring you what belongs to you alone."

"So, Ryder has sent me a geek bearing gifts, then?" the Battle Crow said, wary now and intrigued. "It must be a small present indeed, if you can carry it, little man." She cast her awareness, touched no scent of dragon within her circle. "Where's Ryder?" she demanded.

"Gone," the human said. She read the truth in him. No doubt Ryder had returned to Trier, where Wandalena could hide him.

"What do you carry that belongs to me alone, apart from your own life and limb?" She said.

"This," said Willie Graham, and took a small wooden box from his pocket and held it out toward her.

"Wait." Barbara commanded. "Open it."

"I'm not allowed," Willie said. "Ryder said it is for your eyes only. He said it is the key to your world."

"Then close your eyes and open it," Barbara growled, wearying of her constraining guise.

Willie Graham closed his eyes and lifted the lid from the box. It didn't explode. Willie didn't burst into flame or crumble into dust.

"Give it to me," the Badb rumbled, her human aspect shredding away as she reached out a taloned hand. Willie replaced the lid, opened his eyes, gasped at the apparition before him and dropped the box into her outstretched claw before collapsing into his chair.

Barbara held the box. She could feel the crafter's power in the wood. No ordinary box, this. Lugh, the first and mightiest among the old deities, had made it. Had he been here all along, maybe even before her, near and hidden, all this time?

How perverse are the gods. More inscrutable, even than dragons. "The key to my world, you say?" She rumbled at the little man, who was very much afraid at last. He nodded, unspeaking, his voice swallowed by his fright. She inhaled deeply. Human fear she found as tasty and nourishing as their flesh and blood. Babd Catha lifted the lid, light as a feather, to reveal nestled in a bed of green forest moss a tiny sphere. It might have been a bird's egg, except it was clear and bright as water, and she could see her own reflection imaged perfectly within its depths. Nothing pleasured the Badb Catha more than her own likeness. Lost in her verisimilitude, it wasn't until she felt her power diminishing, draining away, that she saw the stone wall behind her. She knew every stone. She had counted them and measured them and cursed them and beat at them for four hundred years in the dungeon beneath Trier Abbey.

"Close your eyes when she opens it," Simon Ryder admonished when instructing Willie on delivering Lugh's box. But Willie couldn't look away when the dragon woman lifted the lid from the box and indescribable light flooded her scaled visage. He couldn't close his eyes on the thousands of tiny lights that gathered and swirled about her as she gazed entranced at the thing she held.

By the time her expression changed to perplexity to alarm to rage, and she looked out at Willie, paralyzed in his chair, a sphere of swirling light spun around her, obscuring her like a luminous veil as her features seemed to drain away like wax, melting, dripping, flowing like water into the little wooden cube An instant before she disappeared completely, Barbara Battle shot an expression of mad loathing at Willie that struck him like a stone. "You!" she roared. "She can't have it. Yours."

A fire blossomed in Willie's head, blinding him for an instant. When he could see again absolute silence ruled. Years went by. Then he heard the empty box clatter against the floor. His heart began to beat again. He could breathe. After what seemed a long time, Willie decided he was able to move. He stood and walked over by Barbara's desk and picked up the wooden box. It was intact, but empty, the insides burnt black. He replaced the lid and dropped it into his pocket. It would make a nice souvenir of his adventure.

Someone knocked on the door. "Come in," Willie said calmly, as if he were in charge.

Helen looked into the room, "Where's Mother Barbara?" she asked.

"She had to leave," Willie Graham said. "Call your driver to take me home." Helen did as she was told. Willie could tell she was afraid of him. He liked the taste. He wanted more.

Acknowledgments

Heartfelt thanks to Debbie Coulter, David Longley, Scott Derks and Sharon Claybough, who read it rough and set me straight, and especially to Jean Lowd, my publisher and editor at Creative James Media, who rescued Among the Fallen from the author whenever he jumped on his horse and rode off in all directions. Diana Toledo Calçado at Triumph Covers made the spectacular cover art that turns a browser into a reader. There would be no words here to read without the abiding and enabling nurture of Jane Ella Matthews, my Main Muse and co-conspirator in my life-long quest to thwart the Empire.

www.ingramcontent.com/pod-product-compliance
Lightning Source LLC
Chambersburg PA
CBHW030359200726
48286CB00015B/1625